Call of the Sea

EMILY B ROSE

Bug Press

PUBLISHING

Call of the Sea

ISBNs: 979-8-9884836-0-1 | Hardvoer

979-8-9884836-1-8 | Paperback

979-8-9884836-2-5 | eBook

Subjects: Fantasy | Romance

Author Photo: Michael Garcia

Editing: Sarah Pesce, @loptandcropt

Proofreading: Maha Jahingir, @onetruedaydreamer

Formatting: Emily B Rose, @emilybrosewrites

Cover Illustration: Sohisoli, @caspian_interactive

Cover Design, Under Dust Jacket Design, Chapter Header & Scene Break Design: Azura Arts, @azura.arts

To Heidi Goen–Salter, the teacher who changed my life. This might not be what you had in mind when you told me I was an English major, lol, but I hope you're proud nonetheless. I wouldn't be a writer without you.

Call of the Sea

Author's Note

I have to start first by saying THANK YOU to every person who has picked up this book. It means more than I'll ever be able to express that you want to read my story about fat, queer, neurodiverse princesses and mermaids. I want to mention a few things about this book before you dive in.

The main character, Kenna, is explicitly fat. There are no ifs, ands, or buts about it. Because fat people are the heroes of our own stories. She also has ADHD, and she is Demisexual. Her brother, Tristan is bisexual. Her love interest deals with depression. Now, I don't use those labels in this book for a few reasons. I believe that labels hold such power. And oftentimes, they are wonderful things. When I first heard the word Demisexual and learned what it meant, something clicked inside me that had never made sense before. When I was officially diagnosed with ADHD after thinking there had been something wrong with me my entire life, a weight was lifted from my shoulders I hadn't even realized was there.

But that is not everyone's experience with labels, and sometimes they are used to hurt rather than heal. My story is set in a fantasy world, not our world. And so I made the decision that in this world, there is no such thing as homophobia; people are simply who they are. There are no labels for neurodiversity, people's brains just work how they work. But I want there to be no question that Kenna *is* specifically a fat demisexual with ADHD.

Content Warning

There is mild fatphobia on the page, minor injuries on the page, scenes of an explicit sexual nature on the page, death of a character on the page, discussion of demisexuality on the page (without the label), discussion of neurodiversity on the page (ADHD and depression, without the labels).

Kenna's hands were trembling with excitement, her heart pattering in her chest to the tempo of the horses' hooves as their carriage clattered along the path. She wished she could see out the window next to her, but at five years of age she was still too small to reach it. Nevertheless, she stood from her seat, her twin brother Tristan following behind her, as he always did, hoping to catch a glimpse before her mother pulled them both back down into their seats.

"Are we almost there?" Kenna asked, tugging at her mother's sleeve.

The queen looked down at her, love in her eyes and a smile on her lips. She grazed Kenna's cheek, her voice tinkling with laughter as she responded, "You must find patience, *fiadhaich*. We are almost there."

Kenna sighed, stuffing her hands under her legs, trying to keep still. She was simply too excited to contain all the emotions in her small body. Tristan wriggled next to her, equally impatient, and they looked at each other, dissolving into giggles.

They had been traveling for so long, stopping in town after town. Kenna missed her room and sneaking into Tristan's bed in their shared nursery after their parents left so they could cuddle and tell stories when they were supposed to be sleeping. But she knew when they went back home, she would miss this too. It was so exciting, seeing all the new places and people. It was like her and Tristan were living their own real-life adventure, like in their bedtime stories.

Her father leaned over from his spot on the opposite bench and tugged at a piece of her wild, flaming hair. "What are you so eager for, Kenna? You haven't been this excited about any of the previous stops on our royal tour yet."

"None of the other stops have been as fun as this!"

"Yeah!" Tristan echoed. He didn't care about this stop as much as she did, but he was her constant shadow, copying everything she did.

Their parents chuckled in response, shaking their heads.

"And what makes this stop so exciting?" their mother questioned.

They were going to the *ocean* today. Kenna had only ever seen it from the safety of the castle atop the cliffs, never allowed to go down to the shore. But today she was finally going to see it up close. She wondered if it would be warm, like her baths. Or would the water feel like ice, like the rain? It didn't really matter, as long as she got to play in it.

"Kenna?" her father asked with raised brows.

Kenna whipped her head towards him, having gotten lost in her head and forgotten her father's question. She squirmed in her seat. Her parents never usually let her go anywhere near the sea, but this was a different place, so maybe they would this time?

"Because today the village is by the ocean!" she exclaimed, unable to stop the outburst.

Her parents shared a *look*. They always did this, talking in ways Kenna couldn't understand. She couldn't wait until she was big like her parents, and they couldn't leave her out anymore.

She and Tristan shared their own look, communicating without words in the way they only ever could with each other, both of them hating when their parents kept them out of the conversation.

The carriage rumbled to a stop. Kenna and Tristan hopped to their feet before the footman had even opened the door, rushing down the steps without looking back.

Kenna took in the village market in front of her. Booth after booth crowded the cobbled street, people selling everything she could think of. The sounds of crashing waves and seagulls squawking overhead filled her ears, the fresh, salty smell of the water tingling her nose. She grabbed her mother's hand on one side, Tristan on the other, pulling them along in excitement, all frustration forgotten.

She couldn't wait to get to the water, but she knew that first they had to make their appearance at the market.

Along one side of the street the booths all sold different food. There were baskets overflowing with ripe fruit, small jars of sweet honey, dried strips of seasoned meat, and more fish and lobster than Kenna had ever seen at once. Somehow they convinced their parents to let them try everything, watching as the king and queen talked and laughed with the villagers.

After they ate their fill, Kenna and Tristan ran to the booths on the other side of the street where the artisans were. There were gorgeous intricately woven baskets, wool and butter-soft cashmere, and tartans representing every clan of their kingdom Cladach. They wandered, admiring everything they came across, giggling and racing from booth to booth, until one in particular caught Kenna's eye.

The table was covered with wooden carvings of all shapes and sizes and colors. Platters, bowls, and cups, but also little swords and bows and arrows. And lastly, little figurines.

"Ah, have my humble statues caught the eye of the fairest prince and princess in our land?"

Kenna and Tristan grinned up at the older man. His hair was white as snow, his skin tan and wrinkled from a life in the sun.

"They're so pretty!" She picked up the different animals: foxes, fish, dolphins, horses, bears, cats, bunnies, and dogs.

"I make them all from the driftwood that washes along the shore here. Nothing better to do with my time now than whittle away while I watch the waves."

3

Something panged in Kenna's chest at his words, but she didn't know what. She suddenly remembered that they were so close to the sea, and was about to dash away to find it when Tristan moved further into the booth with an exclamation. "Whoa, look at these, sissy!"

The creatures he was looking at were not like the other animals she recognized. Creatures she had only seen drawings of in her story books. Trolls, pixies, dragons, faeries, unicorns. She knew some of them were as real as she was. She hadn't yet seen any faeries or trolls or pixies, as they tended not to leave their own kingdoms often, outside of trading with human kingdoms. And tucked in the back was one little mermaid. Kenna gasped, picking it up delicately in her hands.

"You found my favorite one!" The old man smiled at her, eyes twinkling as she traced the sun-bleached wood of the mermaid's tail.

Kenna turned to find her parents standing behind her, that same look from earlier on their faces.

"Can I have it? Please?" Her heart raced in her chest, daring to hope they said yes. For some reason, they had never liked her fairy tales about mermaids, but those were always her favorite.

Tristan clutched a faerie figurine in his hands. "And I want this one!"

They turned their pleading eyes on their father, who caved after a moment. "It is just a trinket, my love," he whispered to the queen as he passed Kenna to give the old man a handful of coins and a thank-you.

Kenna waved at the man as he bowed goodbye with a gentle smile.

They turned a corner at the end of the street, and the ocean came into view. Kenna's heart leapt into her throat at the sight of all that blue and white stretched out in front of her. The waves roared onto the sand, foaming and thrashing. Seagulls dipped down into the water, fish in their beaks as they flew back out and away. The gleaming sun made the water shine and sparkle, and Kenna wanted nothing more than to jump in.

Her father's hand tightened around hers, but she wriggled out of his grasp and ran to the water, Tristan's footsteps behind her, a shrieking laugh coaxed out of her mouth by the wind. But right as they got close to the lapping waves, her mother scooped her up into her arms and held her tight, her brother swallowed by her father's arms.

"Oh, no you don't, my little *fiadhaich*," her mother lovingly scolded her. "We are meant for the land. Though the sea is beautiful, she is dangerous. We don't test her waters."

Kenna felt her mother's heartbeat quicken and saw the fear shining in her eyes as she walked them away from the water. Still, she pouted longingly at the endless blue that called to her. The waves danced for her attention; the wind sang her name. She knew in her heart that the sea was where she belonged. How could her mother be afraid of something so beautiful? She had thought they might let her near the water this time since they were on tour.

But her mother didn't let her go back to the waves that called to her.

Instead, she walked down the dock, her father and Tristan right behind them. Her father placed his hand on her mother's back and murmured something in her ear that Kenna couldn't quite hear.

She was too caught up twisting around in her mother's arms to stare at the most beautiful ship she had ever seen.

It was massive, taking up all the space in her wide eyes. Kenna looked around in wonder, trying to take in every detail as they boarded the ship.

Her heart settled in her chest as the waves rolled gently beneath them. The sounds of wood creaking, ropes and sails snapping in the wind just felt *right*. When her mother finally set her down, she ran straight to the edge. Tristan wasn't far behind, and they poked their heads over the rail to admire the water that grew darker and darker as they sailed out, until it was a deep, brilliant blue. The hull of the ship cut through the water like a blade, frothy white foam spilling over itself to get out of the way. She was entranced, her eyes never straying from the water, even as Tristan pointed out different things he saw.

That was when something shiny caught her eye.

She leaned out even further, her legs dangling behind her as the top half of her body hung over the rail.

And there it was again.

A flash of the brightest, richest red.

At first, she thought that maybe she was seeing a pretty fish, then Kenna saw the red tail ended with the top half of a woman. She gasped, her eyes flicking between the wooden statue clutched in her hand and the figure just beneath the waves.

"Tristan!" She nudged her twin, pointing towards the figure, but he was distracted, looking out at something else in the water. Even at her young age, she knew not everyone believed in fairy tales. But she did. And this was her favorite fairy tale come to life right before her eyes.

She leaned a little further, trying to catch a better glimpse of the mermaid when her mother's call startled her.

"Makenna!" her mother's panicked shout rang out over the waves as a large swell rocked the ship just a tad too hard.

Kenna's small body fell right over the edge, Tristan's hands reaching towards open air as he screamed her name.

Tumbling through the air, she screamed, but the sound was snatched from her throat by the whistling winds. Kenna plunged into the icy water, the shock stealing what little breath was left from her lungs. On instinct her hands opened, grasping at nothing, her new mermaid figure whisked away by the churning waves. She stared after it, struggling for a moment, but her heavy gown pulled her down, and it was so cold her limbs lost the strength to fight. Bubbles escaped her lips as she slowly sank, her hair like flames fanning her face, hands reaching for the surface she was sure she'd never see again.

Then, that flash of red again, and suddenly there was a face in front of her. The mermaid's hair shone golden in the light streaming through the water behind her, eyes the color of seaweed. She put her hands gently on Kenna's face and smiled, looking like an angel.

"Don't worry, little one. You're going to be alright," the mermaid's words floated to Kenna through the water. A moment later, warmth spread through her, starting in her toes and climbing through each of her limbs. The mermaid wrapped her hands around Kenna's waist, pushing her up until the water embraced her, carrying her up and up.

She looked back down towards the mermaid and saw her smiling, her hands outstretched towards her as if she was still pushing her, though she was far away from her by now. She thought she saw a flash of cobalt scales and gangly limbs behind the mermaid, but didn't get a good look before a cloud of bubbles from above obscured her vision.

Kenna looked up in time to see that her father had dived into the water, scooping her into his grasp. She wrapped her arms around his neck in a vice-like grip. They broke the surface of the water to the sounds of shouting and footsteps pounding on the deck. Kenna gulped in air, coughing the water from her lungs. Her father was crying, cradling her to his chest.

"Makenna! Makenna! Evander, tell me she's well!" her mother sobbed from the deck.

"It's all right, Eileen! She's all right!" he yelled in response, his chest shuddering against hers.

"Get out of the water! Now!" Her mother's voice rang with terror.

A rope was thrown down, and they were hauled up the side. As soon as her father's feet landed on deck, the two of them were swept into her mother's arms, with Tristan at her side, his eyes wide with tears. She sobbed into the top of Kenna's head, holding them so tight it hurt, and she felt Tristan's soft hand take a hold of hers. They took her into the captain's quarters, changing her into warm, dry clothes and wrapping her in a heavy blanket, while Tristan hovered anxiously next to her.

Throughout it all, Kenna didn't cry. She was too enthralled by the mermaid, and no one had given her a chance to tell them about it yet, too caught up in their frantic worry. Finally, the royal physician on board left them, and Kenna was alone with her parents and her twin.

"My sweet girl, I'm so glad you're alright," Kenna's mother murmured into her hair.

Her father, pacing back and forth in front of them, stopped to kiss her brow. "We thought we had lost you."

"A mermaid saved me!" Kenna burst out, unable to keep it inside any longer.

Her parents paused, looking at each other for a long moment before looking back down at her, while Tristan gasped softly at her side.

"What do you mean?" her mother asked, a tremor in her voice.

"I fell in the water because I was leaning over to look at a mermaid! And when I fell in, she saved me. She made me warm and pushed me back to the top."

Her mother smiled tightly at her. "Oh, *fiadhaich*, you have such a beautiful imagination."

"It's all over now, you're safe," her father added.

"The mermaid was there, Mama! I didn't imagine it, I swear!"

Her mother only chuckled in response, squeezing her closer. Kenna kept trying to convince her parents, but they didn't believe her. So she stopped trying, losing herself instead to fantasies about mermaids and pirates and adventures on the sea.

Back at the camp later that night, she climbed into Tristan's bed after their parents left them for the night. It was the first chance that Kenna had had to talk to him alone all day.

"Sissy?" Tristan rolled over to look at her.

Kenna cuddled into him. "You believe me about the mermaid, right?"

"Of course I do! Can you tell me about her?"

Kenna snuggled Tristan tighter, telling him every little detail about the mermaid that saved her. How her tail was the brightest red she had ever seen, and her golden hair looked like a halo floating around her head. Tristan clung to every word, his eyes wide with wonder.

AFTER THAT DAY, anytime sailors came back to the castle from their journeys, Kenna hung onto their every word, tucking their stories into her heart. She wanted to hear about their adventures, and could listen to them talk about the sea forever. Sitting in her mother's lap, she listened with rapt attention, hoping that one of them would tell a tale she wanted to hear about more than anything: the story of a mermaid.

But they never did.

Still, she never stopped believing. Not when her mother and father told her over and over again that mermaids were merely fairy tales, and not when the other kids laughed at her any time she talked about them during a lesson. Eventually, she learned to keep it to herself. Keep that belief, that *knowledge,* tucked away.

Tristan was the only one who always believed her.

On days when he could see her feelings of loneliness and exclusion were too much, he held her hands in his and asked, "*A seòid,* will you tell me about the mermaid again?"

And every time, Kenna would tell him the story again. Tell him about her heart that beat for the sea, called to its unknown depths.

Chapter One

17 Years Later

Standing in the surf along the shore, the warmth of the rising sun bled into Kenna's skin as icy waves lapped at her feet. She went just a little further, until the water was up to her knees. It pulled her, gripping at her legs to suck her down to its depths, but she resisted. She stayed standing as her feet sank deeper into the soft sand beneath, anchoring her where she was.

And as sudden as it came, the pull was gone. In its place, Kenna could see the wave surging towards her, desperate to meet the shore. Crashing into itself to get to her faster, frothing masses of white swarming around her legs. Then the pull came again, and the cycle went on.

But in that moment, the moment before the crash, Kenna's heart thundered in her chest, her senses flooding with everything around her. The only sounds were the rush of water and her own heartbeat pounding in her ears. As dangerous as she knew those waters were, it was the most exhilarating thing she'd ever felt in her life. The most alive she had ever felt. The only time her brain ever quieted enough for her to fully be in the moment, take in and actually process everything around her. And for just a second, she thought about letting that wave pull her. Take her spinning into those unknown fathoms below.

That feeling, that pull, was what Kenna felt every day she stayed away from the ocean. Her heartbeat was the crashing of those waves, her soul forever caught in that riptide. That yearning was only soothed by the cool touch of salt water along her skin.

She didn't know if it had been that way her whole life. If she had felt that longing before she even knew what longing was. Or if it had started that day when the mermaid saved her life. All she knew was she couldn't remember a time before.

She closed her eyes and breathed in the sharp, salty air, trying to soothe the knot of anxiety growing thicker and heavier in her chest. The stress-filled thoughts on a never-ending loop in her head.

She had hoped sneaking down to the waves this morning would help ease her into the day ahead, but even this wasn't quieting her mind today.

Scoffing at her own foolishness, Kenna shook her head, reluctantly pulling her feet from the water's edge and turning back towards the castle. Of course sticking her feet in the ocean wouldn't help. She was being forced to marry. Nothing could help her now.

She glanced over to the small, one-person sailing vessel, shielded inside a small cave and hidden by a long forgotten rockfall, waiting for her.

For one wild moment she considered dragging her boat out now, hopping in, and sailing away. Never looking back. The spiteful side of her thought that if her parents could change their minds, then she could too.

Instead, she forced her feet to carry her back up the cliffside path to the castle, darting through the gardens and up the trellis to her balcony before one of the guards spotted her and ratted her out to her parents.

She made it back into her bed, feigning sleep just in time for her lady's maids, Freya and Martha, to come marching in and get her ready for the day.

Bathing her, clothing her, pinning her hair, and doing her makeup, all the while chatting endlessly about how exciting the day would be, as Kenna's heart sunk further and further into her stomach in dread.

When they were done, Kenna found herself in a beautiful and simple ice-blue dress, her long red waves pulled into an intricately woven knot on the top of her head.

She thanked and dismissed them, making her way to the Great Hall for breakfast where she knew her parents and brother would already be waiting for her.

Her suspicions were confirmed as she stepped into the hall to find them all seated at the head table. Her mother, long auburn hair twisted into an intricate coiffure atop her head, wore a burgundy gown and was eating her breakfast demurely. Her father, with his salt-and-pepper hair and full beard, drank his coffee while he looked over important papers of some kind.

Tristan waved at her enthusiastically with a mouth full of bacon, and she couldn't help but laugh, smothering it with her hand as their parents scolded him for his undignified behavior while she found her seat. Yes, they were twins, but she often teased him about the minutes that separated them, making her the older sibling and him the younger, more carefree one. The twist of fate that had determined the course of her life.

Even with the height difference as he towered above her, along with his curling chestnut hair and light brown eyes differing so much from her own, there was no mistaking their relation. They had the same rounded face, soft neck, and belly. The same red flush to their cheeks, no matter their mood or temperature.

She had just laden her plate with a healthy portion of eggs and bacon when her parents started in. She couldn't remember if she had eaten last night, dinners not being a family affair unless they had guests or important business. And whenever it wasn't a requirement, Kenna often forgot to feed herself. Though she knew her peers would make comments behind her back about how that was possible with her body.

"We want to talk about the men that are coming for the Winchin Festival. To make sure you know what your options are." Her mother's voice broke into the thin layer of calm that had settled over her in Tristan's company.

"I can't even eat before we begin this?" Kenna responded with feigned levity.

Out of the corner of her eye she noticed her mother's mouth tightening, and tried not to feel too vindictive at poking the bear.

Instead she closed her eyes and took a deep breath. She always knew this day would come. She just hadn't expected it would come so soon. Her parents had *promised* her that it wouldn't be so soon. Once the heir turned twenty, they were considered of marriageable age. On her twentieth birthday, she had gone to her parents and begged them for a reprieve. Just because she was of age didn't mean she had to get married right then. She had convinced them to give her more time.

But now, just two years later, war was brewing with the neighboring faerie kingdom, Sithachd. It had started right after Kenna's twentieth birthday, when the faeries halted all trading with Cladach out of the blue. A few months after that, the raids began.

Small parties of faeries sneaking up the shore and raiding their fields and their farms. Stealing livestock and setting fields of food ablaze. They still didn't know what had happened to make the faeries turn on them. Faeries had never been fans of humans, thinking themselves superior. But they had never been outright aggressive, mostly keeping to themselves and ignoring the humans outside of their trading.

Cladach had sent a message to them, calling for a cease of the raids, asking for a meeting to discuss what had happened and try to resolve the issue. That was a year ago, and there had been no response, and no stop to the raids.

Six months ago was when her parents had broken the news to her. They were no longer allowing her to postpone her Winchin Festival. They told her it was for the good of the kingdom. The festival would boost morale with their people, strengthen ties with the clans.

They had taken her choice away, before she was ready.

But whether she was ready for it or not didn't matter; it was here. It might be her marriage, but her parents were still the king and queen, and they still had the final say.

Over the past few months, since telling her they had changed their minds, they'd had this conversation so many times she could repeat the schedule of the entire three-day Winchin Festival by heart. "I know what my options are. But *you* know I do not want this."

"Oh, my *fiadhaich*, my Kenna." Her father sighed. "This might not be what you want, and if I could give you everything you desired out of this life, you know I would. But you and I both have duties to this kingdom, to our people."

"But I don't want to marry for duty, I want to marry for love! Why do I have to sign my life away just because the faeries have decided to start raiding our borders? I want someone to marry Kenna, not Princess Makenna," she pleaded.

"Because they're two different people?" Tristan interjected wryly, his brown eyes gleaming. Kenna shot him a glare, aiming a kick at his shin under the table. She smothered a smirk when he flinched and sent her a dirty look.

"Don't be so dramatic, Kenna, you are not signing your life away. And how do you know you won't find someone you love? You know your father and I didn't know each other for long before we were wed. But we love each other as much as someone can love another person," the queen added, ignoring their bickering and reaching across the table to take her husband's hand.

And it was true. Kenna saw the love in their eyes every time they looked at each other. How they always made excuses to be near each other, to touch each other. How her father constantly surprised her mother with gifts—from a single flower blossom to jewels as big as apples. The gift itself didn't matter to her mother, simply that it showed he was always thinking of her. With them as her example, Kenna had high standards. She didn't ever want to settle for less.

"This afternoon, all of the eligible clan chiefs' sons in Cladach will come to the castle," her mother continued, "and you will spend time with them, picking the man you deem kind and intelligent enough to be your husband, to rule at your side one day. You still have that freedom at least, *mo ghràdh*." Her mother's eyes implored Kenna to cooperate. "You still get to choose."

Kenna huffed a laugh. "Oh, how wonderful I get to choose the least offensive of four men."

"Now, Makenna," her mother retorted, "this is your fate whether you like it or not. We have been sympathetic, but there comes a point when you must accept this. You are a princess. Some princesses don't even have the choice you do, so be grateful for that. We gave you two extra years, but this is the price we must pay to lead the lives we do."

"What if I don't want this life?"

Her question rang in the silence of the room. It was a thought she'd had for as long as she could remember, and had never dared utter aloud before. Kenna's heart pounded in her chest as she took in her parents' shocked faces. She looked to Tristan and found him staring at her in incredulity. He shook his head slightly.

Her parents looked at her with sadness, and a little disappointment. She hated herself for not being the daughter they wanted. The daughter they deserved.

"You have a duty. To this kingdom, to us," her father said softly.

"But Tristan is much better suited—"

"Stop. Kenna, you are the heir, the first-born. There is no changing that. We all must do our duty to serve our people."

"Only by minutes!"

Her parents shared a long-suffering sigh. Tristan looked down at the table, not saying anything aloud, but Kenna knew he would take her place if he could. If there was any other choice.

Kenna knew he would've made a far better ruler for their people than she ever would. She felt suffocated by the thought of being stuck here, tied to this castle forever, when her skin itched for freedom. Yearning for a place that wasn't here, a place where she belonged, a place she would know once she found it.

Tristan, on the other hand, was happiest at home. He cared more than her, enjoyed it more than her; he felt at home here, in his skin, in a way she never had and never would. But her parents wouldn't listen to her pleas. To them, what was done was done. They could not change the fact that she was born first. They wouldn't hear a word otherwise, would never break tradition. Never let her run away to the waters that called her.

But even if Kenna could work up the nerve to run away, she wouldn't. As much as staying made her feel like she was losing herself, she couldn't do that to Tristan, to her parents. She loved Tristan too much to force this responsibility on him without his consent. To force him into a role he didn't choose for himself, even if she believed he would be better at it than her. To disappoint the parents she loved so much. Kenna knew what having your choice taken away felt like. And he wouldn't only have to take on the crown, he would have to take on their parents, and carry their worry and disappointment and fear for the rest of his life.

Kenna closed her eyes, breathing deep and locking her feelings away. "I'm sorry, I won't fight this anymore. I promise. Tell me about the men." She wouldn't fight, but she still wouldn't open herself up like they wanted her to. If this was her duty, then that was how she would go into it. This was a business transaction, and she was here to find the best partner to rule the kingdom with, by her side in title only.

Her parents shared a look, before her mother tentatively began speaking. "Well, first, there will be a change. There are now five men."

"What do you mean? I thought only four of the twelve clans had sons of marriageable age who wished to enter the festival?"

Her father cleared his throat uncomfortably. "There was a fifth."

"Then why was his name not mentioned from the start?"

"We tried to persuade Chief Stewart that it wasn't a good idea, but he insisted they get a fair shot like every other clan, and we cannot afford to alienate any of our clans right now, not with Sìthachd acting out."

No. Kenna's heart dropped in her chest, her mouth going dry as a bone. "You can't be serious." Her voice came out in a ragged whisper, the words tearing at her throat on the way out.

"Now, I know you may not want him to be a part of this, *mo ghràdh,*" her mother tried to interject, "but it was so long ago. It doesn't mean you have to choose him. But you were children then, and Chief Stewart has assured us that his son is different now—"

"I don't care what he says! I meant it when I said I never wanted to see Reid Stewart again!"

"Be reasonable, Kenna," her mother continued in a frustrated voice, "You can't expect us to anger an entire clan just because he was rude to you when you were children."

Her mother's words were like a kick to the stomach, her eyes burning with tears she refused to let fall. This is how it was and would always be. Her parents would never just be her parents. And she would never just be their daughter. They were the king and queen, and she was the heir. They would always put their people first, *had* to put their people first. Of course they had to. *She* was supposed to put her people first as well.

She felt empty, like every cell of her body that had been buzzing to fight for her freedom from this life had given up. What did it matter that Reid had been the final nail in the coffin of her self-esteem? What did it matter that he had single-handedly destroyed the last of her confidence, the last of her hope of finding a person in this world who would love her for who she was? It didn't matter, not when the fate of every person in their kingdom rested on her shoulders.

She was selfish. She was selfish for wanting a different life, selfish for wanting out of something that could help her people.

"You're right," she spoke, her voice barely above a whisper. "I'm being unreasonable."

Her mother looked pained. "No, Kenna, I'm sorry, I—"

But Kenna rose, cutting her mother off before she could say anymore. "I will be there this afternoon when they arrive, and I will do my duty."

"*Fiadhaich,*" her father called weakly, but she was already walking out of the room, silent tears running down her cheeks.

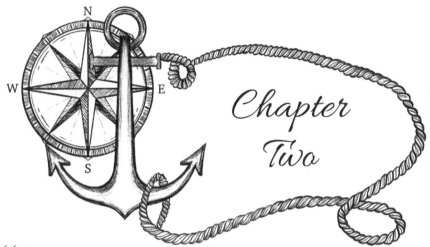

Chapter Two

"Her Royal Highness, Princess Makenna Murdina MacNamera, Crown Heir to the Throne of Cladach."

Stepping into the throne room as the herald called her name, Kenna kept her gaze straight ahead, focused on the throne even as she felt hundreds of eyes on her.

Breathe in, breathe out.

She had spent the last few hours holed up in her room pulling herself together, and then having her maids fix her makeup to erase any evidence of her tears.

"His Royal Highness, Prince Tristan Owen MacNamera of Cladach," was called next. Kenna forced herself not to look back. As much as she might want to meet his reassuring gaze at the moment, she knew she needed to do this without his help.

Longer than it was wide, the hall stretched in front of her, ending in a raised platform. The hall was packed with people, a mix of colors and shapes that Kenna's mind was too overstimulated to decipher, so she continued down the aisle in the center of the room, trying to ignore the looks.

Instead, she focused on the patches of color playing over the ground, brought in by the morning light shining through the stained-glass windows lining both sides of the hall. They depicted the most loved ancestors of her line—queens and kings and monarchs who had come before her and left a lasting mark on their small island kingdom.

People she often felt she would never live up to.

The windows were broken up by grand, white stone pillars shooting up to the tall, vaulted ceiling. The marble floors and cobblestoned walls would make the room feel cold if not for the large windows and the wooden beams crossing the ceilings, which instead made it feel welcoming and cozy. The torches hanging from every pillar as well as the large fireplaces flanking the hall filled the room with pleasant warmth.

Kenna's chest swarmed with butterflies. She still wasn't ready for today, and the conversation this morning had done nothing to make her feel more ready. Kenna didn't think she would ever be ready.

Every step towards that throne, towards the future awaiting her, was another stone on her chest until she was suffocating. This restlessness in her soul was only ever soothed by the sea.

Kenna had little patience for the politics of her court. She felt boxed in by these walls, and the weight of the crown on her head felt like the weight of the whole world. She felt herself wasting away every moment she spent inside training to become queen, instead of out exploring the ocean as she yearned to do. And here she was, willingly walking into the moment that would cement her into this life for forever. This was it. After today, there was no turning back. She would marry, and eventually become queen, and then her life, the life she had always wanted outside the palace, was over.

For a moment, her steps faltered, her body refusing to move another inch. To hell with her responsibilities, to hell with the weight of her parents' expectations. Surely they could find another way to unite their kingdom against the faeries. They could beg another kingdom to fight with them if it came to that; one of the other human kingdoms, or even the pixies.

Her desire to run off to the ocean swelled until it overwhelmed her, until she couldn't think, couldn't do anything but force the breath in and out of her lungs, her mind empty but for the screeching static of her anxiety.

The warm hand on her shoulder brought her back down, and Kenna startled as her brother's voice whispered in her ear from behind, "You can do this."

Closing her eyes, Kenna blew out a breath, expelling everything all on the exhale: her fear, her resentment, her dreams of a different life.

And then she forced herself to keep walking. Forced herself to choose her family, her people, over herself.

She heard every footfall loud as a ringing bell as the room silently waited for her and Tristan to take their seats. Finally, after what felt like ages, she reached her throne. Kenna sat down as gracefully as she could in her gown, her throne smaller and to the left of her mother's, who reached over to squeeze her hand, a mix of sympathy and pride in her gaze.

When she finally gathered the courage to look out at the sea of faces staring up at them, she noticed the five men at the front of the room directly below her. Her heart pounded so hard in her chest she wouldn't be surprised if the whole room could hear it. She took them in briefly; four of them looking vaguely familiar, and at least somewhat close to her age, an array of skin tones from pale white to dark brown. She skipped over the fifth one, feeling like she would lose the contents of her stomach if she truly looked at him.

She met each of their eyes, going down the row—clans Bruce, Grant, Hamilton, Stewart—

Her heart stalled as her eyes tripped over him before she ripped them away. Just the sight of him brought back every memory, every ounce of pain until she felt like she was drowning in it. Kenna closed her eyes, taking in a deep breath and trying to center herself in the moment. She would not let Reid affect her. She would not let Reid have any more control over her or her feelings than she had already let him before.

Forcing her eyes open, Kenna took in the last man in the line.

21

He was wearing the traditional tartan of the clan Mackenzie, the only one of the men entirely unfamiliar to her. She couldn't count the number of times her father had complained about the Mackenzie chief. He was a paranoid old bastard who never left his home, always sending an emissary in his place. His lands covered the largest expanse of farmland of any of the clans, Cladach's main source of grain. It was the only reason Kenna's parents let Isaac Mackenzie get away with never leaving his lands. As long as he upheld his responsibilities, there was no point fighting with him.

His lands covered the northernmost tip of Cladach, the furthest end of the island from the castle which sat along the southern tip, so the royal family preferred to do any correspondence by messenger rather than make the long journey. Especially Kenna. She hadn't been on one since that fateful day she almost drowned as a child. Going on months-long royal tours was an unnecessary danger.

It also happened to be the clan that bore the brunt of Sithachd's raids. Nothing but the Tuamar Sea separated the Mackenzie's land from Sithachd to the North.

Kenna took in the chief's son now as he towered above the other four men, his hair an inky mess of waves atop his head. The second thing that caught her attention were his startlingly blue eyes, the exact cobalt of a stormy sea. His square jaw was covered in a few days' worth of scruff, his shoulders broadly stretching out the fabric of his shirt and coat. His skin was slightly darker than the pale skin of the other white people in the castle, his face and neck the tanned shade of someone who spent a lot of time outside. His lips were full, a shade pinker than his skin.

At the sound of her mother delicately clearing her throat, Kenna realized she had been staring for far too long. Her face flamed with embarrassment. Like most people, she had dreamed of finding a great love someday. But that was all it was—a dream. The idea of ever becoming so vulnerable and intimate with anyone, of opening herself up to be hurt even more than she was by simply daring to exist in her body, terrified her. Kenna couldn't imagine herself being so comfortable with someone as her parents were with each other.

Not anymore.

Her lonely and fraught childhood had crushed all those dreams. *Reid* had crushed all of those dreams.

She may be forced to pick one of these men to marry, but that didn't mean she would open herself to any of them. Open herself up to more hurt.

She quickly glanced to the king and queen, and her father gave her a small smile before facing forward to address the room.

"Welcome! Thank you for being here to celebrate Princess Makenna's Winchin Festival. As you all know, our dear Kenna will spend the next three days getting to know the eligible sons of our clan chiefs, before choosing a partner to wed the following day. Queen Eileen and I were so fortunate to find love at my Winchin Festival, and we have every faith that Kenna will as well."

The room sounded with applause as the king continued, explaining to the crowd how the next three days would work. The competitions, the gatherings, the final ball on the third night where Kenna would dance with all the men and announce who she had chosen. While her father spoke, Kenna found her eyes drifting across the line of men, trying to take their faces in.

When she got to Reid, she forced herself to examine him. This was the first time she had seen him since they were fifteen. Since her father had sent him back to his clan.

He was of average height, the youthful softness of his face now grown out into lean, sharp angles, his limbs thin and gangly. His eyes were still that deceptively warm hazel color. His dirty blond hair was short on the sides, more grown out along the top, and styled in a swooping mop.

He caught her eye and smiled that same smile he used to flash at her, as if it hadn't been seven years since they had seen each other. As if he hadn't taken her tender heart and shattered it into a million pieces.

Kenna swallowed, her dried-out throat sticking to itself painfully, fighting the burn starting in her eyes. She would not give him the satisfaction of a visible response.

She shifted her eyes away from him, as if she didn't even recognize him. As if the sight of him wasn't physically painful. As if Reid meant as little to her as she had meant to him.

Next was Mackenzie, and she found him staring straight back at her. His gaze swept over her from head to toe, and she felt her face heating in response as he grinned at her. The longer his gaze stayed on her, the redder her face got, until she was sure it was flaming. Curse her red hair and fair skin. Every one of her emotions played plainly on her face for the world to see. She hoped everyone assumed the shade of her face was due to general nerves and not the boy—no, *man*—standing at the end of the row.

"Princess Makenna." Her mother's voice brought her back to attention, and she quickly averted her eyes to her mother, who raised an eyebrow. Kenna looked at her questioningly, and the queen smiled at her with humor before talking.

"Would you like to welcome our guests and introduce yourself?" At the response of scattered chuckles, Kenna realized this must not have been the first time her mother asked her this question, and her face flushed again.

"Oh! Um, yes. Yes, of course." Kenna stood up from her throne, folding her hands in front of her.

"Welcome, my noble clansmen. I am grateful you could be here, and I look forward to getting to know each of you." She forced her eyes not to wander to Reid as she spoke. "I am honored you have chosen to accept my invitation, and I hope you find your time here at the castle pleasant." The memorized speech rambled off Kenna's tongue, and when it was done she sat back in her throne to the sound of applause, ready to listen to each of the men introduce themselves.

The first candidate in line stepped forward, and Kenna focused her attention on him. He was taller than her, but not by much. His unruly brown hair was pulled back in a short ponytail at the base of his head. His green eyes sparkled with mirth, bright against his tan skin, and his mouth curved in a friendly smile. Kenna thought to herself that maybe this wouldn't be so bad after all.

And then he started talking.

"Your Highness." His smile deepened into a smirk, his voice slick with barely concealed smugness. "I am grateful for your invitation to this Winchin Festival. My name is James, son of Chief Donovan of the Bruce Clan. I am eagerly waiting for the chance to get to know you, and of course, Your Majesties as well. I couldn't think of better in-laws to have..." Kenna tuned him out as he shifted his focus to her parents and droned on.

At least he wasn't subtle about his reasons for being here. But Kenna had no interest in entertaining men who were here only for social gain.

A man who had no intentions for anything but the throne was not the one who should sit on it.

Her mind drifted as Hamilton and Grant spoke, paying no attention to the sentiments she was sure were identical to Bruce's. Kenna had zero interest in their obvious flattery. She had known this was how it would be. They were only here for the crown, not for her. But what else could she expect? How could someone care for her when they didn't even know her? And yet she still had to pick one of them. She simply had to pick the most tolerable one.

"Your Highness, it's good to see you again." Reid's voice rang through the air, stealing all the breath from her lungs. Her eyes snapped to his, and when they met, he winked at her. *Winked.* Anger coursed through her veins, slowly taking over the pain.

"My name is Reid, of the Stewart Clan, though you already know all that." His grin was sharp, and anyone looking from the outside probably saw it as genuine, but she saw the coldness under his facade. "I'm honored to be here vying for your hand, Princess. And Your Majesties, thank you for having me." He bowed to them, swinging his focus away from her to flash his blindingly charming smile at them, and her blood boiled. Gods, what she would give to spite him right then and there, in front of everyone. If he continued speaking, she didn't hear, the sound of her blood thundering through her veins blocking out any other sound.

He didn't even try to hide the fact that he was here just for the crown. He hadn't changed one bit since she last saw him. The only difference was that now she knew not to fall for his fake niceties.

"Princess Makenna, it is a pleasure to meet you." Her inner turmoil was interrupted by the voice that rang out through the room, deep and confident. It was the first time one of them had actually said her name, everyone else only addressing her as "Your Highness."

It was him. Mackenzie. His gaze was locked on her, eyes intense in a way that made her want to shiver. No one had ever looked at her that way before, like they were looking past her title, looking at *her*. She didn't know what to do with such attention.

His eyes were lit with mischief, as if he could read her thoughts.

"I am honored to make your acquaintance. My name is Cameron, son of Chief Isaac of the Mackenzie Clan. I look forward to getting to know you more these next few days." He smiled then, and it seemed genuine.

"If I may," he continued, "I have brought a gift for Your Highness. I've heard tales of your love for the sea."

Reid and Bruce glanced at each other, smothering laughter at his words, but Cameron paid them no mind as he walked towards her.

Kenna's smile froze on her face. Yes, she had been prepared for the men to all be there only for the crown. But to go out of his way to embarrass her was beyond cruel. She cursed herself for being distracted by her strange reaction to him enough to let her guard down.

Because apparently, he'd heard the rumors about her obsession and was now going to humiliate her with it in front of the whole room. There was no way she could stop him without making it worse.

Now, at the edge of the platform, Cameron revealed the hand Kenna hadn't realized was hiding behind his back, and she let out a gasp.

He held the most beautiful necklace she had ever seen. There were at least a hundred pearls in every shade imaginable—white, green, blue, cream, pink, orange, purple, silver—strung on fine silver chains, looking as if they floated in midair. Several loops of chain carried the pearls, starting shorter near the neck and longer towards the bottom strands. The way they fell longer in the middle made them look like an iridescent waterfall of shimmering color. When worn, it would seem as if the pearls adorned her skin rather than hung from a necklace, and she knew the effect would be breathtaking.

"I hope this pleases you?"

"I—" Kenna struggled to get the words out. "This is the most beautiful necklace I've ever seen. Thank you." Looking into his eyes, she saw satisfaction and pride.

He smiled happily. "Would you like me to help you put it on?" Kenna froze for a moment, before nodding her head and standing up from the throne.

She barely dared to breathe, air moving in and out of her shallowly, terrified to move an inch as he stepped up behind her. His heat radiated all over her back as he reached his arms around her, settling the necklace along her collarbone. She suppressed the shudder wanting to force its way down her body as his fingers softly grazed her neck.

"Beautiful," he whispered for only her to hear, before coming back around to stand in front of her. Then he bowed, returning to his place in the line.

Her head was filled with the pleasant fuzziness that occurred when someone did something for her. No one outside her family had ever given her such a beautiful, thoughtful gift.

It was only when she looked up at him and saw Reid scowling beside him that she remembered where she was. Who was here watching her reaction to this gift. Schooling her features as close to indifference as she could, Kenna barely heard as her parents thanked and dismissed the men, reminding them about the archery competition taking place that afternoon.

In a daze, she stood up and followed her parents out of the hall, Tristan trailing behind. Outside the hall, her guards were ready and waiting to escort her to her rooms. Once safely enclosed there, she shut the door behind her, dismissing her maids. She went to her vanity, carefully taking off and laying down the necklace on its surface.

She stared at it, trying to figure out what the *hell* had just happened.

Reid, Mackenzie, the whole festival—it was all too much. Her body didn't know what emotion to feel, shock and frustration and confusion warring in her overstimulated brain until she shut down, unable to process anything else. And she still had the archery competition to get through.

Chapter Three

T he time in between the presentation of the suitors and the archery competition found Kenna hiding out with Tristan. She knew she was meant to be acquainting herself with the men, but she needed space to sort out her emotions.

Kenna was curled up in her window seat, attempting to read a book on the proper techniques of wayfinding—a different kind of sailing technique used in a country of islands to the south—though her mind kept wandering from the words in front of her. Tristan was sprawled out on the bench across from her, their feet tangled together, reading his own book. She was fairly certain it was one of her romances he had stolen from her shelves.

Every now and then he nudged her leg with his foot, smiling at her, providing her comfort with just his solid presence in only the way her twin had ever been able to. A servant knocked on her door after a short time, announcing they were ready for the archery competition.

Sighing, she bookmarked her page and set it aside, letting the servant lead the way. As they strolled through the castle, Kenna's arm looped through Tristan's elbow, she mentally prepared herself to see the men again.

During the Winchin Festival, suitors participated in challenges each day. Not as a competition, but as a fun way for the crown heir to get to know their options. And the first challenge was always archery.

Yes, shooting arrows at targets was fun when you were the one doing the shooting. But sitting there for hours watching other people do it was *boring.* Not to mention, she was sure most of them would be preening and showing off, hoping to get in her parents' good graces. Didn't they know it was *her* choice, not her parents'? Of course that wouldn't matter to them, though.

She wondered how good a shot any of them would even be.

Kenna reached the field where the competition was taking place, the crowd already gathered, looking to the shaded tent where their parents were already seated.

Tristan grinned cheekily at her, speaking as they settled into their seats.

"Oh no, it looks like we're late!" he exclaimed in mock horror, keeping his voice low so only she could hear him. "That's the second time for you today, dear sister. If you're not careful, people will think you don't want to be here."

"You're a regular comedian, aren't you?"

"Being the spare, I decided to take up other interests to bide my time. I'd make a great court jester if I do say so myself."

Kenna laughed and playfully shoved his shoulder. "You are something else, that's for sure."

"Speaking of humor, do you want to make this competition a little more fun?"

Kenna looked at him sideways, unsure where he was going with this. "And you want to do that how?"

"We place bets on how many of them bring flowers for Mother, or look to Mother and Father every other minute instead of you?"

Kenna tried to smother her laugh, but was only half successful, according to the look their mother gave her.

Tristan opened his mouth to continue, but before he could say anything, the king stood up and addressed the nobles and court members gathered.

"Thank you for joining us for the first event of the festival!" He paused for the scattered applause. "Keep in mind this is just for fun, and the only prize to be won today is a good time." His statement was met with amused laughter; the people of Cladach well used to his cheesy jokes.

"There will be three rounds, one shot each. May the best man win!" Her father settled back into his seat next to the queen, taking her hand in his own.

The crowd quieted down, and Kenna looked ahead to see the first of the men preparing to take his shot. It was the son from the Bruce Clan, James.

Before shooting, he turned and bowed smugly to her parents. Kenna rolled her eyes at Tristan, who sucked his lips into his mouth to hide his own smile.

"They may all be brainless, but at least they're fun to look at," Tristan observed, scanning his eyes over Bruce's lightly muscled frame, dirty blond waves, and light brown eyes glinting in the sunlight.

Kenna scoffed. "Please, you're telling me you would really want to be with any of these buffoons?"

"How do you know they're all buffoons? Some of them seem like they could be sparkling conversationalists."

"I know you've been too distracted staring at their asses to listen to what they're saying."

Tristan grinned. "You know I can't resist a good ass." Kenna snorted, knowing full well Tristan had enjoyed his fair share of both men and women and their asses, and his grin widened, knowing he successfully distracted her. "Now hush and pay attention."

Kenna refocused on Bruce as he turned back to the target and let his arrow loose, hitting the first ring outside of the bullseye. Not bad. Unfortunately for James, his arrogance reflected it.

Didn't men know how unattractive that was?

31

He smirked cockily over his shoulder at Kenna before dropping his bow.

Apparently not.

"He's like a peacock with all that preening," Tristan murmured.

"So, not your type after all?"

"I may like a good ass, but I also prefer a person with a personality to match," he responded dryly.

It appeared as if Kenna would need to lower her standards if she expected to pick one of these men. She only had three other options besides Bruce, after all. If Reid thought he actually had a chance, he was more delusional than he had ever painted Kenna to be.

According to his tartan, the next one in line was Michael Hamilton. He had been rather quiet and polite earlier that morning, and Kenna decided she should probably keep an eye on him as a potential choice. He seemed sweet—although she couldn't trust first impressions—and someone quiet and kind was exactly who she should choose. Someone she could be happy coexisting with, but not risk losing her heart to.

He notched his arrow and took aim, hitting right on the rim of the bullseye. After the arrow hit its mark, he turned around and beamed at her before giving a little bow. Her lips quirked, and she clapped politely along with everyone else.

The next to go was Murtagh Grant. He was short and thick, his light brown skin glowing in the sunlight. His long black hair was pulled into a bun atop his head, and his bright greenish-brown eyes kept flicking to Tristan next to her when he thought she wasn't paying attention. She felt Tristan sitting up straighter in his seat. *Interesting*, she thought to herself, trying to hide her small smile.

After Grant, it was Reid's turn, and she made a point to not give him any of her attention, chatting with Tristan instead, to Reid's obvious displeasure. By the time his turn was over, a frown was tugging at his lips.

Every few minutes, as the competition dragged on, Kenna shifted in her seat, trying to find a comfortable position. She had never been able to sit still, her body constantly needing to be in motion. So whenever she did have to sit for long periods of time, she found herself readjusting in her chair, shaking her legs, tapping her fingers, clicking her teeth, or any other small movement she could do to dispel her energy. She tried to hide her yawn, but the afternoon sun and her full belly were making her sleepy. She wanted a nice, long nap.

Before she knew it, it was the last suitor's turn. Mackenzie.

She straightened in her chair. He picked his arrow up without looking in their direction, and Kenna watched as he took his shot. She was unable to tear her eyes away from the sight of his strong back, the muscles rippling and flexing under his shirt, arms bulging while he pulled the string taut, before promptly letting go with a satisfying *thwang* Kenna felt in her chest.

The arrow thudded directly in the middle of the bullseye.

Mackenzie looked back at her, the corner of his mouth tilting into a grin, a dimple emerging she hadn't noticed earlier this morning. His eye caught hers, and her face warmed.

Oh, she was really in trouble now. Dimples were her undoing.

At the pointed cough to her left, she tore her gaze away from him and looked to Tristan, his brow raised.

Kenna looked down, staring at her clenched hands in her lap, cheeks on fire.

She felt flustered, and she didn't understand why. What was so special about him? This *awareness* of Mackenzie and the space he took up was so out of the ordinary for her; her body had never reacted like this before. She noticed when people were attractive, of course, but she was never attracted to them specifically without forming some kind of emotional connection with them. The few people she *had* been attracted to before in her life, she had known first. Had some sort of relationship with.

This wasn't that, it wasn't exactly attraction. She didn't know what to call it, though. Attraction was too much, but simple awareness didn't feel like enough either.

Why was Mackenzie different? Why did her body react when she didn't know him? Whatever it was, she didn't like it. She had built these walls around her heart for a reason, and someone who held this power over her could break her.

No.

Kenna had already accepted she would marry for reasons other than love, but she couldn't let herself fall for him, even if he seemed different than the others in some way.

But what concerned her the most about it all was that she felt *drawn* to him on more than simply a physical level.

Which was stupid! She didn't know him any better than any of the other men—less, in fact. Could that be it? He was just a mystery that intrigued her? She wasn't usually one to enjoy mystery. She liked the comfort of knowing. She hated being left in the dark, vulnerable to whatever was there left unseen that might hurt her.

The way Reid had hurt her.

The way the girls she'd called friends had hurt her.

At first, all the girls in the castle had been her best friends. They had talked about everything, including which of the boys they thought were cute. Even though Kenna had been a confident child in most ways, she had always been shy about her feelings and crushes. She didn't seem to feel them the way all the other girls did. She only had her first crush long after all the other girls had gone through multiple. She had thought there was something wrong with her, not wanting the same thing the other girls did, or at least not in the same way.

But then she did have her first crush, and she realized she simply didn't experience attraction in the same way. But she was still hesitant to share with the other girls, because feelings exposed her, made her vulnerable.

All she'd had at first was Tristan, and of course she wouldn't trade him for anything; he was her favorite person in the world. But these were friends she had chosen for herself. Tristan hadn't had a choice. As twins, they shared everything. It was nice to have her own thing, her own people. People who had chosen her. Or so she had thought.

When she was fifteen, she had opened up to the other girls about a boy she had started to crush on. Reid.

She told them how handsome and regal she thought he was, and how he always smiled back at her, making her believe he liked her too. It wasn't until one day when she was walking down the hall to her music lesson that she heard what her supposed friends *and* Reid truly thought about her.

She heard voices from a door left slightly ajar down the hall. Curious, she crept closer to see who it was when she heard her name, making her freeze.

"Kenna really thinks I *like* her?" said a male voice she'd recognized. Reid.

"I know, can you believe it?" a female voice laughingly responded.

"As if I could ever like a whale like her. For the gods' sake, she still believes in dumb fairy tales! If I hear her talk about mermaids one more time I'm going to die." His statement was met with a round of snickering.

"No kidding. She's lucky she's a princess with a title to give. Otherwise, no one would even look twice at her. *Especially* not after she opened her fat mouth."

"Why do you think I even bother smiling at her? I could be *king* someday. All I'd have to do is put up with her and her fucking mermaid obsession. I hope it's worth it." That had spurred another round of laughter and retorts, but Kenna hadn't heard them. She'd already taken off, running back to her rooms, desperate to get there before the tears started rolling down her face. Hours later her father had come into her rooms to find her still sobbing. He'd held her tight and demanded to know what had happened. Once Kenna told him, he immediately sent Reid away, back to his clan's territory.

The unknown was what scared her more than anything now. Kenna had never felt a pain like that before. And it wasn't just Reid. It was all of her friends.

The people she had chosen, who had made her believe that they had chosen her too. They had all been using her just to chase the throne. Not a single one of the people in her life who weren't related to her cared about her.

So she built higher walls around her heart. It was the only way to protect herself.

She vowed to herself she would never let someone in who didn't want her for exactly who she was—just Kenna. No one besides Tristan had ever managed to scale that wall around her heart. At this point, she wasn't even sure if she wanted anyone to. It may have been lonely, but it was safe. She was safe.

Her mind, against her will, wandered back once more back to that morning, and the way Mackenzie had looked at her when he'd given her that necklace.

Like he had really seen her.

Like he really cared.

She shook her head, forcing herself to drop the notion. She had to rule him out as an option. She needed someone safe, and Hamilton was looking like the best contender so far.

Reid was still chasing her crown. Still trying to use her heart as a ladder to climb his way into power. There was no way Mackenzie was here for her. She didn't think any of them were, and the sooner she got that through her thick skull, the better off she'd be.

Chapter Four

The men each went two more rounds—Mackenzie, of course, getting a bullseye all three times—and the competition was over. The party moved to the side of the field, and a table was set up with platters of food and drink for everyone to mingle and for Kenna to spend some time with each of the men. She browsed the options, choosing a soft and flaky chocolate-filled pastry before she felt a familiar presence behind her and tried not to roll her eyes.

"So... did I notice you noticing Cameron Mackenzie earlier?" Tristan asked, barely concealed mirth lacing every word.

"I have absolutely no idea what you're talking about," she said airily, continuing to browse the table while nibbling on her pastry. Tristan followed.

"Mm-hmm. Of course not. Because you dislike all of these men."

"Exactly."

"And you definitely don't find any of them appealing."

"Definitely not."

"Even though your face says otherwise."

"Precisely. Hey, wait, no! That's not true!" Kenna turned on him and smacked his arm. He howled with laughter. "Will you keep your voice down? People are staring."

Tristan looked around and sure enough, a few of the guests were looking at them curiously.

They turned back to each other and burst into giggles. Kenna was still bent over in laughter, clutching Tristan's arm for support while he laughed beside her, when Michael Hamilton ambled over.

"Well, you two certainly seem to be the life of the party this afternoon." He smiled at them, his eyes twinkling good-naturedly.

Tristan spoke as Kenna tried to rein in her laughter. "Ah, it's all my sweet sister. She's a true comedian."

"Ha! Very funny, dear brother. You forget you trained as the court jester, so I shall leave the comedy to you." They looked at each other and dissolved into laughter again.

"I'm so sorry, we're being rude," Tristan said, noticing Hamilton's cluelessness. "I'm going to excuse myself now and let the two of you talk." Tristan grinned before kissing her cheek and making his exit.

Kenna turned to Hamilton, the ghost of laughter still on her lips. He stood a few inches taller than her, with thick wavy brown hair falling across his brow. His chocolate brown eyes glowed with warmth in the sun, his skin a rich brown.

His face was soft and open and friendly, and though they stood there in a silence which should've felt awkward, it didn't. With every moment passing, Kenna felt her taut shoulders relax.

They spoke at the same moment.

"Your dress is—"

"You shot very—"

He motioned to her. "Ladies first."

"I was going to say you shot very well. You're a talented archer."

He bowed his head. "Thank you, Your Highness. The bow and arrow are my weapon of choice, so I'm glad I live up to its standards." He smiled. "I was going to say your dress is very beautiful. That blue suits you."

Kenna blushed and lowered her head. "You are too kind."

"I like to think I'm just the right amount of kind." At his joke, Kenna giggled, looking back up to find him already grinning at her. They continued their small talk, Hamilton remaining pleasant and polite and funny.

When she looked at him, though, she felt nothing. No trip in her pulse, no awareness of him. No yearning for him to know her, see her. She felt comfortable, safe.

He didn't set her pulse racing like Mackenzie. Her body didn't seem to get the message that that was a good thing, though.

She opened her mouth to respond to whatever Hamilton had just said when suddenly Reid was walking up behind his shoulder. As Reid began speaking, Hamilton bowed his head and left them to talk alone.

"Princess." Her stomach curdled at the name, the only thing Reid had ever called her. When they were younger, she had thought it sweet, a term of endearment. She had eventually realized that it wasn't anything but a reminder that he saw her as nothing more than a crown. She tightened her grip on her glass until her knuckles were tight. Her other hand still held the plate with the half-eaten pastry sitting atop, and Reid flicked his eyes disapprovingly at it. "Enjoying the afternoon treats, I see?"

On the outside it must have looked like a perfectly pleasant exchange. She was sure no one else could feel the current of tension flowing between them. The hand holding the plate trembled, and heat crawled up her neck at his thinly veiled insult.

No. She would not let this disgrace of a human being make her feel any sort of way about herself. She straightened her back and hardened her eyes, looking at him dismissively.

"I had to find something worthy of occupying my time, didn't I?"

He grazed his eyes up and down her body. "I'd say you didn't need any more *occupying*, wouldn't you?"

Kenna clenched her jaw, her entire body trembling now. Was she truly being forced to endure this? Anger and heartbreak swelled in her chest in equal measures, that her parents would allow this man back into their castle, into her life. The injustice that she was forced to endure this man who was intent on ripping open every barely healed scab over her heart.

"You," she began, forcing her words to come out steadily. Kenna refused to let him see her break. "You will *never* be king. Do you hear me?" The false warmth in his eyes began to cool at her words. "I may be forced to endure your presence here out of deference to your parents, but if you thought there was even a chance that I would choose you, you have lost your grip on reality, Stewart."

Adrenaline surged through her veins, and she turned on her heel, catching the eye of Mackenzie who she hadn't realized was standing behind them, and had probably heard everything. There was nothing she could do about that though, so she deposited her plate and drink on a nearby table, and stormed her way back towards the castle.

As soon as her back was turned to the party on the field behind them, the tears she had been holding back began streaming down her face, but she refused to lift a hand to wipe them until she was fully out of sight.

She forced herself to keep her back straight, her stride unhurried. She would not let Reid get the satisfaction of knowing how much he hurt her.

No, of course she didn't still have feelings for him. If she was honest with herself, she never truly did. It had been the facade she had built up in her head. The boy he had wanted her to see.

But that didn't matter to her brain. It wasn't him specifically that truly hurt her. It was what he represented. It was the pain of rejection. The knowledge that she was too different, too weird, too big, too *much* for everyone, and she always would be.

Reid was her confirmation. Seven years later, and nothing had changed. She was still the lonely, fat girl who couldn't let go of fairy tales, desperate for someone to truly see her.

Once she turned the corner around the side of the castle and found herself alone, she collapsed back against the stones, dashing the tears from her cheeks and trying to calm her racing thoughts. His words from when they were teenagers kept repeating in her head over and over: *as if I could ever like a whale like her.*

She hadn't had these obsessive thoughts in years, but seeing him again, talking to him again, was bringing it all back.

A shadow fell on the ground in front of her, and she looked up to see Mackenzie standing in front of her. Kenna's face heated in embarrassment at having been caught like this, and by no one other than Mackenzie, because of *course* it had to be him.

She did her best to pull herself back together, wiping helplessly at her face and scrambling back up from where she had been slouching against the wall.

"That was quite the show back there," he commented, and Kenna couldn't read the expression on his face. It was something... searching. Like he was trying to find some sort of answer in her face.

Gods, she couldn't take any more of this right now. She could not handle one more person making her feel so small.

"Mackenzie. What do you want?" Her voice was sharp, curt. She never spoke to anyone like this. She prided herself on being kind, on never making someone else feel the way she had felt that day at fifteen.

Mackenzie raised his brow at her, and something that looked an awful lot like approval fitted across his face. "I was coming to check on you." His voice was soft, something that if she was foolish she would call kind.

She turned her chin up dismissively, wanting him to just *go away.*

"That is not your concern, Mackenzie."

He looked confused. "Is it not the right thing to check on someone who is clearly upset? Not that I blame you. That Stewart is—well, he is clearly an arsehole."

Kenna bit her lip against the smile trying to tug at her mouth. She didn't know what game he was playing, but she had no interest in going along with it. She forced a blank expression onto her face. "I have no idea what you mean. I am perfectly fine, and you are free to go."

"That's alright. I'm fine where I am," he responded, ignoring her request like he didn't understand her words for the dismissal they clearly were. Instead, he leaned his large frame against the wall next to her, crossing his arms over his wide chest, casually taking in the view in front of them, as if this was totally normal.

"What," she spoke tightly through clenched teeth, as she turned to face him fully, "do you think you are doing?"

"Enjoying a beautiful afternoon with a beautiful woman. Do you wish to do something else? I would be fine with that. What did you have in mind, Kenna?"

Kenna spluttered at his words, at his flirting and the way he just so casually called her by her given name. No one spoke to her this way. Like she was just a *person.* She didn't know what to do with his complete lack of care for her title. Worse, she *liked* it.

She felt annoyance rising to the surface of her skin. How dare he speak to her like this, and how dare her body *enjoy* it.

"I am your crown heir. You may address me as Your Highness," she responded icily.

He ran his gaze down her body and back up again, landing back on her own eyes. "Kenna suits you better."

Kenna's jaw dropped, and a feeling she refused to name tried to rise in her chest. The longer they talked, the more she forgot about Reid and the way he'd made her feel. Instead a fire was building under her skin, and it had everything to do with the man standing in front of her.

"Who do you think you are?"

"I believe I introduced myself as Cameron Mackenzie, yes?"

"Ugh!" Kenna half groaned, half screamed at his impertinence. Her chest rising and falling with her heaving breaths, her hands clenched in fists at her sides. She hadn't noticed until now that they had both been slowly leaning further into each other until they were merely a few inches apart.

She didn't understand what this feeling was building inside her. She couldn't tell if she wanted to pull him closer or push him further away, which only confused her more. "You are most aggravating is what you are."

"Oh, it's aggravation you're feeling right now, is it?" He smirked at her.

Shock splashed through her system at his words. Mackenzie was right. Kenna didn't know exactly what she was feeling, but it wasn't aggravation. She hated that he saw that, that he seemed to read her so easily.

She stepped back from him, schooling her features and forcing herself to appear unaffected. Something like disappointment ran across his face, too fleeting for her to be sure. Kenna couldn't help but notice how dangerous he felt. How he made her *feel*. It was in direct contrast to the comfortable nothingness she had felt earlier around Hamilton. Talking to him had drawn zero reaction from her or her body. And yet these few moments with Mackenzie had made her feel things she had never felt before, things she couldn't name.

Every time their eyes had met throughout the day, it was like her corset cinched tighter, making it harder and harder to breathe. Her skin heated, not from the sun, but from his gaze setting her on fire. Making her feel things she couldn't allow herself to feel for someone only here for the crown.

All at once she had no more energy for whatever this was. She had to escape, had to get her head back on track. She let her expression shutter, letting go of the fire he had been stoking.

"If you will not leave, then I will. Goodbye, Mackenzie."

His eyes tracked her keenly as she stepped around him, and continued back towards the castle, and the entire way, she felt his gaze burning across her back like a brand. And despite everything, she felt an ember still burning low inside her at the knowledge that he couldn't take his eyes off her.

She needed a bath.

A very cold bath.

Chapter Five

I t wasn't until Kenna made it through the entrance of the castle, her shoulders sagging in relief, that she realized she had all but forgotten about Reid. Mackenzie had so easily wiped the other man from her brain, taking up all the space in her mind himself. Had that been on purpose?

It didn't matter, she resolved to herself. She could spend years trying to understand why other people did things, and she would be left with nothing but confusion and a feeling of isolation. Kenna shook the pointless thoughts from her mind. She was so close to the safety of her room now, where she could hide until it was time for dinner.

It was at that moment that she heard her mother's voice calling for her. "There you are!"

Kenna closed her eyes, cursing before she turned to find the queen walking towards her.

"*Mo ghràdh*, come with me. Let's go talk somewhere, just us two." The Queen linked her arm with Kenna's and led her to one of the many open sitting rooms along the entrance hall. She didn't know what her mother wanted to talk to her about, but Kenna was sure by her tone she wouldn't like it. She didn't have the energy to keep up a positive facade at the moment, not after the overstimulation and emotional whiplash of the last hour.

She had been *so close* to a single moment of peace and quiet, but she tried not to let her frustration show. She had promised her parents she would try, and it wasn't fair to take out her lingering frustrations over Reid and Mackenzie on her. As much as she wished she could blame her mother for Reid being there, Kenna had to remind herself that her mother didn't have a choice. Not if she wanted to avoid conflict with Clan Stewart.

They sat down on a chaise that faced the large windows looking out over the ocean, her mother taking in the view, quiet for a moment. The side of the castle they were on faced the cliffs looking out over the ocean. Outside the windows, endless blue stretched out as far as the eyes could see. Fluffy white clouds lazily trailed their way across the sky.

"You know, this wasn't the life I planned to live," her mother began, still not looking at her. "I know you've heard the story of how my entire clan was ripped from me."

Kenna did know, of course she did. She had grown up on the stories of the Canduine clan. Her mother's had been the thirteenth clan of Cladach. Before Kenna was born, when her parents were the age she was now, Cladach had been at war with a different kingdom.

In the end, Cladach had won, but it had come at a steep price. The already small clan of Canduine had been entirely wiped out. All but the chief's daughter, who had been sent ahead to the castle in fear of that exact scenario playing out.

"I miss my family..." The queen paused, pain lacing her every word. "My clan. Every day I miss them with all my heart," she continued. "And there are times I wonder how different things would be if I hadn't been forced to leave my home and meet your father. But from the moment I laid eyes on him, I knew he was the one. I could feel it, in my heart, in my soul—as if there was a thread tying my life to his."

Kenna's heart clenched in her chest at the pain she could so clearly hear in her mother's voice even now. Kenna felt her throat thick with unshed tears as her mother continued.

"So trust me, *fiadhaich,* when I say I understand what it's like to ache in your soul for a different life. To feel as if you are missing a piece of yourself. But I believe everything happens for a reason. We may not be able to see the reason in that moment, but I know it to be true. If I hadn't lost my family and my home and ended up here at the castle, I wouldn't have your father."

The queen looked at Kenna now, love shining in her watery eyes. She reached over and held both of Kenna's hands in her own, squeezing tight. "I wouldn't have *you.* You and Tristan are both *mo cridhe.*"

Kenna hugged her mother, holding tight while she continued speaking.

"I know you may not be able to see it right now, but I promise you everything your father and I have ever done has been for you. I know you feel drawn to the sea. I know you feel as if you belong out there, and not here, but *trust me* when I tell you it is best for you to stay here. Stay on land, away from the water, and rule this kingdom. In two days you will choose and marry your husband. Try and open your heart to love, *mo cridhe,* because you never know where it will come from, and how it will change you forever."

Tears welled along Kenna's lashes at her mother's words. "I'm trying, Mother. I'm trying so hard to be what you need me to be. What our kingdom needs me to be. But everything feels confusing, and I don't know what I'm doing." At her crumpling face, Kenna felt her mother cup her cheek.

"I know you're trying. And I know it's hard, but that doesn't mean you give up. It simply means you try harder. You've had one afternoon with these men. That's not enough to write them all off already."

"But how am I supposed to ignore my heart? When it tells me this isn't where I'm meant to be?" Kenna couldn't hide the tremor in her voice, her frustration and helplessness building inside of her with no way out.

Her mother pulled back, smoothing Kenna's hair away from her face, tucking it behind her ears. "Your heart will find its home. I know it will."

Kenna didn't respond, too lost in the tangle of her thoughts to try and translate any of them into words. She wanted to believe her mother, but it was hard to imagine a world in which she found happiness here in the castle with one of these men.

She merely nodded to her mother, standing to exit, when her mother spoke again.

"Why don't you spend more time talking to the Mackenzie boy at dinner?"

Kenna froze. "Why?"

Her mother laughed, not realizing the impact her suggestion was having on Kenna. "Don't think I didn't notice the way you've been watching him all day, *mo ghràdh*. I am your mother, after all." Kenna felt her face burning with embarrassment. It was one thing for Tristan to have picked up on her confusing feelings for Mackenzie, but having her mother point it out was so much worse. "Besides, I think he is the perfect choice. It would be good for the kingdom to have a direct line to the Mackenzie clan. Isaac has been much too reclusive lately, and with most of the raids being on the Mackenzie borders it would be extremely beneficial."

Fury surged through Kenna's veins. She nodded stiffly, leaving the room without another word. She could not *believe* this. Betrayal sat like a stone in her stomach. Not only were they forcing this on her when she desperately didn't want to take part, now her parents were trying to sway her choice? The only part of this damn nightmare she had any control over, and now they were trying to persuade her to choose who *they* wanted?

It did not matter that she couldn't stop thinking about Cameron Mackenzie herself. It didn't matter that if she allowed herself, she could admit that she was intrigued by him. She was never going to choose him. She couldn't allow herself to choose, to open herself up to the possibility of more hurt. Because if she had wanted to choose him, and then her parents pushed him on her, she would always wonder in the back of her mind if it had really been her choice.

As she walked, her mind spun over itself so fast she could barely keep up. Part of her wanted to believe in her mother. Kenna knew she was doing what she thought was best for their kingdom. But she wished that just once, she could just be her mother, not her queen.

Kenna shoved the thought aside. It was pointless, because it could never happen. Instead, she focused on their conversation before she had brought up Mackenzie.

Maybe her mother was right about that. Maybe it was too soon to write all of the men off. If Kenna actually allowed herself to get to know them better, she might connect with one of them.

Mackenzie came to mind at that thought.

She still couldn't figure out what it was about him; why she found her mind and eyes constantly drawn to him. Her mind flashed back to the conversation with him before her mother found her. Mackenzie flustered her, and she hated feeling out of control of her body, a predicament she found herself in far more often than she would like.

"Kenna?" The voice startled her, causing her steps to falter. She had been so lost in her thoughts she hadn't heard anyone approaching. She turned and her breath caught in her throat as she saw none other than Makenzie himself striding purposefully towards her.

She groaned. Gods not again. Had she conjured him with her obsessive thoughts? She didn't think she could handle feeling one more emotion that afternoon. But she had already been outright rude to him once already today. She couldn't snub him again so soon.

She elected to ignore the fact that he continued ignoring proper etiquette addressing her by her given name. She definitely ignored the way that she liked it.

Kenna forced a tight smile to her lips, attempting to ignore the fast tempo of her pulse. "Makenzie, what a surprise! I didn't hear you behind me. And so soon after our last conversation."

He smiled good-naturedly in response, ignoring the subtext in her words. "You did seem quite lost in your own mind. Nothing troubling you, I hope?"

Kenna took her time before answering, eyes roaming his face. She didn't know what game he was playing, but she would play along for now.

"Not particularly, no," she finally replied, choosing her words. "I tend to get lost in my mind more frequently than is perhaps appropriate."

Mackenzie gave no response and simply offered her his arm. "May I escort you for the rest of your walk?"

Kenna bobbed her head in acceptance, tucking her hand into the crook of his elbow. She despised the goosebumps running along her skin at his warm touch.

"Where are we headed, if you don't mind me asking?" Mackenzie's voice intruded her thoughts once more.

"Just back to my rooms. I intend to take a bath before tonight's dinner." As soon as the words left her mouth, her cheeks flamed. She hadn't been thinking about who she was speaking to until the words had left her mouth. And now the image of his skin glistening with warm water flashed in her mind, deepening the scarlet she was sure painted her cheeks. These thoughts were the exact opposite effect of the reason she had planned a cold bath.

Either Mackenzie's mind was far cleaner than hers, or he politely chose to ignore the implications. "Ah, yes. Nothing beats being submerged in the comfort of water, does it?"

Kenna turned her head toward him in surprise. "Do you also share an affinity for the water?"

Something flashed in his eyes too quickly for her to read and he cleared his throat before responding, "You could say something like that." He changed the subject abruptly enough to give her whiplash. "So, what is it you do with your free time?"

"Oh, um." Kenna scrambled, struggling to come up with an answer to his sudden question. This version of him was so completely different than how he had acted with her before. Outside, it was almost as if he had been trying to get a reaction from her. But now he was all perfect politeness and appropriate curiosity. Like he had a mental list of questions he was reading from.

Forcing herself to focus back on the question, all Kenna could think of was reading or sailing, neither of which seemed a good response to his question.

"I must confess, I don't often possess much time for myself. But when I do find a spare moment, I have always loved to be outside somewhere. Perhaps enjoying a walk in the garden, or riding horses through the forest with my brother if he is also free."

Gods, but she really was boring, wasn't she?

"How delightful," Mackenzie responded, and Kenna stiffened, waiting for the barb to follow about her 'simple' tastes. "I too always find myself happier when unconfined by walls. Magnificent as they may be." He smiled at her then, and her pulse fluttered in her throat.

"Do you get out on the ocean much? I assume you must, for your love of the sea is so widely known?"

Kenna's steps faltered once more, and she forced her grip to loosen on his arm. Did he know about her sailing trips? But how could he?

Is that why he was acting as if their conversation from before hadn't happened? Perhaps he was only trying to soften her up before he dug in with the taunts about her strange and childish obsessions. Burrowing his barbs under her skin. There was something intense in the way he watched her, waiting for her response.

Kenna straightened her spine, refusing to let whatever it was he thought about her affect her in any way.

Her voice was much colder when she answered, "Not particularly, no. As I've said, I don't often have much spare time." It didn't matter what game he was playing at; she would not feed into it.

His shoulders seemed to relax the smallest amount at her words, only further cementing her anger. So he was relieved she wasn't as obsessed as he had heard?

They finally reached her rooms, and Kenna dislodged her clammy hand from his arm, taking a step back from him. Her face and voice closed off as she spoke to him, "Thank you for the escort, Mackenzie. Have a good afternoon. I will see you at dinner."

He searched her face. "Did I say something to upset you?"

"Not at all." She gave him a tight-lipped smile, bowing her head to him and stepping into her rooms, closing the door on him before he could say another word. She fell against the door, dropping her head back against the wood and closing her eyes, fists clenched at her side.

Well, she had proven herself right. It didn't feel nearly as good as she thought it would. He was just as shallow and judgmental as everyone else, and must only be here for the crown.

A small part of her brain told her she might be overreacting, reading much further into her assumptions about his tone and posture than she should. But to her, they had been a rejection. Proof she was too much, that he wished she were more *normal*. It was all too much; this entire day had been far too much for her to handle.

Her breath shuddered in and out of her chest as she attempted to force her emotions back down. But it had always been this way. The slightest perceived rejection of her or any part of her triggering large emotions she couldn't control. And the past hour had just been one thing after another.

And the worst part?

Even after solving some of the mystery surrounding Mackenzie, she could still feel the goosebumps along her skin where they had touched.

Chapter Six

The next few hours found Kenna in a blur of preparation for the night's feast. It was the first dinner with the men, and she was expected to look her best and act as the hostess of the evening instead of her parents, making her stomach a knot of nerves. It took her two hours and four dresses, but Kenna was finally finished getting ready. She might not have wanted to marry a stranger, but she did on occasion enjoy wearing a beautiful gown, and she would always represent her family and her crown proudly.

The evening gown she had settled on was emerald-green satin, the corseted top cinching in all the right places, accentuating her generous curves and coming to a V right above her navel. The cut was flattering on her full figure, following the soft roll of her middle, and displaying her ample breasts enough to catch the eye, but not so much as to be scandalous. The sleeves clung to her arms down to her elbows, and the skirt fell down to her feet in a rich green waterfall. Black lace accented the dress, running down the middle of the corset, billowing out from the end of her sleeves, and trimming the bottom of the skirt.

Her ruby red hair was half pulled up, decorated with emerald-studded pins holding the top in place, while the rest curled in soft ringlets over her shoulders. More emeralds dangled from her ears on delicate gold chains, and one hung from a black lace ribbon tied around her throat. A dainty gold ring topped with one last emerald adorned the middle finger of her right hand.

The look was completed with a finely crafted golden tiara. The metal was delicate, shaped in swirls and wrapped around a handful of emeralds.

When Martha and Freya finished applying the minimal makeup accentuating her sea blue eyes and concealing the bags underneath them from lack of sleep, she dismissed them and took one last look at herself in the mirror.

Her father had always accused her of growing up too fast. But then there were times like these where she still felt like she was a child, playing dress-up and pretending to be grown. Weren't grownups supposed to be confident and comfortable in their skin? At twenty-two, she wasn't there yet, and wasn't sure when or if she would get there. She had been confident and opinionated in most ways as a child and young teen. Growing up a princess meant people listened to her, respected her—or at least acted as if they did. It's why she had never been shy about telling anyone and everyone about the mermaid that saved her life.

But the older she got, Kenna found people became less and less understanding of her beliefs.

And less understanding of the "baby fat" sticking around far past the age of being a baby.

When they were young, she looked no different than the other children. They played together, and the others would listen, enthralled, when she talked about meeting the mermaid. They believed with her. But as they got older, they lost their baby fat, slimmed down, and became a socially acceptable size. And they lost their belief in Kenna and her story. The children she thought were her friends had turned on her, and she hadn't even realized.

It was so hard to keep that confidence; the self-love Kenna had as a child, before anyone had made her feel as if she didn't deserve that love. It was hard to love herself when the whole world told her that her body should be hated. Even if she didn't quite hate her body, she hated it for making other people hate it. It was a vicious cycle, and even when she told herself what other people thought didn't matter, she could never fully heal from that hurt.

Kenna looked now at her round, freckled face in the mirror, taking in her cheeks, full and soft, no hint of the bones beneath. The fat under her chin, concealing her jawline. Nothing about her was delicate. Not like the rest of the girls in court. She spent every day trying not to notice, not to care. Some days were easier than others.

But today? When she would host these five men for the first time, one of them her future *husband?* It was all she could do not to think about it.

Taking a deep breath, she closed her eyes and braced herself for the dinner to come. She was terrified at the thought of letting one of these men in. Letting herself be vulnerable enough to be hurt more than she already was simply by daring to exist.

But she could do this.

She was Princess Makenna Murdina MacNamera, Crown Heir to the Throne of Cladach, and she could do anything she set her mind to. Damn anyone who tried to tell her different.

Satisfied, Kenna allowed her guards to escort her down to the Great Hall where everyone was waiting for her.

The sounds of echoing voices and clinking dishware welcomed her as she neared the entrance, stopping for a moment before entering. She closed her eyes, pushing her shoulders back and mentally preparing for the socially draining interactions to come. Unlike the archery earlier, this time she wasn't separated from the men. She was sitting with them for a full meal, expected to make small talk and engage with them the whole time.

She had always been able to turn a persona on when she needed to, the cool and collected leader. But these kinds of interactions drained her. Forced into small talk, being so physically close to strangers, no escape—she found it awkward, exhausting, and extremely uncomfortable.

She knew the night ahead was going to be a long one, but there was no getting out of it, so she took one last deep breath before the guards opened the door, and walked into the hall. Everyone stopped what they were doing, standing and looking towards her, and she could feel her pulse pounding in her throat. All the eyes in the room were on her as she made her way to the table at the front, but she didn't see any of them, focusing on a point on the wall at the end of the room.

Unlike this morning, the Great Hall was set up for dining. Four long tables stretched down from the entrance to the end of the hall where all the nobles and dignitaries who lived at the castle or were here to visit were waiting to begin their meal. And at the far end, where the raised platform that usually held the thrones sat, was now one long table stretched from left to right. There her parents, her brother, and all five of the men sat.

Because of course, she had to use the meal as another way to get to know the men, and she couldn't use the distance between tables as an excuse to escape them. Even the thought of attempting to navigate interactions with the men—with Reid and Mackenzie in particular—drained her. But she had no other option.

As she stepped up to the platform, her family, who were the last ones remaining seated, stood to greet her. Once all three of them kissed her on the cheek they sat back down. Before sitting herself, Kenna turned to address the room.

"Thank you all for joining us tonight. The first day of my Winchin Festival has been wonderful, and I have been honored to spend it with all of you. Without further ado, let us eat!"

All of the guests broke into polite applause, and the room was at once filled with happy chatter and the sound of chairs scraping the stone floors as everyone took their seats. A stream of servants entered the Hall, carrying tray after tray of delicious-smelling food until Kenna's mouth was watering and her stomach was grumbling for attention.

With all the commotion today, Kenna hadn't remembered to eat more than the few pastries she had nibbled on during the afternoon picnic, and she couldn't wait to eat her fill of the dinner being served.

"Your Highness, I must say you look beautiful this evening," a voice came from directly across the table, and Kenna found herself staring into bright green-brown eyes. She took in the rest of the face, and found herself looking at Murtagh Grant. His dark hair was swept into a bun atop his head, a thick and neatly trimmed beard covering the bottom half of his face.

If Kenna was remembering correctly, he was the oldest of the men at twenty-eight, and was the quietest of the bunch, not really having spoken to Kenna yet.

"Thank you, Grant, you are too kind."

"Oh, it is no exaggeration, my princess, that gown is quite stunning," James of Clan Bruce chimed in from the right of Murtagh, and Kenna tried not to roll her eyes at the obviously fake and yet still smarmy smirk on his face. She caught the eye roll Murtagh didn't bother to hide however, and covered her smile behind her napkin.

"I believe I must thank you as well then, Bruce." She took a sip of her wine before continuing, "How are you both finding your accommodations here at the castle?"

"Oh, your parents, their Majesties, have treated us most kindly," Grant responded. "I have the most stunning view of the ocean from my room."

Kenna perked up. "You enjoy the ocean?"

"Very much so! As you know, the Grant Clan territory runs along the shore of Cladach. I have sailed with the fishermen of my clan more times than I can count, keeping an eye on the fish we bring in for trade."

Their conversation went on for most of the meal, Kenna quizzing him about everything she could in regards to fishing, sailing, whatever he would tell her about the ocean and his relationship to it. Bruce attempted to integrate himself in the conversation from time to time, but Kenna and Grant both did their best to ignore him.

To Grant's left sat Hamilton, Reid on his other side, and Mackenzie down to the right of Bruce. Hamilton and Reid seemed wrapped up in conversation, but throughout the entire meal Kenna could feel Mackenzie's stare boring a hole into the side of her face. She had to physically restrain herself from looking his way, trying to force herself to actually listen to Grant's words as he spoke animatedly with her.

It was unfortunate, because she could see herself enjoying Grant's company, if it were under different circumstances. Could see herself choosing and sharing a marriage of easy friendship with him, if not for the way he so obviously seemed to prefer her twin brother. But as it was, it hadn't slipped Kenna's notice that his gaze flickered to Tristan more often than not. And by the way Tristan's appreciative gaze wandered back, it hadn't escaped his notice either. She didn't mind it at all, but as much as she loved her brother, she had zero interest in *sharing* a partner with him in any capacity. She shuddered at the thought.

At least she knew he was simply here for the crown, for the political gain being Kenna's husband would lend his family. He probably wished to be in this situation as little as she did.

And she wouldn't be surprised if she caught him sneaking out of Tristan's bed chambers later that night.

After they had finally gotten through all of the courses including dessert—Kenna would never miss a chance to eat chocolate—she excused herself from the Great Hall, begging tiredness from an exciting day and retiring to her bedchamber for the night.

As soon as her attendants helped her out of her dress and into her nightgown, they took her hair down, leaving it in loose waves around her shoulders. When they were done, she sat at the window seat in her bedroom, gazing out at the ocean.

Today had been even more draining than she'd expected. She had not been prepared for Reid, had been given no warning. No time to shore up the walls around her heart against him again. And then there was the matter of Mackenzie, and all the confusion he made her feel. The way he had acted completely different in each of her interactions with him. The way he made her feel, a reaction she couldn't explain or define.

His mysterious behavior aside, it still seemed as if most of the other men, if not all of them, were here for the crown and not her, as she had guessed from the beginning. She thought about her mother's words from that afternoon, that she shouldn't write all the men off from the start before even getting to know them.

Hamilton came to mind, his sweet eyes and soft smile. And then she thought of Mackenzie yet again. Of his deep, cobalt eyes she could drown in. Did she *really* know that he was just here for the crown? She didn't really know him at all, not yet.

No. She cut that thought off before it could fully form.

If she had to choose one of these men, she would choose one she could tolerate. One who didn't make her heart pound, who didn't consume her mind. One who would be pleasant enough to spend her life with, but who didn't have the power to hurt her.

With this resolve in mind, she sat, watching and waiting. Waiting until it was late into the night, and she was sure everyone had gone to sleep.

Chapter Seven

The wild winds pulled at Kenna's hair and nightgown as she quietly shut the doors of her balcony behind her, so as not to alert the guards posted outside her bedroom door. Drifting to the edge of the balcony, she huddled up against the wall with practiced ease, hiding from view of any patrolling guards, before climbing down the trellis into the palace gardens—just as she did every night she was able to, for as long as she could remember.

The gardens were her second-favorite place in the world. She loved the smell of the flowers, the sound of birds chirping, and most of all, the feeling of being free from her responsibilities. Alone in the gardens she didn't have to be Princess Makenna. She could be anyone she wanted to be.

But this wasn't her destination.

If her father ever found out where she snuck off to at night, she would never hear the end of it. Even now in adulthood, she was never supposed to go anywhere without her guards, which meant she never got peace unless she stole moments of it herself, forced to sneak around like she was still a teenager rather than the grown woman she was.

Even though Kenna understood it was for her own safety and the safety of her kingdom, she also knew if she didn't get these moments of freedom, she would go mad. Not to mention that sleep rarely came easy for her, her body longing to wander and explore all night and sleep the day away. She compromised by wandering when she could, sleeping in as late as allowed, and sacrificing her sleep in the process.

As she quickly made her way past citrus trees, berry bushes, and blossoms of every flower and color imaginable, Kenna tried to push all thoughts of the men out of her mind. Tonight, she wouldn't think of any of it, wouldn't let them occupy this time reserved for herself. She had told herself she wouldn't do this again after the men arrived. That she would dedicate herself fully to this festival, to her people. But she needed just one more night to be selfish.

One last night to be just Kenna.

Their castle lay directly beyond the Cliffs of Gaoth, and from a distance, it seemed the softly rolling green hills stretched into the sky forever. But once you got close enough, you saw they abruptly ended, plunging down into a sea so blue it looked like melted sky. This sea had been the song of her heart her whole life—long before the day she saw that mermaid. As she stood now upon the cliffs, she looked out over the midnight waves, the blood in her veins singing, coming alive, just as it did every time she came to the water.

Breathing in the salty air blowing up over the cliffs, Kenna let her long, red hair whip around her face, making her feel wild and free. As if she could touch the sky, breathe in the ocean like air. She longed to cling to that feeling, to never let it go, even when she was stuck in a loveless marriage and trapped in this castle forever. But morning would come, and Kenna would have to let this part of herself go. She couldn't give herself fully to her duty if her heart was still in the sea.

But as she looked out over the water, the ache in her heart intensified. Getting one last look from far away wasn't good enough. If she truly was going to give this up and focus all of herself on ruling Cladach, she needed a real goodbye.

Decision made, Kenna found herself walking down the path laid into the cliffside to the small cove at the bottom. When she got there, Kenna went to the small cave where her boat was tucked away, hidden out of sight.

After the mermaid had saved her, and as she continued to grow older, her obsession with the ocean had only grown, and she had soaked up every bit of information and experience she could. All of those sailors' stories from when she was a child, along with every book about the ocean from the royal library she'd devoured, filling her head with fantasies of adventures exploring the ocean. Searching for the mermaid who'd saved her life.

And then one day when she was ten, on one of her riding lessons, they'd passed the boat shed sitting at the top of the path down the cliff. It housed the canoes and smaller vessels used in the cove when the weather was warm. Kenna had noticed a small, one-person boat poking out from behind the shed. The wood was old and weathered, the paint peeling. The sail no longer the bright white of the sails her kingdom had on their grand vessels.

She hadn't been able to get that boat out of her head, so later that night, knowing the rotation of the guards, she'd snuck out to look at it more closely and realized despite its worn appearance, it was still sound enough to sail. On an impulse, she'd dragged it down to the cove at the bottom of the cliff, pushing it out into the water and clumsily climbing aboard.

First she taught herself how to swim. And then she taught herself how to sail.

Kenna had enough theoretical sailing knowledge to know how it worked, making her believe that meant she could simply jump right in and start sailing.

That first day—and in the months to come—she came to realize just how wrong she was. Knowing how to sail on paper and actually doing it were two very different things, and in those first few months Kenna was dumped into the water more times than not. However, slowly but surely, she learned. It was one of the only things she had ever persisted on, rather than getting bored and giving up as she often did with her many interests.

She now knew every single inlet, eddy, and tide of that cove. She longed to sail out further into open sea, but hadn't yet dared cross that line. She felt too compelled to her duty. And her mother and father had instilled too much fear of the dangers of the ocean to ever go that far.

And now she stood in front of her boat, warring with herself. She knew she shouldn't do it, but she wanted to search the cove one last time, even knowing she wouldn't find a mermaid. She hadn't in the past nine years, so why would that change tonight?

Still, she couldn't help searching one last time. One last time, and then she would give her obsession up.

Dragging the boat out, Kenna pushed it into the water, jumping over the side and onto the deck with practiced ease. Guiding it out into the middle of the cove, Kenna's eyes desperately scanned the waves, wild hope clawing at her chest, searching for something, anything to prove mermaids were real. To give her one last excuse. A way out. If she could prove mermaids were real, perhaps her parents would let her delay the wedding, go on an expedition to find them. Maybe she could even convince the mermaids to ally against the faeries, saving her from needing to marry at all. She laughed at herself for the thought, but still went.

For the next few hours, she sailed in circles around the cove, praying to anyone who would listen.

But she saw nothing.

She didn't realize how much time had passed until she noticed the sky was lightening.

She swung her boat around to face the entrance of the cove, looking out into the gaping, endless expanse of sea. For the briefest moment, she questioned why she shouldn't just sail far away. She knew if she stayed, she might eventually become a shell of the woman she was now, trapped in this life. She closed her eyes, her face lifted to the wind as she imagined it.

Sailing out from the cove and never looking back. Finding her way on the waves, free at last. No parents to tell her it was too dangerous. No brother to care about too much to leave. No responsibilities to nobles that had never cared about her. A country of people who didn't know her. No men trying to tear her down and make her feel small.

But it was a pointless fantasy. She turned the boat around and sailed back to shore.

Running the boat up onto the sand, she hopped out and dragged it back into the cave. Before walking the path back up to her room—to the future constricting Kenna's chest every time she thought about it until she could barely breathe—she went back to the water's edge one last time.

To say goodbye to her heart.

She knew she couldn't come back anymore. There wouldn't be time, and she was already pushing her luck tonight sneaking past the increased security while all the men were there. And then she'd be married. Married to one of the men who only wanted her crown, not her.

Kenna sat down and dug her toes into the wet sand one last time, fighting a losing battle against the tears trailing warm, salty tracks down her cheeks.

Oh gods, in two days she was going to have a *husband*.

Her heart felt as broken as it had the day she learned none of her friends truly cared about her. The day she learned the only boy she had ever fancied thought she was too fat and weird to ever like in that way.

The ocean was the only thing that had never let her down. A wave didn't care what her body looked like when it slammed into her boat. The wind didn't care if she was so big her dresses had to be let out when it pushed her sails. On the water, it didn't matter.

Burying her face in her hands and giving herself a second to sob, Kenna mourned the loss of what she'd always wanted her life to be. Deep inside she had always known she would have to give up her heart for her duty, but she hadn't realized just how hard it would be to say goodbye.

To let go.

As the tears subsided, Kenna tasted the sharp salt on her tongue and calmed herself. Standing, she took one last longing look at the sea before turning her back, squaring her shoulders, and walking up the path to her future.

If she had to give up her heart, she would pour every part of herself into her kingdom until there was no piece left to grieve the life she never got to live.

What she didn't see was the head popping up out of the water, eyes tracking her movements as she made her way back to the castle.

Chapter Eight

S hutting the doors to her balcony as quietly as possible, Kenna snuck back into her room.

"You're coming back pretty late. Or should I say... early?"

Kenna jumped, doing her best not to scream as she clutched her chest, whipping around to see who had scared her. Tristan leaned his tall, rounded frame against one of the bed posts, smirking at her. Humor danced in his light brown eyes.

"Why'd you scare me like that, you *cacan*!" she hissed at him.

He raised a brow in return. "Oh, I'm a little shit, am I? You're the one going off all night. Again." Kenna saw the concern in his eyes, but elected to ignore it.

"What are you even doing in my room?"

"You're not the only one who can sneak about, you know. I came to spend some time with my favorite sister." He winked, continuing on, but Kenna had a feeling it most likely was due to a certain man named Murtagh. "I wanted to make sure you were okay after your first day. I assumed you would be awake. But you told me you weren't going to sneak off to the cove again."

"I'm sorry." Kenna's face flamed with guilt. He was the only one who knew about her secret cove adventures, because she could never keep anything from him. She sighed and made her way over to him, sitting down on her bed and patting the spot next to her, and Tristan complied.

His expression softened at the look on her face. "I understand, Kenna. I know this isn't what you want. But I'm worried about you. One of these days you're going to get caught, and Mother and Father won't be happy. Or you're going to hurt yourself out there and no one will know what happened to you. This might not be the life you want, but it's the one you have. You either need to change it, or accept it, as I have."

"I know, and I have accepted it—I have, I swear. I just... I needed to say goodbye!"

He raised his eyebrow at her. "So, you really are going to stop this time?"

"I am, I swear. I know it's selfish of me, I know it's time for me to grow up. To dedicate myself fully. But now that the men are here and I've met them all, it hit me all over again that this really is the end of any hopes I had for a different life. I had to go in person to let it go. To search for the mermaids one last time."

"And did you see one?"

Kenna laughed dryly. "Of course not."

"You know, you don't need to see one again to prove they're real. I believe you."

A soft smile broke out across her face. "You really are my favorite person, you know that, right? My belief has always been proof enough for you. You have no idea how much that has always meant to me."

"*A seòid*, why wouldn't I believe you? You're my best friend. You've always been there for me."

Kenna wrapped her arms around him, pulling him into a hug she hoped conveyed how much she loved him. "When did you grow so much? I can barely even reach your head anymore, I'm supposed to be the big sister, remember?" She reached up to muss his already messy hair, part of their ongoing joke, but he quickly stood up and out of her reach.

"You're only two minutes older. And *that's* why I grew—right there. So that you would stop messing up my hair." He laughed, smoothing it back in place. "You know this doesn't just happen, right? It takes work to have hair this good."

Kenna laughed in response and shoved his shoulder. "And that right there is why I call you a *cacan*." Smirking, she pushed him towards the door. "Because I know *exactly* how you really got that messy hair." She raised a brow at him.

Tristan flushed. "I have no idea what you are talking about."

"Mm-hmm," she replied.

"Kenna..." His tone turned serious, and Kenna snapped to attention, worried she may have embarrassed him. "I hope you know I would never get in the way of your choice. I'm so sorry, it wasn't right of me—"

"Tristan." She stopped him with a hand on his cheek, looking up to his regretful face. "You have nothing to apologize for. Murtagh clearly did not have eyes for me. If one of us can find some joy out of this situation, that's all I want."

"This world does not deserve you, *a seòid*." As he let himself out of her room, he called back. "Now, go get some sleep before the morning truly arrives, so you aren't an absolute goblin at breakfast."

Instead of responding, Kenna threw a pillow at his head.

"SLEEP WELL?" The question came from Tristan, seated in his throne next to hers.

Kenna had slept through breakfast, making it to her throne right as the caber toss was scheduled to start, to reprimanding looks from her parents. And a smirk from Tristan.

Groaning, she attempted to ignore him. Her head ached from the lack of sleep, and her eyes still felt blurry. Kenna had been woken by her attendants and helped into the day's blush-pink gown with delicate roses sewn along the hem and scattered across the top of the corset, fading down the dress.

The top half of her hair was pulled back in thickly woven braids running along the crown of her head, with smaller braids dangling down her back mixed in with her loose curls. And in the center the two thick braids curled around each other, mimicking the image of the roses on her dress. The look was completed with a touch of berry pink lip stain.

She whispered some not-so-nice words back to Tristan, and then looked out over the field in front of her.

Gone were the targets and rows of bows and arrows from yesterday. In their place, five logs were laid out across the grass. Each one was roughly the length of three men, weighing around eleven stone, and tapered on one end. Half the field was completely cleared, and everyone stood directly in front of the pavilion facing the logs this time. That way, if one of the men lost their hold, no one would be injured.

All five of the men were out of their formal clothing this time, simply wearing their kilts and loose white shirts opening to a V along their chests.

The caber toss was a long-held tradition, rumored to have started with the lumberjacks of Cladach, who would toss the logs across creeks or narrow gulfs in order to cross.

Over time, it became another way to show off and prove who was stronger, thus turning into a game or competition of sorts.

The goal of the game was to lift the log vertically by the tapered end, rest it against your shoulder, and toss it. If done correctly, it would spin end over end, the tapered end facing away from the tosser, and landing as straight out from the tosser as possible. Kenna didn't really see the point of this particular little game, as there was no skill to be learned in the practice of it, but you couldn't have any sort of festival in Cladach without one.

This time, Mackenzie was the first in line to go. Kenna watched as he stepped forward from the line, head tilted down as he spoke quietly with the two attendants there to help each of the contestants get their logs propped onto their shoulders.

The attendants both wore confused expressions on their faces as they spoke to him, before he nodded his head, clapping them on their shoulders and striding to where his log lay with confidence.

He crouched down in front of the log, waiting in position patiently for the attendants to lift the log for him. Kenna couldn't keep her expression from widening with admiration as the log was raised vertically into the air, and placed into Mackenzie's hands.

Mackenzie was crouched on his haunches, like he was sitting in an invisible chair, his hands between his thighs, as the tapered end of the log rested in his cupped palms. The log rose into the air, resting on his right shoulder and supported by nothing else. Kenna appreciated the way his biceps strained at the weight, his thigh muscles pushing against the fabric of his kilt.

Even from this distance, she could see the sweat dripping down his forehead, the veins pronounced on his neck.

The crowd let out a gasp as the log started leaning to the left, and Mackenzie attempted to right it. Once he regained control over the log, he made his move. Stumbling forward in as straight of a line as possible, he rushed forward a few steps before throwing the log in front of himself, his chest heaving as they all watched the log flip over itself end by end.

It landed with a thunk loud enough to shake the dais Kenna and her family were sitting on, and the crowd broke into polite applause. Kenna shook her head as she joined in the applause, chagrined that despite her earlier claims, she couldn't help but find herself impressed at the display, and that the log was nearly straight.

At least this meant he wasn't as perfect at everything as she feared during the archery competition.

Kenna's engagement only diminished as the competition went on, though. She could feel herself nodding off as the caber toss continued with the rest of the men, drowsy from too little sleep, and far less interested in watching the other men as she had been with Mackenzie.

She refused to read anything into that.

The only things keeping her entertained were Tristan's comments and remarks, both of them snickering when Reid almost dropped his caber. His not so subtly crude joke regarding the length of Murtagh's caber when it was his turn to toss.

In the end, all the men had done about the same with their toss, no one getting it quite straight. And by the time they were done, the sun was out in full force, leaving Kenna hot and sweating.

Everyone migrated from the field and into the cool air filling the throne room, where a luncheon feast had been laid out.

Once again, all of the men sat at a long table with the royal family, and Kenna was subjected to more meaningless small talk and obvious, menial flattery.

The one bright part of the meal was that this time, Hamilton was the one sitting across from her. And although her conversation was split between all five of the men this time—Kenna being sure to give as little attention to Reid as was socially acceptable—she did occasionally get to speak with him. He was kind, charming, and easy to talk to. And the best part of all was she felt no attraction towards him.

Yes, he was handsome, but she felt no butterflies when she looked at his perfectly nice face. His grin sparked nothing in her chest.

And that was good.

That was safe.

Unlike the man sitting at the far end of the table. The man who spoke very few words to anyone else, and whose gaze Kenna could feel on her skin for the entirety of the meal, yet again like he was studying her. The one she refused to look at or acknowledge in any way.

She continued pretending he wasn't there as she finished eating. But as she walked away from the table to refresh herself in her rooms before the afternoon activity, she saw him approaching her in her periphery.

She sped up her steps to try and slip away among the crowd that had arisen from the table, breathing a sigh of relief when she made it into the hallway. But her relief was short-lived as she heard footsteps shuffling behind her and a deep voice that sent shivers down her back calling out her name.

Chapter Nine

"**K**enna?" Mackenzie's voice caught up to her right before he did, not even slightly out of breath after running down the hall after her, which was frankly unfair. "I was hoping I could escort you to wherever you were walking?"

Kenna's immediate reaction was to find a way to politely decline, keeping him and the way he affected her at a safe distance. He deserved it for still refusing to call her by her title. *You like it*, a small voice whispered inside her. She ignored it.

Instead, Kenna forced herself to nod in acceptance. She was curious to find out which version of him she would get this time. More of that sly teasing, slipping right under her skin and igniting something in her she couldn't control? More of the perfectly proper and polite chatter?

She smiled at him, hoping it didn't look as awkward as she felt, wrapping her hand lightly into the crook of his proffered elbow. He was so *warm* through the thin cotton of his shirt. She gulped, forcing herself not to react as goosebumps raced up her arm from where they touched. It was getting harder to convince herself that she wasn't attracted to him.

The sound of Mackenzie clearing his throat snapped her back to attention, and she realized she had yet to say anything.

"Oh, um, thank you." She stumbled over her words, her face flaming. He chuckled lightly, and she tensed up, immediately on the defense. But she realized quickly he was laughing *with* her, not at her, and she joined in.

"My apologies, Mackenzie, I often get lost inside my own head."

He smiled, a hint of that mischief he seemed to carry around with him peeking through, "I remember."

All at once she remembered she had already said that the afternoon before, as he had escorted her to her rooms. And he had remembered.

"And no apologies necessary. I was not seeking niceties, merely direction on where to escort you?" He raised his brow at her, and she only flushed further. Of course, he didn't know where she had been heading to; she hadn't even noticed they had been wandering aimlessly, too busy pretending he had no effect on her while she lost her mind whenever she was near him.

His smile was wide and humorous, if a little teasing.

"We are headed to my rooms." At the flirtatious glint in his eyes she realized the way her words had sounded and rushed to correct herself, "I don't mean *we*, I mean—that is to say, *I* was headed to my rooms, and since you asked to escort me that would make us a we, but you wouldn't also be coming in. Because that would hardly be appropriate of course, and—" Kenna sucked in a large breath to cut off her rambling and stared at the ground wishing it would swallow her whole.

Gods, how did he do this to her? Yesterday he had wormed his way under her skin, lighting her up and setting a fire in her with his pestering, his needling. He was lighting a fire in her still, but this time it was a different kind.

His laugh rang out, loud and bright through the hallway, and Kenna bit her lip trying to hold back the giggle wanting to join him. "Whatever you say, Kenna." His eyes danced with warmth, and her stomach clenched at the way her name rolled off his tongue. So she was getting the playfully antagonistic Mackenzie today.

"Why do you call me that?" She couldn't have stopped the words even if she wanted to. And she was finding that around him, she didn't want to stop herself at all. She was always so careful to be the perfect princess when she was in front of anyone other than her brother. Never giving her peers something to use against her. But with Mackenzie, she found it impossible to keep up that mask.

He cocked his head, looking at her questioningly.

"Kenna," she clarified. "You only ever call me Kenna."

"That's who you are, is it not?"

Did he know what he was doing to her? How is it that this man who had known her for less than two days could so easily cut to the core of her, in a way no one else ever had been able to? How is it that everyone in the world saw her as nothing but a crown and never acknowledged her for who she was outside of the throne, and yet this man refused to call her anything but her name? As if it was as simple as that.

She swallowed the lump in her throat, attempting to regain her composure, and responded in a daze. "That it is, Mackenzie."

"You could call me Ca–Cameron." He seemed to almost trip over his name, but it all happened so fast, and she still felt like her head was stuck in a cloud, so she couldn't be sure.

"Cameron," she said his name slowly, warmth rising to her cheeks. Gods, it was just a *name*. What was wrong with her?

Something flashed in his eyes, and she felt the warmth in her cheeks deepen, sure that she was scarlet all the way to her shoulders by that point.

Thankfully, he decided to be nice and save her from herself by continuing their conversation.

"So, Kenna." He shot a devilish smile at her. "Is it just me you dislike, or is it all of us in general?"

"Excuse me?" she spluttered at his words. So much for him being nice.

He raised his brow at her in challenge. "You don't seem to be very happy about this arrangement, and I find you avoiding me whenever you're able."

Kenna kept her eyes trained on the ground, and she weighed her response. She couldn't be fully honest with him. She couldn't even be fully honest with herself. But she had to give him some answer. "I have been rather standoffish, haven't I?" she replied wryly, glancing at him from the corner of her eye only to see him staring back at her appraisingly.

"Someone might say that," he murmured. "But I'd say it feels more like caution."

Kenna's throat tightened. She didn't think that was an observation any of the other men would make, and yet here he was, reading her like a book.

Cameron continued before she could confirm or deny his observation. "I can't imagine how intimidating and exhausting this entire process can be. It must be a lot to take in."

At his words Kenna felt her shoulders loosen, part of her mask starting to slip. Gods, it felt so good to be *seen*. For someone other than her twin to understand her, and she felt that tight grip on her control release the slightest bit. Maybe it wouldn't be so bad to let him in, just a little.

"Yes, it truly is. I'm not—that is to say, I am not always the most outgoing person. I realize that might be odd coming from a princess whose entire purpose in life is to serve her people." She laughed self-deprecatingly, pausing only a moment to consider if she should reveal so much of herself, before blurting the rest of her words. "Social interaction, while something I do enjoy when I choose it, is an activity that drains me in a way that's hard to explain. I know not all people are this way, but it takes a lot out of me."

Bracing herself for his judgment, Cameron simply pondered her words thoughtfully, before responding, "I can understand that. Sometimes it's hard for me as well. To hold up the persona expected of me around other people." Kenna looked down to the floor so Cameron wouldn't see the expression on her face at his words. How did this man understand something about her that no one else seemed to, that she barely understood herself?

"And this is quite a bit of social interaction in a very short time. I imagine you would require alone time to gather yourself in between all of these events. Hopefully I'm not taking up too much of that personal time."

"You're not," she surprised herself by saying. "I mean, I don't mind spending this time with you." She couldn't look at him, terrified to know his reaction to her words, but she thought she saw a smile out of the corner of her eye.

"Besides the fact that it can be draining, how are you feeling? I imagine you have been waiting most of your life for this?"

Kenna knew there were rules and decorum to consider in this situation. You didn't just tell a man courting you that you were doing it against your will, and you had no interest in marrying him or anyone else at the moment. But she also craved to speak openly and honestly, and something about him seemed to crack her open. Maybe this frankness would be what finally drove him off so she didn't have to worry about him anymore.

She chose the middle ground in her answer, tentatively responding, "I did of course know this day would come, even if it came sooner than I thought it would. To be truthful, if it were my choice, it probably would not happen at all."

He stared at her intently, allowing her to continue at her own pace.

"In all honesty, I would much rather marry for choice, when I'm ready. Marry for love, instead of duty." She bit her lip, looking up at him through her lashes, terrified of how he would respond even as she lied to herself that it didn't matter.

"But your parents, they love each other, do they not?" His eyes were focused on her, and she found herself struggling not to drown in them.

"Yes," she breathed, "Very much so."

"And they met in one of these Winchin Festivals?"

"Of course they did, the same as every monarch before them. Surely even all the way on Mackenzie land you all know this."

He chuckled, responding quickly, "Of course. I merely meant to point out they met this way and are still a love match. So could that not happen for you?"

He looked so deep into Kenna's eyes she felt as if he were staring straight at her soul. She couldn't drag her eyes away, like she was hypnotized by them, trapped in his spell.

"I guess... I guess you're right. It's possible I could fall in love with one of the men. With one of you." She hated how breathless she sounded, staring into his eyes as she said she could fall in love, feeling like she was saying it straight to him.

Suddenly, Cameron broke their contact, a wall seeming to come down around him, between whatever connection they had been forming. He cleared his throat, dropping her arm and taking a step back.

"I shall let you continue on to your rooms." He bowed to her, stiff as a board, his shoulders pulled tight.

"I—"

"Hopefully I did not keep you too long." He gave her a small wooden smile before turning on his heel and marching away in the direction they came from.

Kenna continued the short journey to her rooms in a daze, agonizing over what had just happened. What she had might have said wrong. Once safely ensconced in her rooms, she leaned against the door, closing her eyes against the tears that wanted to come. Gods, she had already cried way too much the past few days. But her emotions had always sat too close to the surface of her skin. She always felt too much, felt too strongly. Unable to control her emotions the way everyone else seemed to be able to. The way she was supposed to.

This was exactly what she had been afraid of. She opened herself only the smallest amount to him, and already he had the power to affect her.

To hurt her.

Caught in her torrential thoughts, she barely paid mind to her maids gathering her hair to wrap the ends around the braided rose at the back of her head in anticipation of the heat of the afternoon to come, when she would have to go back for the next challenge. She was stuck in an endless loop, analyzing their conversation from every angle. Imagining that closed-off look in his eyes over, and over.

So caught in the trap of her own mind, she didn't even hear the knock on her door, jumping in surprise when she found Tristan in front of her, a worried expression on his face, as if he had been trying to speak to her.

"How are you holding up?"

"Oh, just lost in my thoughts. You know me." She forced a chuckle out, but this time it was easier. It was always easier when she was with her favorite person.

She took in his clothes, dressed similar to the men, but with breeches instead of his kilt. His soft stomach gently pushed against the fabric of his shirt, hips slightly bulging over the cinch of his waistband. His hair was just long enough to be pulled back in the smallest ponytail at the nape of his neck, a few unruly curls loose and framing his round face.

"Much better now that you're here, of course," she continued, forcing all her thoughts of Cameron out.

"But of course!" He held a hand over his heart, his face a mask of mock modesty. "I don't know how you even function when out of my glorious presence!"

Kenna couldn't stop her chuckle as she walked up to him. Slinging her arm around his waist, he tossed his over her shoulder as they fell into easy conversation about the men and made their way back to the field.

"And do you have a favorite so far?"

"I still don't know..." She paused, collecting her racing thoughts. That wasn't necessarily true. She had spoken to Hamilton a few times now, though she wasn't ready to think anything further of him just yet. And of course her mind wandered to Cameron yet again. After their conversation she was left even more confused. Her gut wanted to say he wasn't here for the crown, but she still didn't know what he *was* here for, and that was even worse.

Kenna had spent her whole life feeling as if she was on the outside of what people were feeling, thinking, saying. She tried her best to learn how other people thought, but she couldn't always figure it out. In those instances she always felt left on the outside looking in, and it frustrated her more than she could put into words.

That was how she felt with Cameron. Kenna didn't know *what* exactly she was missing, but she knew she was missing something, especially after his abrupt exit, and it made her nervous.

She pushed her thoughts aside, realizing she had left Tristan waiting and continued, "I know I only have until tomorrow to decide, but I feel as if I still know almost nothing about any of them."

"It might help if you didn't run off every chance you got." Tristan raised a brow, looking down at Kenna, and her cheeks flushed with guilt.

"I know," she responded quietly, resting her head briefly against his shoulder. "It's just all so overwhelming. I know I promised I would dedicate myself fully. That I would let go of any hopes I had this day would never come. But now it's here and I just... I don't know how to face this future."

Tristan stopped, halting her movements with him, and he turned to face her, placing his hands on her shoulders. "You face it because you are amazing and brave. You face it one day at a time, listening to your heart one step at a time. And you face it with me by your side."

"You know I would do everything forever with you by my side if I could."

He smiled sadly at her. "But?"

She closed her eyes, trying to hold in the damn tears that hadn't fully retreated for days now. "But everyone keeps telling me to follow my heart. And something in my heart keeps telling me this is wrong. That this isn't where I'm meant to be."

"I've already told you, and I'll tell you as many times as it takes you to really hear me, I am with you. No matter what."

Chapter Ten

When they got to the field, Kenna saw it had once again been rearranged. The dais was still in its place, but this time it faced a large circular arena of sorts.

Benches were laid out in a large ring, leaving a wide-open space in the middle. A rope had been laid out in a circle at least twenty feet across. On the opposite side of the ring from the dais was a rack full of swords of all different shapes and sizes.

Now *this* competition Kenna was actually interested in. She didn't know why, but she had always found something about men sword fighting attractive. Sometimes it was hard to decipher the way she felt attraction. She didn't feel attraction specifically *for* someone until she had formed some sort of connection with them, but she did still feel arousal and attraction in general. It was one of the reasons she loved reading her romance books. It was a safe way for her to explore her sexuality in a way that felt comfortable to her.

And one of the things she had learned was that even if she wasn't specifically attracted to them as a person, watching men sword fight, the power and control displayed in the activity, was exciting to watch. And think about later, when she was alone with her thoughts and her hands.

Although these men had mostly proven themselves to be uninterest-ing to her, she wouldn't deny that all of them were marginally attractive. Except for Reid, but she was fairly certain that was more to do with the way she felt about him than what he actually looked like. If she was forced to participate in this, she was glad she would get at least one afternoon with a good show.

As they settled into their seats, waiting for them to appear, Kenna was surprised to have arrived before them, seeing as she was chronically late to everything.

She turned to comment as much, but stopped when she looked past Tristan's shoulder. All five men walked towards the arena. They were all wearing their kilts.

And only kilts.

She snapped her jaw shut and tried to keep herself from looking too closely. She couldn't be caught ogling the men when she was so adamant about not liking any of them. Tristan didn't need any more fuel to tease her. Their kilts all slung low across their hips, and those with hair long enough had it pulled back and tied with leather at the back of their heads.

All of them looked different, their bodies ranging from chests and arms that were baby smooth (Reid and Bruce) to coated in a layer of hair (Murtagh). Bodies small and spindly through round and sturdy. Her eyes inevitably made their way to Cameron, and her brain must have malfunctioned because she found herself continuing to stare.

She already found him attractive, but now that she could see every-thing hiding under his shirt, the muscles she had felt under her hand earlier that afternoon... Well, it was unfair was what it was. Because he was her exact body type preference. Having found herself at least aesthetically attracted to the full range of body types in her life, the way Cameron was built had always been her favorite.

The first word that came to mind was *solid*. He was heavily built, broad and strong—nothing about him was small or skinny. But nor were his muscles majorly defined. His stomach looked firm but smooth, and slightly rounded. His shoulders were broad and strong. Kenna's favorite part, however, were his arms. Large, rounded biceps, and forearms she—

Kenna heard chuckling from Tristan beside her, making her face heat with embarrassment as she tore her gaze away from Cameron. "Oh, don't stop enjoying the show on my account. I'm quite intrigued myself."

She elbowed him, and rolled her eyes, pretending to be unaffected by his comments. In truth, she had forgotten where she was, forgotten all the people around her who could see exactly who she was drooling over.

Which was terrifying. This was exactly what she didn't want, someone who distracted her until she forgot her surroundings, let her guard down.

She needed to remember that.

Tristan must have seen the way her face closed off, because he leaned into her line of sight, whispering, "*A seóid*, you know I was only teasing, yes?"

"I know, you didn't do anything."

"Then what just happened?"

She smiled softly at him. "Nothing, it's fine. Let's just enjoy the tournament."

Tristan looked skeptical, but said nothing more. They both watched as each man walked towards the sword rack, choosing a weapon. The men stood around, swinging their swords, testing the balance and weight. She tried not to notice how Cameron's chest and arms flexed as he swung his broadsword in wide arcs. He concentrated, a look of uncertainty crossing his features as he practiced.

Annoyed with herself, Kenna crossed her arms, forcing herself to take in the other men as they also practiced. Testing their swings, the sound of clanging metal filling the air. Out of the corner of her eye, Tristan stood, pulling his shirt up and over his head.

A laugh burst from her mouth. "And what are you doing, dear brother?"

He grinned cheekily. "You do know how to count, don't you?" She didn't bother dignifying that with a response. "There are only five men here, and you can't have a tournament with an uneven number! I'm going to step in to make it six."

"Well, I don't know if I would call you a man just yet—" Kenna's words were cut off as Tristan threw his shirt at her face, sticking his tongue out at her as he jogged towards the rack of weapons.

As he ran, his stomach and arms jiggled slightly. Kenna had always both admired and been jealous of his ease and confidence in his own body. She didn't know if it was him being male and being held to different standards, or if he was simply more confident than her, but he had never struggled with his body the way she had.

To her knowledge, no one had ever commented on Tristan's body. And he had no trouble finding someone, of any gender, to share his bed. The way she felt about her fatness was the one thing she never spoke about—even with Tristan—so for all she knew, he had dealt with the same bullying she had.

Kenna forced herself to focus as they announced the first match: Tristan and Murtagh. An interesting combination after last night, Kenna mused. Tristan ran into the arena, sword held high above his head, to hoots and hollers from the crowd.

A smile broke out on Kenna's face as she watched Tristan bow around in a circle to the crowd, the attention hound he was. It was times like this her heart ached he wasn't the heir. More than her not wanting it, he was *meant* for it. She couldn't ignore how unfair those two minutes were during moments like this, while the crowd ate his shenanigans up, their cheers only getting louder. Why wasn't he born first?

He was so much better at this; he *wanted* this in a way she never would, never could. It didn't matter what she did or tried, to make herself a good ruler, because it wasn't the idea of being a ruler she disliked. It was that it felt *wrong* being the ruler here.

She watched as Tristan walked up to Murtagh, who had been suppressing a smile of his own this whole time, whispering something in his ear that made Murtagh blush. Kenna chuckled quietly as Tristan shot a wink in her direction. That little *cacan* had definitely said something inappropriate to throw Murtagh off his game.

His trick worked, and Tristan won the match. Murtagh didn't seem too upset though, good sport that he was. He shook his head with a smile before walking off the field to sit on the sidelines, while Tristan wandered off to stand on the opposite side as he waited for the next two matches of the first round.

The next match was called, this one between Reid Stewart and Cameron Mackenzie, and Kenna found herself sitting straighter. Cameron had a broadsword, and Reid was facing him with a traditional longsword; they were fairly matched in weapons. After Cameron's accuracy with a bow, and his brute strength with the caber toss, Kenna was intrigued. And she definitely was hoping Cameron would wipe the floor with Reid.

For a moment, they simply circled each other, neither man making the first move. But with surprising speed, Reid sprung forward with an impressively controlled jab. Cameron's quick reflexes were the only thing keeping him out of the reach of Reid's sword, his swing much too slow to block anything. A look of frustration clouded Cameron's face as he took his first swing, which Reid easily blocked. Kenna found herself disappointed that Reid appeared to be well practiced with the sword, having hoped he would be terrible and embarrass himself in front of everyone.

It went on like this for a few moments, Reid having speed as his advantage, but unable to get past Cameron's better reflexes or brute strength. Though Cameron seemed to have surprisingly less skill than Kenna would have guessed, all of his swings slow and dragging, the main thing Cameron had on Reid was stamina. As the minutes went by, and the sweat started dripping down both of their brows—Kenna ignored how she found the sight of sweat on Cameron very appealing—Cameron began wearing him down. Only moments later, strength and stamina won out over speed, Cameron winning the match to the applause of the crowd.

Kenna fought the smile trying to overtake her face as Reid stomped over to sit next to Murtagh, attempting to smother the anger on his face. He always had been a sore loser.

They called the last match, Michael Hamilton versus James Bruce. Bruce had a smug look on his face, waving to the crowd the way Tristan had.

But the crowd believed it just as much as Kenna did, clapping only enough to be polite. She was glad they also saw through his very thinly veiled act to the rotten person inside, simpering and pandering to them as he had to her parents. Hamilton walked into the arena next to him, a calm and neutral look on his face, and Kenna was glad to see it. Of the men, Hamilton still seemed the safest of the options, and Kenna hoped watching him in this tournament would affirm that belief.

She didn't want a man like Bruce ruling beside her; a man like that should never have power. Hamilton was calm and steady. Not overconfident, nor cocky or obnoxious. But not weak or nervous, either. Ruling required a strong constitution, which she believed Hamilton possessed. *Cameron also has a strong constitution,* her brain whispered.

Watching as they faced off, Kenna's jaw dropped when Hamilton exploded. His movements were so fast and steady she could barely keep up with them. Bruce's smug look was immediately wiped from his face as he struggled in vain to keep up. He could barely hold defense, let alone attempt to get an offensive swing in.

And just like that, only a handful of moments into the match, Hamilton won. He allowed himself a small smile, bowing to the crowd before walking over to where Tristan and Cameron waited. Kenna was very impressed, realizing Hamilton was easily the most skilled sword fighter in the bunch.

As she wondered who he would end up paired with in the second round, Bruce stomped over to where the other two men sat, tossing his sword into the grass and walking off the field, storming his way angrily to the castle. So, Kenna could add 'sore loser' to the very long list of reasons she would never choose him.

She heard a mixture of disapproving sounds and snickers emanating from the crowd as they all watched him stomp away like a child. Kenna did her best to quell her smile, attempting to appear as demure as possible, but she was unsuccessful.

It was time for the second round, and since there were only three men this time, they chose two men at random, the winner of this round facing the third as the finale.

Kenna tried to hide her reaction as they announced the pair: Tristan and Cameron. She could feel her pulse speeding up at the thought, but she could not decipher if it was in nerves or anticipation. Who did she want to win?

She shook her head. How could she even think that? Of course she wanted Tristan to win! He was her brother, her favorite person. And he would win, of course he would. How could he not?

All too soon, Cameron and Tristan were entering the circle. Kenna straightened in her seat, any trace of boredom or tiredness evaporating. She truly didn't know who had the advantage here. They were the same height; the only notable difference being Cameron was more muscle than fat, while Tristan was the opposite. They were both strong, but Tristan had more skill, and Cameron more stamina.

Kenna's breath was caught in her throat, time seemingly standing still as they faced off, both of their brows set in determination.

Tristan, always as impatient as her, struck first. Leading with a step, he struck like a viper, the steel of his sword flashing in the sun, the clang as his blade met Cameron's singing through the air.

Their blades flashed back and forth, dust churning up between their feet as they circled one another. Lunging, parrying, stabbing, but no one gaining the upper hand.

Kenna watched as sweat began beading their brows, their faces becoming more determined with every clash of metal, Tristan's face reddening as each moment passed. The crowd was dead silent at this point, everyone waiting with bated breath to see who would win: this newcomer vying for the princess' hand, or their beloved and favorite prince.

And then it happened.

Kenna was sure no one else would notice, but she did.

She saw the way Tristan's eyes flickered up to her, the way he slid his foot back at an awkward angle, just enough to set himself off balance. So when Cameron next swung, lunging towards him, Tristan had no choice but to fall back and land in the dirt. Cameron's sword point ended directly before Tristan's chin, both men staring at each other, chests heaving, as the crowd watched on.

And then the air was filled with the mingled sounds of cheers and boos, as Cameron and Tristan grinned at each other, Cameron helping Tristan to his feet. They gripped one hand and slapped each other on the back. Tristan murmured something in Cameron's ear, making him glance to Kenna before smiling and bowing to her.

Tristan grinned good-naturedly, bowing in a slow circle to the cacophonous cheer from the crowd, soaking up the attention like the clown he was. Once he had his fill, he jogged back to his seat next to Kenna, mopping the sweat from his brow with his forearm, chest heaving with labored breaths.

Kenna raised an eyebrow at him as he settled into his seat next to her, guzzling down the water handed to him by a servant.

He looked at her, a grin stretching his features. "What?"

"You know what."

A look of innocence crossed his face. "I haven't a clue."

Kenna rolled her eyes, shoving at his shoulder. "Why would you throw the match?"

He gasped in mock outrage, a hand held to his chest. "I'm sure I have no idea what you mean!"

"Oh, please."

"I never cheat."

"Is it cheating if you lose?"

"I am an honest man, sworn to never mislead my people in any way and—"

"Oh, just be quiet, you *cacan*," Kenna said through her laughter, Tristan's ridiculousness finally getting to her. He smiled wide at her, joy and mischief twinkling in his eyes.

"You know you wanted him to beat me."

"I did not! You're my brother!"

"And he is the man you have a crush on."

"How dare you say such a thing! I do not have crushes." She folded her arms indignantly, lifting her chin. Her words, however, were met with booming laughter from Tristan.

"I see we are still set on denial then?"

She scoffed at him, deciding her best option was to ignore him.

"And here I thought I was doing you a favor. Letting your man win so he could look manly and strong."

She glared at him. "He is not my man, and you know it."

"I definitely could have won. I mean, just look at these muscles!" He flexed the muscles in his arm. He poked a finger into the soft indent in her cheek, her not quite dimple. "There she is. Sometimes I think you forget you are allowed to have fun, *a seòid*. You are allowed to enjoy life every now and then, you know."

Kenna's posture softened. "I know, it's just..."

"Hard?"

"Exactly."

"Well, that's what you have me for." Tristan leaned towards her, wrapping his arm around her shoulder, and Kenna was met with a wave of body odor.

"Ugh, get off of me!" She shoved him away as he laughed. "You need a bath."

"This is the smell of victory!"

"You lost!" They looked at each other for only a split second before they burst into laughter, Kenna wiping at her eyes.

Before they could say anything else, they were interrupted by the announcement that the final round would begin, and Kenna snapped to attention. Tristan had distracted her until she had forgotten the last round was still to come.

Cameron versus Michael.

Chapter Eleven

K enna straightened in her chair, watching the two men in front of her. Her head was a mess. Logically, she wanted to only be focused on Hamilton—Hamilton, who was the smart choice.

Who was calm, intelligent, and kind. Who didn't stir any complicated feelings inside of her. Someone who she could pleasantly co-rule with. Someone who she could see herself growing fond of over time, but never losing herself to. Someone who would never have the power to hurt her. Someone who she still thought of in their proper name, versus the man who had her calling him his given name in a way that was entirely improper.

As much as she told herself not to, her eyes still strayed to Cameron as if pulled like a magnet. She still couldn't place her finger on what it was about him that called to her. But she felt it like a tug in her chest, the same tug she had always felt calling her to the sea. There was something... untamed about him. He appeared calm and contained on the outside, but somehow Kenna knew inside of him there was something wild and restless.

It was terrifying how much that thought attracted her. Why couldn't she be pulled to calm things? To safety and reliability, instead of chaos and unpredictability? Sometimes, she felt like there was something untamed inside of *her*. Something restless that was still searching for its place in the world. Something that was never calmed, never satisfied with anything besides the ocean.

Kenna shook the thought from her head. She was being ridiculous. This was just two men having a pretend sword fight. Why did she have to get all philosophical about it?

Hamilton and Cameron—Mackenzie, she reminded herself to call him—were about to begin. Both men stood with their backs ramrod straight, swords in hand, raised vertically across their chest, waiting for the go.

"Begin!"

And then it was like a tidal wave had been released. They surged towards each other, their swords meeting with such power the sound seemed to vibrate the very air, and Kenna felt it all the way down to her bones. Her eyes widened as she shifted anxiously in her seat. This didn't feel pretend anymore.

They glared at each other as they sauntered in circles, moving around the arena like a hurricane, arms swinging, metal glinting. Hamilton had the advantage of pure skill, but he was outmatched by Cameron in size, standing a head taller and much thicker than Hamilton's average stature.

As Kenna watched, the cheering from the crowd began to quiet, leaving nothing but the sound of clashing swords and shuffling people in the wake of their noise. Both men were panting from the exertion at this point, having both already gone two rounds. Kenna loosened her hands from the armrests, not realizing how hard she had been gripping the wood until she began to lose feeling in her fingers.

Her heart pounded in her chest in time to the clang of sword on sword. Their chests were gleaming under the sunlight, and Kenna tried not to notice the rivulets of sweat trickling down Cameron's chest and arms, or the way all her insides tightened at the sight, her mind wondering what other activities he could participate in that would achieve the same effect.

She looked to Hamilton, hoping he would elicit the same thoughts from her, so she could justify them as normal, general dirty thoughts, but nothing happened when she looked at him.

A grunt of pain jolted Kenna out of her thoughts, and she sucked in a breath as she watched Cameron fall to his knee, clutching his shin. And there he stayed, as Hamilton held his sword to Cameron's neck, and the cheers of the crowd blocked out any other noise.

Kenna refused to acknowledge the way her heart fell, just a little, at Cameron's loss. Hamilton made his way to Kenna, bowing to her, and Kenna smoothed her expression into one of congratulations.

"Your Highness," he said, reaching for her hand, which she gave and he kissed the back of.

"You did well." She smiled at him, genuine this time. This was what she wanted. This was how she would be able to survive, with her walls intact and her heart safe. "You are very skilled with a blade."

Grinning in response, he replied, "I practiced every day of my childhood with a sword master. My father wanted me to be prepared for anything. And with the way things are going with Sìthachd, I'm very glad he did."

The reminder of the war was a splash of cold water to the desire still lingering in her as she couldn't help but notice shirtless Cameron watching her from the corner of her eye. She needed to stop losing sight of what this was all about. This festival wasn't just about finding her a husband. It was about strengthening their ties between the clans, preparing themselves for the war brewing on the horizon. Why was it so hard for her to focus on the bigger picture, rather than always getting caught up in her maelstrom of emotions?

She forced herself to refocus on her conversation with Hamilton, thankful for the reminder. "He did a fine job." An idea came to mind, a test of sorts, and she continued. "Perhaps someday you shall test your skill against my own." In Cladach, the days of male superiority were long gone. There was no difference in power between any gender; the crown simply passed to the oldest heir. And though women could hold any job a man would hold—and vice versa—there were some who still clung to those atrocious and ancient ideals, who viewed women as lesser than, for ridiculous reasons Kenna could never fathom. She knew there were even other places in the world that still believed it to be true.

If Kenna were to choose a partner, she would never be able to choose someone who held these beliefs. No partner of hers would ever question her power, her ability.

The tension in her shoulders eased as he replied, still grinning, "I would very much look forward to that."

"Good," she replied with a quiet laugh.

He bowed his head to her one more time, and she returned it with a nod of her own, before turning to walk back with her maids to the castle.

Kenna purposely ignored the way Cameron's bright eyes followed her every move as she walked away.

As PER TRADITION, the second night of the Winchin Festival concluded with a ball. Everyone would dress up to eat, drink, and dance. Kenna was meant to dance with each of the men at least once, allowing her one-on-one time with all of them.

She was dreading it.

However, whether she was looking forward to it or not didn't matter, and so she was allowing her maids to get her ready for the night. When Kenna arrived back to her rooms, she barely said a word as Martha removed her over-dress and corset, leaving her in nothing but her chemise. Freya set to work on the arduous task of filling her tub with scalding water. Once her long, thick hair was brushed out and the bath was full, they bowed and left her bathing chamber.

Kenna stood, slipping her chemise over her head, tossing it to the side. She picked up her favorite rose-scented bath oil, pouring a healthy dose into the water before stepping into it herself.

Sighing as she ducked her entire body under the water, Kenna stayed there. With her eyes closed, wrapped entirely in the warm, comforting embrace of the water, she felt at peace. As her limbs melted into the liquid heat, she felt every thought, every stress, every worry float away until she was nothing. Even as violent and tempestuous as it could be, nothing was ever as still or as silent as when she was in the water. Her mind which never stopped finally found stillness.

Only once her lungs felt they would burst from the need to breathe did she break to the surface, gasping in air as water sloshed over the side. Kenna leaned back on the rim, staring at the ceiling while her hair fanned in the water around her.

Even as uncomfortable as she knew the night would be, she didn't know why she was nervous. Besides the normal fears that centered every ball such as this. Kenna never felt comfortable at events where people gathered as a group to judge each other on how they looked. The kind of situation where Kenna always came out falling short of the physical expectation, the size that she was.

It never mattered what she tried. No matter how active she kept, what she ate, her body had always looked this way, refusing to change. She looked down, grabbing her stomach in her hands and squeezing the excess, wishing for the thousandth time she didn't have to be like this.

No. She corrected herself, and would keep correcting herself until she finally fully believed it. She didn't wish to be any different. She loved her hair, loved her pale skin dusted in reddish-brown freckles, loved the softness of her shape. She was grateful for her powerful legs and strong arms.

What made her feel like she hated her body was the way the rest of the world felt as if she *should* hate her body. The judgment she saw in other people's eyes, the way they stared with derision and whispered when she ate sweets, the disapproval when she dared to wear a dress showing the natural drooping shape of her breasts or stomach.

And if she truly was to marry one of these men, they would be expected to consummate the marriage. This person would see her, with no clothes, no barriers to protect herself.

Kenna trailed her fingers along the surface of the water, watching the way it rippled, the steam rising and curling into the air as her thoughts wandered to the men. She was fairly certain she knew who she was going to choose, who made the most sense. Hamilton would be a good king, a good husband. Nothing she had seen so far made her dislike him. And nothing made her think she would risk losing her heart to him, either. He was perfect.

But what would he think when he saw her body for the first time? Would he still want to marry her? Would he turn away in disgust? The thought made her stomach churn, the thought of rejection physically painful.

She shook her head. There was no use in agonizing over the future. And she didn't know for sure if it was Hamilton she was going to choose. She didn't think she would be sure until the moment came to choose.

A certain black-haired, blue-eyed man came to mind at the thought, but she brushed it off, instead standing from the tub, wringing out her dripping hair, and calling for her attendants to come back.

For the next few hours, Kenna went through the motions of getting ready for the ball. Once it was time for Martha and Freya to put her in her gown, they approached her with excited expressions on their faces.

"What are the two of you going on about?" Amusement shone through Kenna's voice as she spoke to them, a curious smile on her lips.

Martha bit her lip. "We have a surprise for you, Your Majesty." They both seemed ready to burst with anticipation.

"What do you mean?"

Freya spoke this time. "We know how important tonight is for you. And we wanted you to have something you would truly feel beautiful in. Something that was unequivocally *you*. So we asked the seamstresses to create something extra special."

Without another word they rushed into her bed chambers and returned a moment later carrying a large blue and white dress between them, grins stretching across their faces.

"What is this?" Kenna exclaimed, her hand raising to her mouth.

Martha started. "We know of your soft spot for the sea, and that you feel you must let it go."

"We wanted you to be able to bring it with you tonight," continued Freya. "Try it on."

Before Kenna could utter another word, she was caught in a whirlwind of petticoats and corsets, before the puffiest dress she had ever worn was thrown over her head and fitted around her body.

Many people poked fun at her affinity for the sea, it was true. But never Freya and Martha. What if she didn't like the dress? What if she didn't like how she looked in the dress? It was just so *big*.

But when Kenna spun to face the mirror, she gasped, the tears she had been holding at bay finally running down her cheeks.

Kenna was wearing the ocean.

The dress started with the purest white tulle, wrapping around her upper arms right beneath her shoulders, and coming down in the middle to be pinned in between her breasts with blue tinted pearls, making the shape of a V. The bodice was a satin in the lightest ice blue, only a shade away from the white tulle. As the corset went down, it accentuated her soft curves, the blue getting darker, until the bottom V of the bodice at her hips was a beautiful turquoise. The skirt underneath was gathered in layers, getting fuller in volume with each layer, and darkening in color until the fabric brushing her feet was a midnight blue.

The effect was stunning. The white tulle looked like the foam of a cresting wave, the gathered layers mimicking the appearance of a wave, till it got to the darkest blue at what would be the bottom of the swell.

She turned to Martha and Freya, wrapping them in her arms. "Thank you," she whispered, closing her eyes.

Freya broke away first, wiping the tears from Kenna's cheeks. "You're welcome, dear. Now stop crying or your eyes will get puffy, and we can't have that now, can we?"

Martha picked up a box Kenna hadn't noticed, opening it to reveal the necklace Cameron had given her yesterday morning. "We thought this would go perfectly with the dress."

Kenna's heart pounded as she reached out to run her fingers along the pearls. Martha was right, it would look perfect with the dress. But what message would that send? Wouldn't wearing the necklace send the wrong message to Cameron? To the other suitors?

But the longer she stared at the necklace, the less Kenna cared. Because in this dress, she felt more beautiful, and more like herself than she ever had in her life. She nodded, and they pulled the necklace out, draping it across her unpronounced collarbones and chest. Exactly as she had guessed, the pearls appeared as if they dusted her skin rather than hung from chains, and the result was breathtaking.

All of it was perfect.

She put simple pearl studs in her ears to accent the necklace without taking away from it before finding her favorite tiara.

Cladach being an island kingdom, pearls and coral were not in short supply. Her tiara was made from a fine silver, swirled in patterns resembling waves peeking in the middle, where a light blue sapphire was held, studded with smaller blue gems and pearls throughout the waves. Small bits of blue coral were interspersed throughout. Underneath the tiara, her hair was curled into spirals falling down to her hips, the front two pieces pulled back and tucked into the sides of the tiara.

Taking one last look, she was satisfied with her appearance. Growing up bigger than all the other girls, Kenna had always been aware of her presence and the space she took up. She didn't always feel beautiful, but damn if she would ever let anyone know that. Kenna wore beautiful dresses like armor, hoping someday she would feel as beautiful as she found those dresses to be.

Until then, she would take the feelings they gave her and project as much confidence as possible. Squaring her shoulders, Kenna turned and walked out of her room, letting her guards know she was ready to head to the ball.

Chapter Twelve

W hen Kenna stepped into the Great Hall, a soft gasp fell from her lips. Over the years, they'd hosted their fair share of balls. The Great Hall was transformed a million different ways, dazzling and glittering. But this time was different.

This time, it was for *her*.

Usually she was involved in the decoration for the balls they threw, but her mother wanted to surprise Kenna this time, and told her she wasn't allowed to help. And surprised she was. Surprised and awed.

It was magical.

Strips of vibrant turquoise and gold cloth, the colors of Cladach, hung across the cobblestoned walls. The chandeliers were draped with strands of pearls and coral. Though it wasn't a clan anymore in the same sense as the other twelve, her father's MacNamera Clan still had a tartan of their own, vibrant blues and greens and browns, and it hung in banners from the pillars lining the room.

Large streamers in every shade of blue and green imaginable hung down from the ceiling, with random strips of gold interspersed throughout, creating the effect of sunlight streaming through water. Bubbles floated in the air around the whole room, blown through small tubes with soap, by the children running around chasing each other, as well as a few lords and ladies and nobles scattered in groups around the room giggling and clearly enjoying themselves.

There was a full orchestra in the corner playing upbeat music in the background. Two of the long tables that usually filled the space for meals were gone, and the other two were pushed towards the sides of the room, opening up space in the middle for dancing. The back of the room still contained the raised platform and table for the royal family, though none of them were currently occupying it.

People filled the room, dressed in the finest suits and ball gowns of every color imaginable, laughing, talking, drinking, and dancing. Servers wandered around the room with trays of small bites of food and crystal-stemmed champagne glasses.

After a server delivered one of the sparkling crystal glasses into her hand, Kenna searched the room for her parents. She spotted them in the back talking with some of the noble advisors. Making her way over, Kenna caught her father's eye as she neared them. He smiled widely at her, pulling her into his arms before whispering in her ear.

"You are so beautiful, *fiadhaich*." Kenna's cheeks flushed at his compliment. She could always count on her father to bring a smile to her face. "How do you like the decor?"

"It's beyond my wildest dreams. I don't even have words, I feel like I'm in the ocean."

"Your mother and I wanted you to have something you would love. We know this hasn't been easy for you." Her mother reached out, squeezing one of Kenna's hands in her own. Her father cleared his throat, starting again. "You know, it's not easy for me either. You're my baby girl, my little *fiadhaich*. I don't want you to grow up, I don't want you to stop needing me. But that's how it works. Tomorrow, I have to hand you over to someone else and trust them to take care of you the way you deserve. But it's for the best. We both know I won't be around forever."

Kenna swallowed the lump in her throat, holding back the tears welling in her lashes at his words, equal parts of love and guilt churning in her chest. "I know, Daddy. I love you. I'm sorry I haven't been making this easy."

He reached out and tucked one of her curls behind her ear. "You know I love you too. And never apologize for wanting more for yourself, *mo ghràdh*. You just have to learn how to get what you want by accepting what you need to do." With that, he leaned down and kissed her brow before shooing her towards the dance floor, reminding Kenna she was supposed to dance with each of the men at least once.

She'd been hoping everyone would forget that part.

The sooner she did it, the sooner it would be over, so Kenna made her way out into the room, hoping one of them would pluck up the courage and ask her first so she didn't have to. She didn't get far before she heard someone clearing their throat behind her.

Mustering up what she hoped was a believable smile, Kenna turned around ready to fake her way through too many dances, before seeing who was behind her. Her forced grin immediately turned real.

"May I accompany you on your first dance of the evening, Your Highness?" Tristan asked her, a goofy grin on his face, one hand outstretched towards her.

"But of course, Your Highness," Kenna replied playfully as she accepted his offered hand. Tristan swept her into his arms and guided her onto the dance floor.

"How are you doing?" he asked, genuine concern in his eyes.

"I'm okay. I know I have to do this, I've finally accepted it. Now I just have to *pick* one." She grimaced, and Tristan chuckled in response.

"That's the spirit. Though I believe I know someone who you might like to choose," he looked pointedly at the necklace she was wearing, and her face flamed.

"It just... this necklace went best with my new dress! It has nothing to do with Cameron." As soon as the words left her mouth, she realized her mistake.

Tristan raised his eyebrow teasingly. "I find that very hard to believe given you're so comfortable calling him by his given name. Thinking about him so often has made it hard to address him appropriately, hasn't it?"

She took her hand off his shoulder so she could slap his arm with it. "You just be quiet."

"Okay, in all seriousness though, *a seòid.*" He looked at her imploringly. "You know I want you to be happy, and I want you to follow your heart, but be careful. Make sure you give it away to someone who deserves it. I don't want you to get hurt again."

Kenna extracted her hand from his and wrapped her arms around his ample waist, stilling their movement to hug him close. He squeezed her tighter, tucking her under his chin.

"Don't you know life advice is the job of the elder sibling? I have a whole two minutes more of experience to my name after all." She felt his chest rumble against hers as he laughed, giving Kenna one last squeeze before he let go. She grinned at him. "I love you. Even if you are a pain sometimes."

He looked as if he was about to retort before she felt a tap on her shoulder. Kenna turned, seeing one of the men behind her. It was James Bruce. "I apologize for interrupting, but may I ask for the next dance?"

Kenna forced a polite smile and bowed her head in acceptance before he took her hand and swept her up into a dance. It was stiff and uncomfortable, and she suffered through endless, stilted small talk, all the while wishing she were anywhere else. He was constantly looking over her shoulder, in the direction of her parents. Whenever one of them looked back in their direction, what she supposed was meant to be a charming smile crept up on his mouth, and he laughed like they were having a great time.

As soon as the song ended, she excused herself in the guise of searching for something to eat. As she wandered to the edge of the room, however, she found herself face to face with Hamilton.

"Princess Makenna, may I ask for this dance?" He smiled at her, and Kenna found herself smiling back.

"Of course," she replied, taking his offered hand and following him back onto the dance floor. Once there, he took her hand in his, and placed his other on her waist, moving them across the floor to the music.

For the first few minutes they danced without talking, the silence not exactly awkward, but not entirely comfortable either. She felt nothing with his hands on her body, and she supposed that was a good thing.

"Your dress is beautiful. It reminds me of the ocean." The edges of Kenna's lips tilted up, and she quietly chuckled in response. She thought he might say something else, his eyes snagging on the necklace, but he didn't.

"Thank you. You look very fine yourself." And it was true. His suit was a forest green, so dark it was almost black, all the buttons and filaments in gold, popping against his dark skin. His brown hair, earlier curled, was now styled flat against his head, slicked to the sides. He ducked his head at her compliment, murmuring a thank-you.

After that, the tension was broken, and they simply talked. Hamilton told her what it was like growing up in his farming clan, the pressures of being the chief's son with no siblings to help shoulder the weight of expectation upon him. Kenna told him about life growing up in the castle and how close she and Tristan were, and realized how much they truly did have in common.

It was nice to talk to someone so comfortably. She still wasn't ready to fully commit to a decision yet, but she could see herself choosing Hamilton and not being completely miserable.

At the end of the song, Hamilton let go before bowing and pressing a kiss to her knuckles. It was warm and comfortable. But there was no spark. No tingle. Kenna reminded herself once again it was a good thing.

"It was a pleasure, Princess. I'll let you get the rest of your dances in now. But I look forward to spending more time with you later."

"The pleasure was all mine, Hamilton." With that, he gave one last small bow, and excused himself. Kenna accepted a second glass of champagne from a passing server and smiled to herself. She didn't usually indulge this way, preferring to keep her wits about her, but this was a special occasion.

And she had three more dances to get through.

Murtagh Grant made his way up to her next, so she gulped down the rest of her drink and passed it off before he asked her for a dance.

Her dance with Grant passed in pleasant conversation, and Kenna thought again how she could see herself being friends with Grant once this was all over. By the time their dance was done, Kenna was more than ready for a break. Cameron and Reid were the last to go, though she wasn't planning on giving Reid the chance. However, she was definitely going to need a few minutes before it was Cameron's turn.

This would be the closest she had ever been to him, even closer and more intimate than their walk down the hallway, and they would be touching the whole time, far more than just her hand on his arm.

But she couldn't let any pesky physical attraction sway her choices.

Kenna excused herself, making her way out of the Great Hall to walk through the gardens before going back in for her last dance with Cameron. As she wandered the paths, she took in the strong smell of the flowers all around her. She never liked things subtle when it came to the senses, always seeking something stronger. A heavy scent, a flavorful taste, a firm touch rather than light or soft.

The best part about the gardens, though, was the quiet. It was so peaceful. She almost never got to take in quiet spaces, so she cherished every time she was able to.

But with a start, she realized the gardens weren't quiet at the moment. She heard footsteps crunching along the path and the soft hum of voices talking and laughing. Just as Kenna was about to make herself known, she registered what the voices were saying and sank back into the shadows behind a tree.

"You were so right, she is entirely gullible. She's so desperate for affection she'll settle for anyone who's vaguely polite—even if it's feigned." The remark was met with cruel laughter.

The accompanying voice was one she would never forget. A voice she had heard in a situation all too similar to this exact one.

"I'm telling you, when we were kids, I had her right in the palm of my hand. All I had to do was smile. Too bad she caught me talking and had *Daddy* send me away." The derision in his voice was so heavy she could feel it as her entire body locked up.

This couldn't be happening again.

Even seven years later Kenna was embarrassed having had her father handle the situation for her, and had vowed to herself that day that she would handle her own situations from there on out.

Since then, she had put up a brave front through every other negative interaction, determined to fight her own battles.

She couldn't believe this was happening again. Fate's cruel design putting her through an endlessly repeating cycle of hurt and pain. What had she ever done to deserve this? Kenna peeked around the corner to see who Reid was talking to. When she did, she sucked in a shocked gasp, trying to quiet the sound by covering her mouth with her hand.

It was *Hamilton*.

Hamilton was the one playing her? Her thoughts began spiraling, and she could feel her lungs beginning to seize, on the edge of hyperventilating.

She ducked back behind the tree, falling against it, and slammed her eyes shut, hoping against hope she hadn't seen what she'd just seen. Heard what she had heard. Her hands were still at her mouth, attempting to smother the sound of the sobs now wracking her body.

Why? Why did this have to happen to her? Even though she hadn't let him get into her heart, he still managed to hurt her.

They always did.

She had thought Hamilton was the one kind suitor, the one man who really had been there for the right reasons.

Of course, he was the worst one.

At least the other men had the decency not to hide they were only here for her title. This whole thing only confirmed her decision to lock her heart away was the right one. Anyone could hurt her if she let them, which was why she never gave them the chance.

But she was done letting these men have the power to hurt her. She refused to cry anymore over someone who wasn't worth her tears. All of the pain she felt over them was quickly replaced by anger.

She would not give them the satisfaction. She was the Crown Heir, and they were nothing but miserable people desperate for power.

Wiping the tears from her face, Kenna straightened her spine, shoulders back and head held high as she stepped out of the bushes into their path. Nothing had ever felt as good as seeing the color drain from their faces as they stumbled to a halt in front of her. She smiled coldly as their mouths opened and closed, desperately searching for a lie to save themselves.

"There is no use trying to come up with a lie, I heard everything." She looked at them blankly, masking every emotion storming through her. Hamilton at least had the decency to look ashamed, but there was nothing more than anger and disgust on Reid's face.

He opened his mouth, most likely to insult her more but Kenna cut him off before he could. "Don't even try." She stepped forward until she was toe to toe with him. "You are the same inconsequential, desperate boy as you were when we were fifteen. When will you understand that *I* am the one with power here, not you? You may both go collect your things from the castle, and then you will never step foot inside of it again."

Turning around, Kenna gave them no chance to respond as she marched back to the castle. She stopped to take a deep, calming breath before walking back into the entrance hall.

Hamilton and Reid could both walk off a cliff for all she cared, she was done with both of them.

Chapter Thirteen

The moment Kenna stepped back into the entrance hall, Tristan found her, grabbing her arm and guiding her to the side of the room.

"*A seòid,* there you are! Mother and Father sent me to look for you." He must have noticed the look on her face then, because he stopped suddenly, concern filling his face. "Wait, what's wrong?" Tristan looked at her, his brow furrowed in concern.

She schooled her face into what she hoped was believable deniability. "What do you mean? Nothing's wrong."

"Don't lie to me. I can tell when something upsets you."

"It's fine, I'm fine. Don't worry about it."

"I know you're not fine, because you won't look me in the eye." Kenna cut her eyes to his face from where she had been blankly staring. The understanding in his eyes made her want to cry, and the dam broke.

"Why is it so hard? Am I that unlovable?" Her bottom lip began to tremble, and Tristan gathered her into his arms. He stroked his hand down her hair, resting his chin on top of her head.

"Which one was it? Tell me his name, and we'll have him put in the dungeons." Tristan's threat was met with a sad chuckle from Kenna, and she sniffled before pulling away from him. "I'm serious, *a seóid.*" She took in the serious expression on his face, and her own softened.

"I know you are. Do I tell you enough how lucky I got with you as my twin?" Tristan grinned at her, a gleam in his eyes.

"You could always say it more. I am pretty amazing, you know."

Kenna laughed again, punching his shoulder. "Always a *cacan* as much as you are sweet." She sighed, before continuing, "It was Reid. And Hamilton."

Tristan cursed, body tensing as if he was about to run and find them that minute to give them a piece of his mind, but Kenna stopped him with a shake of her head.

"It's alright, I already put them in their place." She grinned at him, and he chuckled in response. "I told them to be gone by the morning. I will let our parents know tomorrow; I just want to enjoy myself for the rest of the night."

Tristan nodded in acceptance before taking Kenna's hand, placing it in the crook of his elbow, leading her back into the Great Hall.

He spoke in a teasing tone, "I believe that means you have just one more dance to get through then."

Kenna groaned in response. "Please don't remind me."

"I thought Cameron was the one you liked!"

When Kenna didn't respond, Tristan pulled them back to a stop and turned to look at her, a question on his face.

Kenna gulped, not meeting his eye. "I can't pick someone I could like."

"You can't guard your heart forever, *a seóid.*" He looked at her imploringly. "There are some people who are worthy of it, I promise you. And one day, someone will earn the right to find their place in it. That person could be Cameron, but you'll never know if you never give anyone the chance." Kenna placed her hand on his cheek, looking up into his eyes. "You have such an honest and open heart, Tristan. I hope that never changes."

He placed his hand over hers and gave it a squeeze, before pulling it back down to his arm. "I just want you to be happy."

"I know. And I love you for that."

They continued to the middle of the room, and Kenna finally looked up, which was when she saw Cameron. As he walked towards her, she took in his outfit, her cheeks pinking at how much she enjoyed the way he looked.

He was wearing the usual attire for a man of his social standing, a collarless silk coat the same color as his eyes and trimmed in gold filigree falling just below his knees, with a matching waistcoat and shirt underneath. The lace ruffled necktie fell down his chest, and matching lace frills from the linen shirt under it all fluttered out of the end of his sleeves. Silk breeches in the same color were tucked into knee-high black boots, polished to a shine.

Yet, he looked anything but usual. His strong shoulders strained beneath his coat as he made his way to her. The breeches were so tight, they were painted like a second skin over his large thighs.

Her face flamed even harder, and she reined her thoughts in, scolding herself and schooling her expression into what she hoped was indifference.

But when he stopped in front of them, she was overwhelmed all over again by how blue his eyes were. They were pure cobalt, the clearest color she'd ever seen, and so achingly familiar in a way she couldn't quite place.

Tristan cleared his throat. "I would love to stay and chat, but I believe I see a beautiful girl over there I wouldn't mind taking for a spin around the dance floor." He shot Cameron a cheeky grin, nodding his head before striding off towards a pretty girl making eyes at him from across the room. Kenna merely nodded, too wound up to speak, but she heard a whispered "Be nice," as he walked away.

A small smile tipped Cameron's lips. "I believe it's my turn to claim a dance."

Cameron gently pulled her in, settling in with one hand on her waist, the other tenderly holding her opposite hand, and the world stopped.

Everywhere they touched set her skin on fire, and as they slowly started swaying to the music, the world spun around her and there was no one left but him. Him, and her, and the way he held her with such tenderness.

Like she was something to be treasured.

As they swirled in circles around the dance floor, their bodies moved apart and together, her breasts and stomach brushing against him every time, and she tried not to notice the way it sent a zing straight through her, down to her core. She cleared her throat, ripping her gaze away from the eyes she had been drowning in.

She needed to stop thinking of him that way. She needed to stop thinking of him at all. She needed to keep this stupid crush under control. She needed to remind herself he was hiding something, and no matter how he looked at her, or held her, she didn't truly know him. Her time was running out, and she had to make her decision in the morning.

But those eyes.

She didn't know what it was, but something about his eyes just *called* to her. It wasn't solely a physical attraction enthralling her. This wasn't something she could ignore.

Whatever this was, she felt it in her soul.

And she didn't understand it—she certainly didn't *like* it.

As they swirled around the dance floor, she feebly attempted small talk, much as she hated it. "So, how have you enjoyed your time here?"

"Well, the castle is very beautiful. And the princess in it is not so bad either."

Her face flamed, but she reminded herself of Reid and Hamilton, and the thought sobered her quickly enough.

As they continued to sway, she looked over his shoulder, searching for a safer place to look than into his eyes. Her gaze settled on her parents, who were staring at them in concern, deep in conversation.

Why could they possibly be upset? She was doing exactly what they wanted. The reminder that her mother had tried pushing her in

Mackenzie's direction helped dull some of whatever she was feeling towards him.

She tried to contain her sigh and looked back at Cameron, smiling tightly. "What a pretty line."

"I'm offended," he said with mock innocence, his eyes crinkling with mirth. "I would never dare use a line on you."

"I'm sure. Because who would ever say what they needed to to try and win a crown?" she muttered sarcastically.

Cameron's face tightened, the humor leaving his eyes. His grip on her hand and waist tightened as well, shooting tingles up and down her whole body, making it hard to concentrate on his words. She could feel every finger burning her skin, even through her corset.

She looked away again, unable to handle the intensity of his stare. But her eyes once again caught on her parents, who were now blatantly staring at them. If she didn't know any better, they looked almost suspicious.

What in the world was going on with them tonight?

She was pulled back to Cameron as he spoke. "I promise you, *ghaoil*, I have no aspirations for the crown. No matter what you think of me, I need you to know that is not why I'm here. And anyone who is here only for that isn't worthy of your breath."

Kenna's mind tripped over his words, wanting to decipher what he meant about what she thought of him, but she was too distracted with how her heart stuttered at the term of endearment, her pulse *thrumming,* blood rushing to her head and making her feel dizzy with pleasure.

She forced herself to take a breath. It was simply a term people used when addressing someone. It had nothing to do with her specifically. But when she looked into his eyes, she saw only blazing sincerity, not a trace of deceit.

Her heart dared to hope it was true.

That *he* was true.

Kenna realized they had stopped moving, his face closer to hers than it had been a moment ago.

"If it's not the crown you're here for, then why did you accept the invitation?" she asked faintly.

Before he could answer her question, Kenna felt two people step up beside them. She leaned away from him, dropping his arms like they were on fire, and turned to see her parents standing together, smiling almost grimly. Cameron dropped into a bow, his smile wide, but not quite reaching his eyes.

"Your Majesties." They nodded their heads in return.

"Cameron Mackenzie," her father began. "I haven't yet had the chance to properly chat with you. We weren't sure you or your father would even accept our invitation." Her father chuckled, and to people looking in from the outside, it would look like a normal conversation, but Kenna could tell something was off in her father's tone.

Cameron's expression didn't move.

The queen addressed him. "We haven't seen you since you were a very young lad, and my, how you've grown. You must be even taller than your father now! And where did those bright eyes come from? I know they couldn't have come from your father. In fact, you don't look much like him at all." They all laughed, but Kenna felt Cameron tense beside her, and could hear the hard edge in her mother's voice.

Whatever was happening was getting on her nerves. She hated—*hated*—the feeling of other people knowing something she didn't.

Kenna didn't even plan on choosing Cameron, but it was supposed to be *her* choice. She would be the one turning Cameron down, not them. She was slowly losing her patience with their intrusion, and didn't think she would last much longer without saying something.

When Cameron responded, there was a wariness to his voice, "I must favor my mother then." But the queen wasn't listening anymore.

"You know, you do remind me of someone else. I just can't quite place who."

"Must be someone from my clan. You know how it is. We all start looking like one another eventually." The king and queen laughed quietly in response, but the queen was studying Cameron closely.

"Ah, it doesn't really matter, does it? Don't mind a mother's curiosity." But the threat was clear in her voice.

Kenna turned back to Cameron, not quite sure what to do next, but he turned to face her with what looked to be an apology. "I regret to say that I'm not quite feeling well. I think I'll retire to my chambers for the evening."

He took her hand, kissed the back of it, and turned around, striding out of the hall without another word.

Kenna stood frozen with confusion, her feet rooted to the spot. She couldn't believe it. He was really leaving her halfway through their dance? Just like that? With some bullshit excuse about *feeling ill?*

All the frustration and hurt and anger welled up inside her until she wanted to scream.

What the *fuck?*

Tears gathered in her eyes, but she refused to let them fall. She didn't understand what she'd done to deserve this. Why was it so impossible for anyone outside of her family to actually care about her? She knew she didn't exactly fit into what society deemed fashionable.

But she was a *good* person.

She always strove to be kind, generous, and thoughtful. She was intelligent and funny, if she did say so herself. She had so many good qualities, and she knew because she constantly reminded herself when no one else in the world besides her twin seemed to remember for her.

Kenna closed her eyes and counted to ten, trying to regain her composure, but she'd had more than enough. She was fed up with people treating her like she was less than.

She was worth more than this.

And she was done holding it in. She was going to tell Cameron exactly what she thought of him and his poorly executed lie to excuse himself. He wasn't dismissed until *she* dismissed him.

But before she gave Cameron a piece of her mind, she was going to deal with her parents.

She opened her eyes to find her parents still standing in front of her. Kenna's mother placed a hand on her shoulder. "*Mo ghràdh*, I—"

She wrenched her arm out of the queen's grasp, glaring at them both. "*No!* You don't get to '*mo ghràdh*' me and make everything better."

"You don't understand, Kenna," her father cut in. "We're only trying to protect you."

"Protect me from *what*, exactly? You told me this was my choice! In fact, Mother, you even tried to persuade me to favor Cameron specifically! I didn't want to do this, but I'm trying. And if I'm going to do this, I need to do it on my terms, but you keep inserting yourselves into the situation, and I've had *enough*."

The queen was looking at her with regret, but Kenna had no patience or sympathy left.

"You don't know the situation—"

"Well, I would if you ever told me what was going on, but I know that won't happen." Her mother opened her mouth, but Kenna cut her off again. "I'm done. I've had enough tonight. Not only did you get involved when I didn't want you to, you did it in front of *everyone*."

She stormed out of the room after Cameron. Kenna made it out the door and around the corner when she heard Tristan call after her. "Kenna! Where are you going?"

"I'm going to go find Cameron and give him a piece of my mind, that's where I'm going," she practically growled at him.

"Whoa." He put up his hands placatingly. "What did he do?"

"He left me on the dance floor in front of everyone, after our parents decided to chase him off."

Tristan looked at her, confused. "Why would they do that?"

"I have no clue, but I'm sick of this. I'm sick of people treating me like I'm not enough. Of doing things and not telling me the reasons."

"Maybe you should calm down a little first. You look liable to kill him right now."

"Don't tell me to calm down—I am calm! I *know* I deserve better than this, and I want an explanation."

"I know you deserve better, alright?" Tristan held her arms, ducking his head to look her in the eyes. "I know you deserve so much better from people than what you've gotten so far in life. But if you go in on the attack, you won't get anywhere. Try to put all of those diplomacy lessons you've had to good use, aye?" He grinned at her. "And if that doesn't work, *then* you kick his ass."

Kenna blew out a breath. "Fine. Now let me go before I lose him, or I'm going to have to kick your ass instead. This anger needs to be let out somewhere." He let her go, taking a step back and raising his hands in surrender.

She called over her shoulder as she stormed past, "And see if you can talk some sense into our parents, would you? They're next on my list." She heard his answering chuckle as she turned the corner at the end of the hall.

Chapter Fourteen

K enna searched for Cameron down the halls. She didn't know exactly where his room was, but she knew all of the men were in the east wing. She took the fastest route there, but when Kenna got to the end, Cameron was still nowhere in sight.

He couldn't be that fast, could he?

She groaned in frustration, taking only a moment before deciding to go back to her chambers and call it a night. It had been a long day, and she was extremely frustrated, so she would go to sleep and confront Cameron in the morning. Hopefully with a clearer head and calmer heart. She turned around and walked back to her chambers, taking off her shoes as she went, because they were killing her. Whoever invented heels must have hated feet.

Once she was in her rooms, Freya and Martha helped her out of the dress, and she dismissed them for the night.

Looking towards her overflowing shelf, Kenna debated which book she wanted to get lost in when a breeze blew the curtains covering her balcony doors, and she caught the scent from the gardens.

Kenna hesitated, clutching her nightgown to her naked chest. She could put the nightgown on and curl up in bed with a book for the next hour, or she could sneak down to the gardens for some fresh air. She promised herself she wouldn't sneak off to her boat anymore, but she'd made no such promise about the gardens.

Plus, she'd had a horrible evening. Didn't she deserve to end it on a happy note? And with how many guards were patrolling, there was no way someone dangerous could sneak onto the grounds.

She was twenty-two years old, and the crown heir. If she wanted to go into the gardens, she would go into the gardens. Damn anyone who tried to stop her.

She threw her nightgown to the side, going to her armoire and pulling open the bottom drawer to fish out a loose-fitting white shirt, held together by laces stretching from the collar to about halfway down, and soft brown breeches. She wore dresses most of the time for appearance's sake, and while she did love her beautiful gowns, she much preferred these far more comfortable clothes.

She pulled out the strip of fabric to secure around her breasts first, wrapping it snuggly around her chest and pulling the knot tight.

While she knew most girls would kill to have her breasts—though they never wanted the stomach that often came with them, of course—and she herself could appreciate the way they looked in a corset, she really wished she didn't have to deal with her breasts most of the time. All they ever did for her was give her backaches and make it hurt to run. And times like these, where she had to rely on only a strip of cloth for support, she really wished she could just take them off instead—they were so inconvenient.

Once she was sure they were secure, she slipped the shirt on over her head and slid the breeches up to her waist, tucking the shirt in and fastening the closures. After pulling her hair into a quick plait, she retrieved a leather cord from her vanity, tying it around the end of her braid to keep it from falling out. Finally, she grabbed her knee-high boots from the bottom of the armoire and tugged them on over the breeches, then made her way towards the balcony, stopping to grab her long, sturdy coat first.

She had just walked out onto the balcony when she noticed movement out of the corner of her eye and stopped.

She dropped her arms to her sides and ducked down, moving as quickly and quietly as she could to the balcony wall. If she hadn't spent so much of her life in this exact position on the lookout for passing guards, she wouldn't have seen it.

Wouldn't have seen *him*.

He obviously knew what he was doing. Moving without a sound, walking in the shadows, his inky black hair helping him blend into them even more.

But nothing could hide the way the moonlight glinted off of his bright blue eyes.

Where was he going? Kenna couldn't think of a single good excuse Cameron could have for sneaking around the grounds in the middle of the night.

Noting his direction led him towards the castle gates, it hit her.

He was leaving, wasn't he? He was going back to his clan without so much as a goodbye. Had her parents' disapproval really scared him off that easily? Didn't he know the choice was hers anyways?

It doesn't matter. You weren't going to pick him, remember?

Anger and frustration built inside her yet again. Every emotion from the day seemed to pile back on her again. Reid and Hamilton, her parents, and now Cameron running away in the middle of the night. She was so *sick* of this. So sick of people treating her like she was an afterthought.

If he wanted to leave—*fine*. But he could at least have the decency to tell her to her face, the *coward*.

Fuming, she quickly made her way down the trellis and crept after him.

He thought he was sneaky? Well, the joke was on him. He could try all he wanted, but he would fail at this game. There was nothing Kenna did better than this.

Being invisible.

She continued to follow after him, dodging the patrolling guards, through the gardens and towards the cliffs. She shivered as she went, pulling her coat tighter around herself, chilled by the wind. She glanced up at the sky, noting the menacingly dark clouds crawling past.

What in the world was he going this way for? Kenna tried to think of what he could possibly be doing as they ventured closer and closer to her pathway. How did he even know about the path, when he was from the other side of the island and had never been to the castle before? There was nothing at the end but the cove.

Kenna ducked into the shadows of a group of bushes at the top of the path, pausing as Cameron looked once over his shoulder before sneaking his way down the cliff. She waited a moment for him to get farther ahead before following, stepping as quietly as possible, and hoping against hope he wouldn't look back again.

As they made their way down, Kenna could just see the bob of his inky black hair, darker than the space around him. She could feel her heartbeat in her throat, stopping every few seconds, making sure she stayed far enough behind, the wind getting stronger the closer to the water they got.

When she got to the beach at the bottom, she found him walking across the sand towards the water.

"What are you *doing*?" Kenna finally called after him, tired of playing this game.

At her voice, Cameron paused mid-step, his shoulders stiffening beneath the tight shirt pulled across his back. And that's when Kenna realized he didn't have a lot with him to be sneaking away back home. He didn't have anything with him at all. No bags, not even a jacket. Only breeches and a thin shirt.

How was he not shivering in the night air?

Cameron slowly turned to face her, a very carefully casual expression on his face. "Princess Makenna!" Only a small amount of surprise colored his voice. "What are you doing out so late at night?"

"I could ask you the same thing, Mackenzie." She raised a brow at him and rested her hand on her hip. She felt her face heat as his gaze traveled down the length of her body, taking her outfit in.

"I like what you've got on here. A lot more practical than that dress from the ball, stunning as it was."

Kenna took a second to collect her thoughts before responding, trying not to be affected by both his compliment and the look he was giving her.

"Yes, well, I can't wear ball gowns all the time, can I? And don't think I didn't notice you avoiding my question."

"Ah, yes. Well, I guess I fancied a bit of a midnight stroll."

"You *fancied a midnight stroll?*"

"I do believe that's what I just said, yes," he responded, a teasing lilt to his voice and a small smile pulling at the corner of his lips.

Kenna tore her gaze away from the aforementioned lips, trying not to stare at the way his biceps shifted under his shirt as he ran his hand through his hair. Or the way the ebony strands painted in moonlight parted to let his fingers slide through them, looking so soft and thick.

He was anxious. There was something he wasn't telling her.

"Well if you're simply going for a stroll, you wouldn't mind if I joined you?" Kenna noted his jaw clenching, eyes glinting with a spark of frustration. "Or would my company prove to be too much of a bother to you? You did have a rather hasty exit earlier this evening, though you've recovered pretty quickly, haven't you?"

"Well, you see, I always find the ocean to be quite the balm to any ailment."

"Is that right?" Kenna drawled, voice dripping with sarcasm.

"Quite right. I know you yourself fancy the ocean—do you not find that to be the same?" He grinned charmingly, and she did her best not to fall for it. Not anymore. Not when he'd so elegantly sidestepped every question she had asked him so far.

"What I know is you never seem to answer my questions."

Cameron hung his head, his shoulders slumping in defeat. "Alright, Kenna, you've caught me."

Her mouth closed with a snap, the retort dying on the tip of her tongue. *What?*

"What?"

"Yes, you've caught me. I lied about feeling ill earlier tonight."

Kenna huffed in frustration. "I knew that. Just how dumb do you think I am? You got scared off by my parents. I'm not sure why they have a problem with you, but it was a coward's move to run because of that."

Cameron paused, closing his mouth before starting again. "Yes, well, they are the king and queen, after all. They can be quite intimidating. However, they are not the reason for this."

"Then what is?"

"I'm afraid my time here has come to an end."

"*Your time here has come to an end?* What does that even *mean?*"

Cameron ignored her question and stepped closer, causing her breath to seize in her lungs. He lifted his hand and brushed the tips of his fingers along her jaw, and her blood thundered through her veins.

"I hate having to leave, more than you know, but it's time. I was never even supposed to get this close to you."

"I—what? I don't understand," Kenna murmured, unable to do anything more with the way he was staring into her eyes. It was hypnotizing.

Cameron hooked his finger under her chin, lifting her face to his, until they were only a breath apart, so close she felt his every exhale. "I hope you find the love you're looking for someday, *ghaoil*. It was enchanting to meet you, Kenna. But I'm afraid I must go."

And then he started singing, so softly and sweetly. Kenna didn't understand the words, but she knew it was the most beautiful thing she had ever heard.

She didn't know where she was, or what she was doing.

She couldn't have even told anyone her name in that moment.

All she saw was deep blue, and all she knew was she was so happy, happier than she had ever been. Her heart swelled in her chest, and she felt any second now she was going to burst.

And then she had the overwhelming need to turn and go back up the path to the castle, and—

What had she even been doing down here?

Confused, Kenna turned haltingly and made her way back up the beach towards the cliff path. But a splash echoed distantly in her ears, and her body felt as if it had been dunked in cold water.

Her thoughts came back to her like fog clearing from a mirror and bringing the reflection back into focus.

Or in this case—snapping her reality back into place.

What the hell *just happened?*

Chapter Fifteen

Stopping to take in her surroundings, the wind was now whipping strands of hair loose from her braid to smack her in the face. How had she gotten on the path to the cove? The weirdest part was she wasn't heading towards the cove. Instead, she was walking in the direction of the castle.

The last thing she remembered was deciding she wanted to take a walk through the gardens before going to bed and then—

Wait, no, that wasn't right, she had already done that. Her brain felt so muddled and confused—why couldn't she remember anything? She buried her head in her hands trying to focus, trying to shake off the fog covering her thoughts.

And then all at once she realized, a gasp leaving her lips.

Cameron! What had he done? He-he had sung, and then—

No. It couldn't be. But what other explanation was there? In all the books she had read about merpeople, a very small number had mentioned something.

That merpeople's voices held power.

If they held eye contact with you and sang to you in the mer language, they could wipe your memory and compel your actions.

She hadn't been sure she believed it, but it was obvious to her now. Cameron had suddenly started singing and—

Which meant Cameron was—

Kenna spun around and ran back down the path towards the cove, skidding to a stop against the lapping waves, frantically scanning the water.

There! There was a flash of cobalt just beneath the water's surface, heading towards the cove.

Cameron was a mermaid—a mer*man*.

She couldn't believe it.

But maybe she could. After all, she had felt drawn to him for some unknown reason from the start. Did her soul somehow recognize what he was? Was that even possible?

What did this mean? How was one of her clansmen a merman? It didn't matter, though, did it? What mattered was that she had *met one*.

She couldn't contain the smile lighting her face, or the giddy laugh tumbling off of her tongue. She was the happiest she'd ever been, and she couldn't wait—

The smile dropped from her face and all the joy she had felt turned sour. Sure, she was ecstatic to have finally met a merman, even talked to one. But that still didn't explain the why, or the how.

Why had Cameron come here?

Why was he leaving now?

And most importantly, *how* was he a merman?

The thought of never knowing was more suffocating than every disappointment she'd ever faced. She couldn't stand to have another thing kept from her, another thing happening behind her back while she was left to stumble in the dark.

This time, she was following her impulse instead of burying it, taking matters into her own hands.

Kenna ran towards her hiding spot, and ripped the covering off her boat. As quickly as she could, she tugged it towards the waves before pausing. She couldn't leave without saying anything.

Her leaving at all would send her parents into a panic, let alone leaving after their fight. But she would have to worry about that later. She wasn't going to sit idly by this time.

She couldn't—not again.

But she didn't have time to go back to the castle and tell someone, and if she did, they would try to stop her.

No. She had to figure something else out. The only one who knew about her boat was Tristan. That was it. She would leave a note for Tristan where she usually stored the boat. Jumping aboard, she rushed into the tiny cabin.

She had thought about running away so many times, had even gone so far as to stock her boat with essentials over time, which meant she would be able to find what she needed in there.

Inside was barely enough space to stand or turn around. It was more like a small hallway, a tiny bed on the right with a thin, lumpy mattress covered in a few blankets and a pillow, with storage cabinets above and below the mattress. They were all latched shut, holding a few changes of sail worthy clothing, towels, bandages, and soap, a few small sealed caskets of fresh water, and lastly non-perishable food.

Kenna rushed to the closest cabinet until she found the quill, ink pot, and parchment she kept for drawing maps of the stars when she was on the water, scribbling a note as fast as she could.

> Dear Brother,
> I'm sorry I didn't have time to say goodbye in person. But I need you to know that I am well. And I will be back, I promise. There's just something I need to do first. You know what I have always believed? Well, I was right. And it was who I ran after tonight! Can you believe it? I need answers, and I'm not going to find them here. You'll take care of our parents, won't you? I've always believed you were better suited to be the heir. Now is your chance to prove it.
> I love you, eacan,
> Kenna

Rolling the piece of parchment up, she corked the ink and shoved it all back into a cabinet before latching it shut. She ran back onto the small deck, the wind even fiercer than it had been earlier in the evening.

She looked up at the sky, taking in the grey clouds far past menacing. But she wasn't going to let a little rain keep her from this. *Nothing* could keep her from this.

Jumping off the deck, she ran back to her hiding spot to shove the note halfway into the sand so it wouldn't fly away, and threw the boat covering over it to shelter it from the rain.

Hopefully Tristan would think to look down here when they couldn't find her in the morning.

Kenna ran back to the boat, shoving it the rest of the way into the water, hopping over the railing at the last moment. Once on deck, she ran to the oars, physically paddling herself out far enough to get into deeper water and let the wind take control.

She fell into the motions with practiced ease. Sailing her boat was second nature to her by this point. She barely even registered her movements, eyes too focused on the water in front of her, desperately searching for that cobalt blue.

Soon Kenna came upon the edge of the cove, the border between her and the open ocean. The line she had drawn for herself and never dared to cross before.

She didn't look back.

Chapter Sixteen

I t had been hours, and Kenna still hadn't spotted Cameron again. The rain was coming down in sheets, the wind snapping the sails louder than even the thunder cracking in the air, setting her nerves on end. Lightning streaked across the sky, illuminating the roiling waves in small flashes before plunging her back into darkness. Every minute the swells were getting bigger, and she was soaked to the bone in freezing water.

Kenna passed *nervous* an hour ago.

At this point she was terrified.

She had never sailed in open waters before, underestimating the difference between it and her cove. She also underestimated the clouds. Kenna knew they had called for rain, but didn't realize how bad the ensuing storm would truly be. As good of a sailor as she fancied herself, she was not experienced enough for *this*. Kenna was losing control of the boat more and more with every passing moment.

Looking up she saw the largest surge yet barreling towards her on the port side, and scrambled to the helm, trying to grab in between the rapidly spinning spokes of the wheel.

Several bruises to her hand later, she finally got a grip on it and pulled with all her might, attempting to turn the stern into the wave, lest it crash over the deck and risk tipping the boat. Her shoulder strained against the wood as she used her whole body to turn the wheel, but it wasn't moving. Not fast enough. Throwing one last look over her shoulder, she found the wave almost upon her.

There was no time left.

When she let go of the wheel, it immediately spun out of control. Kenna rushed for the miniscule cabin, bolting in and latching the door behind her. She looked around the tiny space in a panic, her chest heaving.

What was she supposed to do? She didn't even know if coming down here was the right choice. Maybe she should've stayed at the helm and kept holding on. But what about when the wave hit the deck? It would've been too slippery to hold on with that much water hitting her full force.

Down here, at least she wouldn't be swept overboard.

But it meant the boat was no longer being steered at all. It was already rolling and thrashing, throwing her violently into the walls. She tumbled her way onto the bed, huddling into the corner and pushing her hands against the walls to prevent herself from tumbling about.

It passed like this for another thirty minutes before she heard the first *crack,* accompanied by a bright flash of light.

It couldn't have been anything other than the mast being struck by lightning and splintering.

Kenna whimpered and huddled further into the corner, tears streaming down her face, her breaths catching with terror in her throat with each gulp.

She had made the wrong choice. Once more she had let a man—or in this case, a merman—affect her and her feelings. She hadn't listened to her parents and all their warnings about the ocean.

Why hadn't she *listened?*

And now she would never get to tell her parents she forgave them. Or hug her brother again. It didn't matter what their reasoning had been; deep down she knew they had only wanted what was best for her.

A second *crack* sounded, accompanied by another flash of light.

This one was even louder.

It must have been the final straw to fully snap the mast, because the ensuing crash split down the middle of the deck, ripping open a gaping hole where the door had been only moments before.

Kenna screamed, but she couldn't even hear her voice over the pounding of the rain and the thrashing waves. The crashing booms of thunder made her jump out of her skin every time. The flashes of lightning illuminated the splintered shards of wood, dripping with water, looking like a scene out of one of the horror novels she and Tristan would sneak into their rooms to read together at night when they were children.

She needed to get off the boat. Her best chance now was to pray there was land nearby and hope she drifted towards it and not further out into open sea. If she stayed on the boat while it sank, she would get sucked down too fast to break her way back up to the surface. After stumbling to her feet, she ripped the latches open on the cabinets.

Water was pooling around her feet and Kenna knew she needed to move fast. She grabbed the burlap knapsack and started stuffing it with food.

As she was grabbing a spare pair of clothes she found the set of twin daggers she had gotten for her sixteenth birthday. They were thin, and about the length of her forearm, but extremely sharp. The handle was wrapped in simple black leather, a single gemstone embedded into the pommel of each, the same shade of sea blue as her eyes.

She paused for only a second before throwing them in her bag as well.

Snatching her canteen, icy rain now sliced across Kenna's skin as she filled it with the clean water, throwing it into the bag and cinching it as tight as she could before slinging it across her chest, running towards the hole in the boat.

Once she got to the gaping area where the door had been, she looked down to see the mast had smashed all the way through the hull of the boat. The two halves were hanging together by a handful of boards, and they were liable to split and sink even faster any moment now. The hull had already sunk into the water so that each wave lapped up at its peak onto the floor where she was standing.

Kenna calculated it was about a yard to the safety of open water.

She took a deep breath and clenched her shaking hands. She didn't know if she could do this, but it didn't matter if she could or not.

She *had* to.

Gulping in one last shuddering breath, Kenna walked to the other side until she was pushed up against the far wall. She pressed her back into it and steeled her spine.

She could do this. She was a princess and—

No, she was a *sailor,* and she could do what she needed to survive.

Digging her feet into the deck, she sprinted as fast as she could for the last ledge, gaining what momentum she could to push off and propel herself out to open water.

But a strike of lightning slammed into the railing, setting the wood on fire, and sending a large chunk of the wood spinning through the air and into the back of her head.

The world went black.

Chapter Seventeen

The first thing Kenna registered was the throbbing. She tried blinking, but her eyes felt like they were full of sand.

Eventually, she forced them open, only to slam them shut again in the face of the sun.

What happened?

She had no clue where she was, and the last thing she remembered was the storm ravishing her boat. Terrified for her life, and praying to the gods she would survive—and then nothing.

Licking her dry lips, Kenna forced herself to crack her eyes open once more and studied the beach she was on, squinting from the sun while taking in her surroundings.

She was lying on sand so soft and white it almost looked like flour. It stretched out to the ocean, so clear she could see straight to the sand far beneath it. The clear water turned a stark teal further away, fading to turquoise, and eventually deep navy blue far out. So different from the stormy grey she'd last seen.

She realized her head was resting on something, and she groaned as she tried to sit up, her body aching horribly.

Besides her throbbing head, a sharp pain was running up the right side of her ribs. Once she was finally in a sitting position, she winced and straightened her back, the sensation tugging something along her side that sent another shot of pain throbbing through her.

Looking behind her she found her head had been resting on her bag.

Thank the gods she still had that, at least. But then she froze, looking back down at the clothes she was wearing.

Her chest was no longer bound, and she was wearing a different shirt and pants.

She began to panic. Where was she? Who had changed her clothes? Just the thought made her cheeks flame. She looked around but saw no one.

Behind her, the sand faded into tropical shrubbery. Palm trees scattered randomly until they thickened into a jungle. She was surrounded by water, so definitely on an island.

Kenna struggled to her feet, a groan of pain slipping out from between her lips. She needed to figure out how to get back home.

Slowly, the events right before she blacked out were coming back to her.

She had tried to jump off the boat as it was sinking, but something must have knocked her out.

So how had she gotten here?

The sinking boat should have drowned her. And if by some miracle she had been close enough to the island to drift ashore, she was too far inland from the water. Not to mention her change of clothes meant someone had definitely been there.

But who?

Leaning down to pick up her bag, she cried out at the searing pain licking flames up the side of her ribs. She looked down to see a small red stain blooming across her shirt. Kenna gingerly inched the fabric up her waist until she could see the fearsome gash spanning a handswidth up her side. Grimacing, Kenna let the shirt drop back down, knowing she needed to bind it sooner rather than later.

Her bag in her hands, she rummaged around, finding her daggers.

Aside from the clothes she'd been wearing, only one other shirt was missing. Looking around, Kenna finally noticed the footprints where she had been lying. Her shoulders stiffened when she heard the sound of rustling and twigs snapping from somewhere in the trees behind her. She slowly pulled the dagger out, keeping her movements as small and unnoticeable as possible.

Distinct footsteps were moving towards her now, and her grip on the dagger tightened, her palms sweating, heart racing.

Only when the footsteps were almost to her did she drop her bag and spin around, brandishing the dagger and thrusting it up against the throat of the man in front of her, swallowing down the sound of agony trying to crawl its way up her throat at the sudden movement.

The man came to a halt, holding up his hands in surrender and chuckling softly.

"Whoa there, no need for a knife." His voice held nothing but amusement.

Kenna let her eyes trail upwards from his neck, stopping at his mouth, where his lips were quirked up to the side. She sucked in a breath, her eyes snapping up to find cobalt blue staring back at her, sparkling with mirth.

It was Cameron.

And he was amused.

While she had a *knife* to his damn throat.

"I'm literally holding your life in my hands right now, and you're *laughing?*" She demanded incredulously.

His lips twitched before responding. "Well, you're kind of cute when you're threatening me."

Kenna cursed, lurching back from him and lowering the dagger. And then she was cursing for a whole new reason. She clutched her side and tried to keep her grimacing at bay.

When he moved towards her, she lifted the dagger back up between them. "Don't touch me!"

He raised his hands innocently, taking a step back again, but the smile stayed on his face.

Kenna growled at him through clenched teeth. "How did I get to this island? What are you doing here? *Who are you?*"

"You couldn't have gotten hit in the head that hard. I'm Cameron Mackenzie, remember?"

Huffing a laugh she responded, "Oh, come on, I'm not that dumb. You're not Cameron Mackenzie. You're a *merman*. What's your real name?"

"Now what makes you think that?"

"I saw you! I sailed after you when I saw you transform."

"Hmm, are you sure about that? It sounds a little far-fetched."

Kenna rolled her eyes, groaning in frustration. "Oh my gods *yes*, I'm sure. Even if I hadn't seen it with my own eyes, I would know now that you aren't who you said you were." Her lips curling into a sneer, she continued, "It's why you ran, after all."

"Is that so?"

"Would you just answer my questions?" she shouted.

Kenna was in too much pain to keep doing this back and forth. She could already feel the tears pressing against her eyes, and if he didn't start answering her soon she was going to seriously lose it. More than she already was.

"All right, all right. You need to calm down."

Oh, that was *it*.

She was going to fucking *kill* him. Gut him like a fish.

Noticing her murderous glare and the way her fist tightened on the dagger, he quickly amended, "No, wait... I mean—" He licked his lips, clearing his throat as he started over. "I'll answer your questions, just put your knife away first. You don't need it, I promise. If I'd wanted to hurt you, I very easily could have done so already."

Kenna hesitated for a moment, eyeing him suspiciously. But he was right.

She had no idea how long she had been unconscious, and it was obvious now that he was the one who rescued her from the water and brought her to this island. It didn't mean she trusted him, though. He was lying about who he was, and Kenna was determined to find out why.

She sighed in defeat, lowering the dagger. Walking to the nearest tree she leaned against it, dropping her head back against it and biting her lip at the pain.

She eyed Cameron—or whoever he was—as he cautiously moved a little closer before speaking. "To answer your questions: I saw your boat go down. I watched you get hit in the head and fall in the water. I saved you and brought you here." He paused for a moment, not looking entirely certain, but then continued on, "And my name is Calder."

Calder.

Calder fit him so much better. She shook off her observation. It didn't matter what his name sounded like.

"Ok, *Calder*," Kenna started, hating how much she loved the way his name fell off her tongue. "What were you doing at the castle? Why were you pretending to be Cameron? Why did you leave?" A realization hit her. "Where is the real Cameron MacKenzie?"

It dawned on Kenna that if Calder was the one who saved her, he must have been the one to *change* her clothes. "And why *the hell* am I not wearing the same clothes?" She forced herself not to look away from him—even though the potential answers to her question at once scared and embarrassed her.

Something flashed in his eyes at her question, but it was gone too fast for her to decipher.

"Your old clothes were... unusable. But I promise you, nothing happened." For the first time since he walked up to her, he looked uncomfortable. "I am not that kind of man."

Kenna eyed him warily, the silence thick with tension.

"Well, um... Good. Because I wouldn't hesitate to castrate you if you had." He burst out laughing, and Kenna glared at him. "I'm serious!"

"I know you are," he replied. "I'm laughing at whatever poor bastard would ever dare cross you."

Kenna huffed in annoyance before finally looking away.

Calder didn't answer her first questions, but she never thought he would give that information up so easily. Let him think she hadn't noticed. She would get it out of him eventually.

She shifted her position, and a whimper escaped as the gash throbbed in pain.

Kenna startled as Calder immediately moved until he was right in front of her. He reached his hand towards her, and she flinched. She thought she saw disappointment in his eyes, but she must have been imagining it.

"What are you doing?"

"Do you not feel that trickling down the side of your face?"

As his words, Kenna suddenly realized there *was* a wet sensation trailing down from her temple. She reached her hand up, her fingers pulling away red.

"That's where I was when you woke up. I was soaking one of your shirts in salt water to clean it up." He gestured the hand that had reached towards her, and she finally noticed the dripping shirt clenched in it. "That gash on your ribs needs attention, and you definitely have a concussion. But I was waiting until you woke up to bind your wounds."

"How long have I been unconscious?"

"Most of the day. It was very early morning when your boat went down, and the sun will set within the hour."

"Why are you helping me?" She eyed him, doubtful of his intentions when she still knew nothing about him aside from his name—*if* that was even his real name this time. And that he was a merman. No matter how much he denied it or avoided confirming it, she *knew* what she'd seen.

He stared at her for a moment, hesitating before replying, "I wasn't going to let you die. Let me help you."

Kenna didn't respond right away. Something was still going on here that she didn't understand, and it was eating away at her. She'd followed him to get answers, but now she was completely lost, stranded on an island who-knew-how-far-away from home.

She needed answers. But Calder wasn't stupid—he wasn't going to tell her everything she wanted to know.

She would play along for now. Maybe she could get him to trust her. At the least, he would help her with her wounds.

She nodded her consent silently. Calder smiled his big, bright smile. She refused to acknowledge it, instead looking out over the water, watching as the sunlight glittered across its surface.

It really was the most beautiful ocean she had ever seen.

Kenna had always been in awe of the beauty of the sea. But this was nothing like the sea she had grown up with—the only sea she had ever known. This one didn't even look real.

Kenna could look at this view forever and never tire of it.

As if reading her thoughts, Calder spoke, his voice closer than it had been a moment before, accompanied by the sound of her bag rustling. "It's the most beautiful thing in the world, isn't it?"

Kenna hummed in response, trying not to notice just how similar their thoughts had been. Calder gently cupped her chin in his hand, holding her still. The feeling of his hands on her sent sparks skittering across her skin. She ignored the way her heart picked up its pace, instead focusing on how he concentrated on his task. She felt the soft drag of the cloth as he ran it across her temple.

Closing her eyes she sucked in a deep breath, not paying the slight sting any mind. Nothing was better than this. The smell of fresh air and ocean. Opening her eyes, she stared out to the horizon, watching him from her periphery. His inky hair fell down his brow, curls lifting lightly in the gentle breeze as he concentrated, his eyes never straying from her temple.

Calder dropped his hands and backed up, and Kenna immediately missed the warmth of his touch.

"Thank you," she said quietly. She inhaled a deep breath, grimacing again at the pain it shot through her side, every heartbeat pulsing through the wound.

"You need to bind your gash as well," Calder said as he dug through the bag for the last two strips of cloth.

Kenna's face heated at the thought of taking her shirt off in front of him.

"That's fine." She rushed to take the cloth from him. "I'll do it myself."

"Kenna—"

"No. I'm fine, Cam—*Calder*. I don't need your help for this." She tried to push off from the tree, but cried out when the movement speared the sharpest pain yet through her.

"You can't even move, Kenna. Please, let me help you. I'll stand behind you and I won't look at anything, you have my word. But don't make it worse by trying to do this yourself."

Kenna huffed, muttering under her breath, but she accepted his offered hand and let him pull her upright from the tree. Once she was standing, she turned her back to him, her heart positively racing now. She had never taken her shirt off in front of anyone before. She hadn't even *kissed* anyone yet.

When she had thought Reid was courting her when they were teenagers, she wished nothing more than for him to kiss her. She'd dreamt about it, fantasized about it. Looking back now, she was glad he never had. That she hadn't given her first kiss to someone so unworthy.

And though she often felt shame at being so old and still un-kissed, knowing all the other girls at court had already been kissed—had already done much more than kiss—she tried to remind herself it didn't matter.

Her value wasn't placed in how far she had gone with someone. Her value was in herself, and there was nothing wrong with waiting for someone who deserved her. There was nothing wrong in not being ready for physical intimacy at the same pace as other people.

She had also come to the realization she didn't even feel attraction the way everyone else around her seemed to. Not feeling attraction towards people she didn't know, didn't have a connection with first.

But now she was twenty-two and it still hadn't happened, and she'd begun to fear no one would ever want to kiss her. She'd resigned herself to the knowledge her first kiss would likely be on her wedding day with someone she didn't love.

Maybe someone she didn't even like.

Not that it mattered anymore. She wouldn't be kissing anyone any time soon.

Kenna shook her thoughts away. She needed to focus on the here and now. Attempting to gather her hair to tie up, she quickly realized she couldn't do it with one hand. Warm, rough hands covered her own.

"Here, let me." With her hair held in his fist, he began to work with it—presumably weaving it into another braid.

Kenna wanted to moan in pleasure—it felt *so* good. She'd always loved the feeling of people brushing and combing through her hair. She bit her lip, trying to prevent herself from making any noises. But she couldn't stop the goosebumps traveling down her arms. Hopefully Calder wouldn't notice.

He tied a leather strap around the finished braid, dropping his arms down to his sides.

Kenna took in one last breath before sliding her shirt off over her head and clutching it tightly in her good hand, along with her long braid, keeping it out of the way.

"I'm going to start wrapping it around you now."

She felt his breath on the back of her neck and suppressed a shiver, raising her arms out of the way. Calder wrapped his arms around her middle, passing the bandage across her body to his other hand, before pulling it back behind her, binding it across her chest.

As his hand passed in front of her chest she had taken a breath in, causing his knuckles to brush across one of her nipples. They both froze, and Kenna bit her lip against a whimper as they tightened to peaks at the touch.

"I'm sorry, that was an accident, I swear." He sounded desperate to make her believe him.

Kenna screwed her eyes shut. "I know. Just keep going."

Without another word, he looped it again one more time to trap the loose end down. He started pulling tighter, and the noises Kenna were suppressing were no longer noises of pleasure.

It *hurt*. Every time the bandage wrapped around her, it tugged at the wound.

Knowing it needed to be done, she sucked it up and endured. Every time his hand crossed her back though, his knuckles grazed her skin in a blaze of fire.

It was torture, feeling such pain and pleasure at the same time, and forcing both deep down inside her, refusing to acknowledge either. She couldn't let Calder know she was attracted to him, and she refused to appear weak.

Finally, after what felt like forever, he tied off the end, his fingertips skimming her back as he pulled his hands away.

"There, all done." His voice sounded hoarse to Kenna, but she knew she was just fooling herself.

She quickly pulled her shirt back on and turned to face him, looking at his feet instead of meeting his eyes. By now the sun was almost completely set and their shadows stretched across the sand.

She cleared her throat. "So, um," she began, "where are we going to sleep?" Daring to glance up at him, she was relieved to see he looked almost as flustered as she did.

When he registered her question, however, his eyes lit up. "Ah, that's what I was working on all day while you were sleeping."

"Sleeping? I was *unconscious.*"

"Eh," he waved his hand in dismissal, "same thing."

Kenna opened her mouth to protest before realizing he was joking, mischief dancing in his too-blue eyes. Despite herself, a small chuckle escaped her lips. Calder's face brightened even more, visibly proud of himself for making her laugh. Kenna realized she had been wrong earlier.

That was the most beautiful thing she had ever seen.

Calder grabbed her hand, picking up her satchel in his other, and pulling her along towards the tree line. As they got closer, Kenna noticed two hammocks made of vines, gently swaying in the breeze just inside the trees where they hung. Sitting between the hammocks, surrounded by a circle of rocks, was a pile of sticks and kindling ready to be lit.

Calder smiled, clearly proud of himself, and Kenna's lips curled softly in response.

He lit the fire while she pulled out a small portion of food for both of them. They ate it quickly, taking turns with sips from the canteen.

Soon after, Kenna was suppressing yawns. She may have been unconscious for a better part of the day, but her body was still exhausted.

Before climbing into the hammock, Kenna turned to Calder, hesitantly meeting his eyes. "I never said thank you. For saving me. So... thank you. For that, and for helping me with my injuries, and the hammocks, and just... everything."

His blue eyes glinted in the firelight, softened around the corners. "You're welcome, Kenna. Now, you should probably get some sleep."

She nodded, turning to her hammock and climbing in. She closed her eyes and within minutes drifted into a deep, dreamless sleep.

Chapter Eighteen

When Kenna woke, the sky was rose petal pink, the sun skimming the waves. She tumbled her way out of the hammock, groaning in pain at the movement. She looked to the other hammock, but Calder wasn't there. Walking to the fire, she stoked what was left of the embers.

It looked like another cold meal was in her future.

She sighed, rummaging in the bag for something to eat.

Kenna only had a small portion left, and she realized she would have to ration what little food she had. Who knew if this island held anything edible.

First things first, she needed to find more water. There was almost none left in the canteen.

Deciding to wander the island and take stock of her surroundings, Kenna set off.

The copse of trees where Calder had put the hammocks was separated from the edge of the jungle. The other side of the foliage faded into the white sand, and then the water. However, the island must have been long, because she couldn't see the end of it looking down the beach.

She threw the canteen back into her satchel and slung it over her shoulder.

Before wandering into who-knew-what in the trees, she took the dagger out of the satchel and tucked it into her waistband. Kenna was much better with a bow and arrow, but she had passable skill with a blade. Besides, her people were nothing if not practical. Every child learned how to set traps and hunt, even royalty and nobility.

The days her father took her and Tristan into the woods to hunt were some of her favorites from her childhood. When it was just them surrounded by the quiet of nature, and the smell of fresh air and pine, she never felt like she had to put on the mask of Princess Makenna. Then, she was just Kenna, her daddy's little girl. And she could enjoy him as her father, not her king. He was always so patient with her. His gentle hands guiding her movements, his beaming smile so wide when she got something right, his right eye crinkling just a little more than the left.

She'd puff up her chest with pride and tease Tristan that maybe someday he could be as good as her. His joyful laughter in response to her teasing would fill her heart, and she wished to never leave the forest and go back to the castle.

But of course, they always did. They were the royal family after all.

They had a duty to fulfill.

Kenna shook off the memories and continued trudging her way into the jungle, the trees growing denser as she went deeper and deeper. She marked Xs into the trunks with her dagger as she went. She doubted the island was large enough to get lost, but better to be safe than sorry.

The leaves coating the ground muted the sounds of her footsteps. The small sounds of life surrounded her—the buzzing of insects, the chirping and cawing of birds, and from a distance she thought she made out the chatter of some kind of monkey.

Kenna used her rope to tie a trap to the nearest sturdy tree. After a moment of hesitation, she pulled out one of the spare shirts from her knapsack and tore a strip off the bottom, cringing at the action. She couldn't destroy much more of her clothing, or she would have nothing left.

With a deep sigh, she shoved the now shorter shirt back into the bag before tying the strip around the tree. She needed it to be easy to spot.

When she could no longer see the ocean in any direction, Kenna knew she was deep into the jungle. She could hear more signs of animal life and activity now, and then she heard water trickling, and hastened her footsteps, the sound growing stronger as she went. By now it was almost midday, and the sun was high, the heat almost unbearable. Her mouth was dry, and sweat trickled down her spine. She needed water.

All at once, the trees thinned and she found herself facing a stream of crystal-clear water, tumbling its way past her over rocks and boulders. Kenna dropped to her knees and dipped her face into the water, drinking straight from the creek. The shock of cold was a startling relief, and she gulped the water in, not particularly caring when it trickled down and soaked the front of her shirt.

She filled up the canteen and slipped it into her satchel. Leaning down to take one more gulp of water before getting back to her feet, Kenna winced at the movement and wiped her mouth with the back of her hand.

Taking in her surroundings Kenna saw the creek was fairly wide, the trees coming directly up to the water on her side of the creek. But on the opposite side was a small clearing in the trees, the grass interspersed with hundreds of wildflowers, creating an ocean of colors. Now that she was standing still, she could hear the sounds of nature even more clearly than before. Closing her eyes, Kenna felt calmer than she had since the festival started.

She paused, letting herself simply be for a moment. Her situation was not ideal—she was abandoned on a seemingly deserted island with a merman who had been pretending to be a chief's son vying for her hand in marriage.

What could possibly be the reason for that?

He had to have known he couldn't keep up the ruse indefinitely, so the crown couldn't have been his goal. Which meant he wanted something else. Was he planning to steal from them? Cladach wasn't poor, but they weren't extraordinarily wealthy either. And the gold and jewels they did have were locked away in the coffers and closely guarded. It would be nearly impossible for one man alone to break in and steal from them.

Kenna thought back, but he hadn't really *done* much. Besides their conversations, he had mostly just observed.

His eyes were always sharp and intelligent, tracking everything happening around him. What could he possibly be trying to gain? And what happened to the real Cameron?

Kenna was determined to get the answers out of Calder.

Calder.

Every time she thought or said his name, it gave her goosebumps. She never knew she could be attracted to a name, but it fit him so perfectly. Knowing what he really was now, she wondered if that's where part of her attraction came from. As a merman, he was a part of the sea.

Her heart beat faster at the thought of him. At the memory of his fingers brushing her spine as he tied the bandages around her. His fingers brushing elsewhere. Even now, she could feel the ghost of their heat against her skin.

Kenna pushed the loose hair falling out of her braid off her face—trying to get Calder's dimple out of her mind—only to find her hair crunchy with sea salt, sweat, and dirt. She grimaced, suddenly realizing how gross she felt. She needed a bath. Needed to wash the last day from her skin and gain some semblance of control.

Looking at the creek in front of her, she debated. The water was cold, but the air was hot, so she wouldn't have trouble warming back up. And this water was fresh. She may not have soap, but clean water was still better than how she felt now. Washing out the gash could only do good, she reasoned.

Kenna untangled the leather strap from the bottom of her braid, which most of her hair had already escaped from anyways. She kicked off her boots before carefully stripping off her breeches, and gingerly lifting the shirt above her head, trying to move her right arm and side as little as possible. She paused. It would be nice to get clean water on all of her body, but taking the binding off her chest herself would take time and be painful, not to mention how hard it would be to rebind it. She would probably have to ask Calder to help her again, and that was *not* something she wanted to do.

She decided to leave it on and hope it wouldn't take long to dry. Dipping a foot into the water, she promptly yelped. It was so damn cold. The temperature would feel good once she got used to it, though, and there was no other way to cool off. Squaring her shoulders, she walked all the way to the middle as quickly as possible.

At its deepest point, the stream only reached Kenna's waist. Standing there in the water she shivered, and after a moment, she carefully lowered herself onto a boulder, the water coming up to her chin.

Moaning in pleasure, she closed her eyes at the relief from the heat. She leaned back, dipped her head into the water, and let the current carry her hair out behind her, rippling through the strands. Running her fingers through it, she could feel the dirt and grime wash away as her hair softened in the water.

Once satisfied, she leaned back up and started rubbing her skin under the water, the best she could do for now.

Suddenly, she heard a branch snap from the shore, and her head whipped around, almost throwing her off balance from the boulder. She cringed as the movement pulled at her wound. Coming out of the trees was Calder, his gaze sweeping over her form in the water, eyes sparking with something she couldn't name.

Kenna's face flamed, and she clutched her arms around her legs, drawing them up to her chest. "What the hell are you doing?"

He smirked. "I was following the Xs, and I guess I just found my treasure."

Kenna's mouth dropped open and she spluttered for a second, utterly unsure how to respond to such a statement. "I don't- What are you- Oh my gods, can you please turn around?"

Calder's grin only stretched wider, his dimple appearing as he laughed at her reaction to his words, and she realized he was teasing her. He crossed his arms against his chest, muscles shifting beneath his thin shirt, and leaned his shoulder against the nearest tree. "Now why would I do that?"

"Because you're invading my privacy! This is indecent!"

"There's no fun in decency."

Kenna stared at him in incredulity. "Who the hell are you?"

"Wow, you must have hit your head harder than I realized. We went over this yesterday." Speaking very slowly and enunciating every sylla-ble, he continued, "My name is Calder."

Kenna glared and responded through gritted teeth. "Gods, you are such an ass. You weren't this bad when you were Cameron."

"You already know I'm not Cameron, so why should I still act like him? He was boring."

Kenna stared at him, mouth gaping. "You know what? I don't even give a damn, anymore. All I want is that you please. turn. around!"

Heaving an exaggerated sigh and rolling his eyes much harder than necessary, Calder dropped his arms and pushed away from the tree, turning his back to Kenna and planting his hands on his hips. "Well, at least hurry up. We have things to do."

"What do we need to do on a deserted island?"

She eyed him wearily, not trusting him to keep his back turned. Last night he had seen her shirtless, but it had only been her back. Realistically she knew she looked as big from the back as she did from the front, but it didn't matter to her insecurities. Last night it had been growing dark. And she had been too out of it to really care. Now she was very alert, and very aware of what he could and couldn't see. No man had ever seen her naked before. Had ever seen the soft rolls of her stomach.

She didn't want to see the look of disgust in his eyes when he saw her stomach, her thighs. The look she knew would be there. Knew because of what her supposed friends had said about her when they didn't know she could hear them.

Then there was the matter of her naked, bottom half. She didn't even want to think about him seeing her completely naked, too vulnerable and bare.

Kenna quickly sloshed out of the water, keeping an eye on Calder's back the whole time. But he stayed true to his word, not making the slightest move. It seemed despite his quippy attitude, he was at least somewhat honorable. As fast as she could, she dragged her breeches up her legs, the fabric sticking to her wet skin.

Hair still pouring rivulets of water down her back, she dragged the white shirt over her head. Pulling her hair from her shirt, she squeezed out what water she could. It wasn't much, making her shirt quickly soak through, the damp cloth clinging to her skin. She pulled it away from her body and sighed, realizing this was the best she was going to get.

Calder began tapping his foot on the ground. "My, my, Kenna, you sure do take your sweet time."

Now it was Kenna's turn to huff and roll her eyes. She didn't miss the way he hadn't answered her question, *again*. There was no way for her to slide her boots back on, so she decided to carry them back with her to the camp. She gingerly stepped past him, being careful to look where she placed her feet, following the X-marked trees back in the direction she had come from, heading for the tree with the trap. She heard Calder's footsteps on the jungle floor as he followed behind her.

"Your trap caught a nice fat squirrel. I brought it back to camp already and skinned it while you were playing in the water."

Kenna came to a stop, her shoulders stiffening. *Damataidh*, he was annoying. Without responding, she continued on, stopping when she reached the right tree. She untied the strip of her shirt from the tree and stuffed it into her bag before continuing on back to where they had set up camp.

Sure enough, there above the firepit was a squirrel skewered on a makeshift spit, already cooking.

"Thank you," Kenna murmured begrudgingly, still annoyed with him for the attitude. It didn't help that her stomach was rumbling with hunger, and she was dying to eat.

Calder tipped one side of his lips up with an amused smile. "You're welcome, Princess." Kenna blinked in surprise at how weird it was to hear him call her that instead of her name. A moment later, she realized he was messing with her when his back stiffened, and he bowed overdramatically, sweeping his arm out ridiculously wide as he went. He tilted his face up towards her and winked.

Kenna smothered the laugh trying to bubble up in her chest at his antics. Dear lord, this was going to be exhausting.

Chapter Nineteen

K enna licked her lips, wiping her greasy hands on her breeches, before pulling the canteen out of her satchel and taking a swig. Looking up, she found Calder already staring at her, his eyes glowing from the light of the fire. Kenna quickly tore her gaze away, clearing her throat. She thought she heard a quiet chuckle, but she couldn't be sure.

They ate the squirrel together in silence, and to her surprise, it actually hadn't been that bad. But now that they were done eating, she didn't know where to start. She had so many questions for him, but no idea what question to broach first, or how she was going to get him to answer honestly.

"So," Calder started, "we have some things to discuss."

Kenna attempted to keep her face free of the shock she was feeling. He was going to bring up what they needed to discuss of his own free will? Kenna thought she would have to drag it out of him. But it looked like he was in a cooperative mode—for once.

"Yes, we do," she agreed. "Why don't you start?" She looked at him expectantly, and she could've sworn she saw him quirk his lips before he carefully schooled his features.

After a slight pause, Calder said, "The first thing we need to do is figure out how injured you are, so we know how long it will take you to heal. In the meantime, we might as well establish a secure shelter. If we're going to be here for a while, I want to at least be comfortable."

Kenna stared at him in silence, not sure how to respond. She should've known he hadn't meant talking about the things she *actually* wanted to know. That would've been way too easy. And nothing in her life was ever easy.

One thing she really couldn't figure out, though, was *why?*

Why had he rescued her?

Why was he staying on this island and helping her?

He was a merman—he could swim away and leave her here whenever he wanted to. Which meant he still wanted something from her. That's what she needed to figure out.

"You want us to make a more permanent shelter?" she asked slowly.

"Yes. Or would you rather sleep out here in the open, completely vulnerable to whatever or whomever happens to come across this beach?" He raised his eyebrow.

Kenna looked around them exaggeratingly cautious. "Oh yes, this deserted island seems to be running afoot with suspicious activity and dangerous people."

Calder threw his head back in a full-bodied laugh, and Kenna fought her smile. But gods was he beautiful when he laughed. "You know, you have a *lot* more fire in you than I ever would have expected. Truly, you're nothing like I thought you would be."

Seeing an opening, Kenna asked, as casually as she could, "And what were you expecting?"

Meeting his eyes across the fire crackling between them, she heard nothing but the quiet sounds of wildlife and the waves lapping at the shore. His eyes glowed a deep bottomless blue in the firelight, and Kenna found her body heating more as their stare held. She gulped as he finally moved his gaze, and she heard him murmur, "Not you."

Her not meeting whatever expectations he had shouldn't upset her. Because if they upset her, it meant she cared. And she *didn't* care. She had to focus on the important part of his statement. And it was that he *had* expectations. And whatever those expectations were, they tied into why he came to the castle. "You expected something of me. That means you came for a reason."

"How astute."

Kenna rolled her eyes. "You know, you still haven't even acknowledged me knowing what you are."

"What? Extremely handsome? Remarkably charming?" He grinned, that infuriating twinkle back in his stupidly beautiful eyes.

"You think rather highly of yourself."

"I may not be royalty, like some people, but I'm still pretty great, if I do say so myself."

"How does such a big ego fit into one person?" Kenna shook her head.

"I'm exceptionally talented."

"Oh my gods, how did we even get here? This is not what I was trying to talk about!"

"Then what did you want to talk about?" He blinked innocently.

"You've got to be kidding me. How about the fact that you are a *myth-ical creature?*" By the end of her question she was practically yelling.

"I'm pretty sure I'm not mythical. I'm sitting here with you, aren't I?"

Kenna stood, letting out a noise of frustration somewhere between a groan and a scream. She stormed away from the fire, only to stalk right back over to Calder, jamming a finger in his face. "I am so sick of your damn games! You know you don't always have to be a *toll-thon*, right? Just once you could answer my question straight! I already have enough people in my life who lie to my face every day, I cannot deal with another one!"

Swallowing her rising emotions, she lowered her finger. She hadn't meant for all of that to come out, but the last few days had been too much. The festival, her parents, Reid, and now Calder. She felt like a candle at the end of its wick, and with one last gust of wind she would be burnt out for good.

She couldn't keep a lid on her emotions any longer.

Before she could stop them, she felt the tears building behind her eyes, and she jerked away from him. Turning towards the sea she closed her eyes against the wind, wrapping her arms around herself. She needed to get a grip.

Taking in deep breaths through her nose, she heard sand shifting behind her, and a hand on her shoulder. Her eyes opened to find Calder looking at her gently.

Hesitating one moment longer, a look of determination seemed to pass his face, and then he spoke. "It... It is forbidden. For me to reveal myself to a human. Me doing anything but denying my existence is an act of treason. And I cannot betray my queen."

Kenna's eyes grew wide, her heart swelling.

He admitted it. He just more or less admitted he was a merman.

This was it. It was officially real.

She had known, and she had seen. But to actually *hear* that confirmation was all she had ever wanted. To hear the confirmation she wasn't crazy.

She wasn't weird.

She was *right*.

She could almost cry from the relief of it.

She reined in as much of her reaction as she could, but there was no stopping the smile lighting her face. There weren't just merpeople, there was a whole mer *kingdom*. How did an entire kingdom exist without any of the humans knowing about it? She schooled her expression before responding. "Thank you. I obviously don't fully understand what telling me is going to cost you. But—it means more to me than you could ever know."

He removed his hand from her shoulder, flashing her a stiff smile before shifting awkwardly on his feet, and it was then she realized just how close they were. She could see the flecks of turquoise in his blue eyes.

Calder cleared his throat and looked away. "Why?"

The question threw her off. She looked at him, her face scrunched in confusion. "Why what?"

"Why does it matter so much to you?" When he looked back, his eyes were so intense she was caught in them, forced to answer honestly.

"As a child, I always believed in the fairy tales I was taught. When I was five, I almost drowned." She looked down. She hadn't told this story since she was fifteen. Not since she'd heard those kids talking. Their laughter still echoed in her head. "A mermaid saved my life." She looked back up into his gaze, an intensity in his eyes she couldn't decipher, taking in every word. She thought he looked a little shocked, but she couldn't be sure.

"I thought I saw a mermaid in the water over the side of the royal cruise ship. I leaned over the side to get a better look right when a wave rolled the ship, and I fell into the water. My dress weighed me down, and I didn't know how to swim. I was never allowed to go in the ocean. I was panicking. Then suddenly she was in front of me. I remember her perfectly, even now. She had golden hair and eyes the color of seaweed. A tail the brightest shade of red I've ever seen. She spoke to me, told me not to worry, that I would be fine. And then she pushed me back to the surface right as my father jumped into the water. I looked back one more time once I was in his arms, but she was already gone."

As she finished, she found Calder's eyes wide, mouth slightly open. He schooled his expression so fast she almost thought she imagined it. "I told my parents, but they didn't believe me. I told anyone who would listen, and no one believed me. No one but my brother, that is." A small smile graced her lips. "I kept telling them—telling everyone—until I got past the acceptable age of believing in fairy tales, and people began thinking I was strange or crazy. So I stopped telling people. But I *never* stopped believing.

"And I was *right*. I was right, and all those years, all the people who tried to make me feel like I was crazy were wrong. You have given me my validation, and that means more to me than you will ever know."

Calder lowered his eyes, his thick, dark lashes brushing his cheek-bones, before swallowing hard and looking back up at her. "Good," he said firmly. "I'm glad. And I'm truly sorry anyone ever made you feel like you were crazy. But... " He paused, and Kenna froze as he continued, "You can't tell anyone. They wouldn't believe you even if you did. But please, I beg of you not to breathe a word of this, for my sake. The consequences would be grave."

Kenna clenched her jaw. "Are you kidding me? You want me to go on for the rest of my life, continuing to be ridiculed when I know for a *fact* I've been right this whole time? Why would I do that?"

"You will do it because you must."

"Oh, I *must*," she replied sarcastically. "I find it amusing you think I would ever do what you told me to."

Calder glared at her then, any trace of kindness or understanding wiped from his face. "You will do what I tell you to, or I will *make* you."

"Ha! And how will you do that?" Calder clenched his jaw as Kenna realized what he meant. "Oh, I see. You think you're going to *compel* me?"

"How did you—"

"Because you tried to compel me on Cladach, and it didn't work. Or at least not for very long." She raised her brow in challenge. "What, no clever comeback to that? Now, if you're done being difficult, I'm going to fill the water canteen for the night before it gets too dark."

She snatched the canteen from where it rested by the fire, and started off towards the trees. She was looking forward to a moment alone to relax and breathe, when she heard footsteps coming after her. Without turning, she called over her shoulder, "And what do you think you're doing?"

Calder huffed a laugh, "Calm down, *mo lasair.* I just want to make sure you get there and back. Besides, I need to wash for the night any-way."

Kenna glared over her shoulder. "Don't do that."

"Do what?"

"Give me nicknames, like we're friends."

"Why not?"

"Because we're not friends!"

"Who said we're not friends?"

Kenna didn't deign that with a response, ignoring him as she kept walking.

Chapter Twenty

O n the walk to the stream, Kenna thought more about what Calder had told her, and how she had reacted. Shame burned through her. She had always thought of herself as an empathetic person, but in that moment she had been selfish. Selfish towards someone who had not only been kind to her and helped her, but had quite literally saved her life.

Her cursed brain and short temper had reacted on impulse, being told what she had searched for her whole life had to be kept as yet another secret. But that wasn't Calder's fault. He had told her the truth to ease her pain. She knew she owed him an apology.

"I'm sorry," she said quietly, the sound almost concealed by the crunching leaves under their feet. Calder looked at her with a brow quirked in question. Kenna sighed. "I'm sorry I responded so flippantly when you told me what would happen if I didn't keep your secret. That was selfish of me."

Calder's eyes softened at her words, and he nodded his head. "Thank you. I know it's hard, and I wish there was another way—"

"No, you don't need to say anything. You could have kept on denying it to me. You could have left me to drown, for that matter. So thank you. I promise you, your secret is safe with me." She thought back to the note she had left Tristan before sailing into the storm. "Well, me and Tristan who I left a note for, but he won't tell anyone either, I swear!"

Calder pinched the bridge of his nose, sighing and grumbling something about damned twins not having boundaries, stomping ahead of her and she bit her lip against the chuckle spilling out.

When they got to the creek, Kenna knelt at the water's edge to wash her hands, rinsing the smell of meat from them before splashing her face. She leaned further, ignoring the pain ringing through her side at the motion, cupping the water and bringing them up to her mouth when she heard rustling clothing behind her.

Kenna turned to find Calder standing with his back to her, and her core clenched at the sight. He was pulling his shirt over his head, and Kenna watched as the muscles in his back and shoulders rippled and bunched. His skin was tan, probably from living under the water in the sun. He ran a hand through his hair, his biceps flexing, leaving Kenna even more flustered.

Calder dropped his shirt, and she saw his hands reach for the front of his hips, still facing away from her. It was only when the fabric began lowering, ever closer to his—

Kenna's cheeks flamed so hard she could actually feel the heat. She quickly turned the other way. "What are you doing?"

"I told you I wanted to wash off."

"I thought you meant your face or something! I didn't think you would... you know."

Calder chuckled. "Well, I need to clean my whole body, don't I?"

"But I'm right here! Shouldn't you do that another time? For instance, when you're on your own?"

She heard the splashing of water and assumed he had gotten into the creek. When he responded she could hear the teasing in his voice. "Am I making you uncomfortable, *mo lasair*?"

"I told you not to call me that!" In her annoyance, she turned to glare at him, forgetting for a minute the situation they were in. When she turned she found herself swallowing the end of her words, her mouth drying out. He had ducked under the water while she had been talking. When he emerged, it was a mesmerizing sight.

Standing, he shook out his hair, eyes staying closed as he slicked the dripping hair back from his face with his hand, flecks of water flinging away like sparks of silver. Water sluiced down his thick chest and torso until he stood at his full height, the water cutting a tantalizingly low line across his hips.

Kenna didn't know what to do with herself.

She had never seen anything as sensual as what was happening before her. She tried to fight the way her body was reacting to him, but it was no use. There was no denying she was attracted to him. Very, very attracted to him. And this was the most of him she had ever seen. This was the most of any man she had ever seen.

And Calder was all man.

She may not have any physical experience with a man, but over the years, Kenna had built quite the personal collection of romance novels—her face as red as her hair the first time she read one, even alone in her private chambers. But it had started an obsession, and since that first one, she had consumed as many as she could get her hands on. It wasn't just the physical sexual aspects that intrigued her. It was the emotional connection and intimacy.

By the end of these stories, the characters had shared their entire lives, their entire minds and hearts with their partners. And their partners had loved them exactly as they were. Seen them for who they were at the core of their being, and it was enough.

And then there was the physical aspect as well of course. Kenna was just as intrigued by that. She wanted to be prepared for whatever would come once she was married.

Not that she didn't know the mechanics of it. Her mother had sat her down in what was the most uncomfortable conversation of Kenna's life when she had reached an old enough age, and when they began talking about Kenna's future marriage, the queen explained to her what happened between two people who loved or were attracted to each other.

She had explained that while it was Kenna's choice to decide when she was ready, she had implored Kenna to wait until marriage, being who she was.

But she had also told her of the concoction she could take if she decided not to wait and if her chosen partner had certain appendages. And the importance of using it if she made that choice, as the children Kenna had must be legitimate if they were to someday rule.

But Kenna was curious about the act itself.

What it *felt* like.

What emotions it elicited.

While she knew there was nothing to be ashamed of in enjoying romance novels, and that most people were not shy about these things, she had never been as forward about it herself. Because as much as they were for pleasure, romance novels were also stories of emotion and vulnerability. And Kenna hated being vulnerable.

After reading so many romance novels, she always thought she would be a little more prepared when faced with something like this for the first time. But oh, how wrong she had been.

Nothing could have prepared her for this.

A sound must have escaped her lips because suddenly his eyes snapped open and met hers. She *felt* his gaze zap through her, like electricity running through her veins, and lost all the air in her lungs. She saw something in his eyes—some intense emotion she couldn't place—before a sly smirk pulled up the side of his lips, popping his dimple, barely visible through the scruff that had grown on his face throughout the day.

She blinked rapidly, realizing she was still staring and hastily spun back around, breathing heavily.

"You humans are so sensitive."

"I don't know what you're talking about," Kenna mumbled, hoping the back of her neck wasn't as red as her face.

"It's only skin, you know. Just a body. You humans are much too uptight, if you ask me. So conservative."

Kenna's embarrassment began waning in the face of her curiosity. She peeked over her shoulder to see him still submerged in the water, more at ease than she had seen him since she first woke up on the island.

She almost got distracted again before pulling herself together. "So what? Merpeople wander around naked all the time?" she asked, half sincerely, half sarcastically.

Calder laughed, the sound sure and deep and real. "Not completely naked. We do have tails after all." He winked at her. "But it's not a big deal. We're not nearly so squeamish about bodies." He made his way towards the bank, the water falling lower and lower.

Kenna turned around yet again. She definitely wasn't prepared for *that* sight. As she turned though, she caught a flash of his muscular thigh rippling up from the water, and after she was done drooling over it, a thought occurred to her. She wanted to ask him, but she wasn't sure he would answer. Deciding to ask anyway, she hesitantly called his name.

"Calder?"

"Yes, *mo lasair?*"

Kenna rolled her eyes at the nickname this time, but otherwise ignored it. She assumed it was more in reference to her blushing face than her hair this time, and she wasn't sure why that thought made her skin tingle, but it did.

"How are you still in your human shape right now?

"What do you mean?" The response was accompanied by the rustle of clothing, as Calder blessedly and unfortunately put his clothes back on.

"Well, you were just fully submerged in water. Don't you shift when you're in water? That's what all the books say. And I saw you shift when you dove back into the ocean on Cladach." Her question was met with silence.

As she was about to say his name again, all the hairs on the back of her neck stood up and goosebumps cascaded down her arms. She felt his presence before she felt the heat from his body radiating against her back.

He was so *warm.*

And then his breath fanned across her neck and the back of her ear as he responded softly, "It has to be salt water, *ghaoil.* We are tied to the ocean, not the rivers."

"Oh," she whispered.

And then she felt his fingers at her elbow, slowly tracing down her skin to her hand, a whimper leaving her throat before she could stop it. The feeling of his fingers on her skin shot straight through her, down to her very core.

He removed the canteen from her hand, and then his heat was gone as he stepped around her and leaned down to the water to fill it. She was still in the same position when he stood back up to face her.

Calder stared into her eyes as he handed the canteen back, his eyes the dark blue of the ocean before a storm.

"We should head back to camp," he said, his voice a low rumble.

Kenna nodded her head, but couldn't speak. Calder stepped into her space, the height difference forcing him to bend his head down to look at her. He stood a breath away as he reached to tuck a loose strand of hair behind her ear, his fingers grazing her cheek.

"You keep surprising me," he murmured so quietly she almost hadn't heard him. But if she was surprising him, what had he been expecting?

KENNA BLINKED HER EYES open against the morning sun, groaning as she stretched her limbs across her bed and turned to lay on her back, staring at the ceiling.

Only, it wasn't a ceiling above her, and she wasn't in a bed.

It was the sky, and she was swinging on a hammock woven from vines.

Kenna deflated, having forgotten for that first blissfully half-awake moment where she was. What had happened? Today was her third time waking up on the island. Two days since she had almost drowned. Two days of her parents and brother wondering where she was. If she was alive. She could only hope Tristan had found her note.

She blinked her eyes against the rapidly building tears. This was the longest she had ever gone without seeing him, talking to him, and she missed him so terribly that it physically hurt. Three days. And how many more days would it be until she saw them all again?

If she ever saw them again.

Kenna's whole body froze.

She was supposed to have gotten married yesterday. She would have woken up today as a *wife.*

All at once, a pressure Kenna hadn't even realized had been weighing on her chest dissolved, floating away on the breeze. She gulped in a deep breath and realized what she felt was *relief.*

She was *glad* she'd been shipwrecked.

And when that realization hit her, she began laughing. Laughing so hard her whole body shook. And then she was shaking for a different reason as searing pain shot through her gash at the movement. Kenna clutched at her ribs, forcing her body to still until the pain receded.

How wrong was it that she was relieved she almost died, just so she didn't have to marry someone she didn't want to? She realized in that moment if she ever made it back home, she had to fight this. It didn't matter what she had promised her parents before. There had to be some other way to strengthen ties between the clans. If she would rather drown in a storm than marry, she needed to do something about it.

She should only marry because she *wanted* to. Because she loved someone, and wanted to spend the rest of her life with them. Because they made her happy, made her *feel.*

With that thought, her mind drifted back to the night before at the river. The way she had felt standing so close to Calder.

His fingers on her skin.

His breath on the shell of her ear.

His eyes seeming to see everything she hid so well from the rest of the world.

Gods, she was in so much trouble. She couldn't fall for a merman. Never mind he lived under the sea, a place she could never go. There was only one way that story could end.

Chapter Twenty-One

T he rest of the day had passed in relative monotony, Kenna keeping to herself as much as she could while stranded on an island with only one other person. After her morning ruminations she hadn't been in the mood to talk or pretend like everything was fine when it wasn't. To remember she needed to keep her distance from Calder.

The one time they had spoken more than a few words was when they had seen a ship far off in the distance. Kenna had called Calder over as they debated who might be on the ship, or what they could do to signal it.

Her first reaction to seeing the ship had been disappointment, much to her horror. It should have been joy. Relief she was getting off this island, getting away from this man who consumed her thoughts.

And yet, she had been sad, not relieved. Her heart dropping, thinking that her time with Calder was already at an end. Knowing when she got back home, she would never see him again.

But her confusing feelings had all been for naught, because the ship stayed where it was, just on the horizon for hours, before moving on, never coming close enough to the island for them to signal it.

After that, they had gone back to mostly ignoring each other, Calder sensing she didn't want to talk and respecting her wishes for once.

The next morning, however, Kenna woke to the sounds of Calder stomping around their site, kicking sand over the still-glowing embers from the previous night's fire.

"What are you doing?" Kenna questioned him.

Calder looked up, grinning at her. "Ah, Sleeping Beauty arises."

"The sun is barely above the horizon," she responded drily.

"Well, I have been getting ready for the long day of work we have ahead of ourselves while you've been lounging around."

"Oh, eat sand, you obnoxious man." He threw his head back laughing, and she was unable to stop herself from laughing along.

The sun must be getting to her, making her delirious.

"Well, *mo lasair*, it is high time we built ourselves a sturdier shelter. Which means we need to go scavenging, and I can't very well leave a fire going while we're away from the camp, can I?"

Kenna looked around at their sparse little campsite doubtfully. "Do we really need to do that? How long do you expect us to be here?"

Calder raised his brow at her. "I'm not the one with a gash down my ribs, am I?"

"You could leave me here any time, fish boy." Kenna raised her brow back at him. Calder's lip twitched at the corner for the shortest second before he shook his head, turning away and muttering to himself. "What was that? I didn't hear you."

"I, for one, would like some actual shelter from the sun. If you don't want to join me, then stay here baking. It's your choice."

Kenna watched him, thinking about her options. She could sit here sulking, baking in the sun as Calder had aptly pointed out. But it would be nice to walk around, stretch her legs. Scope out more of the island and see what they were working with. Plus, having a shelter wouldn't be such a bad thing. She didn't respond, but she did get up to follow him when he started walking, and she could've sworn she caught a smile before he turned his face away.

They had been walking for less than a minute before Kenna could no longer help herself from asking questions. "So what is it like growing up in the ocean?"

"What was it like growing up in a castle?" Calder shot back.

Fine, if he was going to play it like that, she would go along with it. But if he thought he was going to get something for nothing he had another thing coming.

"I'll tell you mine if you tell me yours."

Something flared in his eyes as he came to a stop. "Be careful, *mo lasair*, make sure this is a game you really want to play," his voice rumbled lowly, and heat licked up her spine.

Her throat was suddenly very dry.

"Don't chicken out on me now, fish boy."

"You first."

Kenna finally looked away, unable to bear looking in his eyes any longer without feeling like she was drowning again. She cleared her throat, continuing to walk as she gathered her thoughts, unsure where to start.

"It was as pampered as you must imagine. Extremely comfortable and happy. My parents doted on us. My favorite times were when my father would take me and Tristan on hunting trips. Teaching us archery, how to wield a dagger, how to set traps." She smiled to herself at the memories. "Those were the times I felt like I was simply me. Just Kenna. Not some princess who everyone wanted a piece of for their own gain." Her smile began to slip, and she glanced over at Calder. He was staring ahead as they walked, truly seeming to listen to what she had to say.

"I am extremely privileged. I acknowledge that. I am heir to a mighty kingdom, a princess in both title and in my parents' eyes. I never wanted for anything—anything physical, I should say. I already told you about how my peers viewed me for believing in mermaids. Believing in you. And outside of that, it has always been hard for me to truly understand other people. I've just always felt so... different." Calder nodded in sympathy. "It was extremely lonely. People would pretend to be my friends while secretly ridiculing me behind my back, only wanting to be around me for what I could do for them. Tristan was my only friend."

Kenna didn't know what had cracked her open. The way he listened without offering empty platitudes. The way he seemed to actually *see* her. Listen to her the way no one had before. The way something about him made her feel *safe*. But the words were spilling out of her now, unable to be stopped, more honest than she had ever been with anyone besides Tristan.

"It's so hard not to feel alone when everyone but you seems to have that person. That person who they always turn to first, who they always hold space for in their hearts, in their lives. Who will always pick them first back, and not because they have to. I know Tristan would be that person for me. But he's my twin—it's not the same. We didn't choose each other. He has to love me. It's the crushing weight of drifting along in space, alone with no one in sight to pull you back to safety."

She realized they had come to a stop, and when she looked up, Calder was staring back at her. She braced herself for the pity she was sure she would see in his eyes, but instead she saw something else. Something rawer, something like recognition.

He started speaking lowly, his voice soft. "I confess I grew up with lots of friends. I had many people who loved me, and who I loved. And I know they loved me for me, because I had nothing else to give them." Kenna gulped, looking down at the ground. For a second there, she had thought maybe he understood what she was talking about.

But of course he didn't. He was so confident, so sure in who he was, the kind of person who could make a friend wherever he went. Of course he wouldn't understand the crushing weight of her loneliness.

But then he kept speaking.

"And yet, I could be in a room full of people, and feel more alone than I ever had being on my own." Kenna's head snapped up, meeting his vulnerable gaze. "I surrounded myself with people who I loved, people who loved me, hoping they could fill the emptiness I felt inside myself. The boy who always had a smile was not as happy as he wanted everyone else to believe. I was living in a shell, hiding that ache I carried inside myself. But slowly my shell started cracking, and the pain I was feeling began to seep through."

He looked away from her, gaze wandering across the horizon. "And what I came to realize was that no one else could fill that loneliness inside me. It was something I had to fill myself. I learned some people are sad for no reason at all. They feel empty when they have nothing to feel empty about. And that's fine. That doesn't make them any less than. It just means their brains were built differently. And they learn how to fill in those empty pieces of themselves. They fill it with joy. With acceptance that it's alright to be a little broken. That broken doesn't mean less than."

He looked back into her eyes then, his expression fierce. As if he wanted to inject everything he was saying, everything he was feeling straight into her soul. "My parents saw through that perfect facade I was carrying, and they carried the weight that was on my soul for me until I could carry it myself. They proved to me no matter how lonely I felt on the inside, I was never really alone. They were always with me, every step of the way."

At this point the tears were streaming down Kenna's face in earnest. Calder reached up a hand, softly brushing them away, one cheek at a time.

"The way you talk about your brother. You may not have even realized, but it seems like he's been doing the same thing for you this entire time. You're wrong about him. Not all siblings choose each other." Something sad flickered in his eyes at his words. "It sounds to me like you and Tristan chose each other, whether you're related or not. Don't downplay your bond with him, because it truly is something special."

Kenna struggled to breathe through the tightness in her throat at his confession. "I've never heard someone put it into words before."

"Put what into words, *ghaoil*?"

"The feelings my soul has been speaking to me my whole life."

"You are not alone, Kenna. You may be a princess, high and mighty above the rest." He smiled softly in satisfaction as his joke pulled a watery laugh from her. "But I promise you, there are more people who feel the same way as you than you will ever know. We're all just too afraid to speak the truth aloud, in fear no one else will understand. That it will prove we are exactly as alone as we have always felt."

Kenna searched his eyes—looking for what, she wasn't sure. The slightest hint he wasn't being honest? That he was saying what he thought she wanted to hear? But all she saw was bone-deep sincerity. Someone whose soul spoke to hers like they had their own special language. Like there was an invisible string tying her heart to his, stretched across the oceans between them their whole life, taut and pulling, finally able to relax and let go for the first time, now they had found each other.

As she felt herself falling further into the endless depth of his deep blue eyes, she realized their bodies were a lot closer than they had been at the start of this conversation. Her eyes flickered down to his lips against her will, flicking back up only to catch him staring at her lips.

Calder's body swayed closer to her, mirroring her own that seemed to gravitate towards him like a magnet.

Her heart pounded in her chest, warning her this was a bad idea, begging her to close the dwindling distance between their parted lips even faster, when a flash of light lit up the sky above him, drawing her eyes upward. Only a moment later, a boom of thunder made her flinch, and brought her soaring heart crashing back to the ground.

Kenna turned away from Calder, wrapping her arms around her body, attempting to rub away the goosebumps covering her arms as she took in the storm that had snuck up on them. How had she missed it coming? The sky a medley of greys and purples, the rain falling not long after. Her eyes wandered to Calder to find him already staring at her, something like regret in his eyes.

"We should head to the coverage of the trees," he said softly, so softly she almost didn't hear him over the sounds of the storm now raging

171

above them. Kenna nodded, following after him as he jogged into the shelter of the forest.

They huddled under the branches for a short while, the storm passing over them quickly, wiping away whatever moment had been between them, and leaving the sun shining again in its wake, the slate wiped clean.

They didn't say anything more about that conversation as they continued down the beach, making a loop around the island, finding it as small as she had assumed that first day. Along the way they collected as much sturdy driftwood as they could find, as well as a sizable piece of one of the sails from her boat and a small amount of rope.

As they walked they talked more, keeping it to safer, lighter subjects, both of them avoiding the tension pulling taut between them.

It seemed Calder was just as curious about humans as she was about mermaids, asking her question after question about her childhood, about life on the land.

"You truly taught yourself to sail?" Calder asked, his voice impressed.

"Well, my parents weren't exactly going to teach me. They would have locked me in a tower if they knew I ever even went near the ocean."

"Why would you say that?"

"My parents hate the ocean. I don't remember a time when they didn't, but I'm sure almost drowning didn't help matters. I think they fear it."

"Why do you think that is?"

Kenna eyed Calder, wondering why he seemed so curious about what her parents thought of the ocean. She chose her response carefully, cataloging his reaction. "I'm not sure. The ocean is dangerous. That's what my mother always told me. *We don't test her waters.*" She rolled her eyes and chuckled. "Whatever that means." Calder didn't respond, humming his acknowledgement, a faraway look in his eyes. "What about you?"

"What about me?"

"What was it like growing up in the ocean? Do you have any siblings? What are your parents like?"

"It was fine. Growing up as wild as the waves I lived in," he grinned at her, "I was definitely a handful. An only child, thank the gods, for my parents' sake—I don't think they could have handled any more of me. I was always getting into trouble. But they put up with it. Put up with me. They are the most wonderful people in the world. My mother..." He trailed off, a look of pure love crossing his face. "She is the kindest, most giving woman I have ever met. I'm lucky to be her son."

Kenna's heart melted at his words, his obvious bond with his family shining through his eyes. She wished her relationship with her parents could be that uncomplicated. That there wasn't the pressure of their expectations for her clouding the true, deep love she felt for them.

She knew it wasn't fair. She knew it came from a place of love, from a place of wanting her to succeed, to do great things. But knowing that didn't stop the way it sometimes felt like a weight on her heart, holding her back, constricting her from being the person she wanted to be. From being exactly who she was without worrying how they perceived her.

As they kept talking, she couldn't help but notice how... weird it was.

Kenna didn't casually talk with people other than Tristan. Not since she was a child, not since before Reid. What was weird about it was how good it felt to talk to someone. And it was surprisingly easy talking to Calder. He was just so *real*. Sure, he was snarky and maybe a little too arrogant at times, but he never pretended to be something he wasn't.

Even when he was pretending to be some*one* he wasn't, he still acted like himself. Still pushed her buttons, tested her limits. Still talked to her like she was a person, not a princess.

But no matter how easy he was to talk to, and how real he seemed to be with her, there was something more going on.

He was a merman, for gods' sake. He could leave any time he wanted. And she still had no clue why he had come to the castle in the first place. He continued to avoid almost all of her questions.

She was trying to be subtle about her questioning, building up to the heavier topics, like what had actually happened to the *real* Cameron Mackenzie?

She was fairly certain Calder knew exactly what she was doing—it wasn't really her strong suit. But he avoided any question about what the mer kingdom was like. And definitely gave up nothing at all about its location. She had no clue how far from home he was.

The one thing she *had* managed to get from him was the merpeople's connection to the ocean. Merpeople were a part of the ocean. They truly were an extension of it just as she had read, salt water running in their veins.

The ocean was the source of their magic, and they had to be connected to it in some way to use it. If a merperson spent too long away from the ocean, their connection grew weaker and weaker until it was gone. The thought broke her heart, and she wasn't even a mermaid.

But she'd always felt that pull.

That call to the sea in the deepest recesses of her heart.

No breath felt as good as the breath of salty air. No touch felt as good as the spray of the sea. She couldn't ever imagine giving up her connection to the ocean.

Chapter Twenty-Two

Wiping the sweat from her brow, Kenna looked up from where she was weaving fronds of palm trees together and squinted at the sky, gauging the time. The sun was only starting to fall from the midway mark. She rolled her shoulders back, groaning at the pleasure-pain as it stretched her muscles but also pulled the edges of her wound. She gingerly poked at her side and grimaced.

It was definitely much better, but it still hurt.

Kenna let out a long frustrated breath, wanting to just be healed already.

She looked up as Calder walked back into their camp, her mind going blank. He stood in front of her, holding up the frame of a wall made from long stalks of bamboo and tied together with vines.

And he was shirtless. Sweat glistened on his skin, making him practically glow in the golden sunlight. His breeches were slung low across his hips, allowing her a full view of his thick chest and torso. She watched his muscles bunch and contract as he hefted the frame up, propping it against the one already standing.

She tried to force herself to look away, but really, who was she kidding?

He had shaved his beard down to scruff last night, using the blade from one of her knives, short enough now to see the sharp line of his jaw. When her gaze finally made it up to his, he was staring directly at her, a smirk on his face, that damned dimple taunting her. She cleared her throat, looking back down to her work.

"So, I'll take that as a no?" Calder asked, his voice dripping with amusement.

"What?"

"I asked if you were hungry, but you didn't respond. Too busy ogling me. Maybe you're hungry for something other than food?"

Kenna's head snapped up, her mouth dropping open, and she found a wicked gleam in his eyes as he slowly stalked closer to her.

"I—what? No! Of course not!"

But his smile only grew wider. "Are you sure about that?"

"Yes, quite sure," she clipped, refusing to look at him.

Calder stopped in front of her, lifting one hand to brush the back of his finger against her cheek.

"You say one thing, but your cheeks say another, *mo lasair.*" He leaned closer until he was only a breath away. "I think you're lying."

Kenna couldn't breathe. Not when he was this close and all she could smell was him. Sea salt and musk and citrus from the lemons they'd picked earlier that day. She closed her eyes and gulped, unsure what to do with herself.

"I'm not lying," she responded in a whisper. He hooked his finger under her chin, raising her head.

"Open your eyes."

Kenna shook her head.

"Kenna."

She took a deep breath, which was a mistake. All she got was a lungful of *him*, making her head spin. She slowly opened her eyes and met his gaze, his eyes twin blue flames burning with intensity.

"Don't think I don't see the way you look at me. The way you looked at me yesterday walking along the beach, before the storm hit. The way you've looked at me since that first day in the throne room."

Kenna's heart was racing, and she was on the verge of leaning into him when his words registered, stopping her.

The first day she met him.

When he had been pretending to be someone else. Pretending to be Cameron Mackenzie.

Kenna stood abruptly, shoving past him. All the anger and frustration began welling back up inside of her. How did she so easily fall for his charm every time? He was still hiding things from her. She whipped back around, glaring at him.

"That's right. Back when you were in *my* castle pretending to be someone else. Which you still won't give me a valid reason for. It doesn't matter how I looked at you because I wasn't looking at *you*—I was looking at Cameron Mackenzie." The lie burned on its way out, but she couldn't let him think she was attracted to him. That he held any power over her. "And it doesn't matter how I look at you now because I still don't know who I am looking at. You refuse to tell me anything. I don't even know what happened to the real Cameron! Is he even still alive? Did you kill him?" Not how she meant to broach that subject, but she had trouble controlling her impulsive tongue when her temper flared.

Calder looked at her in shock. "Are you serious?"

"Well? Did you?"

"No! Why would you think that?"

"What am I supposed to think, Calder? You pretended to be someone who never showed up. Where was he? What happened to him?"

"We've spent a week together now, and you really think of me as someone capable of murder? That's what you've been thinking this whole time?"

Kenna stepped towards him, shoving her finger in his chest. "I have no idea what I'm thinking. Maybe if you ever actually answered my questions, I would know you well enough to know what you're capable of."

Calder glared at her, his chest rising and falling rapidly against her finger. She could see the muscle in his jaw popping as he clenched it. He moved into her space, backing her up until she was pressed against a tree. One of his hands braced against the trunk above her head.

"You want to know? Fine. I'll tell you. I intercepted a letter Cameron sent ahead to the palace, sending his condolences for his absence, and I seized the opportunity I saw. I never killed anyone. That's not who I am, and deny it all you want, but I know you know that already. I know when you look at me, you see *me*. Because when I look at you, I see you too." Calder leaned further into her until she could feel his breath on her lips, making her skin tingle.

"I also know that even though you try to fight it, try to hide your smiles from me and from yourself, you *like* me. What I don't know is how you haven't yet seen the feeling is mutual, you stupid, stubborn girl."

Kenna sucked in a sharp breath, her head spinning.

"Makenna," he ground her name out, and she had never heard anything sound as good as the way her name did coming from his lips.

He ducked his head down, skimming his lips up her neck as he continued, and Kenna kept her grasp on sanity by a thread. "You are killing me slowly. This is not how it was supposed to go. This was not how anything was supposed to go. You are *ruining* all my plans and I don't even care, because you're ruining *me* at the same time." His eyes flashed at her as he finished speaking, darker than she had ever seen them, the pupils blown wide.

Kenna didn't have time to process his words though, because as soon as they left his mouth, he slanted his lips across hers.

Calder was kissing her.

Calder was *kissing* her.

He was kissing her and her whole world stopped. Every thought but him fled from her mind. She couldn't feel anything besides his lips against hers, the tree pressed against her back, and his hand suddenly in her hair.

And then she was kissing him back.

The world was spinning and her body was going up in flames.

She was burning from the inside out.

Burning everywhere he touched her, and she couldn't stop the whimper that fell out of her mouth and into his. He hungrily took it, using the opening to dive his tongue into her mouth. Sparks crackled through her veins, and she unraveled in his arms. She couldn't take the stillness anymore, her entire body vibrating.

Vibrating with energy. With need.

She wrapped her hand around the back of his neck and yanked him closer. Calder's other hand was now at her hip, molding her body even further to his, and this time it was his turn to groan as he pressed the proof of his arousal further into her hip. All the hairs on her body stood on end, goosebumps racing down her skin at the sound. Was kissing *her* really eliciting such a response?

Kenna had never felt anything like it. She realized there was a feeling of power in it, in making a man want you. And he did really want her, didn't he? She could feel the evidence of that, his hips rolling against her. This man that she hadn't been able to stop looking at since the second she laid eyes on him. That she had always felt some unnameable pull towards. How did this man feel the same way about her that she felt about him?

It seemed too good to be true.

That thought was a bucket of ice water dumped on her head, dousing her desire. She froze, and then shoved him off of her. He backed up with no resistance, and they stared at each other, eyes wide and chests heaving.

"I'm sorry, I didn't—"

"Don't," Kenna bit out, holding her hand up.

She didn't want to hear the rest of that sentence. His apology, whether fake or sincere, was like a punch to the gut. Of course he either hadn't meant to do that, or had only done it to distract her.

"Kenna—"

"No. Whatever you were going to say, keep it to yourself. I really, truly do not want to hear it. That was a lapse in judgment, and it will not be happening again. I am going to the creek now. You will stay here and finish building this hut before it's too dark to finish tonight." Calder opened his mouth, looking as if he was going to argue with her, so Kenna brushed past him before he could start.

Grabbing the canteen and her dagger, she spun back around to point it in his direction. "And before you get any smart ideas, *tolla-thon*, if you follow me, I *will* stab you."

Calder's lips quirked up on one side, his eyes sparking with amusement, and she squinted at him until he held his hands up in mock surrender. "Whatever you say, *mo lasair*."

Gods, the heated way he said that nickname this time was pure sin.

Kenna suppressed the shiver trying to make its way down her body, and spun on her heels, storming away.

Once she was far enough into the trees to be out of sight, she let out the breath that had been building in her chest.

She was so *fucked.*

KENNA WAS STALLING. She knew she was stalling, but she couldn't bring herself to care, she needed the time to sit with her thoughts. Laying back in the creek as long as she could possibly hold the position, Kenna was detangling her hair completely for the first time since getting to the island, her first bath having been interrupted by Calder.

She didn't know what to do, what to *think*. Her lips still tingled, feeling the ghost of his kiss. Kenna closed her eyes, feeling the water run through her hair like fingers, tracing the shape of her skin. Against her will, her mind wouldn't waver from the thought of that kiss.

Her *first* kiss.

"Uggghhh." Kenna sat up in the water, running her hands over her face. She should just drown herself in the creek; it would be easier than dealing with whatever *this* was. That was not how she ever pictured her first kiss going.

At first, she'd pictured it with Reid after he confessed his undying love for her, sweet and romantic and innocent. Then with a husband she didn't want, awkward and fumbling and perfunctory.

But never like this. Like she was kindling and his kiss was the spark that set her ablaze, every inch of her skin burning with need. It was a feeling she had never experienced before, this arousal.

Yes, she had wanted to kiss Reid. But she was a teenager then, experiencing attraction for the first time, and the desire she had felt had been nothing like what it was with Calder. She had not felt attraction for anyone since then, hadn't let herself get close enough to anyone to form that kind of connection. Her desires had grown, of course, but they had simply been desires in a general sense, fulfilled by her own hand and not directed at any one person.

Kenna's face flamed at the thought. At memories of dark rooms and exploring her body until she found relief from the ache that built in her. But with Calder, it was so different. It was intense, a stronger feeling than she could have imagined. And all they had done was *kiss*. What would it have felt like to do more with him? If his hands had explored more of her body, and hers explored him in return?

Just the thought had that ache building back up again in her core, and only the thought of Calder ignoring her request and coming to find her stayed her hand from traveling down her body.

I'm sorry, I didn't—

What had he been about to say? Didn't mean to kiss her? Didn't *want* to kiss her? That he regretted it? At that thought, Kenna's stomach turned. Gods, she was such a fool.

Of course it hadn't meant as much to him as it did to her. It was most likely nothing more than a passing moment for him, one of many he'd had in his lifetime. Most people didn't reach the age she had without having kissed someone. She doubted very much it was his first kiss as well. That he was someone else who only felt attraction alongside emotion. Most people seemed to feel those things very differently, and physical intimacy was simply a normal part of their lives.

She needed to shake it off. To act as if it hadn't affected her. She could not let him know how much he had shaken her, rearranged her very being with his touch. With this conviction in mind, Kenna finally got out of the water to put her clothes back on and head back to camp.

At this point, an hour or two had passed since she had left, and hopefully Calder would let it go. Allow them to move past it and pretend it hadn't happened. They were still stuck on this island together after all.

Kenna had squeezed out as much of the water from her hair as she could by the creek, and by the time she got back to the camp she had twisted it into a knot on the top of her head, a few straggling pieces hanging around her temple.

Calder sat in front of the fire, his skin glowing golden from the light of the flames, and Kenna's stomach immediately clenched, want rushing back through her at the sight of him. Swallowing hard, Kenna looked down to the sand in front of her feet rather than at him. Looking at him was dangerous. Look for too long and she might do something crazy, like throw herself at him and beg him to stick his tongue in her mouth again.

Clearing his throat, he jerked her out of her spiraling inappropriate thoughts when he asked her, "How was your bath?"

"Fine." She kept her response short, not wanting him to hear the desire that she was sure coated her voice, dropping the canteen next to him before crossing and settling on the other side of the fire, still refusing to meet his eyes. Out of the corner of her eye she thought she saw him twitch, as if to come towards her, but he stayed put.

They cooked and ate their food in silence, Kenna stewing in an equal mix of desire and determination to ignore that desire.

Why did she have to feel this way for someone she could never have?

As soon as she finished eating, Kenna said a quiet thank-you before getting up and leaving Calder at the fire, walking into the shelter he had finished while she was bathing. He had used the sail they found washed up on shore as the roof cover, the hammocks now hanging from the bamboo support beams inside the shelter instead of from the trees. Kenna laid in her hammock and turned her back to him. She heard the sounds of him kicking sand over the fire to snuff out the flames, wishing the flames of her desire could be doused as easily.

The creak of his hammock as he settled into it followed, and Kenna squeezed her eyes shut attempting to force her brain into submission. She would stop thinking about him, go to sleep, and start over again fresh tomorrow.

As if the kiss had never happened. As if Calder hadn't opened something inside her with his kiss that she feared she could never shut off again.

A new day for a new Kenna. One who had never tasted Calder's lips, and never desired to do so again.

Chapter
Twenty-Three

A day had passed since the *incident*, and Kenna was trying her best to keep her distance from Calder. She gave up attempting to get answers from him, and was just trying to get by without throwing herself at him.

Or strangling him.

She hadn't decided yet which she wanted to do more.

She could tell Calder wanted to talk about it. To talk about them. But she refused to give in to him. Kenna had no idea what game he was playing, but she couldn't afford to get burned. Her heart couldn't take it.

So, every time he looked like he was about to say something, she found a way to occupy herself. Yesterday, Kenna had bulked up the walls of their shelter, stuffed moss into pillows she'd made out of bits of sail tied together with rope, made wooden bowls and utensils, and built them a more solid and long-term firepit.

Anything to avoid being alone with Calder for too long. Anything to keep him from ruining that kiss for her. Because as much as Kenna wanted to say she regretted it, regretted crossing that line with someone she knew was still keeping things from her, she couldn't. At least not entirely.

She couldn't regret something that felt so *right*.

And gods, had that kiss felt right.

Last night, sitting across the fire from him as they ate in silence, Kenna found her gaze wandering to his lips. The fire made his skin golden, his lips full and inviting, the shadows playing in his short beard, growing out from the scruff.

As soon as she realized what she was doing, she cursed herself and tore her eyes away, but it didn't matter. They always went back.

Kenna forced herself to focus on her current task. She was by the creek, finally taking the bandage off her chest. The gash had stopped hurting long enough that she was convinced it was healed enough to uncover it for good.

Binding her breasts was annoying enough, but having to have her entire torso completely bound every single day was driving her out of her mind. She felt as if she hadn't taken a full breath since she got to the island.

Kenna reached behind her back and grappled for the end of the bandage, but after almost a minute of stretching her arm as far back as she could in a horrible angle, she groaned in frustration and stamped her foot. She never realized how much she took Freya and Martha for granted until she didn't have them.

Suddenly, she felt a large warm hand over hers, and a breath feathered through the hairs at the nape of her neck. "Here, let me." Untucking the end piece, he reached his arm forward as if he were about to unwrap it all the way himself.

Wrenching herself out of his sea salt and citrus scent, she snatched the end of the bandage from his hand, probably a little rougher than she needed to, but she could never function when he was this close, so it was his fault.

"Thanks," she snapped. "I got it. Can you give me some privacy, please?"

She heard a sigh, and then his retreating footsteps accompanied by a mumbled, "I was just trying to help."

Kenna closed her eyes. She couldn't snap at him every time he tried to say or do anything at all around her, but he got her so worked up she couldn't help herself.

She unwound the bandage, and as each layer was removed, she could feel her ribs expanding. All the way off, Kenna gulped in the largest breath she could, oxygen and *relief* flooding her, dizzying her head in the best way.

It felt so good to finally be free. Kenna sucked in deep breath after deep breath, forgetting for a moment she was standing completely topless, alone, in the middle of the jungle, where Calder could pop back up at any moment.

She trusted him about as far as she could throw him, which was not very far at all.

Kenna threw her shirt on over her head, leaving her chest unbound for now. Never mind what it looked like; she had no intention of binding her breasts again for the rest of the day at the least. Stepping down to the water and dipping the bandage in, she squeezed out as much of the sweat and sand and dirt as she could without soap. Once she was satisfied it was as clean as it was going to get, she wrung it out and hung it on a branch to dry.

Kenna was about to slip the shirt back off and sink into the water herself when she had an idea. At this time of day, Calder was usually setting traps to catch their food for the night. Now that her bandage was off, maybe it was time for a proper swim in the ocean.

Smiling to herself, Kenna threw one glance over her shoulder before making her way in the opposite direction. It was a short walk, and in moments she emerged from the trees and onto the white beach, the sand soft and warm beneath her feet.

She wriggled her toes and tilted her face up to catch the sun's rays, breathing in the salty scent of the air.

This right here was her happy place. Yes, she was stranded on a deserted island with Calder, and she wasn't sure how her family was doing, or if they even knew she was still alive. But the ocean breeze blowing through her hair, the sun warming her skin, the sound of the waves softly crashing against the shore, her toes buried in the sand—she had never been happier than in this moment.

Kenna stripped down and prayed to whoever was listening that Calder was nowhere nearby getting a show. She removed her shirt and shucked her breeches to the sand, grinning as she raced towards the water.

She let loose an uninhibited laugh the moment her skin met the water before remembering to keep her voice down so Calder didn't come running.

The water was the perfect temperature—not freezing but cool enough to create a pleasant contrast against the warm air. The best part of this island was how far out the water stayed shallow before dropping off. And it was so crystal clear she could see right down to the ocean floor she was walking on. Could see the multitude of colorful fish darting all around.

Now waist deep, Kenna smiled to herself before spreading her arms wide and falling onto her back with a splash, closing her eyes against the brightness of the sky. She floated on the surface of the water for a moment before rolling onto her stomach and diving beneath the waves in a perfect arc, kicking her feet out.

Once she was under the water, she opened her eyes, letting them adjust to the sting of the salt before looking around her. To her right was a small coral reef, the colorful fish swimming in and out of it, darting around her figure, just out of arm's reach. And straight ahead all she saw was blue. The same cobalt as Calder's eyes.

Kenna groaned, bubbles floating up to the surface. There really was no escaping him in her mind, was there?

It was when she kicked for the surface to release the air beginning to burn in her lungs that it happened.

Her lungs pinched in her chest, and her legs tightened against each other, her skin feeling as if it was melting into itself, not quite painful but not pleasant either. Kenna was still panicking when, in a flash of white light that seemed to come from *her*, it was over. Her brain couldn't register that she was still underwater. In a panic, unable to stop herself, Kenna opened her mouth and sucked in a lungful of water. She knew she was about to choke and drown. She thought how horrible it was that the thing she loved most in the world would be the death of her.

But it didn't happen.

Instead, breathing in the water felt like breathing in air, and it went all the way down her throat, filling her lungs and soothing the burn of holding her breath too long. Kenna didn't know what was going on, but she knew she needed to get to the surface. Kicking out her legs, she found she couldn't move them separately, making her look down.

And then she screamed.

Instead of legs, she saw a glimmering tail, cool blue like a winter sky. Her breaths came so rapidly she thought she might be hyperventilating.

Her breaths that were taking in *water*.

She was *breathing* water.

While she stared at her *tail*.

What was *happening*?

How could she be a mermaid? Yes, this was something she had wanted her entire life, but how was it happening now? *Why* was it happening now? She needed to get back to shore so she could *think*.

She swam towards the shore, pushing the water with her arms and undulating her hips, trying to get the hang of the motion. Way faster than should have been possible, Kenna found herself at the shore and dragged her body out of the water.

Collapsing onto the sand, panting, she pushed her tangled, salty hair out of her eyes to stare at the bottom half of her body. Kenna watched in shock as the flash of white light blinded her again, her lungs pinching for a second once more. When she opened her eyes, her tail was gone, and she again had two legs. She leaned closer to look at them, but there was nothing to show where they had been melded together a moment ago. And no trace of the scales that had gleamed in the light.

Kenna's head spun with questions, disbelief flying through her head. She knew from her conversations with Calder a merperson could transform between their human and mer form as easily as getting in and out of salt water. It was simple: submerged in salt water, they were in their mer form. In air or fresh water, they were in their human form.

Getting in the ocean now was what must have triggered Kenna's transformation. But it didn't make any sense. She had been in the ocean a million times and never transformed before. She had been in the ocean just a few days ago when Calder had saved her.

Calder!

That bastard! He said he had rescued her from drowning after the shipwreck. And he had asked her so many questions about her childhood, and her parents, and even swimming in the ocean. What a fool was she, thinking he asked those questions to get to know her. Of course that hadn't been why.

He *knew.*

He knew, and he hadn't said a damn word.

Kenna grabbed her clothes, jerking them onto her body, too angry to care that her wet skin and hair were soaking through the fabric, verging them on see through, before storming back towards camp.

She was going to *kill* him.

Chapter Twenty-Four

Murder on her mind, Kenna marched into their camp to find Calder sitting in front of the firepit. His feet were planted in the sand, elbows resting on his knees as he forlornly stared at a small piece of wood he was whittling away at.

Calder looked up when he heard her stomping in, and quickly tucked the wood into his pocket, throwing the dagger so it landed blade down. Smart man. She would have been tempted to snatch it out of his hands and use it on him if he hadn't.

When he saw the look of thunder on her face, his eyes widened in shock—and to her satisfaction, a little fear—and he quickly scrambled to his feet, putting his hands up in placation. "Kenna, what's wrong?"

"You! You are what's wrong!" she shouted at him, now close enough to slam her palm into his chest which, she realized only as the sound made a satisfying smack, was bare.

Focus, Kenna.

"I was nowhere near you! I don't even know where you were, what could I have done this time?"

"When were you going to tell me?"

"Tell you what? I am truly lost, Kenna. I have no clue what you're talking about."

Kenna sucked a breath in through her nose, trying to calm down. It was *possible* this was the first time she had transformed, though she seriously doubted it. Dropping her arms, she scrunched her hands into fists, schooling her expression. From the way Calder was raising an eyebrow at her, she guessed she wasn't doing a great job. She ground out, "When were you going to tell me that *I* am a mermaid?"

His eyes widened in surprise for a split second before he regained control of his features, but Kenna wasn't buying it. "I have no idea what—"

"Stop. *Lying!* I know you know. I must have been in mermaid form when you rescued me. Wasn't I? It's why you saved me. Why you've been sticking around, watching me, and why you've been asking me so many questions, why you've been getting to know me. Why you cared anything about me at all." Kenna swallowed the last sentence on a gulp, hating the way her voice cracked on the last words.

Hating she cared at all. That she had once again let her guard down only for someone to use her for their own needs.

Calder closed his eyes, cursing under his breath. After a moment, he opened them and gazed at her. "That's not true." His voice was pleading, but she wouldn't let herself fall for that anymore.

"*Stop lying!*"

"I swear to you! That is not the full truth. I'm sorry, *mo lasair*, none of this is going how it should have. How she told me it would."

Her heart stalled at the nickname, but at the mention of another woman it sped back up again. "What are you talking about Calder? Who is *she?*"

But Calder only looked at her, the depth of emotions in his eyes so deep she could fall in and never find her way back out. They were full of conflict and indecision. He reached out, running a thumb across her cheek.

"Really, this is all your fault," he went on with a small smile, a gleam in his eye. "If you hadn't looked so damn beautiful and been so different from what I was expecting, I wouldn't have gotten distracted."

191

"Gotten distracted from what? Calder, what is going on?" She grabbed his hand on her face, closing it between both of hers and holding it to her chest. "Please, tell me."

"I'm not *just* a merman, Kenna." The breath stalled in Kenna's lungs, knowing the next words out of his mouth, whatever they may be, were going to change her life forever. "I'm a spy for Queen Ailith of Mhariogh."

Dropping his hand, Kenna stepped back and stared at Calder in shock. "You're a royal *spy?*"

"Yes." He looked to the ground.

Kenna's head was spinning. What did this all mean? She walked to the log by the fire and sat down. From the sound of his footsteps, Kenna knew Calder had followed, sitting next to her.

"Why were you spying on my family? What do the merpeople want with humans if we aren't even allowed to know you exist? None of this makes any sense!" Calder opened his mouth to respond, but Kenna cut him off. "And don't you *dare* tell me you can't say anything, because I will go pick up that dagger and gut you like a fish. I am sick of the lies, sick of the secrets."

"*Mo lasair—*"

"Don't call me that. Just start talking." She stared at him, willing him to talk. Telling herself she simply imagined the light in his eyes dimming slightly when she told him not to call her that.

Calder stared into her eyes, searching for something. After a moment, where the world seemed like it was standing still, he began to speak. "The mer people and the human kingdom used to live together in harmony. We had a treaty, ambassadors in your kingdom."

"But that's not possible! If that was true there would be some record somewhere in Cladach. There would be people who remembered!"

"Do you wish me to tell you the story? Or do you wish to keep butting in?" Calder raised his brow at her. Kenna huffed but quieted down.

"Queen Ailith was the youngest of two daughters. She was never meant to be queen—her older sister was. But then around twenty-five years ago, while my mother was pregnant with me, the royal fami-ly—Ailith, her older sister, and the king and queen—went on a royal visit to the human kingdom. When Ailith returned, she was alone, in a panic. She told our people that the king of Cladach had killed them all in cold blood, and Ailith had barely managed to escape with her life. Ailith tried to stop him, but she said it was like he was out of his mind. Cold and cruel and unrelenting. That his people stood by watching it happen, and did *nothing*."

"That's not possible!" Kenna had heard enough. There was no way what Calder was saying could be true. She stood up, pacing back and forth. "I won't stand by and let you talk about my people, my *father*, this way!"

Calder stood and grabbed her shoulders. "Kenna, listen to me. I'm telling the truth as I know it to be. Let me finish." When she still resisted, he ducked down until she was forced to look into his eyes. "Please, *mo lasair*." At his words, she softened the smallest bit, and Calder took that as permission to continue.

"Though there has been peace between us, the humans had never fully accepted us. We were always something just a little too *other* for them, and they felt uneasy that we had ambassadors in their kingdom, but it wasn't possible for their ambassadors to be in our kingdom. So it wasn't that big a leap for us to believe our princess when she described them turning on us. Why wouldn't we believe her?"

Calder let go of her shoulders, taking his turn to pace in front of Kenna, deep sadness lining his features as he continued. "She had come home alone, grief-stricken and terrorized. Ailith went from being a princess who would never take the throne to queen in one day. No time to even grieve for her family." Kenna held her tongue, unable to reconcile this story Calder was weaving with the reality she knew.

"Our royal family has powerful magic in their blood, given by the gods to protect our people. The first thing she did after her coronation was cast a curse to protect our people from further harm. She cursed the human kingdoms to forget about us. To believe we had never existed."

"What about the faeries? Surely they knew you existed as well, then? Were they also under the curse?"

Calder looked weary as he responded. "No. The faeries know about us." Kenna's jaw dropped in shock as he continued, rolling his eyes. "You know how they are, how they think they're above every other species. Ailith bribed them into going along with her schemes. Convinced the faerie rulers to pretend they didn't know about us merpeople, so that they could have another thing to 'hold over' you humans."

At Kenna's glare, he held up his hands. "Her words, not mine! But after that, she made it a law forbidding any mer person from revealing themselves to a human, or in any way letting them know we existed. She feared for our safety. Who was to say they wouldn't kill more of us? She had to do whatever she could to protect our people. And in her grief she banned the names of her sister and parents, unable to bear hearing them."

When Kenna looked like she was about to interrupt again, her face mutinous, Calder squeezed her arms again, silencing her protests. "At least, that's what we were led to believe." Kenna closed her mouth, looking at him wearily, wondering if this was some sort of setup. But Calder shoved his hand through his hair, shaking his head.

"My father is one of the advisors on the royal council. My mother had been friends with Ailith's older sister. Growing up, I was... free-spirited, I guess you could say." He chuckled, and Kenna rolled her lips into her mouth, hiding a smile. According to the twinkle in his eyes, he was on to her.

"It was widely known that I snuck out. Often. And I never got caught. I just... I hated growing up in the castle. I wanted to explore. To spend time with my friends. To meet with girls." He smirked at her as he said the last part, the smile growing wider as a flush bloomed across her cheeks.

"The powers we possess as merpeople, they're different for every merperson. Some have a stronger affinity than others. Some can manipulate our siren song better, stronger than others. Not to brag, but I am very powerful." He winked at her, and Kenna shot him a dull look.

Calder laughed before continuing. "As I was saying, I am more skilled than most with my siren song. A skill very valuable in a spy amongst people who aren't supposed to know you exist. I have been on the royal guard for the past five years, since I came of age at twenty. Two months ago, the queen called me into her chambers and told me the human king had a daughter who was about to marry." His eyes turned serious. Kenna wanted to burst with her questions. How did the mer queen know about her, know she was about to get married? Why did she *care*?

"We weren't allowed to know anything about you humans, so this news made so many things begin to make sense. You see, Ailith has always been a... temperamental and harsh ruler. Not many are fans of her, but what can you do when your ruler is chosen by the ocean itself, tied by magic? But two years ago, it started getting worse." A dark look passed over his face, and Kenna waited with bated breath as he continued his story. Two years ago was when the faeries had cut off their trading with Cladach.

"Her temper was worse than before, and she began acting even more paranoid than usual. She kept going on about how the humans were going to come for her, try to take her throne. It didn't make any sense. You humans didn't even know we existed. And it's not like you could come down into the ocean. But she wouldn't let it go. And then she went back to the faerie king and queen. How much do you know about them?"

Kenna pondered his question. "Truthfully, we don't know that much. They are very secretive about their lives and their customs. The only thing I know is that their typical lifespan is 200 to 300 years. And there are rumors that their minds begin to deteriorate when they age past 300 years."

Calder nodded along to her words, confirming their validity. "It's true, and the more powerful the faerie, the more they lose their mind. The faerie king and queen are the most powerful faeries alive today. And they are almost 400 years old." Kenna's eyes widened in shock as he continued. "It wasn't hard for Ailith to convince them that just ignoring you humans wasn't enough anymore. She convinced them that they should just get rid of you, and take your land for themselves. And she would help them do that."

Sucking in a gasp, Kenna raised her hand to her mouth. The mer queen was the reason for this brewing war? Her head was spinning with all this new information. She didn't know what to do about it yet, but she knew this would change everything.

"I had always been curious about you humans. It actually all started when I was eight." Kenna looked at him warily, unsure where he was going with this. "I was out with my mother, when this little redheaded human fell into the water."

Kenna felt her eyes growing wider, but she didn't interrupt Calder, letting him continue. "It was against the law to help. Even at such a young age, I already knew that. But my mother didn't even hesitate. She saved that little girl, sent her back up to the surface where her father scooped her up." He looked at her fondly, and she realized she was just staring at him in shock.

A memory from that day she hadn't thought about in years came back to her. That flash of cobalt hiding behind the mermaid who had saved her. The exact same shade of blue as Calder's eyes.

"It was you," she whispered.

He smiled at her. "It was. I didn't realize, not until you told me that first day here on the island. I couldn't believe it. I was never able to get humans out of my head after that day. But I was born just after the murder and the curse, so I had never interacted with a human before that day. I had only heard how they were cruel and evil. But I couldn't believe it.

"Ailith asked me if I would be willing to go to the ceremony and spy on the royal family. Gather information to pass along to the faeries to aid them in their attack. I finally had a chance to see the human world for myself. So I said yes."

Calder seemed to be waiting for her reaction to his words. Her immediate reaction was to rage, to assume that was exactly what he had been doing since he met her. That it was all a lie, just as she had feared. Another punch to the gut, another betrayal.

Instead, she forced herself not to react until he was done speaking. Not to jump to yet another conclusion before she knew the full story. When he saw she wasn't going to say anything yet, his shoulders dropped in relief and he continued speaking.

"As I said, Ailith has been getting worse as the years go on. And there are a lot of us who are sick of it. Ailith urging the faeries on to war was our last straw. There are a group of us now, led by my parents." Calder beamed with pride. "We don't know yet how we are going to stop her, but we've been gathering whatever information we could. Biding our time until the opportune moment to make our move.

"So when Ailith asked me to take on this mission, I accepted. But I wasn't doing it for her. I was doing it for *us*. To see what was really going on with the humans that Ailith was so afraid of. I first spent a month spying on one of the port villages. Disguising myself in the mix of your people and foreign trading ships, so I could study you humans. Learning enough about how you worked so I could blend into the castle for the festival. I wasn't sure what to think at first. Sure, a lot of the humans I met seemed enough like the queen had described them. Harsh, unrelenting. But not all of them."

"And no one questioned this man who didn't seem to know how any of humanity worked?" Kenna questioned him, her brow raised.

Calder smirked. "You humans never want to look past what's right in front of you. You want to believe the easiest truth. Anyone who noticed something off assumed I was simply weird, or stupid. And if I needed to, I used my siren song to alter their memory."

Kenna huffed but didn't stop him as he continued. "My original plan was to sneak into the castle with one of the clan parties as a servant or something along those lines, but then I ran into the royal messenger. As you know, I can be charming when I wish." Kenna narrowed her eyes at him, and he smiled in return.

"As I was saying, I got him to tell me what I needed to know. That he was delivering a message from Cameron MacKenzie, apologizing for not being able to make it to the palace for the Winchin Festival. That his clan rarely left their territory and he wasn't sure why the royal family had even bothered with an invitation for them. That no one in the royal family had even seen Cameron since he was a very small child.

"I told him I was on my way there and convinced him I would take the message the rest of the way. That he could spend the extra time staying in the tavern, with the tavern owner he had been eyeing all night. The rest of his clan never had to know. He agreed pretty quickly."

Kenna rolled her eyes.

Men.

"But once I got to the castle—once I met you—Kenna, everything I had been made to believe my whole life began to crumble." Calder stared into her eyes, looking so intense she could hardly breathe. He reached out and took her hand in his, stroking his thumb across her skin as she repressed the shudder making its way down her body.

"You were unlike anyone I had ever known. Mer or human. You were so kind, and so unassuming. I spent those first two days sneaking around the castle, using my song when needed to wipe anyone's memory of seeing me, to observe you. You treated your maids and servants the same as most people treat their own families. You never acted as though you were above anyone, even though you quite literally are. That you held such *power* as a princess, power you did not use against anyone or for yourself. I was... I was mesmerized." He chuckled to himself, before continuing.

"The first thing I thought about you was that you were as soft and changing as the sea, and I felt drawn to you." Kenna's heart stalled, and she knew he could probably feel her thrumming pulse in her wrist. She hoped beyond hope that maybe he thought about her as much as she thought about him. That despite what he was telling her, despite the conflict between their people, he could feel for her. That the connection, for once in her life, wasn't only from her side.

"You contradicted everything I was supposed to know about humans. Confirmed what I suspected about Ailith lying to us for the past twenty-five years. And your parents." He shook his head. "You father is not someone I could ever see killing three people, three *royals*, in cold blood. And your mother? I can't explain it to you, but I felt a pull towards her as well."

Kenna's face contorted and she tried to rip her hand away, the bile already rising in her throat. He was attracted to her *mother*? Understanding filled Calder's eyes, and he held on tighter.

"Oh my gods, *no*! No, Kenna, of course not like that! I wasn't *attracted* to her. The pull was something instinctual. Something in my blood. And she looked so, so familiar." Kenna saw the determination in his eyes, and she thought she knew where this was going. She shook her head, but he kept speaking. "I began to get suspicious. And then the night of the ball, when she told me *I* looked familiar, my suspicions only grew. I have always been told I am the spitting image of my parents."

"No."

"As I said, my father was an advisor to Queen Ailith's parents. And my mother was friends with Ailith's older sister."

"No!"

"Kenna, the similarities are undeniable. And she recognized *me*. There is no other way she could have found me familiar."

The world around Kenna swayed.

"I didn't want to leave you on that dance floor, but I had to go. I *had* to. I couldn't let her realize who I was. I had to get back to my parents and tell them what I had discovered."

Kenna was now gasping for breath, tears spilling down her cheeks, as she shook her head. "No, please, no."

"You have to believe me, *mo lasair*, I never would have left you there. I never wanted to make you feel the way I did. I just didn't know what else to do." Tearing her hand from his grasp she lowered her face into her hands, crying in earnest now, her shoulders shaking from the force of her sobs.

"Kenna, please look at me."

"I can't," she whispered. But she felt warm hands on her own, prying them away from her face. She slowly blinked them open to find the blurry image of Calder kneeling on the sand in front of her. He reached up to cup her face in his hands, brushing her tears away with his thumbs.

"*Ghaoil.* Look at me. When you followed me down to the water, I sang to you. It should have wiped your memory, but it *didn't*. It didn't, and I think we both know why." Kenna closed her eyes again, unable to bear the look of pleading in Calder's eyes. The look said he was begging for her to understand. To forgive him for how he left her. For how he was about to change her life, her world, forever.

"When you followed me, and your boat sank, I should have left you. I was supposed to let you drown. We are not allowed to save humans. But by that point, I was already too far gone. It would have broken my heart to watch you drown. I had planned to leave you on the nearest island and pray someone would pass by and save you.

"But right there before my eyes, you shifted. You turned into a mermaid. And all at once, my suspicions were confirmed."

Kenna clutched at his wrists, preparing herself for the words she knew were about to come.

"Kenna. Your mother is Queen Ailith's elder sister. Your mother is a mermaid, and the true heir to the mer throne."

Chapter Twenty-Five

Kenna didn't know how long she sat like that, crying. All she knew was that a moment after the words left Calder's mouth, she was wrapped up in his arms, her body pressed against his warm chest. In her grief she forgot about everything that stood between them. All she knew was she needed comfort.

She needed him.

And so she wrapped her arms around his waist and pressed her face into his neck. For once in her life she wasn't worried about what she looked like. How much space she took up with her body. She didn't care what he thought of her as she cried.

As much as she had always wanted her belief in mermaids to be proven true, as much as she had wanted to live a life on the sea, she had never wanted it to happen this way. Finding out her whole life was a lie. That everything she knew about herself and her family was false. Her mother had lied to her her entire life.

She wondered if her father knew too. If her father had lied to her as well, or if his memory had been wiped like the rest of the humans.

But no, if that were true, then it wouldn't make sense why *both* of her parents hated the ocean. Why they never wanted her in it. Why she had grown up hearing only tales of its danger.

Grown up being taught to fear instead of love the ocean.

It all made so much sense now that she knew. And she was certain her father must have known, for he feared the ocean just as strongly as her mother. And they had made her feel insane.

Quickly, her grief and confusion turned to anger.

Not only had they lied to her, they had made her feel like a fool for believing in mermaids. Told her what a great imagination she had. Made her feel as if she had to isolate herself from her peers for fear of ridicule and harassment.

There were still some things that didn't make sense to her, though. And she needed more answers. Pulling away from Calder, he let her retreat from the circle of his arms. Kenna took a moment to regain her composure, wiping her face with her hands, before turning back to face him.

Sniffing, she looked at his feet, still too overwhelmed to risk looking into those too blue eyes. "It still doesn't make sense. If your queen's sister was murdered, how could she be my mother?"

Looking deeply troubled, Calder responded, "I still haven't figured out that part. It's one of the reasons I wanted to stay with you. I was hoping either you knew about your mother's past, or maybe even if you didn't realize *what* you knew, you could still help me fill in the blanks. But obviously, Queen Ailith lied to us. She lied to her people.

"I wondered why she hadn't tasked one of her normal court spies for this mission, instead of a random guard. They were all alive before the royal family had been killed—or supposedly killed—whereas I hadn't been born yet. I wouldn't be as likely to recognize your mother." His eyes were hard, unforgiving, and Kenna swallowed down the urge to reach out and smooth his brow, letting him continue.

"My first instinct was that your father kidnapped our princess, and Ailith was simply too horrified or grief-stricken to tell us." He continued when he saw her bristling, "But I quickly realized there was no way that was true. Not with how I saw your parents interact. They are obviously deeply in love."

Kenna spoke quietly. "They've been that way my entire life. We grew up hearing the tale of the war we were in when my parents first fell in love. My mother always told us how much she missed her family, but how she would always be okay because she had us and our father. We were told her clan, Clan Canduine, had been wiped out in the war. She was the chief's daughter and the only one who survived, since she was sent ahead to the castle to protect her and the Canduine line."

When Kenna said the name of the clan, Calder sucked in a breath, and Kenna's eyes shot to his, where she found them open wide.

"What?"

"What did you say her clan was called?"

"Canduine."

His eyes gleamed in excitement. "Kenna! Canduine is not a Cladach clan."

"What do you mean?"

"I mean, Canduine is the family name of our royalty. The Canduine line has been ruling the merfolk as long as our history goes back."

The breath left Kenna's lungs, and she whispered, "So it is true. I mean, I knew it was true the minute you suggested it." She looked into his eyes, hers full of anguish, and a small amount of wonder. "But there really is no denying it now. My mother is the rightful heir to the mer throne."

Her eyes widened even more. "*I* am the heir to the mer throne after her. I can't believe it." At her words, Calder was back on the sand in front of her, this time on one knee. Kenna's heart sped up.

"Calder, what are you doing?"

Instead of answering her question, he took her hand in his, sweeping his lips across her knuckles with a feather light touch. He clenched his other hand into a fist, laying it across his heart and bowing his head until his forehead touched the spot where his lips had just been. "I, Calder Donoghue, hereby swear my loyalty to you, Princess Makenna Murdina MacNamera *Canduine*, heir to the throne of Mharìogh. From this day forward, I will lay down my life at your service. My life is forever yours."

Kenna didn't know what to do other than stare at him, her heart in her throat and tears pooling in her lashes yet again.

No one had *ever* sworn fealty to her before. Lifting his head, Calder searched her face.

"Calder," she choked out. "Why did you just do that?"

"Because," he responded fiercely, "we may not know everything yet, but I do know one thing for sure. Ailith is not our rightful queen. She is not *my* queen, not anymore. If I'm being honest, she hasn't been for a long time. And I know now, deep in my soul, that *you* are. There is a reason you always felt called to the sea. Kenna, haven't you ever wondered *why?*"

"Of course I have! But I thought... I thought it was because I didn't want to be cooped up in the castle. I thought I wanted adventure."

"Kenna, the reason you felt called to the sea is because you *are* the sea. *Mo lasair*, you have salt water in your veins. The ocean was trying to call its queen back home."

Kenna shook her head. "No. No, that can't be. If that were true, it would have been calling my mother."

"Don't you see? We may not know what happened back then, but we do know one thing. Your mother *chose* land. She chose to be human, in one way or the other—it doesn't matter exactly how or why. She gave up her place in the ocean. And the ocean called out to her rightful successor. *You.* It all makes so much sense. You came of age two years ago. Two years ago when Ailith truly started losing her grip on reality and became paranoid someone was coming to steal her throne. She must have felt the ocean calling out for you."

He surged forward, now on both knees in front of her, until their bodies were pressed together, and he held her face in his hands.

"Kenna, you were born to rule the ocean. And I want nothing more than to be there with you when you do."

Kenna couldn't speak, lost in the depths of his eyes. Eyes staring at her, staring into her very soul. Open and honest and vulnerable, the way no one had ever looked at her before. Since the day she had met him, Kenna had been putting all her energy into *not* knowing him, not letting him know her. Doing her best to keep her distance, keep her walls intact, and yet he still found a way to slip through the cracks.

She hadn't wanted him, hadn't wanted to open herself up to hurt, but who was she trying to fool? Despite her best efforts, he was in her heart, and she had a feeling he was there to stay.

"Kenna," he whispered the words against her lips, but didn't move in. Letting her control whatever was about to happen between them. "I started falling in love with you the day I saw you. You were a living flame, so unaware of how brightly you burned, and I wanted nothing more than to stoke that fire and see just what you could do. I wasn't supposed to get distracted by you, but I have been falling more in love with you every minute we spend together. You are beautiful, and smart, and kind, and strong. Gods, you are the best person I have ever met in my life and—"

But Kenna had heard enough. Before he could say another word, she leaned in and kissed him.

Their lips met like crashing waves, and she poured everything she was into him. This kiss was different from the first one, even more intense. A raging storm on the ocean, their lips battling for dominance. She felt like they were both trying to climb into each other. To wash away everything that had come before them.

His fingers were in her hair, tugging at the strands to pull her body closer, impossibly closer. Her hands were on his shoulders, digging into his skin, leaving marks with her fingernails.

But she didn't care. *Couldn't* care about anything other than the way he tasted on her tongue, salt and citrus and *him*.

And then his hands were at her waist and he was dragging her up, standing in front of her, pushing her back until she was pressed against that tree.

Again.

Their lips broke apart, and she couldn't hold back the whimper falling from her mouth as he dragged his mouth down her throat. Down and down and down until it landed at the place where her neck and shoulder met, sucking the skin there.

Clenching her fingers into Calder's biceps, Kenna gasped, dragging her hands up to his head, and buried her fingers in his hair, wrenching his lust-drunk eyes up to her so that he saw her face when she spoke, saw that she meant every damn word. "I love you too, Calder. No one has ever looked at me and seen the person under the crown. Not the way you do. All I've ever wanted was someone who saw me and loved me for who I was. And that's exactly what you've given me."

She slanted her lips across his once she was finished speaking, and he pressed his body even closer into hers, sliding a thigh between her legs. She moaned into his mouth as she moved against him, unable to stop her hips from rolling against his thigh where she ached most, rewarding her with a bolt of pleasure zinging through her body. From the groan he gave in response, he didn't seem to mind.

Hands moving down from her waist, to her hips, he paused at the hem of her shirt.

"Kenna," he panted, lifting his mouth from hers and looking into her eyes. "Can I keep going? Do you want me to stop?"

She hesitated, not answering right away. Of course she wanted him to keep going, how could she not? She wanted him. She *loved* him.

It wasn't merely a physical thing. It never was with Kenna. And with Calder, she connected with him on an emotional level she had never felt with anyone else. When he looked at her, he always saw *her*, which was what her heart had longed for, but had been too scared to accept might be real. That it might not all be an act.

Not anymore.

She knew now he was sincere. But he had still never touched her bare stomach. Had never felt with his hands the way it rolled and folded. How it dipped over her hips.

She stalled, her throat suddenly dry. Sure, he seemed to think she was somewhat attractive. And they definitely had chemistry, but that didn't mean he would be attracted to her body, in all its imperfections. It was one thing to learn to see your own body and accept it. It was another thing to be confident enough to let *someone else* see your body and believe they would accept it too.

Sensing her hesitation, Calder ducked his head down until he was eye to eye with her.

"*Ghaoil*, it's ok if you don't want to do anything else. I just want to be with you, whatever way you'll have me. If that's simply holding you, then I will gladly hold you in my arms all night long." No trace of judgment. No disappointment or impatience, and Kenna's chest couldn't contain the swell of emotions at his words.

She stroked his scruff with her hand, smiling nervously. "Oh, Calder, it's not that. I..." She took a deep breath, her voice shaking. "I do want you. I want you more than you could possibly know." She watched his eyes darken until they were almost black, making her shiver. "It's just—"

"What?" His voice came out gravelly, and she could feel *him* against her stomach, making her flush. Calder seemed to know what was making her blush, and his own cheekbones were dusted pink, but he still grinned that crooked grin. "What can I say? I can't control myself around you."

She giggled, biting her bottom lip, enjoying the way his eyes tracked her mouth. "I want you, Calder. But I've also never done this before. I don't feel attraction the way most people seem to, only after I have an emotional connection with them. And I have never felt this way about someone who reciprocated the feeling. No one has ever touched me. I may act like I'm comfortable in my body, and for the most part I am. But I'm also scared." She looked at him, and for once, she let her vulnerabilities through, let him see every insecurity.

"I'm scared you won't feel the same way about me after you see all of me." Kenna could feel how red and hot her face was, and her eyes swam with tears, more scared than she ever had been in her life, even on her boat in that thunderstorm. Intimacy and vulnerability were scarier than any storm she could ever face, and she was terrified this somehow still wasn't real. She could hear the echoes of mocking laughter in her head every time she allowed herself to believe Calder might actually be attracted to her.

But then Calder was smoothing his hands over her head, pushing her hair back and staring into her eyes. "You are the most beautiful woman I have ever met, Kenna." At his words the tears spilled down her cheeks, and Calder brushed them away. "My Kenna. I don't know why you would ever believe you somehow couldn't be loved. Couldn't be desired. But the way I feel about you, I have never felt before either. Not for anyone. Your body has nothing to do with the way I feel about you. I don't want you because of or despite your body. I desire your body because I desire you. I see you, all of you, and you are perfect."

All Kenna could do in response was stare into his eyes. And his eyes... He was looking at her like he couldn't get enough. Like he never wanted to look away. Like he meant every word he said.

In that moment she felt more beautiful than she ever had before. Not with any fancy ball gown, or jewels glittering at her throat and on her head to draw eyes away from all her imperfections. But here, in a dirty tunic and breeches, her breasts unbound and her hair a wild mess.

She didn't say a word, just grasped his hands and slid them under the hem of her shirt, setting them against the soft skin of her waist. Calder's eyes closed, and she watched his Adam's apple bob on a swallow.

She was still nervous, but even more than that now, she was excited. She was ready. As his hands trailed up her torso, leaving a blazing trail of sparks in their wake, she dropped her head back on a moan.

Calder nuzzled his head into the crook of her neck, licking and nipping the sensitive skin there. "Gods, you have no idea what you do to me, *mo lasair*. What ideas you give me. I want everything with you."

Kenna melted into him until there was no space left between them, and she felt him hard against her. She never wanted this moment to end. Never wanted to stop feeling the way he made her feel. She ran her hands down his back, reveling in the way his muscles shifted beneath her touch, and the goosebumps she could feel under her fingertips.

By now his hands were full of her breasts, his thumbs sweeping the peaked tips of her nipples and her entire body tingled with pleasure and excitement. She gasped as he caressed her until she could no longer think. All she could focus on was how much she wanted him.

She nibbled on the lobe of his ear, enjoying the way it made his whole body shudder, before whispering, "Show me."

Chapter Twenty-Six

A t her words, Calder seemed to lose the last bit of restraint he had, diving back into another devouring kiss. It was like he wanted to swallow her whole, and Kenna didn't think she would mind that.

Pulling away from her lips on a gasp, Calder's heaving chest brushed against her sensitive breasts with every breath, scattering sparks along her skin. "*Ghaoil*, we need to move this away from the tree if you want to go any further. I can't imagine the bark feels good against your back."

Kenna laughed. She hadn't noticed, too wrapped up in him, but he was right. Her back was already starting to sting from the scrape of the wood.

Calder's hands gently cupped her face, his thumb sweeping her kiss-swollen lips, hungrily watching the movement. Kenna licked her lips, enjoying the way it made his eyes darken further.

"Lead the way." Her voice was husky with need.

Calder needed no further prompting. His hands dragged down the sides of her neck, one falling to grip the dip in her waist. The pad of his finger traced down the space between her breasts until it met the laces holding her shirt together. He tugged at it, the movement canting her body towards his, until she landed softly against his chest.

"Can I take you to bed, Kenna?" He punctuated his words with a kiss to her left temple. "Can I show you everything I've been dreaming about since I met you?" Another kiss to her right. "Can I worship you as you deserve to be worshiped?"

A whimper escaped Kenna's lips, her knees going weak as she closed her eyes, sinking further into him. She nodded against his chest, unable to do more, but Calder tucked his finger under her chin, forcing her to meet his eyes. "I need your words, Kenna. We've established we both feel this attraction between us, but attraction is not consent. You said you desire me, but I need to hear you say you want me to act on this feeling before I do anything else."

How did someone like him end up feeling the same way about her as she did? She loved his nicknames for her, loved when he called her *ghaoil* or *mo lasair*, but she loved it most when he called her Kenna. When he showed again that he saw her, and wanted her for her.

Just Kenna.

She reached up, sliding her fingers into his hair before gripping tight and tugging his head down so she could press a kiss to his lips. Her heart was pounding in her chest, words she had never said before sitting at the tip of her tongue, feelings she had never desired acting on sparking to life.

"Calder, I want you to make love to me." Even though she'd said the words boldly, the shyness and fear of vulnerability she had felt her whole life weren't entirely eradicated, but Calder's response had them melting away. Calder grinned and kissed her once more before grabbing her hand and turning to drag her towards their makeshift camp.

They stumbled their way to the hammocks, coming to a stop in front of them. Looking at them, and then each other, they both came to the same realization.

"That is not going to work." He was so adorably flustered, his cheeks flushed with desire, hair mussed from her fingers.

"I think you're right." She shot him a sly grin. "Nothing left to do but cut them down."

"Wait!" He tried to stop her, but she was too quick, darting out of his reach, grabbing the dagger out of the sand on her way and cutting the first hammock down from the shelter.

"Kenna, what are you doing?" Calder shook his head at her, a bemused look on his face, giving up trying to stop her as she went and cut the other down.

"Improvising."

Calder said nothing, simply standing with his hands on his hips, watching her work.

After she cut them both down, she dragged them to the center of their shelter, laying them out on top of each other. She then pulled the sail down from the top of the shelter, laying it over the hammocks to create a makeshift mat.

"There we go." She beamed at Calder, staring at her with wonder in his eyes. "What?" All of a sudden she felt self-conscious again. Perhaps she had appeared too eager, what if he was changing his mind and—

"Gods, you are perfect." His arms wrapped around her from behind, hauling her back into his chest as his mouth met the juncture of her neck and shoulder.

Kenna huffed out a laugh. "You are delusional."

"Oh no, *mo lasair*, I am perfectly in my right mind." His words were spoken into her skin as he nibbled his way up her neck to her ear, making her stomach clench. "And you are perfect for me. My clever girl."

She gasped as he sucked on her earlobe, but it quickly morphed into a whimper as he bit down, soothing the sting with his tongue. He spun her around to face him, walking her backwards towards their makeshift bed.

Calder tugged at the laces on her shirt. "Please, *ghaoil*, tell me I can take this off. I want to see you."

Kenna's heart fluttered in her chest as her desire and nerves battled for dominance inside her. This was the turning point, the moment she couldn't come back from. Calder would never be able to unsee her body, and if he didn't like what he saw then—

She cut off that line of thinking.

If he didn't like what he saw that was his problem, not hers. Looking back into his eyes, she saw nothing but desire and question, waiting for her response. Always waiting to make sure she was alright.

Kenna grasped the hem of her shirt, lifting it above her head and dropping it to the sand at her feet.

Drawing her shoulders back, she lifted her head, standing tall as he took her in. The way her breasts drooped down, falling heavily to her waist. The way her stomach softly protruded, round and rolling, hanging over her hips. Lightning strikes marking the swells of both breasts and stomach.

Calder stalked towards her, his eyes dark with desire as he gripped her waist in his hands, guiding her to lay down. Kenna leaned back, holding herself up on her elbows as Calder stood above her, haloed by the golden light of the setting sun.

"I showed you mine, now show me yours."

Calder grinned wickedly at her, reaching behind his head to grab the neck of his shirt, dropping it to the sand next to hers. It was not the first time she had seen his chest. At this point she had seen it so many times she should be used to it. And yet, the sight still had her salivating. Too busy drooling over him, Kenna almost didn't notice when he dropped to his knees, crawling over her body until he straddled her thighs, and suddenly her mouth was bone dry.

He drank in her bare chest, a hungry look in his eyes.

"You have no idea how long I have wanted to do this." His words had barely registered in her scattered brain before he reached out, scooping her breasts into his hands. He groaned in appreciation when they spilled out over his fingers, larger than he could hold. He leaned down, licking his way from the valley between them up the mound of her right breast until he found her nipple, sucking it into his mouth.

Kenna dropped fully back with a sigh, arching her back, pressing her breasts more firmly into his mouth.

"I feel like a pirate," Calder murmured after letting the nipple go with a pop, before turning to give her other breast the same attention.

"What?" came Kenna's breathless reply, her brain unable to function while he swirled his tongue like that.

"Hoarding my bountiful treasure." Calder emphasized his words with a nip that made her cry out. He soothed the sting with one more lave of his tongue before releasing both breasts, watching as they spilled to the sides of her chest, opening up a path down the middle for him to kiss his way down to the soft rolls of her belly.

It took her mind a moment to catch up and register his words, and when it finally did, she couldn't stop her laugh. "You *eejit*." But her laughter morphed into a moan as he squeezed the flesh of her hips, scraping his teeth along the sensitive skin beneath her belly button, along the bottom swell of her stomach, nudging down the waist of her breeches.

"Oh, an *eejit* am I? Would an *eejit* be able to pull those sounds out of you?"

Kenna's face flamed at his words, and she attempted to bury it behind her hands, but Calder tsked, moving back up her body until he could grab her hands.

"Oh, no you don't, *mo lasair*," he admonished as he laced their fingers together, pulling her hands above her head and leaning further into her. The new angle forced her back up until her chest was pushed fully into his. "You don't get to hide from me, not anymore. And I don't hide from you. I want all your sounds." His tongue delved back into her mouth for another taste. As he rolled his tongue along hers, he rocked his hips in a matching tempo.

Kenna was lost in a world of sensation. All of her nerve ends were on fire, sparks crawling over her skin, her chest felt like it was expanding and contracting at the same time. She writhed under Calder, the feelings somehow too much and not enough at the same time.

It had never felt like this before. Not in her daydreams, not in her bed when she eased her own ache. This was a feeling she couldn't fully describe. It paled in comparison to everything she had read in her precious romance books, the feeling she had been chasing her whole life.

And they weren't even doing anything more than kissing and rolling their bodies together. How would it feel when they did more? Kenna wanted to know. She was desperate for it.

The problem with Kenna was when she craved something, it was never enough. She was all or nothing, and had been her whole life.

And she *craved* Calder.

Breaking their kiss, Kenna detangled her hands from his to push him off her, scrambling to her knees, panting for breath.

Calder jerked back in concern, equally out of breath. "What's wrong? Did I do something—"

"Shush," Kenna cut him off, paying his worry no mind. "I want your breeches off." Before she even finished speaking she was already reaching for them, starting at the fastenings.

"Someone's in a hurry," Calder replied, a smirk on his lips, but still he stood up to make it easier, helping her remove them. They shucked his breeches down, and Calder stood there proudly, not shying away from her curious gaze as she took him in for the first time. The sun now skimmed the surface of the waves, setting the sky ablaze and making Calder's skin glow golden in the light. His chest was dusted with the perfect amount of curling black hair, the firm, slightly rounded plane of his stomach only enhanced with the trail of hair leading from his navel down to his straining member.

Kenna flicked her eyes up to Calder's, only to find him already staring at her with hooded eyes. "Can I—" She cleared her throat. "Can I touch you?"

"Gods yes, please."

Kenna grinned at his eagerness, some of the tension in her shoulders releasing as she took him in hand to give him a tentative stroke. Calder groaned in response, dropping his head down until his chin rested against his chest, biting his lip as he watched her hand move.

"Like this, *ghaoil*." He gripped her hand tighter, moving it at a faster pace that made him lose his breath, dropping his hand as she got the hang of it. Instead, he slipped his hand into her hair, anchoring himself to her. Kenna licked her lips, looking up at him and the lust in his eyes, before impulsively deciding to go all the way.

This was the part of her books she had always been most curious about. Was it something she would enjoy? Would she hate it? Would she be any good at it? She was dying to find out.

Tentatively, she stuck out her tongue, licking the head. Calder sucked a breath in through his teeth, his grip on her hair growing tighter.

"Kenna," he panted. "Are you sure you want to do this?"

In response, she parted her lips, taking him fully into her mouth and sucking. He released a string of curses as he moved his hips in rhythm with her motions. What Kenna hadn't expected was how good doing this for him would make *her* feel. As she bobbed her head, swirling her tongue around him, she squirmed, squeezing her thighs together, trying to relieve the steadily building ache. Seeing the pleasure she caused was a powerful feeling. A feeling she could get used to.

"Kenna. Kenna, I'm going to—"

His words cut off with a moan as he spilled himself into her mouth, and Kenna swallowed it down. She really hadn't expected to do that her first time, but with him standing in front of her looking so perfect, she couldn't help herself. She was surprised how much she had enjoyed it, and based on the glazed expression in Calder's eyes, he had enjoyed it as well.

Her suspicions were confirmed when he dropped back down to his knees and proceeded to capture her mouth in a kiss. She laughed into the eagerness of his assault, and he broke the kiss, laughing with her.

"That was unbelievable." He came in for another deep kiss.

"Oh, was it? I couldn't tell if you enjoyed it or not." She grinned at him, and Calder narrowed his eyes in response.

"Getting cocky already, are we?" He glared at her. Kenna was about to respond when he surged towards her, pushing her onto her back and opening her legs by pressing his hips between them. "Well, *mo lasair*, it's time to return the favor. And then we'll see who the cocky one is."

Kenna released a breathless "oh" as Calder kissed his way down her throat, across her breasts, and down her stomach. When he reached the waist of her breeches, he shot a raised brow at her.

Past words, Kenna merely nodded her head in assent as he pulled the breeches down her legs, taking her in for the first time. Reaching forward, he dragged his knuckle down the seam of her core, and Kenna bit her lip against the whimper trying to break its way out.

"So beautiful," Calder murmured, leaning closer, before flicking his eyes up to her face. Kenna was leaning on her elbows, watching him. With a slow, wicked grin, he inched forward, gripping his hands under the back of her knees before pulling her legs further apart, opening her to him. Calder wormed his way into the now-open space between her thighs, hooking her legs over his shoulders until they were wrapped around him, and his face was directly in front of where she ached most. Kenna couldn't stop her body from stiffening slightly as he looked up at her from this new angle. In this position it was impossible to hide every part of herself the world had tried to make her hate. Even though she tried and mostly succeeded not to think about it, or to care, it was impossible to entirely let go of that insecurity.

Noticing the way she had tightened, pulling back from him, Calder's gaze met hers, full of adoration and desire. Without a word, he started by kissing the side of one knee, making his way up her thigh until he was almost where she needed him most. But he stopped, switching to the other leg and repeating the action. By the time he got back to her center, she was desperate for him again, and didn't even notice herself relaxing into his touch.

Before she could beg him to give her what she needed, he buried his face between her legs and licked up her center. Kenna bit her lip at the sensation, squirming as he licked and kissed softly. The pleasure was there, but it was buried under her discomfort at the softness of the touches. Soft touches had always made Kenna's skin crawl, much more preferring a firm, hard touch.

Calder looked up, noticing that she was not reacting with the same pleasure that she had before.

"*Ghaoil*," he whispered, resting his chin on her thigh. Kenna threw an arm over her eyes, unable to look at him. "If I am doing something you don't like, you have to tell me. This is something you should enjoy, not something that makes you uncomfortable."

She lifted her arm, peeking down at him. He didn't look frustrated, but determined.

"Just as I showed you how to touch me, you have to tell me how to touch you."

Kenna swallowed, building up the courage to speak her desires out loud. "I like firm touches." Her voice started as a whisper, but when Calder simply nodded, encouraging her to continue, her voice grew stronger, more confident. "Soft touches sometimes make me uncomfortable, like ants are crawling on my skin. It is more pleasurable for me if you are firm, hard."

He grinned at her. "I can do hard."

Before she could say another word, he dove back in, this time *devouring* her. She collapsed back, her body contorting at the pleasure coursing through her veins. His tongue stroked firmly against her, doing things that made her see stars. And then he sucked directly on her bundle of nerves, while she felt his finger prod gently at her entrance, causing her core to clench in anticipation.

"Is this okay?" He pulled away only long enough to ask the question before diving back in. Kenna gasped out a quick *Yes*, having no time before his finger was slowly pushing into her, her body tightening at the intrusion.

"Gods, you feel so good, Kenna," Calder groaned into her, the vibrations adding to the pleasure. She cried out, driving her fingers into his hair, gripping tightly and pulling him more firmly into her.

"No more teasing," Kenna pleaded, "*please*. I can't—"

Calder chuckled, resuming his ministrations with his mouth and his finger. He flicked his tongue along her most sensitive spot as he began to move his finger in and out of her in a matching rhythm, soon adding a second one.

The pleasure was tightening in her, every cell of her body vibrating until she felt she would explode with the pressure and pleasure of it. Then he nipped her bud, and it crashed over her like a wave, the tension that had been building in her snapping, losing sense of reality.

She was floating in a sea of stars, light exploding behind her eyelids as her entire being unraveled. Only the feeling of Calder's still-stroking tongue grounded her, until even that was too much and she pushed his head away, panting as she floated back into her body.

"Alright," Kenna begrudgingly conceded. Calder raised his brow at her in question and she grinned ruefully. "You win. You can be the cocky one. I may not have anything to compare that to, but I'm pretty sure I'm a very lucky woman."

Calder laughed as he crawled his way up her body, resting on his elbows above her, before immediately diving his tongue into her mouth. Kenna could taste herself on him, which only aroused her even more. He hummed into the kiss, pulling away with a bright smile.

"I'm pretty sure I'm still the lucky one."

"You're lucky you had to suffocate yourself between my thighs?" She looked at him doubtfully.

"Ha!" He barked out a laugh. "*Mo lasair*, I would happily suffocate myself to death between your thighs. It would be my pleasure."

"Pleasure, really?"

Instead of responding, Calder thrust his hips into hers, his firm member hard and straining once again, and the friction of the movement set her toes curling as she gasped out a surprised "Oh."

"Yes, 'oh.' Did you not feel pleasure while you were attending to me?"

Kenna blushed at his words, self-consciousness trying to creep in, but he had asked her not to hide herself from him, so she didn't.

"Yes," she whispered. "Yes, I did."

"Then are you so surprised it was the same for me?"

"I guess that makes sense," she agreed. Calder smiled down at her, a sheen of sweat coating his brow, one she was sure matched her own. She reached up, brushing a thumb across his lips. "You are too good."

"Impossible." He pressed a kiss to her thumb.

She smiled at him, wriggling underneath his body, the feeling of his weight pressing into her both calming and arousing.

"Am I crushing you?" Calder asked in concern, moving as if to get off her but Kenna snapped her hand out, grabbing his shoulder and stopping him from moving.

"No! No, it feels good. I just..." She blushed, but forced herself to continue speaking. To ask for what she wanted. "I want you to keep going. I want to feel you inside me." She rolled her hips up into his, letting him see the hunger in her eyes.

Calder dropped his head to her chest on a moan, his forehead resting between her breast as he slowly ground his hips down into her, making her lose her breath.

"You are going to be the death of me," he groaned. He reached in between them, positioning himself at her entrance, lining himself up but not moving. Kenna wriggled, trying to get him to move, but he gripped her hip, pinning her down.

"Are you sure you want this?" He looked into his eyes, serious and searching. "You are in control here. We can stop now if you want."

Kenna didn't hesitate one moment, surer in this decision than she ever had been. She surged up to take his lips in a demanding kiss.

"I want this, Calder. I want *you*. Please."

At her words, Calder met her passionate embrace, kissing her with a force that pressed her to the ground. Only then did he start moving, slowly pushing himself in, inch by rocking inch.

At first, there was only pain at the feeling of him stretching her. She slammed her eyes shut, burying her face into his shoulder. But as he kept going, he leaned his head down to take one nipple in his mouth, and the pain slowly melted into pleasure. A pleasure and pressure unlike anything she had ever felt, and suddenly all she wanted was *more*. More of him, more of the drag that made her head spin. She matched his pace with her hips thrust for thrust, urging him on, urging him faster.

The only thing she could feel was him. The only things she could hear were the sounds of their bodies, his sweet words and praise, her own begging; pleading with him, for what, she didn't know.

This wasn't like the first time with his mouth. This was so much more. All she knew was him, and her, and the way their bodies came together like this was how they were always meant to be.

She could feel her climax creeping up on her, but it stayed just out of reach, and she squirmed beneath him.

"I need—" she gasped out, mouth pressed to Calder's shoulder.

"What do you need, *ghaoil*? Tell me what you need." He didn't falter his pace as he asked her, sucking on her earlobe. Kenna had lost all grasp on any more words, so she grabbed his hands, pulling it to the place where they were joined, hoping he would get the message.

He hummed into her ear, immediately rubbing firmly up and down directly over the bundle of nerves above where he was entering her.

Kenna cried out, his touch sending her over the edge she had been torturously teetering on. And then there was only pleasure and more pleasure until she was falling. She fell for what felt like hours, and her release must have triggered Calder's because she felt him fall right after her, his stuttering hips finding home flush with hers as their bodies trembled together.

Kenna came down from the high to find Calder smoothing back her hair, pressing kisses across her face.

She smiled, tracing her fingers across his jaw, and he moved his face into her hand, nipping the pad of her finger.

"How do you feel, *ghaoil*?"

Kenna smiled at him, happier and more content than she had felt in as long as she could remember. "I feel perfect."

Chapter Twenty-Seven

There was a warm, hard surface under Kenna's cheek when she drifted back into consciousness. With a start, she realized it was Calder's chest, and she was draped across his body. One of her legs was slung between his, and she felt the warm weight of his arm thrown over her waist, his hand resting on her hip. Her naked hip.

They were both naked.

Kenna froze, but she could hear his heartbeat, slow and steady under her ear. He was still asleep.

Thank the gods.

She wasn't exactly sure what to do with herself. Just thinking about last night made her cheeks flame, and she had no idea what she would say when he woke up.

Yesterday had changed her life in so many ways.

Not only was she a mermaid, but she was the rightful heir to the mer throne. And then Calder...

Calder swearing fealty to her. Calder confessing his love to her. Calder *making* love to her.

Kenna had never believed she could develop such strong feelings for someone so quickly. Love was something built on trust and familiarity, built over time.

Yet here she was, having known Calder for only a few weeks, and she knew. As she had always known her heart belonged to the sea, she knew now it also belonged to Calder.

A small, dark part of her mind whispered to her that was all it was. That she only thought she had a connection with him because he was a connection to the world she so desperately wanted to be a part of. That as soon as she met other merpeople, the connection she felt when she was with him would be severed. She refused to give that fear any voice. Kenna didn't want to think about what it would feel like to lose Calder now. Not now that she finally had him.

There was still so much they needed to talk about. She still needed answers. From what he had told her, he needed answers too, and they weren't going to find them on this island. Much as Kenna wished they could stay like this forever.

They could, however, stay exactly like this for at least a little longer.

Kenna closed her eyes again, wrapping herself tighter around Calder, soaking up his warmth.

He shifted beneath her, his arm tightening around her waist, fingers flexing into her skin in a way that made her blush.

He hummed a soft noise, his breath ruffling the hair at her brow. "Good morning, *mo lasair*."

Her core tightened at the rough gravel of his morning voice, and she smiled against his skin, before whispering back, "Good morning."

She felt his fingers, sliding up and down her waist, tracing invisible patterns along her skin. "How did you sleep?"

"Better than I have since we got here, that's for sure."

His chuckle sent thrills up and down her spine. She shifted her hips, and then abruptly froze when she felt him hard against her, the breath catching in her throat.

Calder must have felt her freeze because he laughed again, leaning his head down until he could whisper directly into her ear, giving it a nibble for good measure. "What do you expect when this is what I'm waking up to? The most beautiful girl in the world, naked in my arms."

Kenna didn't answer, burying her head into his shoulder so he couldn't see the look on her face. It was mortifying, but it also made her feel giddy. Delirious with exhilaration as much as nerves.

Calder cleared his throat. "How are you feeling? After last night?"

She looked up and saw the look of trepidation on his face, as if he really thought she might regret what they had done.

She reached up, tracing his lips as she smiled, any fear or awkwardness she had been feeling gone in the face of his worry. "I feel amazing. I might not know the right way to act, or what to say, but I want you to know I could never feel anything other than happiness over what happened last night. You make me feel like I'm strong and beautiful, like I can do anything I put my mind to. You make me feel *wanted*. That's something I never thought I would have."

The cobalt of his eyes darkened, and without warning he lifted and pulled her over him, until she was straddling his hips with her weight resting on her knees, leaving her gasping as her hips sat flush with his. Kenna arched her neck as he licked down the side of it, ending with a bite to that place where her neck met her shoulder, before whispering into her skin, "How could anyone not want *this?*" He punctuated his sentence by grabbing handfuls of her ass and squeezing.

Laughing, Kenna slapped Calder's shoulder, and he popped his head back up, a wicked grin on his soft lips. He surged up, capturing her mouth in a searing kiss. Immediately, Kenna shifted her hands from his shoulders to slide into his hair, tugging at the strands before dropping the full weight of herself onto his lap. She moaned into the kiss, loving the way it made him react, pulling her even harder into him, until their hips were grinding together.

"Calder." His name fell from her lips like a prayer as he trailed his lips down while he reached for her breasts swaying between their bodies. Cupping them, he began lavishing them one after another with his tongue. He reached his other hand down to start rubbing against her bundle of nerves while he sucked on her nipples, pleasure zinging through her. Kenna dropped her head back, crying out at the pleasure coursing through her.

A few minutes later Kenna grabbed his wrist, moving his hand out of the way. "I need you inside me," she panted.

He grinned wickedly as Kenna reached down to adjust him underneath her until she could sink down onto him. They both sighed at the feeling of him sliding into her and began to move together, slow and deep and intense until they were falling apart, collapsing back into a heap onto the mat beneath them.

Afterwards, Kenna lay on her back, Calder propped on one elbow beside her as he played with a strand of her hair. She wanted to stay in this cocoon forever and live in blissful ignorance of the world around them. To forget about everything except for Calder. The way he made her feel and the things he did to her.

But she couldn't.

"What are we going to do?"

"You mean for the rest of the day? Well, we definitely need to eat. Replenish our energy, you know. And then we should probably clean off. Go to the creek. Preferably together." She looked at him to find that infuriatingly charming smirk making his dimple pop, and she poked her finger into it.

"You have a one-track mind."

"Only when that track is Kenna."

She groaned, sitting up and turning away from him to pull on her clothes. "You are ridiculous."

"Only when it comes to you, *ghaoil*." Behind her, she could hear the sound of rustling fabric as he pulled on his clothes as well. She did the same then stood, stretching her arms above her head and arching her back. She heard a groan behind her, and turned to see Calder staring at her.

Or more specifically staring at her ass.

"Hey, *tolla-thon*. Get a hold of yourself." She shot a teasing grin over her shoulder before walking away, putting an extra swing in her hips. She swore she heard Calder mutter a few curses under his breath.

As she made her way out of the shelter they had been using for the past week, she stretched out her aching back. Last night she hadn't really thought about or cared how comfortable their makeshift mat was. She had been far too focused on Calder and their activities.

But she was feeling it now. She imagined Calder probably felt even worse than her after she had used him as a pillow all night.

Calder walked up to Kenna, putting a hand at the small of her back and stopping to slide a kiss along her cheek before moving past, her heart squeezing in her chest. Despite everything going on, she didn't know the last time she had truly been this happy.

He pulled out the canteen of water, passing it to her before taking any himself. Her heart warmed at the small gesture, her skin tingling with pleasure. Gods, she could get used to this.

Someone caring about her. Caring for her.

Not because they had to, but because they wanted to.

Kenna took a gulp of the water before passing it back to Calder, watching the way his throat shifted as he swallowed. "So, really. What are we going to do?"

"I was serious about the creek, *mo lasair*. I don't know about you, but I have sand in places where sand should never be." He shuddered exaggeratedly, and Kenna's glare gave way to laughter.

"Are you ever serious?"

"Only when absolutely necessary."

"Well, Calder, I believe we may have reached that point."

He sighed, falling dramatically in front of the log by the firepit, leaning back against it. "I'm afraid you're right."

Kenna followed after him, sitting down at his side. "We need to find out the truth."

"I know."

"I was thinking about it, and..." Kenna hesitated, not wanting to go on, afraid of what his answer might be. But she continued anyway. "I think you should come back with me to Cladach. Back to my parents." She chewed on her bottom lip, waiting for him to tell her she was out of her mind. That he wasn't going back there. But he simply looked at her, searching her face. Using his thumb, he pulled her bottom lip out from between her teeth before running it along her lip.

"You have to know by now I would follow you anywhere."

"So, you'll come with me?"

"Of course, *mo ghràdh*. Anything you wish of me is done. Besides, I agree with you. There are only two places where we can find the answers we seek, and we both know those answers won't be found with my queen." His eyes were dark with anger, the word "queen" falling from his lips in a bitter, mocking tone.

Kenna brushed his jaw with her fingertips.

"Don't let your heart fill with anger when you don't yet know the full story. For all we know, my parents played some part in this. After all, they lied too." Even as the words left her mouth, Kenna knew they weren't true. Angry as she was with her parents right now, she still knew deep down they were good. They couldn't have been at fault for whatever happened between the humans and merpeople. She didn't know everything, but she knew that much.

"Kenna..."

She sighed, closing her eyes. "I know. I know they most likely had a good reason for lying to me. Keeping this from me. But right now all I can feel is hurt. They didn't just lie about the merpeople. They lied about everything. Making up a war and a clan. Forcing me into the Winchin Festival knowing I didn't want it, using their own festival as proof that it could work. But they didn't do the Winchin Festival. Not if my mother was a mermaid princess."

As she spoke, all the anger came rushing back, until it felt like a living flame in her chest. The betrayal of her parents hurt worse than Reid or her fake friends ever had.

"I know they'll give you a good reason, *mo lasair*. And then you can forgive them. You don't want to hold such anger in your heart. It will hurt you as much as it will hurt them."

Kenna smiled at him with watery eyes, his words calming the storm in her chest. "How do you always know the right thing to say?"

"Because I'm amazing."

She burst out laughing, his remark made even funnier by its deadpan delivery.

"That you are." His eyes brightened, so she continued, "But don't let it go to your head."

"Wouldn't dream of it." He grinned at her, and she felt herself leaning towards him. A gravitational pull she could resist no more than she could resist pulling air into her lungs. As her lips were about to meet his, though, a bird squawked loudly, breaking the spell. Calder chuckled, leaning his forehead against hers instead.

"So we're leaving paradise?"

"Oh," she said, drawing back to cock her brow at him teasingly. "You call this paradise? No real shelter, no real food, no bathroom?"

"Well, aren't you spoiled?" She gasped in mock outrage. "I'm serious! What more could we need? Warm sand under our feet, the ocean two feet away. You by my side. Paradise."

"Anyways..." Kenna dragged the word out, knowing they weren't going to get anywhere if she didn't ignore his quips. "Yes. We need to go back. How long would it take us to swim there? Now that I know what I am, we can shift and swim, right?"

The humor faded from Calder's face, replaced with seriousness. "Theoretically, yes."

"What do you mean?"

"It would only take us a few hours if we used our magic to propel us through the water, faster than you could ever swim as a human."

"But?"

"But Ailith is the queen of the ocean. She has eyes everywhere. We lucked out when I saved you from the thunderstorm. Most of her eyes would have been in shelter, and obviously none of the ones still out saw us, or we would not have been left here in peace for so long. I should have been back by now. Ailith will have sent people out looking for me, and they will have figured out I'm not at the castle by now."

"What would they do if they found us?"

"That's the problem." A dark look crossed his features. "I don't know what they would do. They wouldn't know you on sight, but our kingdom is not that vast. They would know they *don't* know you, and that is enough for suspicion."

"So what do we do?"

"We have no other option. We must swim."

"And what do we do if we get caught?"

"We don't get caught."

Kenna glared at him. "Yes, but what if we *do?*"

"Let's hope we don't find out."

She didn't know if she wanted to risk getting caught, but she knew they had no other choice. They had to leave, and soon. At least with their magic they could swim faster. And then it hit her, making her feel so stupid for not having wondered before.

"Calder?"

"Hm?"

"You said it's as simple as a merperson being in salt water for them to transform, right?"

"Yes, why?"

"Then why have I never transformed before the day you saved me?"

Calder took a moment before answering. "I've been thinking about that, and I believe I have a theory. You said you've been in the ocean many times before, right?"

"Yes, I have."

"But have you ever been that close to death in the water before?"

Kenna opened her mouth, but stopped. She didn't think so. But what about when she was five and had almost drowned? That fateful day when she had seen her mermaid. "Just that time I almost drowned when I was five."

"But how close were you, really?"

"What do you mean?"

"I mean," he shifted closer to her, getting more animated as he spoke, "were you seconds away from death? Could you feel your life slipping from you?"

"I... I don't know. I was only five. I don't think I even knew what death *meant* yet. I just remember looking up to the surface and thinking I would never see it again. Never see my parents, or my brother. And then she was there."

Calder paused, seeming to consider her words before he spoke again. "I've been told before the curse, when our people still lived in harmony, there were a few times when a merperson and a human would fall in love and have a child."

"Really?" Kenna's eyes brightened, full of hope. "So Tristan and I are not the only ones?"

"No, but I don't know where any of the others are. If they are in our kingdom, they never speak of their human parents. I'm sure they would be shunned if they did. It would be seen as an act of betrayal against our people to talk of them. And I'm sure there are some in your world. Ones who have either forgotten where they came from, or are too scared to ever speak of it."

"Then what does it matter?"

"Because when human and mer blood mix, it is not a perfect split. In most cases, the children are born without any of the powers of their mer blood."

Kenna's brow scrunched in confusion. If the mer blood didn't often manifest in children of both worlds, then how did that explain her being able to shift?

Seeing Kenna's reaction, Calder continued, "But there are rare cases where the merblood is strong enough, and the children have the powers of their merparent. But the magic would lie dormant in their blood until awoken. Obviously, with your bloodline, it is powerful enough that it would still be there. And what triggered it was your near–death experience.

"A merperson cannot die from drowning. The magic in our blood will not allow it. We cannot be claimed by the ocean, because we are a part of it. When you were about to drown, the magic in your blood responded. It woke up and shifted you so that you wouldn't drown."

Kenna didn't respond, trying to absorb it all. Her whole life, everything she'd sought had been hidden in her own blood. All she had to do was almost die, and there it was. She laughed at the irony of it all.

"What?" Calder asked her, his smile bemused.

"I spent my whole life searching for mermaids, to prove they existed. And the whole time all I had to do was almost drown."

Calder cracked a smile, laughing with her. Kenna knew she should still be angry. She should be a lot of things. But sitting there laughing with Calder, all she felt was joy.

Chapter Twenty-Eight

A few hours later, Kenna and Calder had bathed in the creek, hunted, and eaten. Calder had also gone out into the ocean and come back with kelp. Apparently all merfolk ate this at least once a week to prevent unwanted pregnancy.

Now they stood at the shore, staring out over the water, holding hands. Kenna closed her eyes, trying to calm her nerves.

This was it.

They were finally leaving the island. Leaving their bubble of happiness and safety. She had no idea what would happen when they got back to Cladach. Would her parents tell her the truth? How would they react to Calder?

And what the *hell* were they supposed to do once they did know the truth? What was knowing going to change?

Calder squeezed her hand in his, and Kenna opened her eyes, looking at him with a nervous smile.

"Are you ready, *mo lasair*?"

"As I'll ever be."

He laughed quietly, letting go of her hand and moving closer to the water.

Kenna closed her eyes, steeling herself for the day to come. She had always wanted this, an adventure on the sea—and here she was, living her dream. She was terrified of what would happen if they were caught, and what would happen if they weren't, and they made it back to Cladach.

But she couldn't stop now. The only way forward was through.

She took one last breath of air before walking into the ocean and diving under the water.

The surface broke around her, the cool water washing over her skin until she was fully submerged. The water was crystal clear, and Kenna could see her hair floating around her head in a fiery halo. Under the sea was a whole different world. One she would now be able to explore to her heart's content. She opened her eyes, letting them adjust to the sting of the salt, taking in the world around her.

After only a moment, she felt the shift start again, saw a flash of light, and she was a mermaid. She took in a tentative breath—swallow?—to test if she really could breathe the water, and it flowed in and out of her lungs easily, just like air. Kenna would never get past her fascination and curiosity over exactly how it worked.

She stretched her arms straight ahead of her, giving her hips a powerful flex to test out the motion. She easily shot through the water, moving yards in the time it took to blink.

Kenna grinned, a laugh bubbling up from her mouth. She straightened herself with ease, and spun her hands around in the water in front of her, marveling at how *right* it felt. Like this was where she was meant to be. Like the piece of herself that had always felt missing had finally clicked into place. She spun back around and faced where she thought Calder was behind her, but the water stretched out towards the shore in front of her, empty besides a scattering of small sea creatures.

She spun back around again, her hair fanning out after her, and came face to face with him.

She let out a scream, and the fish around her scattered. She clutched her hands to her pounding heart, and watched as Calder doubled over in

233

laughter. She could hear it as if it were drifting to her on the air instead of through water.

"You scared me, you *cacan!*" Kenna glared at him.

He bit his lip as he floated closer to her, his eyes dark and dancing. "You're cute when you're mad."

"I'm about to get much cuter if you don't knock it off."

However, she realized he wasn't exactly listening when she noticed where his eyes were. She tried to cover herself more fully with her arms but it was no use. "Hey! Eyes up here."

"Well, what did you expect of me?" He shot her a mischievous grin.

"It was you who said merfolk were less modest about these things."

Calder leaned into her, wrapping his arms around and gliding them smoothly up her back to wind through her flaming locks. "Yes, *mo lasair,* but you have to give me an adjustment period now that I get to see all of you." He punctuated his remark with a quick but deep kiss. Kenna's head was fuzzy with pleasure when he pulled back, and she found herself chasing his mouth, but he didn't yield.

"As much as I would love to continue this—and trust me, I would—we need to be on our way."

Kenna pouted but acquiesced, listening as he explained to her how their magic worked. It was very simple, and it took Kenna only moments to master it.

All she had to do was concentrate and compel the ocean to do her bidding. The stronger the bloodline, the easier it came to the merperson. Her Canduine blood, even mixed, was still the most powerful.

Especially being the sea's chosen ruler.

When concentrating on the water, merfolk could compel it to move around themselves, boosting their body through it. In concentrating on a certain material, merfolk could compel it to form the way they wanted it to, which Kenna did with a band of red seaweed a shade lighter than her hair, wrapping it around her chest.

Calder protested, of course, but Kenna simply rolled her eyes and ignored him.

Once it was on, she looked up at Calder, and the way he looked at her sent a thrill through her. He looked at her almost as if he was seeing her for the first time again. Wonder, and awe, and want.

"What?" Kenna asked.

"You just... you look like this is what you always should have been." He wrapped a floating strand of her hair around a finger, tugging on it as he spoke.

She beamed at him, but then a thought crossed her mind. "Wait! What happened to our clothes when we shifted? Yesterday when I shifted and realized what I was, I had taken my clothes off first."

"No one really knows. It's part of our magic, tied to our shifting. When we shift forms, whatever we were wearing disappears, and when we shift back it's there again." He shrugged, seeming unbothered, but Kenna had a million more questions.

"No. I know that look, and we do not have time for that right now." He glared at her, and she burst out laughing. He raised his brow at her, but she just shook her head, laughing.

"It's nice to be the one annoying you for a change." Calder dropped his jaw in mock outrage, but before he could respond she flashed her eyes at him in challenge. "Race you," she called out as she streaked past him, in the direction of home. She wasn't sure exactly how she knew—assumed it was part of her connection with the sea—but she sensed exactly which direction to go.

"Oh, you're on."

An hour later, Kenna still wasn't out of breath or the least bit tired. She was shocked. She didn't know if it was the energy of the water feeding into her, or the magic in her veins. The only place she really felt it was her abdomen. Kenna's body was used to moving side to side, not waving down the length of her body. Her abdomen muscles were getting a workout every time she undulated her hips to propel herself forward.

Looking over, she smiled at Calder, warmth flaring in her chest when he smiled back without hesitation. "You're a natural."

235

"I feel like... like I've finally found where I belong." She looked forward again, watching where they were heading. "I always felt out of place in that castle. I love my parents, and my brother, of course—he's my favorite person in the world. But there was always this feeling I was missing a piece of me. That I never truly belonged. And now I know it's because this is where I belong."

Kenna felt a subtle shift in the water around her, and looked over her shoulder to see Calder slowing to a stop. She doubled back to where he was now floating in the water, looking around them sharply.

She pulled up beside him. "What is it?"

"Someone is coming."

Kenna stared into the murky dark blue. There were a few random schools of fish, a pod of whales off in the distance, but other than that she didn't see anything. "How can you tell?"

"The more you learn the water, the stronger your connection becomes. You'll be able to read the shifts in the water, and tell from far away." He swam closer until he was right behind her. He trailed his finger lightly up her forearm, and whispered in her ear as she repressed a shudder. "Just trust me, and follow my lead."

She felt then there were indeed two figures ahead of them, materializing as if by magic from the blue. A moment later they were upon them, and Kenna immediately understood Calder's warning.

Kenna took in the two formidable mermen.

The one on the left was tall and built like a wall. His muscles rippled beneath his pale skin, bulging across his chest. His hair was a blond so light it was almost white, and he had a short, neat beard to match. His shoulders were broad and he bore a staff strapped across his back. His face was stern and imposing, lightly lined with age. His eyes were a hard, dark brown. Kenna guessed he was around the same age as her parents.

The one on the right looked to be but a few years older than her. He was shorter and slimmer, but no less intimidating. His build was compact but strong, and he wore the same staff strapped to his back.

His hair was a shock of orange on his head, matching the color of the freckles almost completely covering his light skin. His hair was just long enough to sway slightly in the current, and he was clean-shaven. His eyes, piercing and green, scrutinized her with no depth of emotion behind them. Completely indifferent, as if she were nothing but a passing creature that posed no threat to him.

Calder straightened to his full length, shoulders pulled back, spine stiff as a board. He nodded first to the ginger, and then the bigger one. "Graeme. Murray."

Murray spoke first, clearly the lead of the two guards. "Calder, the queen has been looking for you."

"I expected she would be." Calder's voice carried an arrogance she had never heard in it before, and her skin crawled.

"Your mission ended almost a week ago," Graeme remarked.

"There were... unforeseen circumstances." As Calder said this, he looked at her out of the corner of his eye in a dismissive way that was still loaded with meaning, and Kenna bristled. She knew he was only playing a part, but the attitude was too familiar.

"I can see that." Murray raised a brow, looking her up and down before looking back to Calder. "And this is?"

Kenna suspected Murray knew, but was waiting for Calder to confirm it. None of them had been expecting *this* from her.

"This is Princess Makenna."

Both looked at her more closely.

"This is the human princess?" Graeme asked.

"As you can see, she is not exactly human," Calder responded dryly.

"And where have the two of you been this past week? You weren't at the castle when we sent Andrea there to search for you," Graeme retorted.

"This"—he looked her up and down, disdain in his eye, and Kenna struggled to keep her face impassive—"*princess* decided to go for a leisure sail in the middle of a thunderstorm. Not very smart, are they?" He grinned conspiratorially at the soldiers, as if they were in on some secret together at her expense. Kenna's fists clenched. "Anyways, I was going to let her drown, but then right there in front of me, she shifted. I have no idea how it's possible. But she was injured in the sinking of her boat, and she wouldn't have made it back to the palace in her state. I took her to a nearby island until she healed, and I was just now bringing her back for the queen to interrogate."

Neither Graeme nor Murray spoke for a moment. Kenna didn't know where Calder was going with this exactly. How he thought pretending to be on their side would help them, but he had told her to trust him, so she would. She lifted her chin, glaring down her nose at them in her best impression of a snobby royal. Though she had never been that way herself, she had seen it in many of the nobles at court.

"Well, then." Murray gauged Calder's reaction as he spoke. "We'll escort the two of you the rest of the way."

Calder didn't miss a beat. "Oh, thank the gods, I've been stuck with no company but this dreadful bore for a week." He threw an arm over Graeme's shoulder and began asking after news from the palace, if any new pretty mermaids had shown up since his absence.

The glare Kenna shot Calder at his last comment was very real, as they fell in formation around her, leading the way. Calder shot a wink over his shoulder, discreet enough that the other two wouldn't have been able to see it, and Kenna rolled her eyes.

He was such a drama queen.

Chapter Twenty-Nine

They continued swimming for another hour or so, and as every moment passed, Kenna became more anxious. The entire time she wondered what would happen once they got to the mer palace. She had no idea what this Ailith was like, or how she would react to Kenna's existence.

Did she know exactly who Kenna was? Did she know she could shift?

The exhaustion of swimming for hours was finally catching up to her body, her limbs feeling heavier and heavier. Though it didn't seem to matter to the mermen, who barely acknowledged her existence. She tried to ask a few questions—like how long it would take or what the palace was like—but they ignored her.

Every time she opened her mouth to ask a new question, she could see Calder shooting her looks from the corner of his eyes, wanting her to stop pushing the boundaries. But Kenna couldn't help herself. There was so much she still wanted to know.

They were swimming through a kelp forest, tall green stalks swaying with the motion of the water, sea creatures drifting in and out between them. Kenna couldn't yet see what was ahead of them when she felt a shift in the water. She still couldn't tell when a creature was nearby like Calder and other merfolk could, so whatever she was feeling this time must have been the size of a village, at the least. Colorful fish darted in and out of the seaweed around them, and when Kenna looked down, she could see coral and other bright sea creatures on the seafloor.

When they broke through the edge of the kelp forest, Kenna came to a halt. The castle in Cladach had always been imposingly beautiful to Kenna. Large and sweeping, the stone facade standing out sharply against the green of the hills and the blue of the sky, rugged yet inviting.

But her home was *nothing* compared to what stood in front of her now.

The castle was beautiful—all arches and pillars and open hallways, short, elegant spires built of glistening white stone filigreed in gold, merpeople swimming in and out and around. Kenna realized there would be no reason to have them enclosed, because there was no risk of weather or danger of an attack happening. The palace wasn't tall, but it sprawled, slowly morphing into what looked like homes of varying sizes to either side, in what appeared to be a mermaid city of sorts. On the ocean floor in front of the palace was a reef, the mer palace's equivalent to the royal garden back at Cladach.

Calder noticed Kenna had stalled and swam back towards her, taking her by the arm. His grip looked tight from the outside, but his fingers were gentle on her skin. "Come along, Princess, no stalling."

She glared at him, sticking her tongue out after making sure the other two weren't looking, and his eyes gleamed with amusement.

"Is there a problem, Calder?" Murray stared at them with his arms crossed over his chest.

"No."

"Then let's go."

Calder pulled her along, falling in line behind Murray and Graeme, his hand still around her arm. Kenna wasn't paying attention to where they were going, too busy staring in awe at the beauty around her. As they got closer, she could see that while the hallways were open, they had awnings across the top to line the pathways, and all of the rooms were enclosed, with tall, grand doors. The most fascinating part, though, were the bright red flames lining the walls inside ornate golden sconces.

"You have *fire*? How do you have fire underwater?" Calder merely grunted with dismissal of her question, unable to indulge her wonder with their audience. But he gave her arm a loving squeeze, and Kenna knew he understood what a monumental moment this was for her.

She was so busy admiring the palace she didn't notice the stares at first. But as they passed more and more merpeople—of a variety of sizes and hair, tail, and skin color—she noticed every single one was staring at her.

Calder was right. People immediately knew she wasn't one of them.

How few merpeople *were* there?

"They're staring," she murmured quietly to Calder.

"It's 'cause you're so pretty," he whispered back.

Kenna tried her hardest not to roll her eyes, knowing everyone was watching. Instead, she ignored him and looked ahead as they came to a stop in front of a gigantic door. The wall was made of rough, white stone with bits of coral and shell embedded. Pillars were carved into either side of the doors, coated in gold. The doors themselves were made of the same stone, with carvings resembling waves etched into them.

Two guards were posted outside of the door, floating with their backs straight and staffs held in their hands at their sides.

As the four of them came to a stop in front of the guards, the one on the right—a merman with ebony skin, hair in dreadlocks down to his waist, and a bright yellow tail—nodded to Murray.

"We have someone here to see the queen," Murray said to the guard, who shot Kenna a glance before turning back to Murray and nodding once more.

He turned to the door behind him, pushing it open. He must have been using his powers to compel the water as it opened with no resistance, even though the heavy stone must have weighed tons. Murray and Graeme led the way, Calder following immediately behind with Kenna in tow.

The inside was just as grand as the outside. It was almost a mirror of the throne room at her castle. Long and narrow, pillars lined the sides. But in this throne room, the pillars were made from the same stone as the outside walls, and the ground was laid with large chunks of blue stone, interspersed with swirls of gold.

A few clusters of merfolk lingered, talking in clumps throughout the room, but Kenna paid them no mind, because at the end of the throne room sat the queen.

The back of the throne she sat upon took up most of the wall behind her, and was made of sharp, spiked coral in every shade imaginable, melded together and interspersed with shells, pearls, and gems. It looked both fierce and beautiful, and Kenna couldn't tear her gaze away from it, or from the queen who sat on it.

Ailith was not what Kenna had been expecting.

Although Ailith was supposedly only a few years younger than her mother, she appeared to be about Kenna's age. Her face was soft and sweet, with dark brown eyes that looked warm and inviting. Her lips were soft and plump, stained a fiery red, the color of Kenna's hair. Her tail was a deep, shimmering violet, but most shocking of all was her hair. It was white as snowfall, and the strands floated around her head in waving locks.

Atop her head sat a large crown matching the throne she sat on, and in one fist she held a trident, so gold it looked like sunlight in physical form.

She didn't say anything, staring intensely at Kenna as she and Calder swam towards her. When they came to a stop, Ailith spoke without removing her gaze from Kenna. "Leave us."

At once, every single merperson in the room left, leaving Ailith alone with Kenna and Calder. Kenna didn't take her eyes off the queen, though.

She couldn't get past all the similarities between Ailith and her mother. The shape of their faces, the slope of their noses. Their eyes may have been different colors, but the shape was identical, and they held the same beauty. If Kenna had any lingering doubt about her family's history, it was gone now.

The three of them floated in silence. Kenna had no idea what was going through Ailith's mind, her face a perfectly blank mask.

Finally, after Kenna thought she might burst from impatience, Ailith spoke. "So, you are Princess Makenna MacNamera?" Ailith said Kenna's name like she was tasting something particularly unsavory, and any hope Kenna had for getting out of this easily went down the drain.

"And you're, what? Some sort of fish queen?"

Kenna's chest tightened at the anger flaring in Ailith's eyes at her words. She wasn't sure when she decided to play this on the attack. Maybe she was sick of being the nice one. Being soft and kind while everyone around her took what they wanted without apology.

But she realized that, here and now, in this place where no one knew her, she could be her own person.

A new person.

A *strong* person.

And Kenna knew she couldn't let Ailith know that she knew who she was. Because the only place she could have learned it from was Calder, and they still needed Ailith to believe he was on her side.

"You, child, will address me as queen. Seeing as you appear to be one of my kind," she sneered as her eyes slid up and down, taking in Kenna's appearance in displeasure, "that makes me *your* queen." A cruel smile tilted her lips.

Kenna bristled at Ailith's words. "I have one queen. And she is not you." Ailith's knuckles went white around the staff of the trident, and the water in the room churned.

For the first time since entering the room, Kenna truly feared her. Ailith wasn't simply a queen.

She was a queen with extreme power.

Ailith spoke, her words quiet yet all the more powerful. "You will *not* speak of them in my realm." She spat the word "them" with more venom than Kenna had ever heard.

So her parents were a sore subject, apparently.

Ailith narrowed her eyes at Kenna. "What are you doing in my kingdom?"

Kenna bit her lip, thinking of how to answer. If she told the truth, Calder could be in serious trouble. She had to tread very carefully. "I'm guessing you already know what was going on in my castle." Kenna sent a pointed look at Calder, her brow raised. "Well, I wanted no part in it. So I left."

"You... *left*."

Kenna raised her chin, "Yes, I left. I sailed away. But I didn't see the storm coming, and my boat was wrecked. You can imagine my surprise when the next thing I knew, I was on a deserted island with someone who I believed to be a clansman of mine. I gather now, obviously, he is one of yours?"

Ailith ignored her, moving her gaze to Calder. "Care to explain what happened?"

Calder dipped the upper half of his body into a deep bow. "Your Majesty. Do you wish me to explain my... excursion in the presence of these ears?" He shot a sideways glance at Kenna, his eyes clouded with wariness.

He was a good actor.

So good, Kenna couldn't help the niggle of doubt in the back of her mind, but she crushed it down before it could grow roots.

Ailith nodded, and Calder continued. "As per my assignment, I took on the guise of one of the clansmen's sons, there to vie for the Princess' hand." At Ailith's growing expression of anger, Calder hurried on. "I was going to sneak in as a servant or such, but I intercepted the messenger informing the royal family that the chief's son was not going to be in attendance. I figured this was an opportunity to get that much closer. Once I gathered the humans did not know of us, and nothing other than a courtship was taking place, I excused myself. I was coming back to make my report when the storm hit, and I found the princess shipwrecked. Before my eyes, she shifted." Calder began to look nervous but continued.

"When I realized what she was, I decided to rescue her. Nurse her back to health and see if I could figure out what was going on, but I learned nothing. Either the princess knows nothing, or she is the best liar I have ever met. She went into the ocean before I could stop her and realized what she was. At that point, I decided to bring her back here to be questioned by you. That's when Murray and Graeme found us."

Ailith was silent for a moment, before nodding her head toward Calder. "You did well, boy. You are dismissed."

Calder hesitated, and Kenna knew he didn't want to leave her alone with Ailith. But she prayed he would hold his tongue and do as the Queen asked. The last thing they needed was her to get suspicious. To Kenna's relief, he said nothing, instead bowing to Ailith before turning and leaving the room. Kenna forced herself not to throw one last look at him over her shoulder.

"So the human princess is really a mermaid."

"Apparently." Kenna would give her *nothing*.

"How long have you known?"

"Since yesterday."

Ailith's mouth was a hard line. "Do not be smart with me, girl. You could never comprehend the power I wield. I would not push me if I were you." Accompanying Ailith's words, the water shifted around Kenna, and she found she could no longer move. The water pressed in around her on all sides, almost as if it were solid. Just as Kenna began to panic, feeling as if she was being suffocated, she felt the pressure ebb away. She looked up to find a satisfied expression on Ailith's face. Kenna clenched her teeth.

She would *not* be intimidated by her.

She would not bend.

"I am doing nothing but telling you the truth." *At least about this,* Kenna thought to herself. "I have only known I had mer blood in my veins since I discovered it on the island. I didn't even know that mermaids—that *you*—existed."

"Oh, really? And why am I supposed to believe that?"

"Why would I lie about it? Humans do not believe in mermaids. Sure, there are fairy tales, but they're just that."

"You expect me to believe your mother never told you anything?"

Kenna's heart pounded in her chest. Here it was, the confirmation Ailith knew her mother was the human queen. That she knew her sister had not been murdered and had lied about it. And now, Kenna would find out how good her own skills of deception really were.

"Why would my mother know anything about you?" Kenna waited, hoping her face showed the right amount of suspicion and confusion. She tried to read the queen's expression, but it revealed nothing.

"You're right. She wouldn't know anything. Which means you are useless to me."

Kenna's shoulders sagged in relief. Maybe Ailith was done with her and would cast her out.

But Kenna knew that was wishful thinking.

Her thoughts were confirmed a moment later when the queen raised her hand, and with a twitch of her fingers, the grand doors behind Kenna whooshed open on a current. The two guards from before swam into the throne room, coming up behind her.

"Take her to the dungeons until I decide what to do with her."

Kenna's heart pounded a staccato rhythm in her chest, but she refused to let Ailith know she was scared.

Instead, she lifted her chin and stared directly into Ailith's eyes, not uttering a word as the guards behind her each grabbed one arm before swimming her out of the room. The last thing she caught before her back was forced towards the queen was a small, arrogant smirk pulling at the corner of Ailith's lips.

Chapter Thirty

K enna didn't say a single word as they floated through the palace, but her eyes consumed everything around her in awe. It was the most beautiful place she had ever seen. And that wasn't a small thing, as she found her island kingdom stunning. But Cladach was nothing compared to this underwater palace. Everything shone glittery and gold, all built from a mixture of rock, coral, gold, and gemstones.

If the palace were broken down and sold in pieces, it could keep her entire kingdom fed for years.

But to tear down this work of art would be a crime. Elegance and grace were etched into every pillar, every arch. The open hallways allowed light from the sun to stream through the water, reflecting off the shimmering walls and giving the entire area a warm, ethereal tone.

Kenna was ushered through a maze of passageways and saw plenty of merfolk swimming past, all stopping to look at her. Some of them didn't seem too happy to have a stranger among their midst, but most of them held nothing in their gazes but open curiosity. She wondered how often it was they got visitors, and guessed it was fairly rare, if not completely unheard of. At least since the curse went into effect. She didn't blame them for being distrustful of strangers if all they knew was the story Ailith had told.

Kenna found herself hauled to a stop in front of a long stretch of empty wall. She watched in amazement as the guard to her right—a mermaid with light brown skin, more freckles than even Kenna had, brown hair coiled around her head in a halo, and an iridescent tail like a shining pearl—hefted her trident and leveled it perpendicular to the wall, touching the longer middle spoke against the stone and coral.

Kenna's eyes widened in astonishment as the wall melted into nothing, leaving behind a perfect archway, past which was a long, dimly lit hallway. This one, unlike all she had seen so far, was covered by a roof of the same material as the walls. Along these walls were long, glowing stripes crisscrossing over one another across the whole way, providing the only light. She looked closer, letting out a soft gasp.

The glowing lines were some sort of algae. Kenna had never seen anything like it. She didn't even know there was any type of sea plant that glowed in such a way, and she was instantly fascinated. She longed to ask someone how it worked, but knew she would get no answers from her current companions.

The guards shoved her forward, and she continued in, noting on either side of her were cell after cell, each separated by rusty, metal bars, covered in barnacles and algae. Most of the cells seemed to be empty, but one or two had vague shapes lingering at the back, and Kenna couldn't help but wonder who they were—what their reasons for being locked in here were.

Moving her forward, they stopped at the end of the hallway. The same guard who opened the wall with her trident let Kenna's arm go. She moved in front of her, lifting a ring of keys and unlocking the door of the cell in the right-hand corner. She swung the door open, moving out of the way for her partner to shove Kenna inside the cell before slamming it shut and locking her in.

Neither spared her a second look as they turned and swam back towards the exit, and Kenna's pride wouldn't let her ask them any of the questions she so desperately wanted to ask. Instead she floated, watching in silence as they left, the wall melting back together after the last fin was through the opening.

Kenna closed her eyes and leaned her forehead against the bars. She was so *tired*. Twenty-four hours ago she didn't even know she was a mermaid. She'd not only spent hours underwater, but was now trapped in a mermaid prison. She had no idea how she was going to get out of this one. And Calder...

She didn't know what happened to him. Had the queen believed his act? Was he safe? Or was she currently questioning him? Was she torturing him?

Kenna squeezed her hands tighter around the bars until her knuckles groaned in protest.

No. She refused to let her mind go there. Calder was fine. He was fine, and he was figuring out how to escape at this very moment. She just needed to be patient and have faith. Not typically her best qualities, but she could do it.

She let go of the bars, turning to take in her cell. It was as she imagined any cell to be. A small corner cell, it was surrounded by two solid walls and two walls of bars. In the corner, where the two solid walls met, was a low stone bench. On one end lay a bundle of what looked like seaweed, and Kenna concluded this was what they passed for a bed.

Great.

Aside from the bed, the cell was completely empty. Kenna floated over, sinking onto the bench. She wasn't sure how this worked—her being able to sit under water. It was more like hovering. There must be an explanation, but Kenna didn't currently have the capacity or energy to think about the technical aspects.

She rested her elbows on her knees—or rather, the bend of her tail where her knees would have been—and cradled her head in her hands.

How had she gotten here?

A mermaid, locked in the prison of her apparently evil, long-lost aunt, who just happened to be the queen of the merpeople.

With a jolt, Kenna realized these were technically *her* people. The crown was technically hers, if they could get Ailith off the throne and convince the people they had been lied to all this time. They would need to see her mother, alive and happy, to no longer believe the lie. But she knew that distrust would be hard to break. Kenna could hardly expect an entire kingdom of people to change their minds when they knew one thing to be true their whole lives.

Was that even something she wanted, though?

To rule Mhariogh?

She had spent her whole life longing to do anything *but* rule. But Kenna realized, despite the arguably less than ideal circumstances, something felt... *right* being here. Ever since they crested that ridge and she saw the palace for the first time, her heart felt settled in a way it never had in Cladach.

It seemed like it was trying to tell her, *this is home.*

Maybe she hadn't spent her whole life yearning to do anything but rule. Maybe her heart had just been trying to bring her here, to the kingdom she was *meant* to rule. Maybe Calder was right. Maybe the sea *had* been calling to her.

Kenna shook her head, realizing her thoughts were getting ahead of her again. Tristan had always said her mind was stuck too far ahead to see what was right in front of her.

Tristan.

Kenna's heart ached at the thought of him. She was a terrible sister. She had barely thought of him since she'd been gone, too preoccupied worrying about Calder, and then preoccupied by Calder in... other ways.

She wondered what Tristan was doing now. He must be sick with worry over her.

Did he think she was dead?

She could feel the tears welling as she thought about him. She missed him. More than she ever knew she could miss someone. He was the other half of her heart, and without him, she was lost.

All at once Kenna realized she could never rule the mer kingdom. She could never leave Tristan behind. Even if she could get past the ache in her chest at the thought of no longer seeing him, she couldn't force such a huge responsibility on him, of ruling Cladach. Not without knowing absolutely that he wanted it.

Kenna was pulled out of her thoughts by the sound of a metal chain clinking against stone. She whipped up her head, squinting into the gloom of the dungeon. The strips of glowing algae weren't enough to illuminate the whole dungeon, however, and she could only see down a few stalls clearly before the water melted into a murky black, unidentifiable shapes concealed within the darkness.

After another moment of silence, she heard the same noise again, and she rose from the bench, swimming to the wall of bars separating her from the next cell. She pressed up against them to gaze into the dark.

"Hello?"

Kenna floated there, hands wrapped around the bars, staring into the dark as a figure slowly began to materialize. She couldn't make out all the details, but she saw the silhouette of a tail and a torso and long hair floating around their head. She wondered what the clinking sound was as the figure became clearer, the closer they drifted to the edge of their cell, two down from Kenna.

It was a mermaid bound in chains. There were cuffs around both her wrists, the chains connecting them fading out of sight behind her. Attached to the floor or wall, Kenna assumed. Her wrists were thin and bony beneath the cuffs, red and scarred. She must have been cuffed for *years*, and Kenna's heart ached for the mermaid.

Her gaze traveled from the mermaid's tail—some nondescript dark color too hard to make out in the dim lighting—up her warm brown skin. Kenna wondered how old she was, her face worn down with who knew how many years of pain and suffering, while her hair stayed jet black without a trace of gray to be seen.

But her eyes... though they gazed at Kenna with what appeared to be cautious hope, they were also sharp with intelligence. This mermaid had not given up.

"Who are you?" Kenna asked, her voice soft and tentative. For all she knew, this woman could be even more evil than the queen. What did someone have to do to end up locked and chained in this prison for so long?

She waited, but the mermaid simply stared at her, studying her.

"Hello?" Kenna tried again. She wondered if she was deaf, but she didn't believe so. The other woman's eyes glinted in response to her questions.

Just as Kenna was about to give up and go back to her bench, the woman finally spoke. Kenna's entire body froze, because the words weren't spoken aloud. She heard them *inside her mind.*

Hello, daughter of Eileen Canduine.

Chapter Thirty-One

Kenna shook her head forcefully. Surely, she was imagining things. You couldn't speak into people's minds; that was impossible.

Not impossible. Just rare.

Kenna's entire body went rigid. There it was again. She looked at the woman, her eyes wide. "Is—Is that you?"

She only smiled in response. *Do you see anyone else?*

"But how are you doing that?"

Under any other circumstances I would explain, but I'm afraid we don't have long.

"Don't—" Kenna began, but the woman shook her head, cutting her off.

Speak in your mind, not out loud. We don't know who listens.

Kenna snapped her mouth shut, continuing her questions in her mind. *Don't have long until what?* Kenna was thoroughly confused by now, another thought occurring to her. *Wait, how do you even know who I am? Who are you? Why don't you talk out loud?*

In response, Kenna heard a tinkling laugh in her head. *Just as curious as your mother, I see.* Kenna's eyes snapped to the woman's, and they sparkled with mirth. *My name is Isla, and I promise, I will answer the questions that are necessary. But we only have a short time until you must go.*

I don't know if you've noticed, but I'm kind of stuck in here. I don't think I'll be going anywhere any time soon.

Isla continued as if Kenna hadn't spoken. *I knew your mother, child.* Kenna watched the light in the woman's eyes dim. *I was her lady's maid, and her friend.*

Kenna's heart cracked open. *You knew my mom?*

You are the spitting image of her. Besides the hair, of course. That comes from your grandmother.

It does? Kenna questioned, her heart swelling. She always wondered, since neither of her parents sported the bright red. She had mourned never knowing either set of grandparents, and her parents never talked about them. Kenna always assumed it was too hard, them having all passed too soon. Now she was thinking there was another reason.

She was known with great renown for her flaming hair. And her flaming personality.

Kenna smiled, a grin to match Isla's.

What happened to them? My mother told me there was a war before I was born, and that her whole clan was wiped out. I know now that wasn't true, that she came from here—Mhariogh. But what happened? How did Ailith become queen if my mother was the heir? How did my grandparents die? Why did my mother leave and Ailith curse the humans? Why did my mother lie to me my entire life?

I don't have all the answers you seek, Isla replied, *but I do have some. For a long time, our two people got along very well. We were allies. As with two groups of people who are so drastically different, however, there was tension. In an attempt to smooth it over, a marriage was proposed, between the human king and our youngest princess, but no one was told. Both our people and your people believed it to be a regular royal visit. In reality, it was a chance for Princess Ailith and King Evander to meet.*

I don't understand. Ailith and my father? But we have a festival where the heir marries from within our own kingdom. My father and my mother always said that was how they had met and married. I know now that was a lie, but what reason did they have to break that tradition?

There was an exception made on behalf of the humans. A break of tradition in order to more solidly unite all of our people, Isla responded. *The only reason I knew any of this was my close relationship with your mother. We told each other everything, and I accompanied them to Cladach for the meeting. When we got there, your mother and Evander fell in love. It was unavoidable—fate's design. But Eileen was the heir to our throne. She couldn't go off and marry the king of another kingdom.* Isla's expression became dark, and Kenna shuddered with a feeling she knew where this was going.

The other problem was Ailith had fallen in love with Evander as well. At this point, Evander and Eileen had come clean to our king and queen, trying to convince them this was a good thing. That the two of them could make it work. That if it came to it, there was always Ailith to take the mer throne. But Ailith had always been... Well, she had always had a temper—an edge that never softened. Isla paused, her face growing somber.

Your parents hadn't yet told Ailith of the feelings between them, even as they began sneaking around her. They were talking with our king and queen one day, while Ailith was off taking a tour of the gardens, telling them they were in love, they would be wed, and Ailith could take the throne. Your grandparents said they would not allow it, as they did not trust Ailith to wield such power. Ailith overheard this conversation and lost herself in a fit of rage.

Kenna could practically feel the sorrow rolling in waves off Isla as she spoke, waiting for the rest of this story she knew would end horribly.

Ailith didn't know I was there, that I saw everything. Saw as she screamed and raged, as your parents and grandparents tried to calm her, but it was too late. Her entire life, Ailith felt as if she lived in the shadow of your mother. Always the second daughter, always second best. These things together were too much. Your mother taking her love, and their parents saying she wasn't good enough to take the throne. Discussing this all behind her back. I watched as she picked up the bow and arrow, and fired. Right at your mother. Evander pushed Eileen out of the way, just in time.

Kenna knew if they weren't under water, her tears would be spilling down her cheeks. As it was, she could feel her shoulders shaking while her breaths shuddered in and out of her.

Everyone stopped what they were doing and stared at her, but she didn't look remorseful, only angry. And so they took her, your grandparents. They wanted to bring her back here, lock her away until they decided what to do. They were horrified and heartbroken. This was their little girl.

I was meant to stay with your mother, but when a week passed and we still hadn't heard from her parents, I volunteered to go see what had happened. I was accosted by guards before I got anywhere near the palace. I asked them why, but they refused to answer and threw me in here. I heard the whispers passing in the hallways, though. The people believed the king, queen, and heir were dead. Finally, Ailith came to me, demanding to know what I was doing.

I pleaded with her to tell me where the king and queen were, but she didn't answer. Instead she cut out my tongue. She decided to let me live, condemning me to a life in this cell. I believe she enjoyed the fact that I was right here, underneath her reign the whole time, unable to tell a soul the truth of how she got the throne.

Kenna gasped, her hand coming up to cover her mouth. *So, does that mean...*

Isla's expression was grim. *I never found out what happened for sure. But they never came back, so I assume she... disposed of them. Killed her own parents to take the crown, and told our people the humans had turned on us—poisoned our people against them. I still don't know how she cursed the humans to forget we exist, but I felt when she did it, right after I came back here. It was a wave of magic, stronger than anything I had ever felt before.*

And you've been imprisoned here since? Kenna asked. She couldn't imagine an existence such as this for so long. She had always felt trapped in Cladach, trapped in her duty. And now she burned with shame, in the face of someone who was *actually* trapped. Twenty-five years of this tortured life. Isla nodded.

I'm so sorry. I can't imagine... When I get out of here I will bring you with me. I'll get you free, even if I cannot give you your life back. She stared into Isla's eyes with fierce determination. She was going to make this right.

Isla only smiled. *You really are your mother's daughter. She must be so proud of you.*

Kenna flushed under her praise. Isla's expression quickly turned serious, though. *Now listen. I don't know if your mother ever found out the truth of what happened, but I know she is a smart woman, and she has avoided the ocean this whole time. I'm sure she figured if she stayed out of Ailith's way, she could stay safe. Keep Evander and her future children safe. But Ailith knows you exist. She knows the ocean calls to you, and she will stop at nothing until you are destroyed. She will not let any threat to her power stop her. You must warn your parents.*

But how do I break out? How do I get back to my parents? Kenna clenched the bars so tight her knuckles went white.

You needn't worry about escape. Your charming young man will take care of that for you. A small smile played on the corner of Isla's lips.

How did you....?

I am what you would call a... seer of sorts. We are a rare merperson that pops up once every long while. Luckily, Ailith never knew of my true nature, or she would not have let me live. But my true powers were kept a secret—no one but Eileen and the late king and queen knew. It was the reason I was chosen as her lady's maid in the first place. Being locked in here, being deprived of my tongue and my ability to communicate has let my power grow in other ways. It's how I know we don't have much longer before you will be out of here and on your way home.

Kenna still had a million questions, but before she could ask her first, the archway melted open once again, light streaming into the dungeon. She quickly swam away from the bars she had been pressed up against, Isla having melted back into the shadows of her own cell. Kenna glared towards the entrance, ready to put up a fight in any way necessary, when she was instead met with the face she would never forget.

Chapter Thirty-Two

"**I**t's you!" Kenna gasped.

In front of her was the mermaid who saved her life all those years ago, green eyes sparkling with mischief, her blonde hair plaited down her back, one of the gleaming tridents all the guards carried in her hand. She broke into a bright smile, a dimple carving out a space next to her lips.

"You're Calder's mother!"

"Hello, darling. You can call me Coira. My, my, you really have grown into such a beautiful woman. I can see why my Calder cares for you so."

"How did you get in here?" She tried looking over her shoulder and out into the hallway beyond the door.

"I have my ways." Coira grinned wickedly, the mirror image of her son. "But right at this moment, an explanation is not as important as *speed,* darling. Calder's waiting for us, and we only have so long before the next round of guards come this way. We must get you out of here before Ailith notices you're gone."

Coira unlocked the door to Kenna's cell while she spoke, pulling it open. The rusted hinges squeaked in protest as it opened and they both flinched, throwing furtive glances past the door. Luckily, there must not have been anyone within hearing distance. Kenna rushed out of her cell, moving quickly towards the exit, stopping when she noticed Isla out of the corner of her eye.

The mermaid was hovering in the shadows at the back of her cell, smiling at her. Kenna paused in front of her cell door. *Thank you. You have given me more than you know. Please, come with us. We can take you from here, back to my mother!*

But Isla declined. *No, it is not my path to go with you now. But don't fear; we will see each other again.*

But—

You must go now, Kenna. But before you leave, go to the palace gardens, and take with you feamnach purpaidh. *It's a purple kelp. Your young man will know the one. You will need it.*

What for?

Isla only shook her head. *Hurry.*

Kenna wanted to argue, but Coira grabbed her hand, urging her on. "Darling, there is no time to waste. We must leave now."

Kenna went with her, throwing one last look over her shoulder at Isla. *I promise, I will be back for you.*

Then they were out of the dungeon, the wall melting into place behind them. Coira slowed to a stop at the corner, poking her head around to check that they were clear, before ushering Kenna ahead and racing down it.

"Why don't we just swim up?"

Coira laughed. "You think Ailith would leave the water above her palace unguarded? She has eyes everywhere, my child."

"Wouldn't it be safer than making our way through these open hallways, though?"

Calder's mother grinned over her shoulder at Kenna. "No one would ever be stupid enough to sneak around her home ground. Inside the palace is much less guarded than the outside."

"Well, that's reassuring," Kenna muttered.

They passed the next few minutes in silence, sneaking their way through the many layered hallways, until they finally found themselves at one edge of the palace.

She gently pushed Kenna out of sight behind a pillar. "This is the quickest and easiest way out of the palace, but it's also the most heavily guarded. Stay behind this pillar and wait for Calder. After this, it's up to the two of you. Ailith is queen of the ocean, which means she is more connected to it than any other mer person. She knows everything that happens in her waters, especially this close to home, so you *must* be careful getting back to your parents." Coira focused her gaze on Kenna, smoothing her hair away from her face in a move that made Kenna ache for her own mother in an unexpectedly fierce way. "You are going to make a wonderful queen, darling."

Kenna opened her mouth to reply, her eyes suddenly stinging with tears that would never shed under the water, but Coira only leaned in, placing a kiss on her forehead before swimming away. Kenna peeked her head around the pillar to watch as she swam down the hallway at a brisk pace.

A pair of guards turned the corner, and Kenna froze. *Shit.* They couldn't afford any mistakes. What would happen if the guards caught them? What would Ailith do to Coira for helping her—

"Relax, *mo lasair*, this was all part of the plan." The words were whispered, and she felt a solid chest press up against her back. She almost screamed, but a warm hand clamped over her mouth, another arm wrapping around her waist and holding her body tight against the chest. Her body relaxed into his, recognizing the safety of Calder's arms before her brain could catch up.

"I'm sorry, I didn't mean to startle you," Calder apologized. "But if you scream, that's when our plan really will go to shit."

Kenna couldn't stop her smile, and Calder must have felt it against his palm, because he loosened his grip enough for her to turn around in his arms. She hungrily drank in his face, his eyes bright with joy and love.

"Calder." His name was barely past her lips before his mouth was on hers, and everything inside her that had been wound up so tight settled. Her body melted into his until she couldn't tell where she ended and he began. They stayed like that for another moment, until she remembered his mother and reluctantly pulled back.

"As much as I want to keep doing that, what about your mother?"

"Ah yes, I love talking about her while I'm kissing you," Calder said in a wry tone, and Kenna glared at him.

"*Cacan.*" She rolled her eyes at him before turning back and peeking her head around the edge of the pillar.

Coira was talking with the guards, waving her hands in large gestures, while the guards leaned in, worried expressions on their faces.

"What is she telling them?"

Calder leaned his body up against hers from behind, peeking his own head over hers. "She's telling them that she saw a pack of electric eels making their way towards the other side of the palace where the nursery is. They'll want to go with her to make sure all the young ones are safe. That's when we make a break for the kelp forest." He gripped her hand in his, tugging her back around before taking one last peek into the hallway to watch as the guards left with Coira in the opposite direction. "Ready?" He grinned down at her, and Kenna couldn't stop herself from smiling in return.

"With you, I'm ready for anything." She felt embarrassed as soon as the words left her mouth, but the feeling quickly vanished when his grin softened, and he looked at her in that way that made her toes curl—when she had toes, that was.

Calder moved out into the open water above the gardens, her hand still gripped in his, when she remembered. Kenna stopped, tugging on his hand. "Wait!" Calder looked back at her and she continued, "I'm supposed to find some *feamnach purpaidh*? "

"What for?" He looked at her quizzically, and she shook her head.

"It will take too long to explain. Do you know where to find it?"

He paused only a second longer before nodding and pulling her to the right. They swam down into the garden, and he pulled her to a stop in front of a patch of purple kelp. "Quickly, we have to get out of the open."

She let go of his hand, breaking off as much kelp as she could. She didn't know exactly what she needed it for, and wanted to make sure whatever it was she had enough. Once her hands were full, she turned back around to Calder.

"I guess I didn't fully think this through. Where am I supposed to put all of this?"

Calder's eyes twinkled with mirth as he took the kelp from her, wrapping it around his wrist into a cuff of sorts. "I'll carry it for you, *ghaoil*."

"Gods, I love you."

Calder only grinned in response before tugging her towards the kelp forest. He didn't relax his pace until they were hidden inside it.

"This is where we need to be careful. Ailith knows the kelp forest is an easy place to hide, so she keeps guards on it at all times. We need to stay as close to the ocean floor as possible, and be careful not to disturb the kelp."

Making their way through quickly and cautiously, Kenna couldn't quiet all the thoughts in her mind. She still had no clue how Calder and Coira had managed to break into the dungeon in the first place. What would happen to Coira if Ailith learned she had helped Kenna escape? Calder's parents had been waiting for the right moment to overthrow Ailith for so long now—if they got caught, ruining everything, Kenna would never forgive herself.

And when they got back to Cladach, what was Kenna supposed to do once she told her parents she knew the truth?

Her thoughts kept tumbling through her mind as they went, while she tried to focus on not alerting the guards to their presence. Now that Ailith knew Kenna knew about the merfolk, she must realize all her lies were about to come crumbling down. So what happened now? How would Ailith retaliate? Obviously, they had to find some way to break this curse on the humans, but how? Was it even possible?

She was brought out of her thoughts when Calder stopped in front of her. She leaned around him to see what was ahead. "Why did we stop?"

"We've reached the end of the kelp forest."

Sure enough, the kelp thinned out until nothing but open sea was left. Besides the normal sea life, there was nothing past the kelp as far as she could see, the water fading into murky darkness.

"So, this is the last of our cover?"

"I'm afraid so," Calder replied, looking down at her.

"What's next?"

"We swim as fast as we can to Cladach, and hope no one sees us before we get there."

Kenna rolled her eyes. "Perfect."

Chapter Thirty-Three

S ome god must have been looking out for them because Kenna and Calder made it back to Cladach with no trouble at all, arriving in the twilight hours between midnight and sunrise.

The fact that they hadn't come across any merpeople was more worrying than if they had. What was Ailith up to, leaving her ocean completely unguarded?

A prickle of unease crawled down Kenna's spine, but she shook it off. If something was going on, there was nothing Kenna could do about it at the moment. She had other things to worry about.

They made their way onto the dark beach, illuminated only by the moonlight as they waited a moment as their bodies shifted and their clothes reappeared. When they were standing, Kenna turned and looked towards the path up the cliffside, her brow creased. Calder reached up, smoothing out the wrinkles with his thumbs, cupping her face in his large hands.

"Are you ready?" He leaned into her, kissing her brow, and she couldn't stop the hum of contentment making its way out of her throat. She closed her eyes, burying herself in his warmth for a moment. His safety. She inhaled his scent, which was starting to smell like home. Once she had built up enough courage to face what they were about to walk into, she pulled away.

"No, but I never will be, so let's go."

Calder cracked a smile. "There she is."

The corner of Kenna's lips tilted up, and she made her way up the path. Neither of them spoke as they neared the castle. They didn't know what reception they would get, but they knew it wasn't going to be a good one. Especially not for Calder. The last thing she had told them, if Tristan had found her note, was that Cameron was a merman. And with that thunderstorm, she was fairly certain they thought she was either dead or kidnapped.

But as they got closer to the castle and still didn't see a single soul, Kenna's unease grew. There should be people out and about. When the Winchin Festival was in full swing, the castle had been full of people. When she went missing, Kenna assumed not everyone had stayed, but it wouldn't have emptied entirely. At the very least there should be guards roaming the grounds. For a fleeting moment Kenna wondered what her parents had told the people. If anyone outside her family even knew she was missing.

"Something is wrong," Kenna murmured to Calder. He made a noise of agreement and gripped Kenna's hand in his. They continued on, Kenna's palms slick with sweat, her heart beating a fierce rhythm. When the castle came into view, it fell out of her chest completely.

The banners flying from the parapets were not the tartan of Clan MacNamera. They were solid black. The color of mourning.

Oh gods.

Panic seized her lungs as all other thoughts left her. She didn't know how she knew, but she could feel it, something had happened to Tristan when she left.

She left him. Left him to bear the burden of their entire kingdom so she could chase a fucking fairy tale. If he was gone, she would never forgive herself.

Kenna dropped Calder's hand and ran, faster than she had ever run in her entire life. She couldn't do this without Tristan. He couldn't be dead. He couldn't be.

She could see nothing through the tears blurring her vision. She barely heard Calder calling her name over the sound of her feet as they hit the ground, the blood pumping through her veins.

She burst through the front doors of the castle and was met with utter chaos. Servants and nobles alike were running in every direction, no one noticing her as she burst through the doors.

Every single person was dressed head to toe in black.

"No. *No, no, no, no, no, no,*" she cried to herself, tearing past them in the direction of Tristan's bed chamber.

Reaching his rooms she threw the doors open, not even flinching when they banged against the walls. She didn't stop until she got to his bed, paying no attention to the small group of people standing around it, looking at the body lying there. But before she could get a good look at him, she was wrapped in two sets of arms, her name sobbed over and over.

Her reaction was delayed, her brain too stalled to comprehend what was happening, but then she realized it was her parents. The sob that had been lodged in her throat came out, and she was crying with them, hugging them, gripping as tight as she could, sobs wracking her entire body.

Kenna hadn't realized until that moment just how much she had missed them. Even though they lied to her, they were still her parents, and she loved them more than anything in the world.

As much as she wanted to stay in their embrace and pretend everything was fine now, she couldn't. She pulled away, ignoring their questions.

"That doesn't matter right now." Her voice cracked on the words, her throat sore with her tears. She took a fortifying breath before turning back to the bed.

Back to Tristan.

He looked like a ghost. His skin was pale and emaciated. His normally full cheeks were hollow, cheekbones more prominent than ever before. His lips were dry and cracked, tinted blue. His clothes hung loosely off his large frame, making him look like a boy wearing his father's clothing.

Kenna would never get this image out of her mind. This unmoving shell of the twin she loved would haunt her forever, as would the knowledge that she was responsible. Would he have gotten sick if she hadn't abandoned him to deal with the kingdom on his own? The stress of her disappearance and the weight of the responsibilities now on his shoulders triggering some kind of illness?

Kenna fell to her knees beside the bed, gripping Tristan's limp hand in her own, pressing it to her forehead as her tears soaked the mattress.

"This is all my fault." She didn't know if anyone heard her. If they responded, she didn't hear it, only gripping his clammy hand tighter.

His hand was *clammy.*

Bodies weren't clammy when they were... when they were dead.

Which meant that—

Kenna gasped. "He's still alive?" She wrenched up her head, standing and leaning over Tristan, brushing the hair off his forehead. She stared intently at his chest, waiting for the telltale sign—the slightest rise and fall of his chest. Her tears began falling again in earnest.

She wasn't too late.

"—doesn't have long."

With a start Kenna realized her mother was talking to her in a shaky voice.

"What?"

"I said, yes, he's still alive, but he doesn't have long. He could go at any moment. We've been standing vigil all day."

"Why aren't you doing anything for him? Why are you just letting him die?"

"There's nothing left for us to do, *mo ghràdh.* We have tried everything." Her father's voice was thick with tears.

Before Kenna could respond, there was a commotion from the hallway. She could hear the sounds of a scuffle and shouting voices. She started for the door when it slammed open, two guards hauling Calder in between them, who was complaining very loudly.

"—why you won't listen to what I'm saying, you *riatach*! Kenna! Will you please tell them to let me go?'

"We found him in the Great Hall. I believe this is the miscreant who disguised himself as Cameron MacKenzie during the Winchin Festival."

"I *told* you, I came back here with Ke— Princess Makenna. Ask her yourself, she's standing right there!" Calder wrenched his arm out of the guard's grip and spun out of his reach before the guard could grab him again.

"It's fine! It's fine." Kenna put herself between them. "He's telling the truth, he's with me."

"Kenna?" She turned at the sound of her mother's tight voice. "What's going on here?"

"This is Calder. He's from Ailith's court."

At Kenna's words, her parents froze. Her mother looked like she'd seen a ghost, and her father sighed wearily, before turning to the guards. "Leave us."

The guards bowed, sharing a look before exiting and leaving the four of them alone in the room. Kenna stared at her parents, willing them to break the silence. To speak first and admit the truth—they had been lying to her her entire life.

But they didn't. All they did was stare at her in pained silence.

"You aren't going to say anything?"

"*Mo ghràdh*, you have to know that everything we have ever done was to keep you safe." Her father stepped forward, raising his hand to touch her, but she stepped out of his reach.

"I hate to interrupt this heartwarming reunion," Calder intruded. "But shouldn't we be worried about him?" He pointed to Tristan, and immediately the tension drained from Kenna's body. Her face flamed with shame at her attention being so easily torn from him.

She rushed back to his bedside, sitting on the edge, clutching his hand in her own. Leaning forward, Kenna brushed the hair off his forehead, blinking back tears for what felt like the millionth time that day.

"Oh, *cacan*, how am I supposed to live without you?" She felt heat at her back, a moment later warm hands resting on her shoulders, squeezing them in comfort. Calder wrapped his body around her, lending her his support, taking in Tristan's still form lying in front of them.

"What are his full symptoms?" Calder's words held a slight edge.

"He got very weak, developed a fever. He can't retain food or water, and he became lethargic to the point that he sleeps more often than he is awake," the queen replied.

Calder's eyes shone with realization, and he turned sharply to look at her mother, his tone hard and incredulous. "Did you not consider he might have the mer sickness?"

The queen looked at him, opening her mouth as if to respond, before stopping, the color draining from her face. "I never even thought..." She trailed off, her voice shaking. "But... He's human. I renounced my mer blood a long time ago. He has never shown any signs. How is it possible?"

"He is not human. And neither is Kenna. You should have realized your blood was too powerful to disappear completely," Calder shot back, his voice laced with thinly veiled anger.

Kenna's mother held one hand to her stomach, the other at her mouth, looking as if she might be sick. Calder didn't wait another moment before walking to the door and pulling it open. The guards standing on the other side looked at him in distrust, but Calder paid them no mind, barking orders.

"I need someone to fetch a mortar, pestle, and salt water!" When they didn't immediately follow his directive, he continued, "Now! If you want your prince to have a chance of surviving."

The guards continued ignoring him, looking over his shoulder into the room. Kenna had no idea what Calder was up to, but she trusted him completely. After ordering them to listen, they were gone, and the only sound was fading footsteps running down the hall.

A few short but tense minutes later, in which no one uttered a sound, the guards came running back with exactly what Calder had asked for. He took the mortar and pestle, placing it on the stand by Tristan's bed before pulling the kelp from the pocket in his breeches, where he had stuffed it when they got to land.

Isla's warning came back to her. *You will need it.*

She had known.

Somehow, Isla had known Tristan was sick, and she had known what his ailment was. Kenna vowed then and there, no matter what happened, she *would* return to the mer palace and free her. She owed Isla everything for this kindness.

Kenna was pulled from her mind with the sound of the mortar scraping the sides of the pestle. Calder was grinding the kelp into a fine powder. He stopped after a few more turns of the mortar, pouring a small amount of the salt water onto the powder, mixing them together.

He did this a few times, until they combined to make a soggy-looking plum-colored paste. He moved to Tristan's side, bringing the bowl and leftover water with him.

"Help me lift him, Kenna."

She sprang into action, coming to the opposite side of the bed as Calder. She helped lift Tristan, leaning his back against the headboard until he was in a sitting position. Calder then lifted the cup of water to Tristan's lips, and realizing what he was trying to do, Kenna helped him open Tristan's mouth enough to pour the water down his throat.

A few weeks ago Kenna would've questioned forcing Tristan to drink salt water. But she reminded herself of what Calder had said. The ocean was a part of merpeople, and merpeople a part of the ocean. Salt water was in their blood. After they managed to get a small amount of the salt water down Tristan's throat, Calder lifted a spoonful of the paste

271

to Tristan's lips, forcing it into his mouth. They massaged his throat, helping it go down, and then gave him more salt water.

They did this until the paste was gone. Calder set down the bowl and backed away from the bed, allowing the king and queen to take his place at Tristan's side. He came around to where Kenna was sitting, again lending her his strength.

And they waited.

Chapter Thirty-Four

J olting awake, Kenna blinked the bleariness out of her eyes. She looked around, trying to remember where she was, the room bright in the afternoon sunlight.

She was slumped on a settee, a warm body lying behind her. That must have been Calder, and with the way his chest rose and fell in equal measure, she could tell he was still asleep. She looked across the room and saw her parents asleep in chairs on the opposite side of the bed directly in front of her.

The events of the previous day came rushing back to her. She shot up, scrambling off the settee and over to Tristan. Yesterday they had waited for hours, never leaving his side. But eventually, Kenna had succumbed to sleep. She'd tried to stay up, wanting to be right there when Tristan woke, but she hadn't slept in almost an entire day, her eyes aching with exhaustion.

As she stepped up to the bed, she realized what had woken her up.

Tristan was awake.

Tristan was awake.

"*Mo cridhe?*"

Tristan groaned, his body shifting and rustling the sheets before his eyes fluttered open. Kenna brushed the curls back off his forehead, sitting gingerly on the edge of the bed, trying and failing to choke back her tears. They silently rolled down her cheeks, splashing on the mattress.

Tristan opened his mouth as if to speak, but the only sound that came out was a croak. Kenna leaned to his bedside table, picking up a cup of water—this time without salt. She tilted it to his lips, a small trickle entering his mouth.

She watched as he swallowed the water down, licking his dry lips before trying to speak again.

"Took you long enough," he whispered with a weak smile, and Kenna burst into a wet laugh, so happy she thought her heart might explode.

"Oh, my *cacan*. I can't believe we almost lost you." The smile slipped from her face. "I never would have forgiven myself."

"There is nothing to forgive, *a seòid*. You did nothing wrong."

"I left you." The tears were streaming down her face in earnest now. "I left you with the responsibility of our entire kingdom, and I did it for a fantasy."

"Listen to me, Kenna. You are not responsible for me. You didn't do this *to* me. You left, and I got sick. There is no other correlation besides bad timing. I'm just happy you're back." His lips began to tremble, but he continued, "I wasn't sure if I would ever see you again. The storm hit, and we didn't know—we didn't know what happened to you. And then pieces of your boat washed ashore, and they thought you were dead."

Tristan clutched her hand then, his grip stronger than it should have been in his frail state. "But I knew. I knew you were still alive. I could feel it. And I wouldn't let them give up on you. I would have never given up on finding you."

They were both sobbing, and Kenna laid next to where he was propped up, her back against the headboard next to him, so she could curl herself around his body, wrapping him up like she did when they were young.

"I'm so sorry, I'm so sorry," she kept repeating, as they held each other.

Tristan pulled away from her, wiping the tears from his eyes, looking at her imploringly. "What happened? How did you get back to us?" He averted his gaze then. "I thought I was dying. I... I thought I would be dead by now." Kenna's heart broke at the resignation and acceptance in his voice. "Why do I feel so good? How is this possible?"

"Oh Tristan, there's so much I need to tell you."

She placed a kiss on his curls before standing up. Yawning, she stretched and looked around the room. They had been talking quietly, not wanting to wake anyone. Not yet. She wanted Tristan all to herself for a moment before they had to speak with their parents. It was going to be a heavy talk, but she knew it was necessary.

Kenna looked over where they were still asleep. She guessed they hadn't gotten any real sleep since she'd disappeared, and couldn't blame them. Then she looked to the settee to find Calder awake, staring at her, a small smile on his face. She walked back over to him, sitting on the edge.

"Hi."

"Hi." His grin widened. He leaned up onto one elbow, and Kenna bent down to meet him halfway. Gods, she didn't think she would ever get over kissing him. The moment their lips met, she melted into him, immediately forgetting where she was and what she was doing.

Until the sound of a throat clearing behind her brought everything rushing back, and she froze. She pulled away from Calder and looked over her shoulder to find Tristan staring at them with a huge grin on his face, his eyes sparking with laughter.

"Well, well, well, will you look at that?"

Kenna bit down her smile. "You *cacan*, be quiet."

"No, really. I'm happy for you." His smirk had melted into something more sincere, and Kenna felt herself smile in return. Tristan cooled his expression into what he probably meant to look stern, but what was all too soft on his face.

"I don't care if I'm half dead—you hurt her and I'll find a way to kill you."

She heard Calder's quiet laugh behind her, but all he said was, "Yes, sir."

"Since Kenna has deemed you worthy of her attention, and she is capable of determining who to trust on her own, I'm guessing whoever you are and whatever you were doing parading around as one of us wasn't too bad. So I will forgive the intrusion. You're welcome."

Kenna rolled her eyes. "Speaking of that, it's time we wake up Mother and Father."

NONE OF THEM SEEMED to know where to start, so they sat in silence, tension thick in the air.

But Kenna was sick of the silence, sick of the waiting.

So she told them everything. How she had seen Calder leave and knew he was a merman, that she had to follow him. She told them about the shipwreck and how Calder saved her, nursed her back to health on the island—leaving *certain* parts out of the story.

When Kenna caught up to the part where she discovered what she was, she looked her mother dead in the eye.

"I think you know what I discovered next." Kenna let the frustration and hurt and anger shine through her eyes when she stared at her mother.

The queen closed her eyes, bowing her head. Her voice croaked out, soft and pleading. "You have to know, *mo cridhe*, that everything we did was to keep you safe."

"So you've said," Kenna muttered.

"What are you talking about?" Tristan's voice interrupted. When their parents didn't answer, he turned to Kenna. She took a fortifying breath, knowing what she was about to tell him would change his entire life, as it had hers.

"Tristan, do you remember Mother's clan?"

"Canduine? It was wiped out in the war before we were born."

"Well, that's not exactly the truth."

"I don't understand."

"Canduine is actually the family name of the royal mer family." Tristan's eyes widened. "Mother was not from an extinct human clan. She was a mermaid. The heir to the mer throne, Princess Eileen."

Tristan looked to their mother. "But... that means... Is it true?"

The queen looked at her son and nodded.

"But you made Kenna feel like she was crazy for believing in mermaids! You forced her into the Winchin Festival, using your own as an example when it never even happened!"

"Tristan, you have to understand," the queen pleaded, "I only wanted—"

"I don't care what you wanted!" Tristan struggled into a sitting position, swinging his legs over the side of the bed, standing up, swaying on his feet. The queen looked as if she was going to reach for him, but he held out his hand to stop her. "I don't care what your intentions were when the result was making Kenna feel like she would never be good enough, because no one ever believed her. Believed *in* her."

Kenna's heart ached, overwhelmed by how much Tristan loved her. She stood up and wrapped him in a tight hug. Calder had been right. They did choose each other, and she would never take his love for granted.

"Oh, *mo cridhe*." Tristan's arms squeezed around her, gripping her back just as tight. She pulled back, far enough to clutch his face in her hands. "I don't know where I would be in this world if I didn't have you."

Tristan's angry eyes softened at her words, and he opened his mouth to speak, but she cut him off before he could. She had thought she wanted to rage and scream at her parents when she saw them again. So many years of hurt and resentment had built up inside her. If her parents had simply been *honest* with her, she might be a different person. Maybe she would have been more confident. Maybe she would

277

have been content in the life she had, just knowing this other world was out there. And her parents were a large part of that, yes.

But she also realized now they were the victims as well. Her mother had lost her entire family, everything she had ever known. Stranded in an unfamiliar world for the rest of her life, never to see her home or her people again.

Left with a fear that at any moment, her past could come and take away her future and there was nothing she could do about it. Unable to even speak of her true self to another soul besides her father. Her mother must have lived a very lonely life. That was something Kenna could understand.

Was she still angry with them? Of course.

But she now understood *why*, and knowing Tristan felt the same anger as her softened her own to something dull. Something she could put aside until other, more pressing matters were dealt with.

"To know I have you in my corner means I know I can face anything. But as much as what they did may not have been perfect, they are not the enemy here."

"But Kenna—"

"No, listen. If you think I wasn't livid when I found out, you really don't know me as well as I thought you did." A laugh huffed out of him, and she continued, "But the time to be angry is not now. Right now we have much bigger problems than how they made me feel as a child."

"What do you mean?"

"Sit back down, Tristan. This tale has only begun."

Tristan looked confused but did as she said while Kenna told him everything. The false history Ailith created. The real history that Isla told her. How Ailith had slowly been losing her grip the past two years. That she was behind the raids from Sìthachd.

When she finished, a tense silence hung in the air between them.

"So, this Queen Ailith, our aunt," he shook his head, an understand-ably dazed expression clouding his face, "who is extremely dangerous and wields the power of the ocean, hates us and wants us dead? Am I getting this right?"

Kenna shot him a wry look. "Pretty much."

Tristan shook his head. "Well, that's just perfect. So, what's the plan?"

Chapter Thirty-Five

K enna looked to Calder, who gave her an encouraging nod, letting her take the lead. "We have to go after her."

There was a brief pause, before three voices spoke out at once in varying degrees of dissension.

"Kenna, you can't be serious. You just told me how evil and dangerous she is!"

"We've spent the past twenty-two years protecting you from her, we will *not* lead you right to her!"

"*Fiadhaich*, you cannot expect your mother to go back into the ocean she was run out of?"

Kenna held her hands up, stopping their protests.

"We don't have a choice. Whether we like it or not, she *will* come for us. She won't be content waiting for Sìthachd to attack anymore, not after realizing that I know about her and her kingdom. And our best chance is catching her unawares. She would never think us bold enough to confront her in her own palace. Which is exactly why we have to. She may hold the power of the ocean, but Mother, you are the *true* heir. The true queen."

Kenna remembered what Calder had told her. That when her mother had chosen a human over the ocean, the ocean had no longer chosen her as its queen. But she had to hope it would take their side in this battle. They couldn't afford to go up against Ailith *and* the ocean.

Her mother opened her mouth to respond, but Kenna continued, speaking over her. "It's the only path I can see forward that ends well for us. She may know that castle, but so do you. And so does Calder. He can help us."

"In her power, Ailith has grown complacent and cocky. She doesn't think anyone would dare challenge her, so she has grown somewhat lax in her defense of the castle," Calder added.

"Plus we have a secret weapon." Kenna grinned at Calder, and he smiled back, his eyes crinkled with adoration.

Her mother looked back and forth between them, confused. "A secret weapon? What do you mean?"

"My parents," Calder responded. "My mother was a friend of yours. Your Majesty," he tacked on belatedly.

The queen gasped, a hand to her mouth.

"Of course," she whispered. "I knew you looked familiar, but I couldn't figure out why. It's what set me on edge, especially at the ball. You move just like she always did. With the grace of a mermaid. I should have realized." She gave him a small, wry smile. "Your mother is my dear Coira, isn't she?"

Calder smiled softly in return, and Kenna could see the love he had for his mother in his eyes. "Yes. She misses you dearly."

"She was pregnant with you when I saw her last. And look at you now. All grown up." Tears welled in her eyes. "And I missed it all. My dear friend gave birth to her child, believing I was dead."

"But she didn't. She never truly believed the lies Ailith told everyone. She held onto hope you were out there somewhere. But she kept quiet all these years to protect our family, with the hopes she would have a chance to learn the truth and set our kingdom to rights. Ailith inciting Sìthachd to war was the last straw for both of my parents. They've gathered a group of merfolk who are over Ailith ruling the ocean the way she has been. A few other merfolk in the royal guard and I have been collecting whatever information we can and funneling it back to my parents, biding our time. My mother is the one who helped Kenna and I escape, and she will help us when we go back."

Kenna's father reached over, squeezing her mother's hand. "I know it's scary, *mo ghràdh,* but I think they're right. We have no other choice."

Her parents looked into each other's eyes, communicating in the way only two souls who have been bound for as long as they have can. Her mother slowly nodded.

"So when do we leave? How are we going to play this?" Tristan asked, his face grim and determined.

"Tristan, you can't join us," the king replied, face set in stone.

"What the hell are you talking about? If you think I'm going to sit aro—"

"Tristan, Father is right."

"Kenna!" Tristan looked ready to burst, his face red in anger.

"No! You're too weak right now. You just regained consciousness after being close to death. It's too dangerous."

"But how can I sit back and watch as you all risk your lives?"

"Oh, my sweet boy." The queen cupped his cheek in her palm. "You never did shy away from anything, did you? You can't understand how proud I am of you and your courageous heart. But courage is not all this mission will take, and strong as your spirit is, the truth is simply that your body is not strong enough yet."

The king jumped back in. "And if something happens to us—"

"*No,*" Tristan cut him off. "*Nothing* will happen to any of you."

"We have to face the fact that not all of us might return," Kenna said gently. "And if that happens, one of us needs to be here to keep our kingdom safe and rule. Someone needs to tell the people about the mer kingdom."

Her father cleared his throat, and they looked up at him. "About that." Kenna cocked her head at him. "We're not sure what happened. But yesterday morning, every person in Cladach woke up with their memories of merfolk restored."

"How is that possible?" Kenna gasped, but her parents just shook their heads.

"We have no idea how, but it seems the curse was broken." Her mother looked anxious, and Kenna could understand why. If the people remembered the merfolk, they remembered she was one of them. That she was not from Cladach, there was no Canduine clan, and their queen and king had been lying to them for the past twenty-five years.

No one spoke, everyone sitting in a tense silence as the news sunk in.

Tristan closed his eyes, fists clenched so hard his knuckles turned white. "I hate this," he whispered. "I hate not being able to go with you all."

The queen grasped his hands in hers, bringing them to her lips. "I know you do. But everything happens as it's meant to. And if, gods forbid, the worst happens, no one would be better suited to take care of our people, our home. No one so courageous and kind as you."

Kenna couldn't agree more with her mother's words. And it would tear her heart in two to leave Tristan again, but her parents were right. This was the way it had to be. She would have fought in Tristan's defense, but not this time. Not when he could barely stand for more than a minute at a time.

And they didn't have time to debate it any further. As if he were reading her mind, Calder cleared his throat, gaining their attention. "We need to discuss what the rest of us will do once there. I believe it would be too hard for us to sneak into my family rooms once we get to the palace. I assume Ailith will have posted more guards than usual if she has realized Kenna and I are gone, but even so, she would never expect us to come back so soon."

"And she wouldn't expect me to come back at all," Kenna's mother added. "Not after I let her spread her lies with no objection for so long. She is safe in her assumption I have willingly given up on the ocean. On my people." Her mother's eyes turned to steel. "But my neglect ends now. I have turned my back on them for too long."

Calder looked at Kenna's mother with new respect. As much as she was terrified about what they had to face, her heart couldn't help but warm at the sight—all the people she loved together in one room, getting along.

He shot Kenna a small smile. "Once we get there, we will find my parents. They can fill us in on what Ailith has been up to since we left, and we can figure out where to confront her. She usually spends her afternoons in the throne room, pretending to care about her people's concerns. Then she takes her lunch alone in her offices. She'll have three or four guards posted inside the room and two outside of the doors.

"If we're quick, we can take them, but when they see you," he said to the queen, "I don't think we'll need to fight them. They believe you were murdered by the humans. If they see you, it will be a miracle. They will most likely welcome you. Ailith has only held her power by making you a martyr. You would not be a threat to them."

"Then we use that to our advantage. Maybe she'll realize she can't win. Not against us all, or against the truth." Her mother sounded hopeful, but unconfident.

"I doubt it." Calder's eyes darkened in hatred. "She believes the throne is hers. She will not give up her power without a fight. She has only gotten crueler with each passing year."

The queen swallowed hard. "Then fight we will." Kenna saw the pain in her mother's eyes. Her father saw it too, and he held her hand tighter, lending her as much comfort as he could. As he always did.

Her mother may have known Ailith was evil, but she was still her sister. This couldn't be easy for her. Kenna tried to imagine ever having to face Tristan being evil. That he had lied and killed and stolen the throne from her out of jealousy.

She couldn't.

She looked around at all of them. Their drawn faces, lined with exhaustion and pain. They may need to move quickly, but they didn't need to move at that very moment. All of them could use some rest to regain their strength. She looked out the window, the sun halfway up its climb.

It was midmorning now. They could take the rest of the day to sleep, eat, and mentally prepare, then leave the next morning.

"We've all had a long night. A long week, truly. We should rest and recuperate, then leave in the morning."

"That's a good idea, *fiadhaich*." Her father stood, walking over and squeezing her shoulder. "We should all get some sleep. We can reconvene here to eat dinner and continue strategizing tonight."

Tristan bade them all goodbye, attempting to stand tall and proud, but she could tell even the talking had worn him out. She was sure he would fall asleep the moment he laid back down, and she smiled to herself. He always could fall asleep faster than anyone she knew.

As the four of them stepped into the hall, there was a moment of awkward silence as they stood there, seemingly unsure where to go from there.

Her father cleared his throat and looked at Calder. "I'll show you to one of our guest rooms, son."

"That's all right, Father. He'll come with me." Kenna's face was on fire, but she stood her ground, not shying away from her parents' gaze. Her father's face was also slightly red, and she could tell both her mother and Calder were trying to suppress their smiles.

Her father cleared his throat, trying to regain his composure. "Oh, yes, very well. Er, I guess we will see you both at dinner."

He jerked toward her, as if to wrap her in a hug, but seemed to stop himself, unsure. Kenna's embarrassment receded, and she stepped into him, wrapping her arms around his middle, the tension releasing from her shoulders when he returned the embrace just as tightly. Her father's hugs were one of her favorite things in the world, and she was glad that wasn't changing, no matter their complicated feelings at the moment.

"I love you, *mo fiadhaich*," he whispered before pressing a kiss to the crown of her head.

"I love you, too, Father."

He released her, smoothing back her hair, before turning and taking her mother's arm and walking down the hall, the queen shooting Kenna a grin and a wink over her shoulder.

T he bedroom door clicked shut behind Kenna, and she slumped against it, closing her eyes on a long breath. Everything was going so fast. They had barely gotten back, and they already had to face Ailith again?

She knew it was her and Calder's idea, but that didn't make it any less daunting. Did she really think she could take on the queen of the ocean? Her aunt, who had killed her own parents, Kenna's grandparents, who she never got to meet for that very reason.

Not to mention that somehow the curse had already been broken, and the humans now knew about the merfolk again. For better or worse, Cladach was forever changed now. It was all so much to take in.

Warmth radiating in front of her pulled her from her thoughts, gentle fingers stroking her cheek. She opened her eyes, instantly drowning in cobalt waters.

Calder trailed his fingers down her face, burning a path to her chin, tilting her face up to his. Slowly lowering his head, he gave her plenty of time to push him away.

But she wanted him. Him and the comfort he provided her.

She tilted her chin up those last few inches, melding her mouth against his. She opened her lips under his, sparks shooting through her veins as his tongue met hers.

Slowly, he moved his body until it was pressed against hers, pushing her shoulder blades into the door at her back. His hands, which had moved down her arms in soft caresses, now clutched at her waist, pulling them impossibly tighter together.

She delved her hands into his hair, the silky strands sliding through her fingers like water, letting out a groan.

At the noise, all the softness in their kiss disappeared, unbridled passion taking its place. Calder devoured her, and Kenna gave back as good as she got. Her hands tightened in his hair as his hands dug into her hips.

She gasped for breath, tilting her head to the side while Calder licked and kissed his way down the side of her neck, paying particular attention to the sensitive spot where her neck and shoulder met, his tongue tracing her pounding pulse.

"Calder," she whimpered. With the slightest tug at his hair, Calder lifted his head from her neck, his chest heaving as much as hers.

"Do you want me to stop?" He looked into her eyes.

"Yes." She leaned in, stealing another kiss, pulling his bottom lip with her teeth. "No." She kissed her way across his face, making her way to his ear, nibbling on the lobe. "Ugh, yes."

"Gods, Kenna. You are going to be the death of me." He put his hands on her shoulders, pushing himself out of reach of her mouth.

Smart man. She didn't think she could stop herself if he was within mouth range.

His lips quirked to the side, that damn dimple making an appearance again. "What is it, *mo lasair?* Talk to me."

She let her head fall against his chest. "That's not fair. You know I can't think when you call me that." His chuckle reverberated through his chest and against her cheek as he wrapped her into his arms. She snuggled into his warm, firm body. All of his hard planes melted into her soft, round curves, her head tucked into the curve of his neck. She breathed him in, his ocean scent soothing her racing heart.

They stayed like that for a few moments, simply holding each other. Calder didn't push her to speak, only smoothing his hands in slow sweeping circles across her back. She squeezed her arms once more around him before pulling away. She trailed her hand down his arm, taking his hand in hers and leading him towards the couch nestled into the corner by her bookshelves.

She dropped onto it, sighing in contentment as she sunk into the soft cushions. Calder sat next to her, and with his added weight, they dipped towards each other. Instead of fighting it as she would have just a week ago, she curled into him, weaving her arm through his, lacing their fingers together and leaning her head on his shoulder.

Kenna was continuously amazed at how comfortable she felt with him, how strong their connection had grown in a matter of days. She felt like a whole new person. Confident where she used to question and obsess over every move. Calder made her feel safe. Safe to be exactly who she was.

He made a hum of contentment, resting his cheek atop her head. "I feel as if I could sleep for a week."

Kenna laughed. "I couldn't agree more. I can hardly wrap my head around everything that's happened. Everything I've learned in such a short time."

"I imagine it's overwhelming."

"Ha!" Kenna belted out a laugh. "That's an understatement. Everything is moving so fast, I feel like I can hardly keep up with it all." At her words, she felt his body tense beneath hers. She lifted her head to look at him, but he wouldn't meet her gaze, instead looking at the ground and chewing his lip.

Kenna brushed her fingers along his jaw, tilting his head towards her until she could search his gaze. "What?"

His throat bobbed on a swallow. "If things are moving too fast, if *we* are moving too fast, I would completely understand. I don't want to—"

Kenna really did laugh then, and Calder looked at her in surprise. She simply shook her head, leaning up and kissing him.

"You are the one thing I never want to slow down. Calder, I love my kingdom. I love Cladach. But my heart has always belonged to the ocean, and it's found its home in you. I love you."

Calder's eyes shone, a look of wonder and admiration on his face. He shook his head. "I will never deserve you, but I love you anyway." He met her halfway this time, and she lost herself in him once again. They were supposed to be resting, but she didn't think they were going to get much sleep.

Calder's hands were splayed over her waist, under her shirt. Every-where his skin touched hers was on fire. As his fingers inched higher, she couldn't stop herself from lifting her hips against his, where she felt him hard and ready for her. As she moved her body against his, he moaned into her mouth, his movements becoming frenzied. She dragged her hands down his back, until she cupped his backside, hauling him firmly against her core.

"Kenna. *My Kenna.*" He spoke her name like a plea, and Kenna's blood sang in her veins.

"Please, Calder. Please touch me before I burst."

He needed no encouragement, his hands immediately finding the hem of her shirt and lifting it up.

But right as he began dragging the shirt up her torso, they were interrupted by a bang so loud it rattled the windows in their frames.

Calder's head shot up, his body suddenly tensed, as if ready to spring to action. Kenna lifted herself onto an elbow, looking around the room in alarm.

The sky flashed a bright white outside the windows, rain suddenly pounding the castle, before another boom of what they now understood to be thunder cracked through the air.

"What in the world was that?"

"I don't know." Calder's voice was grim. "But it can't be good."

They ran out of her room, rushing down the hall, passing both servants and noblemen milling around in confusion. A moment later they arrived in front of Tristan's rooms, when the doors flung open and Tristan stumbled blearily into the hall.

"What's going on?" He took in Kenna and Calder's nervous expressions and cursed under his breath. "This storm came on so suddenly, you don't think—"

"That's exactly what I think." Calder paced the hall, shoving his hand through his hair.

Kenna anxiously chewed her lip. "How could she have gotten herself together and come on the attack already? It hasn't even been a full day since we got away!"

Calder stopped pacing and took one of Kenna's hands in his, the other cupping her cheek. His thumb swiped under her bottom lip, pulling it from between her teeth, his other rubbing soothing circles across her knuckles. "I don't know, *mo lasair*, but all that really matters is she's here now, and we must face her."

Kenna wrapped her hand around his wrist before kissing his thumb. "You're right." She took a deep breath. "Let's go."

The three of them continued on, finding the king and queen in the Great Hall.

"She's here!" The queen's eyes shone with panic as she and the king rushed in.

"We know." Kenna met them in the middle of the room with Calder and Tristan. "What are we going to do?"

"I don't know, but we need to figure it out soon." Her father's expression was drawn.

"I'm surprised she made a move so quickly," Calder spoke up. "She may be insane, but she's not stupid. Usually her actions are more methodical. She must be angry."

"If I remember her temper from when we were children, I would say she's well beyond anger. We need to think about this carefully. We only have one chance," the queen replied gravely.

"How should we play this? How many guards should we bring with us?" They all looked at Tristan carefully, and his expression turned to thunder. "No! No way am I sitting up here in the castle while you all risk your lives. Now that we don't have to travel to Mharìogh, you can't expect me to sit this out!"

"Travel or not, your body is still too weak to fight. We will not put you in harm's way."

"But—"

"No! I am your father *and* your king, and this is an order from both. You *will* stay in the castle, and you *will* stay alive."

Tristan's shoulders drooped in defeat, his expression miserable. "What am I supposed to do while you are off fighting Ailith?"

"You will be preparing the castle."

"Preparing the castle?"

"If we should fail, who knows what Ailith will do to our kingdom. You must meet with the council and prepare to defend the castle. You should round them up now, fill them in on the situation, on Ailith's history and her dealings with Sìthachd. We have to be prepared for war on both sides if this does not go well." The king walked up to Tristan, resting his hands on his shoulders, and looking into his eyes. "We're counting on you, son. I know you will lead our council well."

The king pulled Tristan into a quick but firm hug, the queen next. Kenna walked up to him, wrapping her arms around him, tucking her head under his chin.

"*A seòid,*" he whispered in her ear, "make me proud. I know you can beat her. You're too stubborn to let anyone else win."

Kenna chuckled wetly, gripping his shoulder after she pulled away. "You *cacan.* I know you want to be out there with us, but this is what's best. Your greatest strength has always lain in your strength of mind. In your conviction. You are *meant* to lead. You always have been."

Tristan smiled at her one last time before turning to Calder and nodding to him, a gesture Calder returned. Then Tristan walked briskly from the room, the rest of them turning back towards each other.

"So what's the plan?"

"We need to draw her out of the ocean and onto land." Calder paced. "She can still wield her power on the sand, but she'll be much weaker."

"How do we do that?" Kenna asked.

"We make her even angrier." Her mother's words were grim.

Kenna turned to her mother, incredulous. "Are you serious, Mother? You want to make her even *more* mad?"

"No, that's a good plan! Making her angrier is risky, but it's also brilliant," her father joined in, looking more and more convinced as he spoke. "The angrier she is, the less rational she'll be. We can bait her onto the beach."

Kenna took a deep breath. It was really happening. There was no time to be nervous. No time to obsess and worry about all the ways this could go wrong. That this might be her last moments with her family. With Calder.

"We need to move quickly. We've already given her too much time to familiarize herself with the cove. Our best hope is to lure her in, then overwhelm her." Her mother was all business. As if she weren't discussing going to kill her sister, and Kenna's gut clenched with pain for her.

"Come, we should stock up in the armory, and then it's time to go." They followed after the king as he swiftly made his way down the hallways, not pausing to heed any question thrown at them as they went. The people would hear about it all soon enough.

Only moments later were they in the armory, outfitting themselves with as many weapons as possible. Kenna felt a brief moment of gratitude her parents had seen to it she was trained in the use of all manner of weapons growing up, and wondered if they had been planning for a moment like this all along.

Kenna went to the far wall where the bows were hung and pulled down her favorite. It was made custom for her, and it fit her perfectly. She pulled the matching quiver, filling it with as many arrows as would fit, before sliding both the quiver and bow across her chest. Next she went to the wall of swords and daggers, fitting her sword belt around her hips and sliding her sword into the scabbard. Lastly, she fit three throwing knives into their respective sheaths attached to the strap across her chest.

Sliding the last dagger into place, she looked up to find Calder staring heatedly at her.

He stalked towards her, and Kenna felt the breath whoosh from her lungs. He had leather straps crisscrossed over his chest, plastering the fabric of his shirt to his strong chest and shoulders. Then she noted the two massive sword handles poking out above each shoulder. A belt slung low around his hips, holding a number of throwing knives himself. That should not look as attractive as it did.

She ripped her gaze back up from his hips as he crowded into her space, lifting a hand to tuck a lock of her flaming hair behind her ear. "You look incredibly sexy covered in weapons, did you know that?"

Kenna laughed, shoving his hand away. "You are ridiculous."

"You love it." There was that damn dimple. She smiled, shaking her head at him. How did he always do that? Make her forget her worries with a smile and a few dirty words?

She leaned into him, planting a chaste kiss on his lips, aware of her parents close by. "I guess I must be ridiculous too. Because damn if you don't also look sexy beyond reason right now." Then she sent him across the room to grab her a leather strap as she braided her hair, the plait falling down to her lower back after she tied it off.

She looked up to find her parents similarly decked out in weapons, standing by the door with solemn expressions.

"It's time."

Chapter Thirty-Seven

T he four of them raced out of the armory, making their way outside. They were met with a storm that put the one that shipwrecked Kenna to shame. The rain was coming down in icy sheets, immediately soaking them to the skin, plastering their clothes to their bodies. The wind ripped at them, coming from all directions at once. The sky was an angry riot of gray and purple, streaks of lighting forking across the mass of clouds and setting the rain aglow every few moments. Booms of thunder louder than any cannon accompanied it all.

They quickly and carefully made their way down the cliffside path, feet sliding in the mud. When the water came into view, Kenna's heart dropped. This was not the cove she knew so well.

The usual peaceful blue waters were gone, a raging dark mass of white-capped waves in its place. The sea and sky were both in such an angry state she could hardly tell where one ended and the other began, the rain coming down so thick she could barely see.

But what waited for them in the middle of the cove was impossible to miss.

Ailith sat on a throne made entirely of roiling gray water.

It swirled, funneling down into a whirlpool, before shooting up the middle, unnaturally formed into the shape of an opulent throne. Ailith sat, lounging arrogantly against one arm of the water throne, her purple tail twitching, the only sign of her agitation. She held the trident across her lap, her sharp eyes tracking them as they closed the distance to the water.

The four of them drew to a tense stop a few feet from the water's edge, waiting for the slightest reason to draw their weapons and begin fighting. They knew they couldn't go right into it. Ailith had a major upper hand, and they had to be smart. Let her get comfortable before drawing her out.

Looking at her blank expression, Kenna wanted nothing more than to start raging.

This was the person who had kept her from knowing half of who she was her whole life. The woman who had caused her mother so much pain. The reason she never got to meet her grandparents.

But since she could do neither of those things, she spoke instead.

"Hello, *Aunt.*"

Ailith's eyes flashed in response, no doubt angry at the insult of not being addressed by her stolen title.

"So." She moved eyes full of hatred and contempt to Eileen. "You finally told the little brat the truth."

"I didn't need to tell her the truth. She already knew." At that, Ailith shot a murderous look to Calder, and Kenna shifted subtly closer to him. "And even if she didn't, it's all over, Ailith. The curse is broken."

Ailith ripped her gaze back to her sister.

"What are you talking about?" Ailith snapped, leaning forward on her throne.

"Cladach remembers, Ailith. There is no more hiding what you've done. One way or another, your reign is done."

But Ailith wasn't listening anymore. "But that's not possible. The curse can only be broken if—" She whipped her head back to Calder. "*You!*"

"Ailith, what are you even doing here?" Kenna's mother demanded, drawing the attention back to her.

Successfully distracted, Ailith attempted to pull herself back together, falling back on her haughty anger. "Well, dear sister, I'm visiting my family. After all, family comes first, does it not?"

Eileen huffed and rolled her eyes, projecting an attitude Kenna had never seen from her before. One she probably hadn't used since she was a child, arguing with her little sister.

"And we all know how much *you* care about family."

"Oh, please. You don't get to pin this on me. Anything that happened was because of the two of you." She gestured angrily between Kenna's mother and father, and watched as their jaws hardened.

"Ailith, I understand that what we did hurt you. But we never meant to, and what happened between us does not excuse every action you have made since then," her father spoke in a calm but firm tone.

"You," she spat at him. "Do not even speak to me."

"Ailith, it's not as if we shared some great connection. We had only just met. It was twenty-five years ago."

"It does not matter how long we knew each other, you ungrateful wretch!" As she spoke, Ailith's voice got louder and louder. It apparently wasn't going to take much to set her off. "All that mattered is you were betrothed to *me*, and yet I caught you with *her*!"

"Ailith, that is enough! Why are you always such a drama queen?" Her mother rolled her eyes to further anger her sister, but Kenna could see the nervousness in her stiff posture.

"Oh, you're one to speak! Everything was about you! It always was. And yet you still had to go and take the one thing that was mine!"

"He is not a possession to be had, he is a person, and you are being insane."

"Don't call me insane!" Ailith swept her trident, and a funnel of water shot out of the ocean and landed directly on Eileen's head, drenching every last inch of her that hadn't already been soaked from the rain. Kenna, Calder, and her father had all reached for their weapons, but her mother hadn't even flinched. She calmly spit out the water, pushing back the wet strands of hair clinging to her face.

"I'm already wet, you *eejit*."

Ailith screamed, sending another wave of water, this time hitting them all. Kenna was not as collected as her mother, spluttering when the water hit her. It was somehow impossibly even colder than the icy rain still pelting them.

"You do realize that throwing water at us isn't doing anything, right?" Calder chimed in lazily, a bored expression on his face. Kenna tried not to smirk. He was born to antagonize people.

"Ahhh, so the half-breed's new pet speaks at last." Kenna stiffened at the insult, but Calder subtly brushed his hand against hers, reminding her to stay unaffected. The less emotion they showed in the face of Ailith's taunts, the more enraged she would become.

Calder did smirk, however. "Beats being your pet."

Even from this distance, Kenna could see how Ailith's fingers tightened around the staff of the trident until her knuckles were as white as her hair. The wind whipping around them increased in its intensity, the only other clue they were getting to her.

"You men. None of you know anything about loyalty. I shouldn't be surprised you chose her over me, that you fell in love with my sister's brat."

"I chose her over you because she is better than you. Honestly, that's something you should be used to hearing by now," Calder replied lazily.

"Watch your tongue, boy."

"What are you going to do? Splash me again?"

Ailith's expression was thunderous as she lunged from the chair, the water now forming around her waist, holding her up straight, as she whipped the trident in circles around her head. The mass of dark clouds above them swirled in answer. Swinging the trident out of the circle, she pointed it directly at Calder with a roar. As she did, lightning streaked through the air, following the path of the trident, directly towards Calder.

Kenna moved before thinking. She heard her mother screaming her name, but she wasn't stopping. She wouldn't stop for anything. Her body slammed into Calder's, and they flew through the air before dropping to the sand, not a moment too soon. Kenna landed on top of him and heard the breath whoosh from his lungs the same moment it went from hers. There was a boom, followed by a spray of sand falling across her back. Kenna scrambled off him, looking to the spot where he had been standing a moment before.

In his place was a smoking hole.

"Oh, now she's done it," Kenna growled to herself as she got to her feet. "Playtime is over, *galla*."

Kenna slung the bow off her shoulder, reaching back to grab an arrow before stringing it. She pulled it taught, until the feathers on the shaft brushed her cheek. Taking a deep breath in, she lined the arrow up with Ailith's heart, letting the string go as she breathed out. The arrow shot straight and true.

Until it was blown to the side by the wind and fell harmlessly into the water.

Kenna cursed, pulling out another arrow, starting the process over again, her father—who had his own bow and arrows—joining her this time.

They knew they wouldn't actually be able to hit her like this, as much as they wanted to, but it was a good distraction. And a good way to keep riling her up.

She batted each arrow out of the air with wind and water.

"Are you actually going to come out and fight, you coward?" Kenna shouted into the wind, growing angry as her stockpile of arrows dwindled.

"You really think that's going to work, child?" came Ailith's unbothered response, and Kenna ground her teeth, a quiet growl coming from her throat.

"I know that look," Calder murmured next to her, only loud enough for her ears. "She's going to get it now." His voice was full of laughter, and Kenna shot him a glare over her shoulder.

"Maybe you want to actually help in some way instead of standing there?" she snipped at him.

"What? And miss the show? No way. You're cute when you get angry."

"Seriously, Calder? You think this is an appropriate time for your jokes?"

"When are you going to learn I'm never appropriate?"

"You are so infuriating!" Kenna turned to him fully now, exasperated by his flippant attitude, but as soon as she took her eyes off Ailith, the mer queen sent another streak of lightning arcing towards them. This time Calder yanked her by the hand into his chest and out of the way.

"What, am I boring you?" Ailith's voice was icy, and Kenna could tell they were finally wearing on her patience. Kenna suppressed a smile as she met Calder's eyes, his shining with smugness.

Oh, that *cacan*. He knew exactly what he was doing.

"I think I made it pretty clear I was bored of you when I left you to come back here with Kenna," Calder responded in a dry voice.

"I will enjoy killing you as much as I will enjoy killing them," Ailith's voice seethed.

"*If* you can kill us, that is," Kenna rebutted, shooting another arrow at her, which she batted out of the air with the trident this time.

"Why do you keep trying? Your little arrows can't touch me, fools."

"Yes, but it's so fun to shoot at you," Kenna called back sweetly.

"You taught your insolent spawn to speak this way to her elders?"

"Not to the ones who actually deserve her respect," Eileen responded nonchalantly, and Ailith whipped her head to look at her sister.

"Careful, sister. You are not the only queen here."

"Ah, yes. Queen of Mhariogh. You had to copy me one last time, didn't you?"

"Watch your mouth! I am the only queen here with power. You are *nothing*."

"If I am nothing, then what does that make you? You always did love to stand in my shadow." Ailith threw another lightning bolt at Eileen, but she missed by a good few feet, her chest heaving in anger as Eileen kept speaking. "You are, and always will be, nothing more than my little sister who wanted what was mine. You couldn't even fight us yourself to start. Having the faeries do your dirty work for you was low, even for you."

Ailith's scream was so loud the sound pierced Kenna's eardrums. She flew through the air to the sand, her mother's words finally doing it. Finally making Ailith angry enough to forget strategy and act on pure, enraged impulse instead.

The four of them rushed back from the shoreline, making sure to go far enough from the water to make Ailith truly leave it if she wanted to engage them.

Ailith made it to the sand, dropping down, and in a flash of white she was in her human form, covered head to toe in leather armor, layered over itself like the scales of a mermaid's tale.

"Um, how did she shift so quickly?"

Her mother responded, "Whoever sits on the throne and wields the power of the ocean can shift at will. They do not have to wait like the rest of us."

"How convenient for the insane person," Kenna mumbled, and her father snorted in response.

"You and your brother have always been too sarcastic for your own good."

"The apple doesn't fall far from the tree, Father," Kenna sang back at him.

He opened his mouth to shoot something back at her, but stopped, the color draining from his face. Kenna turned to see what might have caused that reaction, her mouth drying out at what was before her.

Ailith stalked toward them, her face a mask of fury, but that wasn't the scariest part. In one hand, she brandished her trident, the other stretched out to her side, palm open and fingers splayed wide. A thin rope of water with floating bits of coral, rock, and glass shot out of the ocean, forming in the air above her hand. It kept forming until she held a large sword made out of those bits, held together magically by the water.

"Well, there's something you don't see every day," Calder said in awe.

"My sister always had a flair for the dramatic," Eileen responded.

The four of them pulled their swords out, getting ready to face her. It should have been easier now that it was four against one, and they had lured her from the water. And it would have been.

But the surprises did not stop there. Behind Ailith, three soldiers made their way out of water, melded from the ocean in the same way Ailith's sword had been made, walking up the sand holding magical swords of their own. How in the world were they supposed to fight *water?*

But Kenna didn't have time to think about it, because a moment later, Ailith and her soldiers were on them, and they were all fighting for their lives. Eileen was facing off against Ailith, their skills fairly matched. In between clashes with her own water soldier, Kenna shot glances at her mother, trying to keep them in her line of sight. The two women lashed at each other again, and again, neither getting the upper hand.

Ailith was fighting with pure rage, making her stronger but sloppier. Eileen was fighting for love, for family. And Kenna had to have faith that would be enough.

Something bit into Kenna's shoulder, and she cried out. In her distraction, the soldier managed to swipe at her, and she redoubled her efforts. The problem was the soldier didn't defend itself at all. It was made of water, and Kenna's sword did nothing but glide through with no resistance, not affecting it at all.

Kenna was left to do nothing but defend, blocking attack after attack. She could hear the clashes of swords on either side of her and knew Calder and her father were going through the same thing.

"How are we supposed to beat these things?" she yelled in between swings.

"I have no idea," came the panted reply to her right, and she could tell Calder was getting annoyed. It was one thing to fight for your life against an opponent that could feel the bite of your weapon. But what did you do when your opponent would never injure or tire?

Kenna was wrenched from her worries when she heard a cry of pain, followed by her father's voice bellowing her mother's name. She whipped her head around to see her mother cradling the hand that had been holding her sword, blood dripping between her fingers, the sword lying forgotten on the ground.

"Did you really think you could beat me, Eileen? You were never fierce enough to lead. You never could do what needed to be done. And now, you will pay for that weakness with your life."

Kenna watched in horror as Ailith lifted her sword, and Eileen did nothing to get out of the way. She simply stared into her sister's eyes, daring her to do it.

Ailith thrust the blade, Kenna's scream blending into her father's, who ran towards the sisters. But Kenna was too far away. Instead, she could only watch as her father dove in the path of the sword, taking the blow meant for her mother.

Chapter Thirty-Eight

Kenna watched Ailith's expression turn from shock to anger as Eileen sobbed her father's name.

"You fool!" Ailith screeched.

But Kenna paid her no attention, seeing only her father. The way he slumped to the sand, a dark red stain spreading across his chest. Her mother was next to him, her hand forgotten. She dragged the upper half of his body onto her lap, cradling him in her arms as she sobbed over him, pushing the hair off his face.

"Evander, Evander, *mo ghràdh*, don't leave me. You can't leave me," Eileen sobbed.

Kenna fell to her knees, unable to hold herself up any longer as she looked at her father's lifeless body. Vaguely, she could still hear screaming, and she thought it might have been her, but she was past thought. Ailith looked at Kenna's mother and father with contempt. Arms wrapped around her from behind, and she could hear Calder speaking reassuringly into her ear, but she didn't register a word he was saying.

"If he was fool enough to get in the way of my sword, then he deserved to die. Are you ready to join him, dear sister?" Ailith asked in a mocking tone.

At Ailith's words, something inside of Kenna snapped.

All the anger and the grief welled up in her, too much to contain. She needed it *out*. It was too much, everything was too much. She couldn't sit there and watch her mother holding her dead father for another second, while Ailith stood over him without an ounce of remorse. She *wouldn't*.

"*Enough!*" Kenna screamed, breaking out of her stupor and wrenching herself out of Calder's arms and onto her feet.

Kenna would not stand by. She would not let Ailith get away with what she had done. For too long, Kenna had brushed everything aside, instead of standing up and facing it. But not again. Never again. Ailith had taken one too many things, and Kenna was changed forever. She was fatherless. And she would *not* let Ailith take her mother, too.

Her chest heaved as she faced Ailith, her emotions overwhelming her until she stopped trying to suppress them, instead letting them go. Letting everything go.

And it was like a flip switched inside of her.

A wave of *something* rushed through her veins, and she gasped. She felt more like herself than she ever had before, but she didn't understand what was happening. Belatedly, she realized the rain had stopped, the dark clouds still there, but no longer roiling across the sky.

"No," she heard a gasp, and looked up to see Ailith staring at her in horror. "It can't be. *No!*" She turned to scream the last word at the ocean, and Kenna looked to Calder in confusion.

"What just happened?"

But Calder was not standing behind her anymore. He was kneeling in the sand, and when he met her eyes, he murmured, "*Mo bhanrigh.*" Then he held his fist across his heart, and bowed his head.

The breath woodshed out of Kenna's lungs, and she stumbled back a step.

My queen?

What was Calder talking about?

But the words felt *right*. They felt true, and suddenly Kenna recognized what she had felt unlock inside her. The power she had felt rush through her. The ocean. It had chosen her, just as Calder had said.

"You have no idea what you've just done," Ailith growled, before charging. But Kenna only smiled, feeling the power of the ocean answer to her will. She reached her sword up to the sky, calling that power to her, before slinging it in an arc at Ailith, and watched as the lightning streaked through the air.

Ailith dove to the side, rolling back to her feet.

"How dare you use my own powers against me!"

"I believe they are *my* powers now, Aunt."

Ailith roared in anger, charging again. Kenna met her this time with her sword, and they traded blows. Ailith continued to hurl obscenities at her, but Kenna did nothing in return, simply smirking darkly, enraging her further. Ailith's blows got sloppier and sloppier, while Kenna's became more and more precise, the new magic flowing through her veins replenishing her strength and energy.

With every clash of their swords, new bits of Ailith's sword broke off, her hold on the magic weakening as Kenna's strengthened.

A movement behind Ailith caught Kenna's eyes, and she looked past the mer queen's shoulder to find her mother advancing towards them. Grief welled back up in Kenna in full force at the look on her mother's face. Her eyes were dark pits of despair, her mouth slashed across her face in fiery determination.

Kenna purposefully weakened her blows, letting Ailith think she was gaining the advantage to keep her distracted as her mother approached them. As angry and heartbroken as Kenna was, this was Eileen's blow to deal. Ailith had caused her more pain than Kenna could ever imagine. Kenna couldn't take this from her.

She let her foot slip, sending herself off balance, and Ailith's eyes glowed with triumph as she lifted what was left of her sword above her head, ready to swing down onto Kenna.

But the strike never came.

Instead, a silver blade stained red plunged through the center of Ailith's chest. Her eyes widened in shock, the sword above her head dissolving back into water, the rocks, coral, and glass raining down over her head as she looked at the sword in her chest.

Ailith fell in what felt like slow motion, first to her knees, before slumping to the side. Blood poured out of her wound and pooled beneath her body as Eileen dropped to her knees beside her sister. Her mother pulled the sword out, turning Ailith onto her back. Kenna watched as Eileen pulled Ailith's head onto her lap, wiping away the drizzle of blood leaking from the corner of her mouth.

"I always loved you, you know," Eileen whispered in a shaky voice, and Kenna realized she was crying, her tears dropping to Ailith's face. "You were my baby sister."

Ailith's breaths were so shallow her chest barely moved, and her eyes were unfocused, but she looked up roughly in Eileen's direction. "That was the problem, wasn't it?" And with her last word, her chest stopped moving, her hands falling lifeless to the sand, her unseeing eyes pointed to the sky.

Eileen's shoulders shook as she sobbed over Ailith's body, mourning the baby sister she had loved. The one she had lost twenty-five years ago, and was losing all over again now. Kenna realized tears were streaming down her own face, and she lifted a hand to dash them from her cheeks.

Kenna had never known Ailith, and she did not deserve Kenna's tears, but she didn't cry for Ailith. She cried for her mother's pain. Her mother who had now lost not only her sister but her husband at the same time.

Father.

Chapter Thirty-Nine

Kenna rushed past her mother and Ailith, falling to the sand at her father's side, the sobs wrenching from her throat in earnest now. She couldn't believe he was gone.

It wasn't fair. As she cupped his face, leaning her forehead against his, she didn't know how she was supposed to move on from this. How her mother was supposed to move on. How she could ever find a way to tell Tristan he would never get to hug his father again.

And then she felt the lightest brush of air across her face. She jerked her head away, looking down to her father. Her trembling fingers desperately searched for a pulse at his throat, her eyes straining to catch any movement in his chest.

There! He was alive!

"Oh my gods! Mother, Mother, he's not dead!"

Suddenly, Eileen and Calder were kneeling on the sand next to her, all of them crying now.

"What do we do? We need to get a healer, we need to save him."

"There's no time," her mother said frantically, grabbing Kenna's arm as she made to stand.

"We can't just give up on him!"

"We are *not* giving up, but there is no time to get the healer. Kenna, you must save him."

"What do you mean?" She looked up, her mother's words making no sense to her grief-addled brain.

"*Mo lasair*, you are the queen of the ocean now," Calder interjected, his voice full of reverence. "You have all of its powers running through your veins. I told you, you can use the water to heal. Did you not wonder how your cut healed so quickly on the island? I used the salt water to speed along the healing process. You are more powerful than I am. You can do this."

"But—how? How do I do it?"

Eileen grabbed her hands tightly, her own slick with blood, looking desperately into Kenna's eyes. "I know you can do this, *mo cridhe*. It has been inside of you all your life. You always said you felt called to the ocean, now you need to call it back. Dive into the power inside of you, and *call it to you.*"

Kenna's heart tightened in her chest, and she shook her head. She didn't know how to do this. How was she expected to wield such power she had just gained? Her lips trembled and she could feel the tears welling again, as she started to hyperventilate.

"It's okay, it's okay. Shhh." Her mother smoothed her hands over Kenna's hair, tucking the loose strands that had escaped from her braid behind her ears. "Close your eyes," she whispered. Kenna obeyed.

The world went black, and Kenna tried to focus on nothing but her breathing and the sound of her mother's voice as she continued. "You are part of the ocean, and it is part of you. It *chose* you. If you call, it will answer. Just focus. Tug on that connection you have always felt inside of you."

Kenna tried, but it kept slipping from her grasp every time she thought she had figured it out. She growled in frustration and panic, about to tell them it was hopeless, and they needed to run for the healer before it was too late. And then she felt a hand warm on her back, and words whispered against her ear. "*Mo ghràdh, mo bhanrigh.* You can do it."

Warmth rushed through her entire body at his words, and suddenly she could feel it, her connection to the water.

She pulled on it. Hard.

She heard a gasp of breath and opened her eyes to see a swirling mass of water detach from the ocean and float over to them. Pride bloomed in her chest.

"That's my girl." She felt a kiss on her cheek and could practically feel the love coming from Calder in waves.

With renewed vigor she refocused on her task. Concentrating on the water, she called it until it hovered over her father's injury.

"Now what?" Kenna looked to her mother.

"I knew you could do it." She smiled. "Now, focus the love you have for your father on the water, and will it. Will it into him, will it to heal him. Pour your love, yourself into that connection, and bid it do your will."

Kenna nodded, turning back to the water and calling to it. It lowered to her father, funneling into the wound, disappearing into him. Kenna hovered her hands over him and closed her eyes in concentration.

She thought about her father. Thought about the way he had read to her and Tristan as children. The way it felt to be held in his arms. The way he kissed her forehead. The way he called her *fiadhaich*. The ways his eyes glinted with love and pride when he looked at her. And she channeled all of her feelings, all of her love, down through that connection, and into her father.

Heal him, she demanded with all her heart and soul. *You have to heal him.*

She opened her eyes, not daring to breathe as his wound began to glow. The light flared brighter and brighter, until right before her eyes, the wound sealed itself, nothing left but a hole in his shirt and blood glistening on his skin.

With a gasp, her father's eyes flew open and his body jerked up. Both Kenna and her mother sobbed in relief, launching themselves onto him, and he had no option but to hold them in return as they cried all over him. He clutched them back, tucking his head on top of her mother's.

"She's really gone? It's over?" he asked.

"Yes." Her mother kissed him, holding his face, her smile filled with joy and relief. "It's finally over."

Kenna looked at Calder standing to the side, tears falling down his face, smiling at her softly, his eyes warm and clear. Eileen saw where Kenna's attention had gone, and she looked to Calder as well.

She grinned. "Get over here, son." And as soon as he was close enough, she yanked his arm, pulling him into their pile, all of them laughing.

They stayed like that for a few minutes, holding each other and basking in the joy of their victory. When they all pulled away, it was to find the sky clear of clouds, the cove once again a calm, blue sheet of water. The sun was setting as they walked back up to the castle, setting the sky aglow with golden light, making it feel as if they were ascending into the heavens. When they got to the top of the cliff, Kenna looked back to the ocean, watching as the sun painted the water in glowing pinks, oranges, and golds.

"You feel it more now, don't you, Kenna?" her mother asked, standing at her shoulder. Kenna realized Calder and her father had continued walking, giving them a moment. "The pull."

Kenna nodded. "I've always felt drawn, but it was never like this. This is... physical. It's like there's a cord connected to my heart, and the farther I walk from the water, the harder it tugs."

The queen smiled. "I remember the feeling. Before I gave up my title, before I gave up the ocean, I felt that every time I left the water. It's stronger for us. The Canduine line. The more powerful a mermaid, the more powerful the pull."

"How could you give it up? If you felt what I'm feeling now, how did you walk away?"

Her mother's smile softened, and she glanced over her shoulder to her husband.

"It's easy, when your heart belongs elsewhere." She gave Kenna's hand a squeeze full of affection before walking away.

311

Kenna sighed, staring out to the ocean for another moment. She still had a lot of feelings to sort through. She still felt anger and resentment for what her parents had kept from her. But it had lessened, after learning the truth. After watching the pain Ailith put them through. After watching her mother grieve her sister in spite of that pain. Maybe it wasn't the perfect solution, but her mother had only done what she thought was right.

She could forgive her mother the pain she had caused, knowing the pain she had prevented her from feeling.

A MOMENT LATER KENNA was stepping into the castle entryway, looking for her family. She spotted them just past the front doors, Tristan wrapped between her parents. He lifted his head at the sound of her footsteps, and when he saw her, he disentangled himself from their grasp, running to her and squeezing her tight.

"*A seòid!* They told me what happened!" He pulled away from her, grinning widely at her. "I heard you have some cool powers now." His eyes twinkled with mirth, and Kenna pulled him in for another hug. She couldn't remember the last time she was this happy. With Ailith gone, and now knowing the truth, it was like a weight had been lifted from her shoulders. Like for the first time in her life, everything was exactly as it should be.

She pulled out of the hug, and grabbed his face, pulling it down and going on her tiptoes, to kiss his forehead. "I love you."

Tristan's smile softened. "I love you too."

She released him, giving his hand one more squeeze before turning around and searching for Calder.

She found him, leaning a shoulder against the closest wall, his arms folded, one foot kicked over the other. He was watching her with a hungry gleam in his eyes, tracking every movement, and she sauntered over to him, grinning.

"Whatever would we do without you to hold up the walls in this place?" she teased as she sidled up to him, smoothing her hands up his chest and leaning into him, tilting her face up to his.

"You would just be lost without me, of course," he murmured against her lips as he melted into her kiss. His hands cupped her cheeks, the tips of his fingers tangling in her hair. She got lost in him, oblivious to the world around her until she heard a throat clearing behind her.

She broke off the kiss, her face flaming, and hid her face against his chest.

"Sorry to break up the fun," she heard Tristan's teasing voice, "but Father wants us to gather in the Great Hall."

Kenna turned to find that her parents were no longer there, the three of them the only ones left.

"Why? What's going on?" Her stomach dropped, her mind racing to figure out what could have gone wrong now.

Tristan noticed her panicked expression, and raised his hands in a placating gesture. "It's fine, nothing's wrong." Kenna's shoulders dropped, and she let out a sigh of relief. "It's just time to tell the people everything. Come on, they're waiting for us."

When they got into the Great Hall, they found Kenna's parents standing on the raised dais, a large group made up of the royal council, as well as most of the people who were currently staying at the castle, standing in front of it, asking questions all at once.

"If everyone would calm down, we can give you the answers you seek," her father said, trying to tame the crowd. But they continued talking over him. Calder, Kenna, and Tristan reached the dais, stepping onto it and walking over to the king and queen.

Kenna's mother rolled her eyes. "We've been trying to get them quieted down for minutes now, but they won't stop."

Kenna looked out over the loud crowd, seeing the expressions of confusion, hurt, and anger. Before all this happened she would have stood back, let someone else deal with it. But she wasn't that girl anymore.

She stepped up to the edge of the dais, standing with her back ramrod straight and her head held high. "We need quiet!" she yelled over the crowd, projecting her voice to the back of the cavernous room. It took a moment, but the voices stopped one by one until everyone stared up in silence to the royal family. Kenna turned to find her parents looking at her with shocked but pleased expressions, while Calder and Tristan were both beaming in pride.

Kenna stepped back, allowing her parents to take the lead. She stood right behind her mother, while Tristan did the same with their father, and Calder took his place directly beside her.

"I'm sure you are all very confused right now, but I promise you, we can answer your questions," the king spoke in a placating tone.

And so, over the next hour, they explained to the people everything that had happened. What Ailith did twenty-five years ago, the curse she put on them. How she instigated their conflict with Sìthachd and sent Calder to spy on them, not knowing he was part of the group fighting against her.

How Ailith died.

It wasn't easy, and there were many, many questions, but eventually everyone was satisfied enough to at least call it a night.

This would not be an easy change to make. There was a whole generation of humans who did not know about the merfolk. And those who had been alive at the time had lived the past two and a half decades not remembering. There would be a long road ahead of them.

Kenna's parents dismissed everyone but the council. While the rest of the people filed out, the king and queen turned to Kenna, Calder, and Tristan.

"We have to meet with the council, have them send messengers to each of the clan chiefs to spread the word. There will be people all around Cladach right now needing answers," the queen said. "But we do not need you three for this. Why don't you go rest? We can talk more in the morning."

"Wait, mother." Her mother looked at Kenna questioningly while her father continued on to call the council together, and she continued. "How *did* the curse break?"

Her mother's tired eyes softened and she flicked her gaze between Kenna and Calder. "A curse of that magnitude cannot exist unchecked. There has to be a caveat, a way to break it. When you two were on the island, something happened, didn't it?"

Kenna's face flamed. Having this conversation with her mother while Tristan and Calder were standing right there was not something she ever imagined. At the look on her face, Kenna's mother laughed.

"Not that, *mo cridhe.*" Kenna's face flamed even harder as her mother continued. "I meant you two fell in love. You admitted that you loved each other, yes?" Kenna looked to Calder, to see him already looking at her. His cheeks were dusted pink, probably just as embarrassed as she was, but there was nothing but love in his eyes.

"Yes," she murmured, not taking her eyes away from Calder's.

"I thought so," the queen responded softly, tucking a piece of Kenna's hair behind her ear. "I'm sure my sister thought she was being clever," she continued, her voice thick with a mix of fondness and melancholy. "Cursing humans to forget merfolk, and outlawing merfolk from speaking to humans. She thought it would never be possible for a merperson and a human to fall in love."

Realization washed over Kenna. It was yesterday morning that the people woke up remembering. And the night before was when Kenna and Calder had admitted their love for each other. Had made love that first time.

Her mother kissed her on the cheek and bade all three of them a good night, and they walked out together.

Outside of the Great Hall, Tristan turned to them. "I will see you wild kids in the morning. I have to escape before you two pick up where you left off and leave me scarred for life."

"*Cacan!*" Kenna lunged to whack him on the arm, but he ducked out of her reach and ran away cackling. She yelled after him, "How many times did I have to walk in on you doing something I didn't want to see!" He didn't turn around, simply flipping his finger up at her. Kenna shook her head, laughing at Tristan's antics, before turning her wide grin to Calder.

"Oh, whatever shall we do with our time?"

Calder's grin turned wicked as he crowded her against the wall. "I can think of a few things," he spoke into her ear, before sucking on the sensitive skin right behind it.

Kenna tilted her head. "Only if you can catch me first." She bit his earlobe, then ducked out from under his arms and ran off down the hallway, her laugh echoing in her wake, squealing when she heard his footsteps pounding after her.

Chapter Forty

Sunlight was streaming through the windows when Kenna woke the next morning. The first thing she registered was the warmth of a firm chest beneath her head instead of a pillow. As her brain slowly woke up, she relived everything that happened yesterday.

She still couldn't believe they had done it. That they really didn't have to worry about Ailith anymore. The work was far from over—in fact, it had just begun. There was the mer kingdom to reintroduce to Cladach. There was still a war brewing with the faeries. But that there *was* work was a good thing. The humans and merfolk would interact with each other again. Kenna had woken up to a brand-new world.

She had also woken up to a beautiful man in her bed, and that felt almost more unbelievable than the merfolk. She folded her arms across his chest, resting her chin on her hands, watching him sleep. He looked younger when he slept, his face slack and peaceful. The thing that aged him was the scruff already starting to grow back, the sunlight bringing out its almost unnoticeable ginger tint.

She loved that scruff.

Kenna brushed her lips over his, and he sighed, murmuring her name.

Leaning on one elbow to the side of him, she ran her hand down his chest, watching the goosebumps raised in her wake, loving how his body responded to her even in sleep. When she got to his waist, she moved her hand to the side of his body, and began tickling.

"Wake up, sleepyhead," she whispered in his ear, watching as his face broke into a smile, and his body jerked, trying to get away from her wiggling fingers. He woke with a laugh, and after taking a second to figure out what was happening, he growled at her, rolling over until he had her pinned underneath him.

"Oh, you're going to pay for that, *mo lasair*." He kissed and bit a path down her neck, and she tilted her head back to give him better access, her body squirming beneath his.

"Oh no," she gasped out sarcastically. "This is terrible."

With one last nip to her neck, Calder kissed his way down the front of her body, stopping at her breasts to give them some attention before he continued on downwards. Without warning, he gripped her hips, flipping her over and pulling her thighs towards him until he could bury his face between them.

Kenna cried out, the sound muffled with her face turned down into her pillow. He was relentless, a starved man feasting for the first time. It didn't take long before she was coming undone under his tongue. It wasn't enough, though. It was never enough.

"Calder," she panted. "*Please*, I need more."

"I'll give you everything, *mo bhanrigh*. Everything." And he did. With one motion, he thrust into her, seating himself to the hilt, trailing kisses down her spine while he kept up a steady, deep rhythm.

Needing to be closer to him, Kenna surged up to her knees, leaning back until she rested against his chest, balancing on her knees and meeting his pace with her own. She drove her hands back and into his hair, holding him, while he wrapped his arms around her, holding and squeezing her breasts in his hands.

"I need—"

"I know," Calder panted in her ear, sucking the sensitive skin of her neck. He needed no further prompting, moving his hand between her legs, circling his fingers firmly where she was most sensitive.

Kenna bit her lip from crying out at the feeling, not wanting to be overheard. And then she was falling apart, clenching around him with such force he had no option but to follow right behind her.

They collapsed to the sheets, chests heaving. Kenna turned in his arms, still wrapped around her, laying her head back on his chest, planting kisses there, while he stroked a hand idly through her hair. She was filled with that warm, fuzzy, buzzing sensation, the soothing calm of happiness.

Closing her eyes, she simply took in the sensations, basking in the warmth and comfort of Calder's arms. The longer she spent with him, the more she came to realize this was exactly where she was meant to be.

"*Mo Iasair?*"

"Hmm?"

"I hate to break the peace and quiet, but there are some things we need to talk about," Calder's voice was hesitant and unsure, and Kenna stilled, realizing his hand had stopped its movements in her hair.

She rolled to the side, stretching out next to him instead of on top of him, leaning her head up to rest against her hand. Calder looked at her and smiled, but he seemed nervous.

"What's going on?" she asked softly.

"I think we need to talk about what comes next."

"With us?"

"Well, yes. But also with *you.*"

Kenna's heart squeezed in her chest. She had known this was coming, but she had wanted to pretend for a while longer that she didn't have a life-changing decision looming ahead of her. She wanted to spend the rest of eternity right here in this bed with Calder, ignoring the rest of the world.

But she couldn't.

She picked at a nonexistent thread on the sheets. "I know." She looked up to Calder, moving a hand to trace the edge of his jaw. "I never wanted to be queen." Calder's eyebrows went up in surprise, and she laughed. "It's true! I always felt like I wasn't meant to rule. As much as I love my kingdom and my people, I felt like they were holding me back, tying me down. I thought I wanted to live a life of adventure on the sea. I realize now that wasn't what I really wanted. It was just the ocean in my veins, calling out to me."

"Calling its queen." Calder looked at her with reverence.

"I've realized it wasn't that I didn't want to rule. It's that I knew I was never meant to rule *Cladach*. I think Tristan is going to be an amazing king."

"Does that mean...?"

Kenna grinned at the hope in his face, leaning into him. "Yes. I am going to accept that call inside of me, Calder. I will take the throne and rule Mharìogh, once I talk to Tristan, and make sure he is alright with this."

"*Mo bhanrigh.*" A laugh of pure joy boomed out of his chest as Calder swept Kenna into his arms, laying her body across his and covering her entire face in kisses while she giggled and squealed.

"Wait!" She pulled her head back to look into his eyes. "I have something I need to ask you." Her heart pounded in her chest, her hands growing slick with nerves, but she pushed on. She wanted to do this. She *could* do this.

Calder took in her suddenly nervous expression, and his face smoothed out, brows lowering in concern.

"What is it? Is something wrong?"

"No, not at all." She placed a hand on his chest, directly over his heart. "Everything is very, very good. But it could be better."

"How do you mean?"

"I mean..." She took one last, deep breath before asking the question in a rush. "I know we've known each other only a short time, but that's how most royals do it anyway, and I love you, so if you want to, I am wondering if you, maybe, wanted to rule alongside me?"

It took a minute for him to make out her jumble of words, but then a grin slowly made its way across his face.

"Kenna, are you asking me to marry you?"

"Um, yes?"

Instead of answering, Calder rolled himself on top of her, kissing her fiercely into the mattress.

When he broke away, Kenna asked in a breathless voice, her head spinning, "Is that a yes?"

Calder bit his lip, staring into her eyes, his brimming with love, and if Kenna wasn't mistaken, glistening with an unshed tear or two.

"I would be *honored* to be your husband, *mo lasair*."

AFTER MORE TALKING—and kissing, of course—they decided they should leave that day. Just as there was much upheaval in Cladach, there was much to be done in Mhariogh. The merfolk would have no idea Ailith was dead. Kenna and Calder had no idea what their people were thinking. Where they believed Ailith was. It would take them time to adjust to a new queen, especially one they had never met, who was the daughter of a human and the princess they thought dead for twenty-five years.

It wouldn't be easy. Healing never was. The distrust in humans had to be managed, and a relationship between the two kingdoms had to be rebuilt. But as much as the merpeople might be shocked and confused once they learned the truth, they could not deny Kenna as their queen.

She was the rightful heir by birthright, and beyond that, the ocean had *chosen* her. No one could argue against that.

Hopefully with Calder—one of their own—by her side, it would be easier to accept. And with the support of Calder's parents and their group of merfolk who did not like what Ailith was doing, hopefully they could convince the rest of the merfolk that the way Ailith had been ruling was wrong.

But now came the hardest part. They had to break the news to her parents. To Tristan. Every time she thought about leaving him, her heart broke a little more. But she knew this was right. This was the way it was always meant to be. And it didn't mean she would never see her family again. It wasn't a long trip with her powers to come back and visit whenever she pleased.

The two of them finished dressing, Kenna in a simple, pale pink gown, and Calder in a plain but finely made shirt and breeches they had stolen from Tristan. Calder grabbed her hand before they left her room, bringing it up to his lips, and kissing the back of it, giving her a reassuring smile.

"I'll be with you, always. I love you."

He always knew exactly what to say to ease her pain and anxiety. She brushed her fingers against his cheek, giving him a sweet smile before opening the door.

The guards posted outside her door fell in line behind the two of them as they made their way down the hallways towards the private royal dining room, where she hoped Tristan and her parents were still eating.

When the two of them walked into the room, Kenna had to laugh. Her parents were calm, eating like the dignified royals they were. Meanwhile, Tristan was stuffing his face, his plate one large pile of eggs and sausage.

The three of them looked up at the sound of Kenna's laugh, and when Tristan saw it was her, he shot her a large smile. Which only made her laugh harder, as he still had a mouth full of eggs. He quickly swallowed, his smile sheepish.

Her parents smiled at them, exchanging *good mornings.*

Kenna and Calder sat down, piling food onto their plates and devouring it, having worked up an appetite. Kenna was stalling, not sure if she was ready for this conversation, but she was fairly certain her parents had an idea of what was coming next.

Eventually, the food was eaten, and Kenna had no more excuses. She straightened the fork next to her plate for the hundredth time, and Calder put a reassuring hand on her knee, giving it a light squeeze. Kenna put her hand over his before looking at her parents to find them already looking at her. Their faces beamed with pride but also sadness, and she realized they already knew.

"I'm sorry," she whispered, the tears building in her lashes and threatening to fall.

"You have nothing to apologize for, *fiadhaich.*" Her father smiled at her. Her parents shared a glance before turning back to her, and then her mother spoke.

"We knew this was coming. I told you that your heart would find its home, and I was right. It's just not with us."

"What do you mean?" Tristan looked back and forth between Kenna and their parents. "What's going on?"

"Oh, Tristan." Kenna gave him a watery smile. "Leaving you is going to break my heart."

"Leaving me? What do you mean?"

"I want to renounce my claim to the Cladach throne and take my rightful place as queen of Mharìogh."

Tristan stared at her in shock, his mouth hanging open. "But—but you can't leave. This is your home."

Kenna smiled at him sadly. "No, it isn't. You are half of my heart, but the ocean is my home. It always has been. I simply didn't know the true reason until now. I was never meant to rule Cladach. My soul is too restless to rule this kingdom the way it should be. I was born to rule the ocean. And you, *mo cridhe.* You were *meant* to rule Cladach. If you can accept this, you will make the most wonderful king." The tears were falling down Kenna's face in earnest, but she pushed on. "You will make a better ruler for our people than I ever would have, because it was never meant to be me. Can you accept this?" Kenna bit her lip, nerves circling in her gut for the first time since she had decided this was what she would do. "I would never leave if you truly did not wish to be king. I would never force this on you."

"It's not being king I am worried about, *a seòid*. It's saying goodbye to you." He stood, pulling her into a tight hug. They stayed in each other's embrace for a long moment, until Tristan pulled back, looking down at her and taking her hands in his. "But I would never hold you back from where you're meant to be. I will just miss you more than I could ever say."

"I am so proud of the man you are, and that will never change. This is not goodbye forever. It's time to rebuild both our kingdoms. Time to reconcile them. You and I will rule side by side, be the bridge between them."

Her parents stood, walking around to their side of the table.

"We could not be prouder of you both." Their father beamed at them, their mother brushing tears from her eyes. "You've grown into such kind, compassionate, and intelligent adults. You will *both* make great rulers. We could not leave this world in better hands."

The four of them piled into a group hug, all of them clutching each other tight, staying that way for a long time. When they did pull away, the queen put a hand on each of their shoulders, bringing their attention to her one last time.

"Do not think of this as an ending. This is just the new beginning."

She squeezed their shoulders, before letting them both go.

"Calder and I are returning today. We need to tell the merfolk what happened. Both yesterday and what happened twenty-five years ago."

Her parents nodded, a knowing gleam in her mother's eyes. "And?"

Kenna swallowed the lump in her throat. She was fairly certain her parents approved of Calder, but how would they react to her choosing to marry him without first getting their blessing? She squared her shoulders. They would approve because it was *her* choice, and they didn't get to have a say in this.

"And Calder will rule by my side, as my king. I have asked him to marry me, and he said yes."

All three of them broke into wide smiles, pulling her back in for one last group hug, tears being shed all around.

After that, they talked for a while longer, planning how they would go about healing the rift between the two kingdoms, how they could form a new plan to end whatever this was with the faeries. Kenna couldn't wait for the day she could teach Tristan how to shift. To see his mer form and explore the oceans with him. But there was work to do first.

Her mother also wanted to go back. To see her home, her friends again. Show the people she was alive and well, and confirm Ailith really had deceived them all. Plead for help in ending this tension Ailith had started with the faeries. She would join Kenna and Calder in a few days, since Cladach needed her at the moment.

Finally, it was time. Calder had snuck out of the room long ago to give her time alone with her family, and she was grateful to him yet again. She wandered back to her room once they were done speaking, looking for him. He was standing on her balcony, resting his forearms on the railing. Kenna took a moment to appreciate the view before walking up to stand next to him, placing a kiss on his shoulder before resting her head there.

"Thank you. For giving me that time with them. We all needed it."

Calder shifted his position so he stood behind her, arms wrapped around her shoulders, resting his chin on top of her head.

"I get the rest of my life with you. I think I can spare you a few moments with your family."

She smiled, looking out over the royal gardens. As excited as she was to start her new life, she would miss this. The smell of the flowers, the way the breeze flitted through the air, lifting her hair, rustling all the leaves beneath her. It was a sound she loved. But she was ready.

Ready to go home.

They changed into simpler clothes, knowing they would not need finery in the mer kingdom. Then they walked to the entrance hall to find her parents and Tristan waiting. They exchanged hugs one last time, her family seeing them off. They would let them start this new chapter on their own, just the two of them.

At the top of the cliff, Kenna turned back one last time to take in the castle that had been her home her entire life. Her heart was a mix of joy and grief. But she was done repressing her feelings and denying herself, so she allowed herself to feel it all. The good and the bad.

She turned away from the castle, toward the ocean.

Toward her future.

This felt more right than anything ever had in her life, and she couldn't help but smile. She turned to Calder, finding him already smiling back at her with such love in his eyes it filled her heart to bursting.

"Are you ready, *mo bhanrigh?*"

Kenna's grin turned mischievous, and she leaned into him, tilting her head up towards his face. Just as he leaned in to plant a kiss on her lips, she yelled in his face, "Race you! Loser eats squid!" She rushed down the cliff path, her laughter floating on the wind.

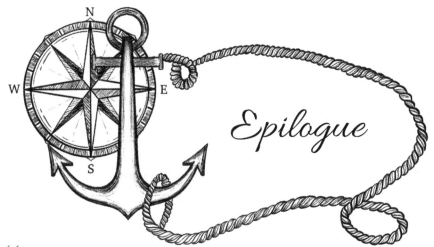

Epilogue

"Where are you taking me?" Kenna laughed as Calder dragged her along behind him. They were making their way through the paths in between the homes and shops that spread out from the castle in Mhariogh.

It had been a week since they'd arrived back, and although it had been one of the best weeks of Kenna's life, it had also been the hardest. The first thing she had done upon arriving was go to the dungeons and release Isla. She finally got to hug the woman who had helped her, who had saved Tristan's life. Kenna couldn't erase the last twenty-five years of pain Isla had lived through, but she could give her a new life.

Kenna had offered her a position in her court, but Isla had declined, which Kenna understood. She had done more than her duty for her kingdom.

After that it had been non-stop. Kenna had met with everyone in Ailith's court, every noble, every merperson close enough to the castle and available to come. So far she had only heard small rumblings from some of Ailith's closest advisors.

But no one could outright argue. Not when they learned the truth of how Ailith got her throne. Not when the ocean had chosen Kenna.

The meetings had been non-stop strategizing and planning and getting accustomed to this new life, this new world that was now Kenna's home. If she wasn't in a meeting she was being shown around her new kingdom, learning the castle and the ocean that was now hers.

It was incredible. It already felt like home in the way Cladach never quite had. Though she missed Tristan so much it hurt. Thankfully, Tristan would be here tomorrow.

Kenna smiled at the thought, so excited to show him around her new home.

She was brought back to the moment when Calder shot her a mischievous grin over his shoulder. "With all the commotion of the last week, there's one place I haven't shown you yet."

Immediately, Kenna knew what he was talking about. They hadn't had time to visit Calder's home yet, and she had been pestering him about it ever since they arrived. Calder had been staying at the castle with her, never leaving her side for more than a moment. But she wanted to see the place he called home.

Calder brought them to a stop in front of a small home, on the edge of the innermost ring of buildings that circle the castle, open water behind it. Just like every other building here, it was made out of that same material as the castle, stone embedded with corals and pearls and gems. The door was a curtain of seaweed that Calder parted as he made his way inside.

It was a small open room, with a small bed pushed into one corner. Opposite the door was a window, looking out over the drop-off behind the home. The ocean stretched out behind it, a deep endless blue. On a level directly below them sat the next ring of buildings.

Kenna turned in a circle taking in the walls, which were carved with beautiful swirling patterns mimicking the motion of waves. And on a shelf ringing the full room sat hundreds of small, human trinkets. Kenna glanced at Calder, who was watching her, biting his lip in trepidation as he watched her take it all in.

"Is this all human stuff?"

Calder rubbed the back of his neck, nodding sheepishly. "I told you I've always been fascinated by you humans. I kept anything I found."

"Can I?" Kenna motioned to the items closest to her, and he nodded his head. She floated up to the wall, picking up an old rusted fork from the shelf. It must have been decades old, far out of fashion from the current cutlery in Cladach. There was a golden gravy boat, a weathered paint brush, and a bright green pendant hung on a necklace of shells, carved in a pattern native to the kingdom of islands to the south of Cladach. A three-pronged candelabra next to a small wooden clock. A beautiful blue glove held down with a small golden green pendant strung on a black ribbon.

She made her way down the line, finding object after object so lovingly placed on this shelf. Finally, she got to the end of the line and let out a soft gasp.

There, sitting on the edge of the shelf, was a small mermaid figurine carved out of wood. She delicately picked it up and traced her fingers down the intricate carvings of the mermaid's swirling hair, suddenly transported to five years old, standing in a booth full of wood carvings in a village by the sea.

She looked up at him, that familiar burn in her eyes now the only sign that tears were floating from her lashes. "Calder," she whispered, too overcome to say any more.

Calder floated up to her, wrapping his hand around hers holding the figure, his other hand finding its way into the floating mass of her hair. He leaned his forehead against hers, brushing their noses together.

"*Mo lasair, mo ghràdh, mo bhanrigh*," he murmured against her lips. "It was always you."

Glossary

These words are all Scottish Gaelic, translated and spelled phonetically here to the best of my abilities, based on the research I was able to find online. Some words I made up combining Gaelic words with relating meanings. Gaelic (GA–lick) is a part of Scottish culture that was erased and stolen from Scottish people beginning in the 1700's, and is a beautiful and endangered language. I set out to include these words in my story with the utmost respect, and any and all mistakes are my own.

Mo ghràdh: My love (moe g–RAH–gh)

Fiadhaich: Wild one (FEE–uh–ee–kh)

Cacan: Wee Shite (KHAA–k–ehn)

A seòid: My Hero (ah sh–oh–d)

Mo cridhe: My heart (moe KHREE–uh)

Ghaoil: Love (g–ue–lh)

Damataidh: Damnit (DA–mah–tee)

Tolla–thon: Arsehole (T–OW–luh–hon)

Mo lasair: My flame (moe l–AH–seh–d)

Riatach: Bastard (VEE–air–tah–kh)

Galla: Bitch (g–OW–luh)

Mo Bhanrigh: My Queen (moe v–AH–ree)

Magairlean: Bullocks (m–A–kar–lee–ehn)

Eejit: Idiot (EE–jit)

Mhariogh: Mermaid Kingdom. *Maighdeann–mhara* (mEYE–chum vAH–neh) for mermaid, *rioghachd* (REE–aa–kh–K) for kingdom. (vAHn–ree–gh)

Claddach: Shore (kl–A–taw–kh)

Sithachd: Faerie Kingdom. *Sitheanach* (SHE–aw–nah–kc) for Faerie, *rioghachd* (REE–aa–kh–K) for kingdom. (SHE–aw–kh–K)

Gaoth: Wind (g-ooew)

Feamnach purpaidh: Purple seaweed (FEM-nah-kh PUSH-pee)

Tuamar Sea: *Tuath* (t-OO-ah) for north and *mar* (mar) for sea. (t-OO-ah-mar)

Acknowledgements

Wow, ok, hi! I don't even know where to start. This book would quite literally not exist without so many people!

First of all, the biggest thanks goes to my parents. You both have always told me I could do anything I wanted to, and somewhere along the way, I started to believe you. I can never give enough thanks for the emotional, financial, and physical support you've both given me my entire life. I love you more than I could possibly express. And dad, Pug Press is for you.

My second thanks HAS to go to the best CP I could have ever asked for. Maha, you and I were always meant to find each other. I can't imagine my life without you. Thank you for proofreading, thank you for every writing session, brainstorming phone call, encouragement, and answer to my panicked texts asking you to fix my entire plot for me. I love you so much, and I wouldn't be here without you.

Thank you Heidi Goen-Salter for being one of the best teachers I have ever had. You truly cared about me and every student that's ever come through your classroom. You saw the English major in me before I did, and you changed my life for the better. This book would not exist without you because I would not be a writer without you. *Thank you.*

To Jenny Howard, thank you for your encouragement and knowledge of craft, for helping me get this book started. I don't think I ever would have taken my little short story and turned it into a novel if it weren't for you and your class.

Jan Osborn, I don't even know what to say. You not only are the reason I finished this story, you are the reason I graduated college. You are one of the kindest and most encouraging souls I have ever met, and I'm so grateful I ended up in your class.

Thank you to Evva, Taylor, Lindsay, Colby, and every other beta reader who read and helped with any piece of this book.

Thank you so much to Chloe Liese who gave me such beautiful and wonderful feedback!

Thank you to my editor Sarah for really seeing the heart of my story and helping me make it better than I ever could have on my own.

Thank you to Shelby Mahurin and Jen DeLuca for putting up with my endless shouting of love for you and your words. You both have influenced and inspired me and my writing in a way I'll never fully be able to express. Thank you for being such kind and wonderful people, and for writing such beautiful stories.

Thank you Sarah Estep for answering all my questions, and every late night writing sprint, it would have taken me a LOT longer to get through my revisions without you.

Thank you Courtney Kae, Leanne Schwartz, Lizzy Ives, Hazel St Lewis, Jessica Joyce, Jordan Gray, RM Derrik, & Jes McCutchen for every encouraging word, and answering every question I've had about publishing. An extra thank you to Ray for helping me figure out this whole formatting thing, this book only got formatted as well as it did because of all your help and answers!

Thank you to Jack and Lira, my furry children for cuddling me on every hard night, and being the best writing assistants a girl could ask for.

Thank you Sohisoli and Azura for giving me the absolute cover of my dreams, I am beyond obsessed with it, and I couldn't have dreamed of a better cover. I am so incredibly blessed especially to have you, Azura, in my life. You made so much of the visual aspects of this book what they are, and are also the best business partner. You have always been so supportive of me and this dream of mine, and I love you.

Thank you to my IRL friends and support system. KT, Meghan, Carina, Kaitlyn, Christiana, Erin, Michael, Kendra, Sarah. I love you all so much, and I'm so grateful to have each and every one of you in my life. Thank you Michael for being my first sensitivity reader, and for taking my incredible author headshots. Thank you Kendra for being one of the first people I talked to about this story, encouraging me so much over the past four years, our wonderful and very short writing retreat (lol), and helping me take so many of my best cosplay photos including of my girl Kenna.

Thank you to Adrienne Young and Kristin Dwyer for Writing With The Soul. It's such an encouraging community, and helped me meet some of my favorite people, including Maggie Rapier and Jamye Smith. You both are so incredible and supportive and I'm so glad to know you.

Thank you Julie Murphy and Talia Hibbert for being the first authors I read whose stories told me it was ok to love my body. Thank you to Chloe Liese and Mazey Eddings for writing stories that told me it was ok to love my brain. Thank you to Ali Hazelwood and Alison Cochrun for introducing me to demisexuality and helping me understand a part of myself I never knew.

Thank you to every author writing fat characters, neurodiverse characters, and queer characters for making me feel seen and valued and loved. I hope everyone who reads my story will feel the same way I have felt reading those books.

Last but definitely not least, thank you to every single person online who has told me they are excited to read this book, and thank you to every person who DID read and stuck it all the way out until now. There were many, many times I wanted to quit. That I didn't think starting and FINISHING a book was something I was capable of. (All my ADHD folks I'm sure you understand). But I DID IT. I DID THE DAMN THING. And the biggest part of it is due to every single person who encouraged me to keep going. I wrote this story to see myself reflected on the page in ways I never had, and in ways I know other people never have either. I hope that Kenna made you all feel less alone, like she made me feel.

About the Author

Emily B Rose grew up addicted to storytelling in all its forms, and always knew she would have a career in something creative. With a bachelor's degree in creative writing, she settled on books as her favorite form of storytelling, though you will still find her glued to the tv watching her favorite sitcom or nerdy movie series, or belting show tunes in her apartment (to the annoyance of her cats).

California born and raised, she can be found wherever the closest beach or bookstore is, or curled up at home trying to convince her cats to cuddle with her 24/7.

Emily is a proudly fat, demibisexual, ADHD woman who wants her stories to reflect people often ignored, especially in love stories. She hopes her books will make people feel less alone, and affirm that everyone deserves the love story of their choosing.

Connect Online

www.authoremilybrose.com
◎ ♪ @emilybrosewrites

Printed in the USA
CPSIA information can be obtained
at www.ICGtesting.com
LVHW090613090324
773809LV00010B/172/J